THE
BLOOD - BORN
DRAGON

BOOK ONE
of the
EVERLANDS CYCLE

J.C. RYCROFT

BATTLEWARRIOR
PRESS

Copyright © JC Rycroft 2023

First ebook edition April 2023 | First print edition April 2023

Cover by Fay Lane

Illustrations by Myfanwy Cadwallader

Developmental editing by Cameron Montague Taylor

of The AuthorShip Publishing and Editorial Services

Copy and line editing by Rachelle Wright of R. A. Wright Editing

Proofreading by Nay of That Grammar Gal

Ebook ISBN: 978-0-6456228-4-3 | Print ISBN: 978-0-6456228-5-0

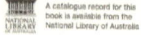

A catalogue record for this book is available from the National Library of Australia

A BattleWarrior Press book

First published in Australia in 2023 by BattleWarrior Press

BATTLEWARRIOR
PRESS

Visit the author's website at www.JCRycroft.com

For mi novia, with so much love, and the warm recollection of reading this to you aloud as I wrote it in a hut beside a beach in Thailand.
Thank you for your love and care and support—it means the actual world.

AUTHOR NOTE

T his novel is not all puppies and sunshine, I'm afraid, and there's some naughty language, dark events, and explicit content.

For a full content note (including a comprehensive set of trigger warnings), which I'd encourage you to check if you're wondering "what exactly do they mean by dark, though?" please see the very final page of the book or visit the book's online home: www.jcrycroft.com/the-blood-born-dragon

WESTERN ELIAR

SEREN

AREDOMA

ASCELIN

SERALIN →

DAGNON →

HATHWAY

TYRASENE

JAM

ROATH

SCYLESS

CYLINA

TIBALT

MARCO

RESCALIN

WROSK

ASHERE

VALENTA

LAKE
SUNRISE

BELLIS

ENISHAE

KRIA

GREAT
RED
DESERT

PASTIRA

HELT

DELYPHA

CHAPTER ONE

The meaty knuckles swing toward me. I duck too late, the unexpected backhand sending me tumbling from the saddle. I sprawl into red dirt, face pounding. *Ouch.* All I wanted was to get to Valenta, the next town. I hear they have baths, and fuck knows I reek after crossing this desert.

The three dismount, laughing and exchanging what I'm sure is witty repartee I can't make out through the ringing in my ear. My cheek is split inside, the blood slick, salt, and copper on my tongue. I spit into the dust. The air smells like heat, and I'll bruise to blues on that hip tomorrow.

I scan the horizon, a red line carved against deep blue sky. No one else in sight, and with my blade unhelpfully strapped to Liza's saddle instead of slung on my back.

Well, that one was my choice. My fault.

I squint against the sun at them. Hefty. The blade'll help if I can get to it, much as I wanted to not use it. But it's probably not enough on its own. I'm good, but I'm not *that* good.

But there's no one else.

Right. *Fuck.*

Any decent swordsman will tell you half the game is in the head, and the best place to play that game is out on the stage.

I level my gaze at them, unveiling the challenge in it. "Really? That's your best offer?" I grin, knowing my teeth are outlined in red. The second-in-command blinks. An iota of fear. I can work with that.

The leader, a brawny man with a scar carved from eyebrow to chin, grins back. He opens his mouth to speak and glances at his two goons. They always do this—take a moment for their audience. As the goons return his look, smirks dawning, I move. I toss a handful of sand across their faces, kick hard into the leader's belly, and turn immediately to feint left but hit hard on the right with an elbow into the first goon's crotch. He grunts, folds in half, and I stumble as I spin away from the second.

Their mounts panic, kicking up heels and bolting along the road to Valenta. Liza, my own horse, stands firm, thank fuck. She's the best.

My burst of violence is not going to be enough of a head start. No mercenary or highway brigand would hire backup less than raised to the kill. I need a weapon.

I roll backward through the hard-packed red dirt, sparing a sad thought for my glossy new silk jacket as I spring up next to Liza. The sword is there, tied into my blankets like only a fool would do. I grab the hilt, and with a swift tug that sends poor Liza skittering sideways and whinnying in protest, it's out of the scabbard.

I grin. It's been a while, but the leather-wrapped, sweat-soaked hilt welcomes my touch like a mother's arms to a prodigal son. Well, not my mother. Then again, I'm not her son. If I'd been a boy, it might've made all the difference.

Making my entrance, I lick the blood off my front teeth and spin the blade casually from hand to hand. A juggler's trick. The bright sunlight glints off the blade. The three have recovered, and are spreading to flank me. The second-in-command is closest. He'd been coming for me, full of bravado, making up for the stab of fear earlier. But now, he hesitates.

Intensify, bellows Picton in my memory. *They mustn't be able to look away!* I add an extra half-twist to the juggle of my blade, opening my eyes a little too wide, and the goon glances back at the leader, uncertain.

"Look, I get it," I say, after a decent spell of silence bar the whistle of my sword. "I do. You thought I was easy prey. Here I was, riding along, looking for all the world like a weaponless fool in a pretty silk jacket. You made me an offer based on that assessment. But none of those things are true ... except for the pretty silk jacket."

I pause for a moment, making a show of scanning the desert horizon, blade still spinning in the light. "So why don't we just leave it here? You can go home with all your limbs, and I'll be on my way. Better deal than the one you offered me." The traditional deal of highway brigands everywhere: give us everything and we'll kill you anyway.

Silence. It sounds like a fight coming. I spit on the ground, red on red, and try again. "That can be the measure of blood spilled here. Sum total."

The leader's craggy brow draws even tighter, and his face gets ugly. "So the fucking bitch has a sword," he snarls at his men, his disdain clear. It's always a marvel to me, the way men will loyally follow those who mostly show them contempt. "She's still a fucking bitch. Take her out!"

I'm decent with a sword, but truth be told, I'm a better player. I'd hoped the juggled sword would be enough to at least open negotiations. Wishing for the seven hundredth time that Petrus was still at my back, I draw up strength I haven't used this way in a good long while. Time to lean in to what I *do* have.

As the two goons rush me, I duck to cut swift across the middle, then spin right around to cut low, slipping below their blows. The dry air scalds my lungs. Their axes clash against each other above my head and my ears ring, but they are both bloody across the thighs. I might be a better player than fighter, but that is true of these two too. They tumble against each other, moaning as long spurts of blood chunk the dirt of the road. They won't be getting up anytime soon, but it won't stop them from screaming at me. I tune them out.

I shuffle back, soft boots stirring up the dust. The leader curses and strides toward me. He raises his blade, and a wily gleam lights in his eye. I meet the sword, eyes on his. We're beyond chatter now.

They stomp toward me. It's a bit of fancy talk when people compare a sword fight to dance. It's not like any dance I've ever done. My dances are all swaying hips and playing at sex. But then it's nobles, with their dances full of intricate footwork, who wax that kind of lyrical about fighting, trying to give it a swanky gloss. Really, it's all pretty stories. Sword fights are grim.

The swing is hard. I wince in anticipation and renew the grip on my hilt. The blade comes hard against mine. My shoulders complain at the impact, and I grunt aloud, locking my knees for a moment. He thinks where he holds it over me is in strength, and he's not altogether wrong. I shove back panic. Not helpful.

But I've known what looks like weakness on me for a good long while now, and know how to handle those trying to use it against me. I slip sideways, scuffing through sand, and turn my body toward the blade with my own sword for protection, letting his force slide past me.

I slice down his back as I dart backward. He's almost quick enough in his recovery, and the tip of my sword only cuts through the thick leather of his belt. It tumbles about his feet. I grin again, and he grins back.

"Flirting with me, girlie?" he growls, cupping his balls. I almost roll my eyes, but that would mean taking my eyes off him.

"Oh, for fuck's sakes." I feint high and then swing the blade to cut low. Both are feints, really, and he blocks both, but the third is a slice across his collarbone, near enough to his face to make him flinch. I want to crow, but he's not there yet. I draw back, knowing he'll be wary now, then shuffle sideways toward him, driving him back, forcing him to turn. Just a little further...

I go for two easy, ugly beginner's swings, moving a bit faster than he can shift that rough, weighty blade, and he's where I want him.

I grin, then yell, "Liza!" The horse raises her head abruptly with a noise of protest—I think she'd been napping—then grumpily points her rear hoof.

He hesitates, glancing sideways at the horse, and I rush in, driving him even closer to her unhappy hindquarters. She tosses her head and kicks back. She doesn't hit him, but she doesn't need to.

He leaps out of the way and into my swing. It's not fancy, but my blade carves through the leather straps of his vest and deep into his ribs, curving to tear upward through cartilage, into lung and bloody heart. It hurts my everything—the force of him falling toward me, the hilt driving towards my belly. My whole body howls in protest, then I struggle to hang on to my blade as he falls away from it. I stagger back to keep my balance.

"It was a bad deal," I say, almost sad as blood bubbles up to his lips. A hundred times over, this could've been me. It's actually *been* me a good dozen; I've just been luckier with wounds and companions and jobs. His eyes go wild for a moment, then they're still. "You'd've found I'm not disinclined to business, but I'm damned if I'll be fleeced."

"Fucking bitch! You killed him!" A roar from the two standing off to one side makes me look around, assessing.

The road is a mess, blood congealing in the ocher sand. The stink is already starting in the hot sun. This isn't exactly the note I'd choose for entering Valenta—bringing raging bandits in my wake. I don't need this kind of trouble.

I need money, and for money, I need work. And for work ... well, since I put away my sword, I've been leaning hard on the Rogue—doing minor theft and sex work, mostly. I can't afford to have this lot telling terrible tales about me, especially to the Rogue King himself.

I swallow, stumble across to catch up the leader's sliced belt with its big, heavy purse, then pause, returning to crouch beside the corpse. He's an ugly bugger, grimy from the road. Probably been two-week since he's cleaned his hair.

I narrow my eyes. The blade is better than he is, though, and the sheath has pretty patterns burned into it. Strange combination, but maybe he'd lucked into a new patron or one of those jobs I used to dream about that pays enough to kit you out forever. Well, luck is one word for it. I can only hope for my sake that whoever sent him wasn't too attached. How is it that since Petrus and I split up, trouble seems to stumble into my path?

I slice the rest of the ties on the front of his vest and yank the two sides back to reveal a small blade tucked into one side—also a bit too fancy for a simple mercenary—and a purse tied tightly to the other. That'd be right. Most traveling swords keep the good stuff close. I myself have a pouch tucked between my breasts with the few things I've kept precious.

The goons roar curses at me. Guess they know where the good stuff is. I tug the small blade from its sheath, toss them a salute with it, making them bellow even harder, and use it to cut away the purse. It's smaller, but falls open in my hand to reveal three gold coins mixed in with a button, a carved stone, and some sand.

A drop of blood falls from my face into the little collection, and I catch my fist back against my mouth. Still bleeding. I shake my head, and another drop falls. I shove the small purse inside the bigger one and tuck the blade into my right boot. Waste not, want not.

I glance over toward the two sidekicks as I wipe the blood off my sword on his legs. They snarl curses at me. Unlikely to be the forgiving type. I should kill them now, but my stomach roils at the thought of putting the blade to helpless men. I mean, I hadn't even killed Cap, and he'd deserved it far more than these two. They just followed a poor leader, and gods know I've done the same. I shake my head. Maybe the sun will make my decision for me? They wouldn't be the first to die in this desert.

I go over to pat and calm Liza, shoving the purses into the pouch tied to her saddle. "You're such a wonderful girl," I say, smoothing my sweaty hand against her neck, streaking the dirt. "Too wonderful for words." She gives me a look that is half preen and half haughty disgust, and I know I'm forgiven.

I blow out my breath as I untangle the scabbard from the roll and sling the blade across my back, strapping it down. It settles into place easily—too easily—and my mouth tightens. Easy is discomfiting, given the reason I'd put the sword away in the first place. That poor fucking kid.

"It wasn't meant to play out like this," I add, as I haul myself into the saddle. "Peaceable was the aim." I reach a finger inside the pouch, reassuring myself about the coin I've just taken. Enough to keep me for a while. Something sharp catches on my finger, and I yank it free. "Ow!" I put my fingertip to my mouth, tasting copper yet again.

I unhook my water skin, rinse my mouth clear, and spit. My mouth tightens. Can I really just leave them here to die? I scowl. They roar as I leave them behind me in the dirt.

"Not carrying a visible sword was meant to keep us safer!" I mutter as I urge Liza forward. She harrumphs in response as if she could have told me how silly that idea was.

CHAPTER TWO

V alenta feels more familiar than I expect. My first glimpse is of a low, dark bulge on the horizon, stark against the blue. Beyond it, to the north, unfolds the slow green-gray growth of farmlands, interspersed with crops of a yellow so bright it hurts my eyes. As I near, the town resolves into a chaotic brown mess. Shanty houses mark its edges, along with a stench that makes my nose twitch.

There's not a whole lot of town. Probably a fifteen-tavern place—big enough to visit if you're needing a place to stop, but not big enough to entice that many newcomers. It's much like any other town, but as I approach, I realize I know the layout better than I'd have expected. I frown. Had Petrus and I spent a night or two within its bounds and I've forgotten?

I follow the road, alert but playing at relaxed. If any of the brigands have friends expecting them, I need my bloody clothes to not be noticed. The thought of those goons out there under the broiling sun makes my gut turn over. Can I really leave them there to die? What if someone else happens on them, and they tell a tale about me that brings trouble for me into Valenta? The desert road isn't that sparsely populated. It could happen.

To either side of the entrance stands a tall wooden watchtower—the sign of a town large enough to sustain a border guard. The only story I've ever heard about this custom that makes sense is that, once upon a time, our sovereigns couldn't be relied on for aid, so towns that were large enough constructed these tall buildings and funded the soldiers to keep the town safe. Safe from what was never quite clear, though some say there were now-extinct beasts that used to attack humans. I'd seen the skeleton of a wombat taller than a man once, in Pastira, the capital.

The four guards shelter from the sun in the shadows of one of these towers, playing a game of royals. Doubtless they're supposed to be keeping an eye to the horizon and challenging visitors, but they barely cast me a glance, fixated on the game. A woman showing enough shoulder to clarify her trade leans over the game board as well, smiling. I wrinkle my nose as the wind shifts and wafts the scent of sweated-out beer.

I leave the towers behind, thankful no one felt the need to use me for any other kind of game today, as often happens at smalltown watchtowers.

By the messy line of shanties, boys kick a ball in the dust, a noisy cluster of energy in shades of tan and gold and brown. One disappears as soon as he's given me a good scan. That makes them Rogue kids, mostlike. Had Petrus and I presented ourselves to the Rogue here? I can't remember—probably a sign I've spent more time here drunk than not.

I narrow my eyes as an idea strikes me. I could send them to fetch the goons, calling them my friends—say we were all attacked together. I'd likely have to pay to get them healed up, but I'd be on the front foot telling the story with the Rogue, before their version starts to circulate. It'd pull the teeth of any plans for vengeance they had, and avoid anyone stumbling on them on the road and carrying them and their story about me this way. Coz their story would *not* endear me to the Rogue.

The goons were just that – goons. They shouldn't die because their boss made a foolish call. Gods know I've made bad choices for leaders before—I'd just been lucky enough that it hadn't meant own death. I swallow at the memory.

This country carries enough risks in the unpopulated areas between towns that the care of strangers has stood between me and death more times than I care to recall. At this point, it's almost a professional courtesy to keep other swords-for-hire from dying beside the road.

These lads'll make perfect storytellers for me. I guide Liza over and say, "You boys look like smart lads. Want to make some coin?"

They eye me up, and the dark-eyed, dark-skinned eldest lazily slaps a long stick in his hand. I oscillate between grinning or rolling my eyes but pick neither.

"Yer offer?" asks the biggest one, his long, curling dark hair hanging in greasy clumps.

"Two men on the road. Injured. Friends o' mine. I want you to go and help them back into town so's they're not dead 'fore morning. I'm sure smart lads like you will know where to get a barrow or a horse and dray." It sounds like I'm too easy a target to believe, so I curl my hand into the sign used by Rogues everywhere, and bare my teeth. Now they don't know what to make of me.

Half of me agrees with their original assessment. But this is the best plan I've got. I miss the gigs Petrus and I used to get, dancing more on the "in" side of the law than the out. They didn't have me casting a weather eye to the road every two seconds.

"Arright," the smallest says, tanned golden brown with blond curls tangled and gleaming. "How much ye offering?"

I smile. "Two silvers each now, and three when you come and tell me where they're housed so I can make sure they're taken care of."

They glance at each other, still suspicious. "And if we don't?" says the biggest one.

I smile even broader. "Then your friends' pay goes up," I tell him bluntly.

He glances at his mates, and we can both see they're willing. He nods, so I put two silvers into each grubby hand.

"Best place to lay my head?" I ask of the smallest, who lingers a moment with his canny gaze on my face.

"Reckon you're best at Indron's," he says. "Their place is clean and safest for a traveler like you. Take the second to the right and then the first left. Can't miss it." I nod a brusque thanks, and they're on their way.

As I head down the slight incline into town, the road changes from red dust to pale sand. This town's clearly got folks that still care to keep the place tidy.

The streets are busy but not packed—enough to give me some anonymity, at least.

I catch sight of the long trailing red-and-gold flags that designate a players' tent, billowing lazily above the rooftops. I've planted enough of those flags, cast in green and gold, my own self, in another life. My heartbeat kicks up. Killeen's lot those colors signify, if I remember right, and I know I do.

My mind skitters away from going further down that track, and firmly reminds me I need somewhere to sleep. I worry my tongue against the gash in my cheek again and wonder...

I inspect Indron's from afar and decide I'm not being played. It's well lit and a bare block away from the main street. I like the look of the stern, broad owner standing outside the door, in charge of the youngsters scrubbing at the pale stone of the steps.

The room is as I expected. Smaller windows than I'd ideally like but big enough to get out of in a pinch, overlooking a laneway and the back courtyard, and it's clean and recently painted. The bed's made for more than one. Blessed heavens, a mattress.

Tossing my pack down on a chest, I undo the buckles on my sword-harness and let it slide to the floor, ignoring the ache in my back from the unfamiliar weight. The bed groans as I sit down and glance down at my boots. Too much work. With a sigh, I let myself fall back across the bed, resigned to getting it dusty, and give my recalcitrant mind its head.

Killeen. I met him when I was traveling with the Picton crew. Salt-and-pepper hair and a waxed mustache, he was the head of another players' troupe, one that did a bit better than ours for patrons and pay. But when two companies of players meet on the road, no matter their differences, they tend to make nice, lighting a campfire and spending a night in playful competition, gossip, and performance.

Those nights had been the most fun of all—with an audience who could see the tricks and the illusions; who noticed the tiny bits of brilliance expressed in a subtle gesture of a hand or a breath; who knew precisely how hard the tumbling or juggling act really was, no matter how we labored to make them seem the easiest thing in the world. They usually ended with vast quantities of alcohol, some dancing, some sex, and sometimes even romance. After all, who better than a player to know how to inject a passing favor with all the fervor of a forever love.

But when we'd encountered Killeen, I'd been Liv's shadow, still awestruck over her beauty and blazing spirit and, oh gods, her caprice. Liv, Liv, Liv. She'd changed the whole of my world in ways that made my old life unrecognizable. My mind wanders away from thinking about Killeen, the path too well trod to deny another slow meander to where Liv and I began.

I'd been barely grown, really, looking back. Considered fully an adult by my little hamlet but country born and bred, I hardly knew my letters and had never spent a night away from home.

And then her troupe had come through the little village where I lived. I'd seen her perform some comic piece about a beautiful young man enchanting a string of girls with his bravery and heroism and charm.

I had been half in love with the young man she was playing, with the innocent way he played on the girls' affections and his dashing way of bowing—his feathered hat, which should have been ridiculous, scooping low.

But when, in the story, the young man is scandalously unmasked as a woman, the dark cascades of Liv's curls tumbling around her shoulders and her long lashes framing green, green eyes gone suddenly feminine, fierce want tugged between my legs. I'd known desire before, but not like this.

I have no doubt I was a hilarious sight when I approached her after the performance. Later, I would chuckle with Petrus over the other naïfs who did the same. I was speechless, but Liv must have recognized the helplessness of the desire in my eyes—she was the best at that. She smiled almost gently and led me, laughing toward the starry skies, back to her caravan.

I would eventually see that place as small and cramped and ragged, layered with devastations of a thousand kinds. But at that point, it was more opulent than anything I'd ever seen. Cushions were scattered all over the brocade bed, and as she swooped the hat from her head into that bow, making me one of the gorgeous girls from the play, I grinned foolishly. But that was nothing to the sex.

I'd had my fair share of tumbles with the local lads and enjoyed them, even occasionally seeking them out.

This ... this was different...

Finally, I had been left dangling from the hook set in the ceiling of her caravan, my knees no longer able to hold me up, as she threw herself down on the bed, worn out and pleased. She had released the catch that let the hook loose and sent me tumbling to the floor, turned over, and went to sleep.

I still remember the slow process of untying my hands with my teeth in the dim light, my mind unable to compass what had happened, thighs still soaked with my own damp and her saliva combined. I fell in love there on that floor, replaying impossibly beautiful images in my head, massaging the feeling back into my poor hands. I fell in love, and Liv slept on.

Which was to be, more or less, the nature of our relationship, at least for most of the time I spent with her.

In the morning, I softly and sincerely told her I loved her, and she lost the wicked gleam she'd had in her eyes the night before and responded in kind. It was more and other than I'd ever dared to dream of, and I couldn't imagine how the world could *not* be changed by the *us* we'd discovered.

But when I went home, love-drunk and still dizzy with desire, it all changed. My mother, thinking I had been with a boy, was happy and teasing, trying to get the tale out of me—already looking for marriage and grandchildren, no doubt. When I finally confessed I had been with a woman, she threw me out of the house with nothing but my ragged clothes. Few in this country will countenance talk of women lying with one another, though I've found, over the years, that there's more hypocrisy in that fact than is usually thought.

Brokenhearted and red-nosed from sobbing, I'd made my way back to Liv's caravan, shouted at by the villagers I'd spent my entire life alongside. I'd beaten on her door, almost howling with the loss. The tale about us was circulating so fast I had nowhere else to go. All my friends, all those families who had been almost like my own ... all repudiated me.

Liv was wide-eyed and sympathetic, rubbing my back until I calmed enough to speak. She swore to take me with her when they left, and I'd kissed her 'til I fell dizzily against her pillows. Together, we dreamed of a wild, heady, nomadic future.

I had thought all of this—not least what I'd lost to be with her—made me special, and I do believe that, at least for a while, she loved me. But it didn't take long before I realized Liv was still leaving behind a string of broken hearts—not just mine—and often broken heads, no matter what she whispered to me in the night.

I loved Liv for three long years, and she loved me, in her capricious, complex way, for, I'd estimate, eight months of that time. Fortunately—or perhaps not—I had made my place amongst Picton's troupe by then and was already a contributing player earning my way. I had a place in the world. After losing my home and my family and my village, that counted for something. And so, I'd stayed, despite the way she oscillated between seduction and devastation, until Petrus convinced me to leave.

I sigh, letting the back of my hand rest against my eyes. *Liv.*

The tavern bed is a little lumpy, I realize.

I shove my thoughts in another direction. Killeen. Not Liv, not the Picton troupe. Killeen's flags marked the street here in Valenta.

The night the two troupes had met by the campfire has its own special sting, even after all the hurts Liv was yet to do to me. I was likely almost eighteen and still achingly in love with Liv while she vacillated between being "madly" in love with me and begging me never to leave her, ordering me to go, and telling me to stay but that she couldn't ever love me. She took up with numerous others, driving Picton wild with the chaos she perpetually sowed in his crew.

And on this particular night, it was Killeen himself, mustachioed and brown-skinned and probably three times her age. She was three years older than I, lithe and long and gorgeously curved. He was older.

Killeen prided himself on the beauty of the members of his troupe, and he had long tried to talk Liv into joining his crew. Their allure meant they were given some of the best gigs available—wealthy folks seeking slightly naughty entertainment for their parties, and princes and princesses who, rumor had it, invited players to perform both onstage and in the bedroom. They were the kind of troupe I would never be invited to join—not incandescently beautiful enough.

On the other hand, it would have been the perfect place for Liv. But she knew Picton gave her liberties Killeen would never have allowed—like me joining the troupe—and if there was one defining thing about her, it was that she wanted her way, whatever that might mean.

After denying his request that she sign up with them, she'd mollified Killeen with sex, and I'd curled up and sobbed on the bed we had sometimes shared. I'd not yet learned the power of seeking out affirmation with other lovers. As Petrus told me later: it might not fix the situation, but it sure makes it easier to deal with. Knowing that even if the one who seems the world doesn't want you, the world actually might.

We'd not encountered Killeen and his company again before Petrus finally talked me into moving. I'd been with Picton's crew for nearly three years by then, in an agony of love. I've no idea what had happened to Picton's troupe since then, and Killeen and his crew ... well, it would have been, what, a good six or seven years since I'd seen them? They might not even recognize me.

I roll onto my side with a sigh, focusing on the grain of the wooden bedhead. If I'm honest, it isn't seeing Killeen again that makes me anxious. Hell, there might even be a chance to revisit the possibility with Joseph, a player from Killeen's troupe I'd turned down in order to weep over Liv. I'd regretted that choice a few times since. Joseph was beautiful, all narrow limbs and grace. No. I blow out a breath. That's not what's scaring me.

I force myself to say it aloud to the bedhead. "I'm worrying that Killeen's talked Liv into joining him. That she's here. In Valenta."

The words are stark. I've refused to let her name cross my lips for a long time. I take a deep breath. They're a wealthy company, Killeen's, and Liv knows the power of money. It wouldn't be that surprising if she had eventually exchanged Picton's latitude for Killeen's gold.

I pull myself up to standing. Liv's stage presence means she'd be in every performance, even among Killeen's talented crew. I need to go along, part of the crowd. Then I'll know.

I ignore the voice in my head that wonders why knowing would help. No matter how much I try to dismiss Liv from my mind, the possibility of her appearing will be like an aching tooth I worry at if I don't get my head clear. If Liv is in town, I need to get far, far away, and this plan with the Rogue, the goons, and making some coin will all be convolutions I can leave in the dust. Distance. The only safe way to deal with Liv is distance.

I stare down at my sword, wondering whether to take it with me. Next, I wonder whether the silk jacket I'm still wearing looks right after my tumble in the dirt earlier. Then I'm thinking about how Liv had loved the bottle of scent I'd bought off a traveling merchant and speculating about whether it's still tucked into the corner of my pack. I sigh, scrub a hand through my short hair, stare at the mirror, and try to channel Petrus.

"Are you really going to do yourself up for her when you don't even know if she's there?" My hazel eyes narrow at myself. "Of course not. Because she doesn't matter. Not anymore. She hasn't mattered in a long, long time." My mouth quirks at me, almost a betrayal, and I bite down on my tongue until it hurts.

I screw my nose up at myself. "Besides, Des," I say, calm and firm now, "you know that if she's there, she'd know in an instant you'd dolled yourself up for her. And then she'd know exactly how to wiggle back in."

Before I can tidy my hair or rub the smudges from my face, I sling the sword into place, buckle it, and lock the door behind me. "Just don't think about her," I murmur as I head down the stairs, almost at a run.

CHAPTER THREE

The sun's gone golden with late afternoon and it gleams on the tavern's whitewashed walls. It'll be hours before the daylight disappears altogether. As I come around the corner at the bottom of the stairs, still trying to rid myself of the memory of Liv's green gaze, I almost run into the tavern keeper, Indron.

And they're holding a familiar young lad firmly by the scruff of his shirt. Tthe situation I've managed to get myself into with the bandits on the road reasserts itself. "Ah. Says he's looking for you," Indron says measuredly to me, before the boy can spit out a word. "Says you owe him. This true?"

I force a smile to my lips. "I apologize if he has been disruptive." I keep my voice quiet to encourage Indron to do the same. "I sent him to help some friends of mine earlier, and he was to report back to me."

"I'll thank you," Indron says, "to keep your business within proper bounds. Hiring children for adult work is ... cheap."

I smile again, determinedly. "It *was* a bargain."

Indron sniffs and stalks away. I turn to the boy. "Excellent work, young man," I say, dripping sarcasm. "Don't tell me Indron's not got a reputation round here. You knew exactly how to avoid getting caught."

"Sure they do." He gives me a quirk of a smile. "But their reputation is 'alf growl, 'alf sticky rice with mango an' pity for us poor kids. They thought they caught me, but this way, I'm sure to get rice, prob'ly for the four of us."

I grin. "Smart man. So, did you find my ... uh, friends?"

He grins back, eyes sparkling behind his greasy hair. "Yes'm, though they told us tales about a bitch in a black silk jacket as killed their boss." I smile faintly and don't respond. His critical look only lasts a moment. "Ah, yer business is yer own, after all. They're no worse'n they were. We've took 'em to the healer, Rositus, what's over on the Street o' Flowers. They's not got much money, though. Not sure as he'll give 'em the herbs they need after he's stitched 'em, 'less they pay 'im. Calls it 'enabling,' he does."

I nod, but my heart sinks a little. "I'll go see them, then." I pause. "Do they not have money because you took it? Surely they had some on them." His eyes grow shifty, and I shake my head. "Those who steal from my friends... Well, the Rogue will surely have something to say about those who kill a man and steal his goods, and without his permission. Or his cut."

He gets my meaning in less than a moment. "We've not stolen nuffink! Nuffink! I was gonna give it you all along."

I raise my brows, letting the cynicism show. "So give it me, then."

"Not 'tils we get paid. We hold his stuff 'til you pay for us helping yer ... friends."

I bite my lip, keeping back a grin. "It is a sad, sad thing to see so much distrust in one so young," I say, playfully overacting mournful.

He looks taken aback for a moment, smirks, then puts on a mask of utter dejection. "'Tis a cruel world." He glances at his toes and then up through his lashes.

The memory flashes in my head—one of Liv's favorite characters says precisely that line. I shove the feelings away. "Save it for the stage, young 'un," I say affectionately. "Where are your mates, then?"

He leads me out into the sunshine and down to the corner, where the three others are back to kicking the ball around. I fish inside one of the three purses I'm carrying—the small one—and carefully count three coins into each hand. I doubt any of them had seen five silvers together in their short lives. It's a thing I like: overpaying the truly poor and haggling hard with the seriously rich, with all the skills of player and gambler at my disposal. "So, show it to me, then," I say, looking down into pleased faces.

They hand over two small dirty purses, little more than drawstring leather pouches cut from the two men's belts. I know they are probably somewhat lighter than they had once been, but that's as it should be. I run my fingers through the coin, but it's clear there's nowhere near enough here to care for the goons. Lucky I scrounged the leader's purse before the kids got to it.

"Such kind souls, the kids of this town!" I overplay sweet, making them grin, half-abashed and half-proud. "Generosity to shake the gods free from their heavens. So let me beg one more prize from you, my young friends."

They're almost laughing now, poking each other in the ribs and bowing low enough to grace a king. Perfect moment for it. Time to lay the groundwork for my way in with the Rogue and hope to blessed heaven either the injured goons are as unfamiliar as I am, or that I at least get to tell my story before they get to tell theirs.

"It's been some time since I've drunk with the Rogue here, and honest, I'm on the road so much that these little towns... Has there been a change in leadership? Is ... now, what was his name, the Rogue I knew here?" I tap my lip, performing as though I were racking my brains. "Ah... hmm..."

"Harman," the young blond one says helpfully. "Harman's dead, but. Killed two summers ago by the new Rogue."

"Harman!" I play at epiphany. "Ah, I'm sorry to hear he's gone, but these things do happen. What's the new Rogue's name, then?"

"Armand." The lank-haired one has a canny look in his eye. "We could innerduce you, if yer like."

I grin conspiratorially at him. "For a fee, I don't doubt," I say with a wink. They all laugh. "That would be good. Can you make a time for me this evening? I'm sure savvy lads like you know all the right ways to get before him. I need to present myself proper-like, see if there's any work for a traveling sword like me."

That ought to do it. With the story I've told these chatty boys about the goons being my friends, there shouldn't be too much suspicion on me, even if they wax lyrical about a woman with a sword. They look doubly pleased now. Being the center of this small drama in their town is a bit of a boon for them, mostlike. "But for now, I have to visit my friends. Street of the Flowers, you said, yes?"

Lanky nods and adds, "The Rogue holds court at Kitchener's. We'll be there after dark. That's when he sees supplicants. We'll make sure you're on the list."

I nod solemnly, giving them respect. "I'll see you there." I turn to walk away. "Oh, and don't forget Indron's sticky rice. Silly to set 'em up and not knock 'em down."

I'm a little worn as I walk away, like I usually am when I'm feeling something entirely different to the mask I'm trying to keep in place. Gods. I tie the two extra purses inside my jacket, making it bulge a little, and pull out the goon leader's moneybag to check whether there's enough money to pay for their care. Can't half-ass a rescue; gotta plant enough doubt in the Rogue's mind for when those men heal up and tell their own story. Yep. More than enough coin.

I run fingers through the rounds again, over and over, finding comfort in the feel and clink, calming my breath. Until something cuts me and I almost drop the whole bag. "Ow!"

I cautiously withdraw my hand and find a long, thin slice along one side of my middle finger. It oozes a drop of blood, and I catch it quickly to my mouth. I glower at the bag a little more, then tie it to my belt. Time enough to investigate its contents later. I've reached Rositus's door.

I slowly open the creaking door to find a small wooden room lined with shelves, stocked with glass jars full of herbs and seeds and icky things. A counter runs the width, and the doorway behind is draped with a curtain. Likely the treatment room. I walk in, letting my footsteps resound as if I'm a good deal more solid than I am.

"Hello?" I call.

"Ah, you'll be the kind friend who sent those boys back to save these men's lives and goodness, not a moment too soon! They were really bleeding out and I'm not sure I could've done anything if they'd arrived much later though of course they'll be alright now." A little man hastens through the curtain, finally pausing to draw breath. "I assume?"

The rush makes the silence sound deep when it's gone. I nod, smile, and stick out my hand to shake his, hoping they don't hear me. "I'm Des. Desta Mildue. Thanks for taking care."

"Rositus. Elmo Rositus. It'll cost a pretty penny, likely," he warns, scanning me head to toe. The two purses at my waist reassure him. "Want to see the patients before we settle things?"

"Oh, that's alright. I don't want to disturb their healing. What do I owe you?"

Rositus mutters over a scrap of paper, adding figures and scrawling totals. I glance around as he does, hoping we don't disturb the goons behind the curtain. I'd really rather not have the confrontation with them right now, especially about the purses still hanging about my person.

Rositus is taking his time over the sums. I wander over into a corner, away from him, so I can count out some of the goon leader's coin. I cup my hand around the little sack, untie the bindings, and pull them loose. The purse falls open in my hands, revealing a goodly amount—more gold than I remember, and enough silver. It should more than cover the goons' treatment if Rositus isn't trying to rob us blind.

A strange glimmer beneath the gold and silver catches my eye, and I remember the button and the stone I saw earlier. I poke at it gently, and there's a searing pain on my fingertip, just like before. Stifling a cry, I yank my finger away, bite my lip, and squeeze my eyes shut for a second against the pain. That's the third time! The pain settles quickly, and when I glance back, Rositus is still working away. Clearly, math is not his strong suit.

I peer back at the little pile of coin, and something shifts. I cover a finger with the leather of the purse this time and awkwardly stir the pieces against each other. Two things that look a bit like thimbles are actually two halves of a tiny, very thick carving of an egg, I realize, patterned with rainbows that glimmer in the light. I reach to pick up one of the halves, wondering how the stone could have broken.

Then I see it.

I stand very, very still, trying to force my mind to make sense of what it's seeing. Coiled in the little pile of money is a minute but very complete statuette of a lizard curled around itself. Cast in a dull silver, perhaps even pewter, it's about the size of my thumb.

But it moves.

My heart beats like a punch. In fact, if my eyes aren't deceiving, its little sides heave in and out. I blink and stare and try to clear my vision, or my mind, or whatever it is making me see impossible things.

And then the lizard isn't just breathing. It uncoils its head and peers up at me with tiny sapphires for eyes. Except they're not sapphires, of course, because sapphires don't move around, taking in their surroundings.

I lick my lips, my heart beating in my throat. The little lizard stares, then spreads broad, faintly rainbowed wings and, beating hard, flies awkwardly up toward my face. I react as if an insect were coming at me—I make a muted cry and swat at it with the hand holding the purse.

Coins go everywhere, and I hit the little dragon—*dragon!*—right out of the air and send it skittering across the floor.

Rositus doesn't even look up, clearly in the middle of a calculation. "Did you say something?" he asks absently. "Won't be a sec."

"No, sorry, just dropped something." Convincing.

I slide to my knees. The slight shimmer of the dragon glistens in the shadow of the shelves. As I bend toward it, it picks itself up, and I'd swear anger and indignation line its body. It turns to face me and rears up on its hind legs with its wings spread, clearly aiming for fierce and terrifying. And it is, even if it's tiny.

The little jaws open, and I nearly fall backward as I retreat from its darting bite. "I'm sorry," I whisper, soft and desperate. Am I talking to a moving dragon statue? Why is there a dragon statue, and why is it *moving*? Alright, probably not a statue.

Why is there even a *dragon*?

If Rositus sees it ... I have no idea what will happen if Rositus sees it. I'd always thought they were myth! Clearly not, but ... of all the places, what would a dragon be doing in a brigand's purse? I think of the lead brigand's fancy blades, and my heartbeat kicks up. I need some space to work out what to do about this latest obstacle in my path. "You startled me."

It cocks its head to one side, for all the world as if it were considering my words, and its wings slowly fold. It's brightening, still gray, and it shimmers with every movement. I hesitate for a long moment, then offer it the purse I grip tightly in my hands. It rears back up on its hind legs, chirruping in indignation, and I pull my hand away.

"Sorry, sorry, I didn't think," I whisper, frantic. "But you can't just walk around. Someone will see you." And that would necessitate far too many explanations. Like where it came from.

Where *did* it come from?

The tiny creature bows its head, almost frowning, then abruptly takes off again, still clumsy in its flight. I control my surprise a little better than last time. It hovers up around my head, staring into my eyes, so close I go cross-eyed, then lands on my head, its sharp talons gentle against my scalp.

I hesitate, then put a hand up to take it back down and get a little nip for my trouble. It's not angry anymore, but it seems to be warning me it could get that way again. I swallow. Is this enough to hide it? I rise slowly to standing, worried I'm going to unbalance it.

I'm not sure what to do about my new hairdo, so I slowly collect up all the coins and put them back in the purse, holding my head like I'm balancing a book on it. The last couple of things I find in the shadow of the shelves are the halves of the small egg. I peer at them. There's a spot of blood on one side of one piece. The shell is thick. Anything that came out of that must have been damn strong to break it in two.

And now, it's clutching at my hair. Not very comforting.

"Don't suppose you want to get down," I suggest softly, trying to see my new headdress in a window. It's too bright outside, though, and all I can see is a hazy outline of my head. I can only hope the tiny dragon looks like some kind of extravagant and out-of-character hair clip.

And not a moment too soon. My heart leaps back into my throat as Rositus finally looks up and announces triumphantly, "Four gold pieces!"

I spin and blink at him. "Four?" The price *is* steep. I regret my generosity already.

"Including everything, yes." He flicks his pen, clearly used to this kind of surprise. "Four days' care here, along with enough herbs to get them healed."

I hesitate a moment, still holding my head stiffly, then stick my hand back into the leather purse. I pull out money and begin counting it, and the bell at the door tinkles behind me.

"Hello?" says a musical voice, and I freeze.

It can't be. Dread can't make people manifest, can it? Fuck.

"I'll be one moment young lady," Rositus says hastily, in his habitual run-on way. "I need to finish up a transaction with this young woman and then I will need to get back to my patients though all I really need to do is check whether they're awake and then I can help you with whatever you need so long as they don't need anything first."

I stand, frozen, still holding a palmful of coins, and I have one in hand to count onto the long counter, but I have no idea what number I was up to. I suck in a large breath, but it's not enough. The fear, already scotching its way through my veins from the dragon's attack and, well, existence, redoubles. I struggle for air a little, breath coming short. *Fuck, fuck, fuck.*

I'm only putting it off. I know exactly who is there. Part of me wonders, just a little, how much and how little has changed in six years. Who am I kidding? That part of me is most of me, or at least all of me that's not thinking about the creature of myth tangled in my hair.

And if my pounding heart is any measure, nothing has changed. Nothing at all. Curse every god there has ever been.

But, fuck... There's a dragon perched on my head. I have to get out of here so I can work out what I'm going to do.

I steel myself and prepare to play, reaching for a casual charm I hope will cover my tumult. I glance toward her as if I hadn't recognized her voice, then fake a double take. "Gods!" I exclaim, all light surprise, as if seeing her is not like a tent peg through my heart. I've said it before; I'm a decent player. "Liv Equitor? Is that you?"

She's barely changed. Her skin is still impossibly pale, and her dark brows slant over those green eyes. I can see the stress—I've only seen those lines between her brows when she is truly vexed or anxious. She is more than startled to see me here. I've caught her off guard. I haven't ever seen that on her. It's surprisingly heartening.

"Des?" she says disbelievingly. "You're here? I thought you were dead!"

I open my mouth to reply, but a cloud of dark curls covers my face as Liv's arms wrap around me—not tight, but our bodies know precisely how we fit together. My breath stops. "Oh, my dear," she whispers in my ear in that same low lilt. "I have missed you so!"

My heart pauses for a beat, then races on. My facade fractures, and I buy some time to compose myself by returning her embrace. Which is a mistake, of course. The heat trickles down to a place between my legs.

"Nope, not dead." My voice cracks a little. She notices and softens a bit. I curse her ability to read people so easily, to read *me* as if I were a book. "Just been traveling around ... seeing a little of this, a little of that. You know."

It's not quite the truth, but it's hardly a lie. After leaving Picton's crew six long years ago, I spent two years dressed as a boy, learning swordplay. It was hard work—not just the swordplay, but the playing at being a boy. Fortunately, Petrus had been there with me, and my time in Picton's crew had left me player enough to maintain the deception.

Petrus and I had traveled a while after that school, but about a cycle ago, he'd abandoned me on the road without warning. I understood. He had learned to love me over the years, and I was a mess. Even after four years, I still couldn't help it—I spoke of Liv almost every day. Malicious words, always, but it didn't really matter, one way or another. I wasn't speaking of him. He raged at me—the kind of anger I had learned was the only thing that could buy your freedom sometimes—and I left him with it.

I've been on the road alone for more than half a cycle since. I've sometimes performed: tumbling and juggling for crowds in marketplaces, keeping fifteen oranges in the air and then high-kicking into the middle of the flow. Sometimes I've danced for crowds, occasionally wearing shockingly little. Sometimes I've joined mercenary groups, paying my way in violence, though the past half cycle I've traveled without the sword on my back. That kid's face was like to swim in my dreams for a while yet. Only Liza knew the story, but even so, she still disapproved of me putting my sword away.

And sometimes, I had sex for money. It's been enjoyable, and oh-so-bad at other times, but it can be almost as fun as being on the stage, and it pays well if you know how to work the job. My purse still jingles with coin from last week's three clients. And birthing dragons, I think a little hysterically. A little of this. A little of that. Not quite a lie.

Slowly, Liv nods, as maddeningly knowing as ever. I can't even name the emotion that makes my gut knot and roil. "I see. You look very well. Stunning, actually. You've grown some curves to match that height."

Few would be able to recognize it, but there's a cruelty hovering behind her words. I've spent so much time thinking about this woman that I can spot it off the bat: a compliment and the tiniest hint that she might even find me more attractive now. That's her way. Always the promise. Right now, it doesn't even touch me. I'm desperately angling for nonchalance, hoping she won't notice the dragon.

"You look well too. Coming into your prime." The barb catches, and her eyes narrow slightly. It's ferociously satisfying.

"And that's a gorgeous decorative piece," she says. I catch my breath as she reaches out as if to touch the dragon. *Shit.* No. I can't even work out the risks of her knowing about the dragon.

My palms grow sweaty, and I lean away from her touch, hoping the dragon won't move. Her gaze is amused, the knowingness spun up to vanity. That dark, practiced rage unfurls in my gut, a counterpoint to the anxiety. "It doesn't seem quite like you, Des! Although I must confess, it sets off those green flecks in your eyes beautifully."

I half smile, then frown a little, having to hold myself back from racing out the door and away. This is too, too much. I clutch after reason and turn back to Rositus. "My apologies, good sir. My friend and I have not seen each other in many years. Do you remember where I was?"

Turning away from those green eyes helps, but I can feel Liv's body behind me. The warm length of it, those curves. The sardonic smile that could turn pouty at any moment, and the satiny tumble of curls. I struggle to concentrate as Rositus wends his way through his response. "I'm afraid I don't young miss and I do apologize but I was taken by surprise and really it's not surprising is it now, with such a beautiful young lady?" This last is directed to Liv, who I know is smiling that smile that is mostly kind and holds a hint of promise—enough to keep him generous to her.

Fuck. I need out of here. I bite the inside of my lip hard. The pain galvanizes my attention, and I manage to count out the coins into his hand. I thank him profusely, tell him I will be back to visit my "friends" soon, then turn to Liv. "It is great to see you," I gush before she can speak. "Such a shame I'm here so briefly, and I'm sure Killeen's schedule keeps you run off your feet. Still, wonderful to see you again. All the best!"

She smirks. Fuck. I've screwed up. Saying I'm only here briefly when I've just arranged with Rositus to visit the invalids? And that casual reference to Killeen means she knows I saw the troupe's flags, and it made me think of her, and so, of course, seeing her probably wasn't quite the complete shock I'd pretended it was. And no doubt she's putting all of my edginess down to her appearing, when really, I have a fucking dragon sitting on my head. These mistakes will look to her like a way back in. If she wants it.

It feels like the time I'd made it to the top of the pyramid of bodies Picton had arranged, only to mess up the jump down, which I'd practiced over and over off the high board. It had hurt, that fall.

This one feels potentially messier.

I walk toward the door, hasty now, giving up on the illusion of being fine. I need out. The dragon shifts a tiny bit on my head, and I force myself to slow my step. If it falls...

"You should bring your friends to the show," she says, confirming how obvious my mistakes are. "Perhaps we can go for a drink afterward. If you can spare the time, of course."

I nod, smiling ferociously. "Sounds wonderful. See you soon, then."

And then, thank all the gods, I'm in the street. I glance back to make sure she's not looking out after me and take off at a dead sprint, kicking up a pale cloud of dust, while one hand cups the dragon to my head.

CHAPTER FOUR

I reach the inn as the sun begins to set. A cluster of customers sit around eating, and the food smells great. I make myself notice so it doesn't start thinking on Liv. My heart won't quit racing. Indron nods to me from behind the bar before I make my way back up to my bedroom. My hand shakes as I press a taper to the hall lamp to light my own lantern. It's tempting to fall on the bed and weep—today has been a fucking shitshow, beginning to end—but I'm not alone.

I stand before the mirror and turn my head. How convincing would it have been, pretending it's a hairpiece?

The dragon clutches my hair still, balancing. It looks for all the world like a miniature version of the beasts I've only ever seen depicted in fancy tapestries in some of the more salubrious joints the Picton troupe performed in—aristocratic halls or merchant.

Well, I've seen a dragon represented in one other place—that one play we occasionally performed, *The Slayer of Pastira*. I'd only ever played a member of the townsfolk, but we'd had an enormous dragon head made of papier-mâché that appeared onstage when Petrus, as the dragon slayer, chopped the beast's head off. The story was supposedly about the last dragon that ever lived. Some scribe had been sent by some aristocrat from the west coast to watch us repeatedly in one of the towns—said he was recording the details from the play for a collection about the Era of Storms. I mostly remember how annoying the prop was to cart around.

But this dragon is tiny and intricately wrought, and hardly seems capable of the devastation the play described. It is less silver and rainbows now and more of an aquamarine hue, and has arranged itself aesthetically, catching back a little of my hair in its claws. It does look for all the world like an overly ornate hair comb. I swallow, imagining what might have happened if Liv really had touched it.

"Smart little thing, aren't you?" The dragon raises its head and preens in the mirror at me. Its sapphire eyes are focused on mine. Intelligence comes off it in waves. "I wish I could understand what the hell you are." I cautiously reach up a hand.

It doesn't attack, just releases my hair and steps onto my palm. I put my hand on the desk, and it clambers down carefully, even that tiny distance seeming enormous. It is so little. I pull up the chair before it.

For a long moment, we stare at each other. My mind is almost blank, still trying to make this whole situation make sense. Where the fuck did this little thing come from?

"So," I start, "you're a dragon." It sounds laughable, and I get the distinct sense that the dragon thinks so too. "Yes, alright, stating the obvious. But I can't really ask you questions and get answers, can I?"

The dragon rears back on its hind legs and stares at me.

"Why do I get the feeling you're about to tell me how to get answers out of you?" I say uneasily. "And why not? If I'm going to try to wrap my head around your very existence, I may as well go the whole hog. Get all the impossibility out of the way at once, yeah?"

The dragon moves dartingly fast, then, faster than I've seen it move yet. It flies up toward my face, and when I open my mouth to protest, it weaves and slips inside. I jerk forward in shock, but a moment later it's out again. Pain drifts down my throat, my tongue freezing and on fire.

I haul in a breath, heart racing.

Then my whole body shudders, every muscle slamming tight. I crash onto the floor. Fire licks its way through my veins, burning me from the inside out. *Fuck.* I thought I'd known pain, but this outstrips it all.

Slowly, it fades to a tingle.

Just as I sit up, my ears fill with pain—deafening noise resounds in them.

I glance up. Hundreds of people are packed into my bedchamber.

Shit! I scramble backward until I hit the wall and yank my sword over my shoulder. My heart hammers. It makes no sense. The room had been empty. Now, distinctly, hundreds and hundreds of people, more people than could ever fit in this room, move around in it. They don't seem to be aware of me at all. Few of them seem to be aware of each other either. It's terrifying. They're not ghostly—they look as solid as I am—but they're passing through each other as if they're not.

A woman mops the floor, looking exactly like the fifty other women at various cleaning tasks, and her mop simply passes through the legs of the person at the washbasin, shaving and humming to herself. The sound disappears into the cacophony. I try to focus on this one image, try to make it make sense, but it's impossible.

I glance over at the bed, and somehow, in a way that I can't explain, hundreds of people lie in it. Asleep, wakeful, having sex—overlapping but not overlapping at all. Impossibly in the same space, but also somehow not. I shake, my teeth chattering.

My heart pounds in my ears, and I can't help the whimper that rises in my throat.

I leap up, fling my sword out. It passes through twenty overlapping people as if they aren't even there. But they *are*. I can hear them, see them, smell them. The smell! It stinks like fifty thousand battlefields, with wafts of perfume too intense to be pleasant.

It makes no sense. First my mind and then my body rebel against impossibility. The sword clangs to the floor, my fingers gone nerveless. I cover my ears and slide down the wall.

I can't close my eyes, but my mind won't compass what I'm seeing. My gorge rises in my throat. Somehow, the vomit passes through boots piled untidily against the wall.

The crowds begin to disappear. One by one, they simply are not there anymore, as abruptly as they had appeared. The noise settles too, along with the smell.

Apologies, sounds a snarky voice I don't know. *I didn't know, but it makes sense.*

I scramble to my feet as the last of the people in the room wink out of existence. The smell is gone, all but the stink of my vomit. The room is quiet. I stagger over to the bed and ease down onto it, trying not to recollect the hundreds of people all piled together onto the same mattress.

This must be insanity.

Shaking, I take long, deep breaths, staring down at my upturned palms. My heart still batters against my ribs. There's a quiet whir, and the dragon lands in my right palm.

I am sorry, repeats the voice. *I didn't even think of it.*

"Is that you?" I ask softly, somewhat afraid of the answer.

What? This voice? Of course. You told me you wanted to communicate with me. This is me communicating.

This last is sardonic, as if I'm an idiot. Irritating little thing. I straighten my shoulders. "You can cut the tone. In case you missed it, I'm already believing too many impossible things, and now you're behaving like I'm a backward child. You might be smart and impossible, but I'm still bigger than you." I peer at it. "Actually, have you grown?"

The dragon's sapphire eyes are pinned to mine. *Oh, well spotted.* The sarcasm oozes off the little creature. *Of course I'm growing.*

I swallow hard, trying to digest that one. "I... alright."

This is the arrangement. Sorry I couldn't explain it to you earlier, but, well, until the bond is complete, communication is impossible. And that's hardly my fault. The ordering of time is not my problem. I'm not built for it, that's all.

I close my eyes against the dizziness. It's like shuffling cards, trying to make sense of a hand in a game I don't know. I can't even work out what question to ask first.

Ah, goodness, mortality does make one's anxieties intense, does it not? the voice says, a cool and detached observation. *Interesting.*

I scowl. "Glad I'm so fascinating for you," I snark back. The anger is a relief. "How's about you explain what's going on instead of treating me like an extraordinarily mediocre new species you've discovered?"

Goodness, the dragon echoes itself. *Well, alright then. I suppose it can't hurt to have you understand a bit. After all, we'll need to leave soon. As if we haven't already left.*

I close my eyes and take a deep breath against exasperation. The little dragon's eyes sparkle up at me when I open them. *So. It was your blood that birthed me. I don't know how that happened because I was obviously not alive then. Which is ridiculous, but that seems to be the way it is. So here I am. And I am blood bonded to you. And now you are blood bonded to me. Well, really, you always were.* It hovers up near my face for a moment and places a cool claw against my lip. *I put some of my blood inside you, and you can hear me, as well as the other way around.*

I blink. Does it mean that I'm communicating nonstop? Without speaking? Like it is with me?

Indeed. It tips its head on one side. *Why? Is that bad?*

I go through everything I've thought in the last hour and sigh. "Pretty bad," I murmur aloud, running a hand through my hair as I contemplate Liv. "Some of that stuff is private."

Such a strange concept, this private. *She did interfere with your ability to think, which is interesting. I know everyone you know had rejected you, but it was still a strange decision to stay around someone who has that effect on you.*

The old hurt—older than the scars Liv left me—resurfaces, and I close my eyes to manage it. My heart aches, and a moment later I reach anger. Who the fuck is this dragon, sorting through my entire history and passing judgment?

Yes, very odd, privacy, it continues. *I sincerely don't know how you hu-mans came up with it in the first place. But then, maybe it's part of this whole chained-time thing.*

"Does it matter?" I snap. "Could you get on with it?"

You blood-birthed me, and with you Incorporating a drop of my blood, we're blood-bonded. Which means you have to help me get to Calindrina. As soon as possible. I don't know enough, and I can only know more by getting there. Which, again, ridiculous, but I can't be blamed for how you've chained time.

"Like not knowing about privacy?" None of this makes any sense.

Indeed. It seems not to react to my tone, but I know it notices. *But I need to get there, and soon. It is too strange I was birthed out here when I need to be there. And, of course, I am there, which is the most frustrating part. Or I could be. But goodness, this will take some time, I suppose, so we should get on with it.* I stare at it now, my mind refusing the nonsense. *But yes, we should leave. Sooner would be better. Sooner! As if I've the time for sooner!*

I harrumph and dump the dragon roughly out on the bed. It hisses up at me. "Enough," I announce, to it and the room. "I need dinner. I need to think. There are men out there with sharp weapons—the fucking Rogue, for one!—and I need to think about how I'm going to manage that. This"—I gesture wide—"is ridiculous. I'm going to eat, and you're going to stay here."

It glances mildly at me. *I might be too small to talk to you from afar,* it responds calmly, *but I can certainly speak to you downstairs from here.*

I stare at it a long moment, then turn on my heel and close the door, locking it behind me. It'd better not try to talk to me. I'm in no mood.

The name is Esquidamelion, by the by.

I sigh and narrow my eyes at the wall. A bearded man unlocking his door further down the hall turns his head toward me with a frown. I grin far too brilliantly, and he recoils. Then I head downstairs.

CHAPTER FIVE

I skip down the last few steps, almost grateful to be losing myself in the ordinary hustle and bustle and noise of the tavern. Big tables with long benches seat dozens of hungry and thirsty folks. My breath comes easier here, and my heart slows.

This I can manage. Most people nurse a beer, and many are also digging in to the stew. It smells great, and in this moment, I want food more than anything. And not only to get the taste of vomit out of my mouth.

I settle on a stool by the bar, ready to order, but as I start sorting through everything that's happened today, my gut plunges. The boys—they'd promised to arrange for me to present myself to the Rogue. This is key to my plan. I need cover with the Rogue, and I need money, which means I need the Rogue's approval to work this turf. Ugh. I huff out a breath, wondering whether it's best to leave Valenta.

We should leave. The Rogue is irrelevant, as is that woman you can't stop thinking about. The thought is clear, and my irritation kicks up. Does it think I'm its servant or something?

I shake my head and climb off the stool, earning a strange look from Indron, who was about to ask if I wanted food. I raise a hand in farewell. "Forgot I have plans," I say.

I set a swift pace out into the evening, stalking through the dust and lamplight until I find the sign for Kitchener's. It's big, and a worryingly large man with two scars on his broad face stands by the door, like a mascot to the danger within. It makes me second-guess my plan again, but it's better to get this done with. Plus, the smell of dinner wafting out of the tavern makes my stomach gurgle in anticipation, and I can't resist anymore.

I collect a beer from the keep behind the bar, and she nods brusquely at my request for dinner, demanding more silver than I'd have liked. But my head is too full for negotiation, so I count the coins out.

My purse is getting far too light. I'm going to have to hope Armand is willing to let me ply my trades here. Long-ingrained habit sends me to a seat tucked in a corner with my back to a wall. It helps settle my anxiety some.

The beer is good, and I gulp down half the large cup. It washes away the lingering taste of spew, and the alcohol calms the ragged edges. It can't unmake the memories of the dragon—the *dragon*—in my room, but it helps. A careless teenage boy with greasy hair dumps a big wooden bowl in front of me with broth, noodles, and meat within, and I'm in heaven.

The thoughts in my head won't leave me alone, though. I've relied on my wits for too long to let this be. The egg—the dragon egg—was in the brigand's pouch. Did he know it was a dragon egg? What was he doing carrying it like it was any old trinket? I chew my food mechanically, trying to straighten it all out in my mind.

The egg hadn't looked like anything much, had it, before? I rub my fingers against my head, trying to remember the brief glance I'd had of it out there on the sands. I'd thought it was a gray carving of an egg. I recall the drops that fell from my mouth into the pouch. That must've been it. The blood-birthing.

I'm jerked out of my train of thought when four young faces appear and pull up seats next to me. It's the boys. "You found it, then," says the leader. "Was worried my directions weren't clear."

I close my eyes for a moment, trying to rally my flagging wits. "Got caught up with our dear friends," I say a bit roughly. "Thanks for that, by the by. Looks like they'll be alright. Were they meant to be meeting anyone here, do you know?" Anyone who might have known the egg was not an egg…

Four faces look at me in puzzlement, then the eldest shakes his head. Clearly they'd thought they were meeting me. A pause, then one of the younger, with blond curly hair, declares, "You're a strange one, mistress, if you don't mind me sayin'."

I raise my brows at him. "And whose script are *you* borrowing, lad?"

He flushes red, and I grin to gentle the sharp edge. I take a deep breath. "I'm guessing, though, you've been sent to round me up, is it not? The Rogue?" Best to know where I stand; I'll have to leave if I can't earn coin here. Gotta play it right.

The leader—the one with the greasy hair—nods, dark eyes glimmering. "He wants a word."

I half smile, half grimace. "I have a few to spare." I brace my hands on the table and haul myself upright. "What are your names, anyway?"

The leader clears his throat. "I'm Smit Carlon." He dips his head awkwardly, somewhere between a courtly bow and refusing it. "This is my brother, Kelt." The two are similar, both brown as brown, but the smaller's hair is shorter and greasy, and beside his brother, he doesn't look as lanky. I shake their hands seriously.

"Scarface McGraw," says the sweetest-faced one proudly.

I have to swallow a giggle. "Quite the name you've got there, young 'un."

"Rogue named me," he says, with a satisfied nod. "Better name than I used to have, anyways."

The tiny blond one grins at me, his teeth flashing white in his tanned face. "I'm Twisty Rogers. And Scarface is really Davo, but since the Rogue named him, he's been all proud."

"And I'm Des—Desta Mildue." I nod greetings around. "Alrighty then, lads. Let's meet this Armand."

They lead me to a dark and smoky room with two minimally clothed women dancing in front of the fire. It's clear who Armand is. He sits carelessly in a throne-like chair, one leg looped over the arm and a cup spilling beer onto the floor. All the bodies in the room—his sizable court—are oriented toward him.

I've seen a lot of Rogues in my travels. He appears to be drifting toward the dead soon end of smug, but it's tempered with a canny look. I wonder how much of that is performance. I've seen Rogues play at arrogant to encourage disloyal underlings to make themselves apparent. It's effective. When it's an act.

I draw myself up tall, bow very low—low enough for a duke, but not for a king, so as not to appear to be mocking—and make the sign. "And who do we have here?" the Rogue drawls, a sardonic look in his eye. "I'm not sure I've seen your face before, milady."

He's insulting me, so I play along, drawing out pretend skirts and fluttering my lashes. The crowd smirks. "I'm Desta Mildue, your roguishness." It's meant to be playful, and most of the other Rogues I know would grin and clap a hand to mine for not taking offense. Armand doesn't move. There's a small giggle from a few of the less wise thieves lining the walls. "Just a visitor to these parts, come to pay my respects and ask for go-ahead to work your patch."

"And your dues, yes?" The Rogue's eyes are on mine, assessing. Shit. I've misstepped; off my game tonight.

My eyes want to narrow, but I school my features. "I learned my manners in Pastira, milord. No trade nor tricks within the Rogue's claim without permission. I've no dues to pay as yet. I'm here to learn the lay of the land and beg that permission."

Armand twists, leaning forward in his chair. "None to pay, hmm? I've heard otherwise." When he lets his eyes drift toward the boys who led me here, I have to quash a sigh. Squabbling over territory is always painful, and it rarely goes the visitor's way. If they know I've injured the brutes on the road, then me trying to explain paying for medical care of menfolk I'm not acquainted with is likely to be complicated. Especially if they're known here. My whole plan to undermine their story in advance is evaporating, thanks to my small accomplices. "But no matter. Let me introduce myself."

He rises, and he's a graceful man. Practiced sadism whorls through that grace, but sexuality does too. It half reminds me of Joseph, my regret of Killeen's crew, except talking to Joseph never felt like playing with a blade.

The Rogue picks his way across the room to me and extends a hand. "Bazel Armand." He glances into my eyes and then away as I slide my hand into his grip.

Even this feels risky, and a moment later, as I'm beginning to say, "Pleased to make your acquaintance," my instincts pay off. He squeezes my hand, twisting down so that I let out a gasp and trail off with my words. It's never a good idea to play at not feeling pain with a sadist. They go looking for what *will* make you react. So I go with it, crumpling to my knees and letting my face curl in agony. "My lord?" I gasp out.

He glances down at me, eyes not even cold, just uninterested. "Welcome to Valenta, Desta Mildue," he says, then releases my hand. "You have my permission to turn whatever tricks or trade you wish, so long as dues make their way to me within the week."

He turns and stalks back to his seat. Every eye is on me, but the fact he's prepared to leave it there is promising. If he knew the brigands I'd fought, the boys bringing word of them to him would've made this interrogation more, well, pointed. It's a good sign.

Time to suck it up. I draw a breath, stand, and bow at his back once more, deeply enough to hopefully demonstrate that my first bow was habitual courtesy, not mockery. "I thank you, Bazel Armand, for your welcome." I can't keep the edge out of my voice, even if I know it's unwise. I see the hesitation in his step as he angers, but he's already made his demonstration of authority for this round, so he lets it slide. He slips into the throne and nods once. The crowd falls back into chatter and noise.

I turn away from the room full of thieves staring at me and sigh as I make my way down the hallway and back into the front room. The four boys are with me, silent and wide-eyed as I pause to collect another cup of beer and shake out my wrist. It might be unwise to drink more, but after my day, I have other priorities. I gulp down my beer. It's half-gone before I take a breath.

"He doesn't like you," Twisty says finally. "He doesn't like you at all."

I nod, mouth tight with regret. It's rare I do this poorly with Rogues, and it's annoying. I think blackly of the dragon and Liv and the mercenaries on the road. How did this mess get to be my day? "It happens."

Smit looks shamefaced. "It might have been because of what I told him."

I drink deep once more. "What'd you tell him, kid?" I'm too weary now to play them.

Smit traces the grain of the table for a moment. "That you paid us to get those friends of yours what got attacked outside the gates to a healer."

I sigh and drink the rest of my beer. "Ah." The dregs are bitter.

"I didn't think it would matter," he adds, bemusement in his face. "I mean, it's a strange thing, right? That you survived and got to Valenta on your own? I don't get why it would make him angry."

"Armand doesn't like things he can't control." Little Twisty's blue eyes are mild. "And it's hard to control things you don't understand."

I smile at him faintly. He's sharp for his age. If he makes it to adulthood, he'll likely be in Armand's place, so long as he can work out how to make others respect his wits. "Alrighty, boys. I'm done proving I'm not put off by Armand's welcome. I have to go."

Smit looks wary. "Probably shouldn't show you the ropes..." He's uneasy in his chair—can't even work out whether they're risking the Rogue's ire by sitting at my table. He's got good instincts at least, wanting to put space between us. "That alright?"

I stand and smile at them all and ruffle Twisty's hair. Smit's lost his bravado. "'Tis fine, lad. I might see you at Indron's if you come seeking sticky rice." I'm about to leave when I glance at Scarface. He looks anxious, and it makes my nerves sing. "Something wrong, Scarface?" I ask.

He hesitates, ducking his head, then reaches a decision. "There's folks. They're asking after the ... after ... your..."

I nod once, licking my lips. "After my friends, you mean?"

He nods, and all their eyes are wide now. It's beyond what they understand and, to be honest, I can't get my head around it right now either. But at least

I can ease their mounting anxiety, though it does nothing for mine. "Thanks, Scarface. They're probably more of my friends. Good to know. I'll see if I can find them."

I walk away from Kitchener's tavern deeply weary. Soul-worn. I'm also fiercely awake. I kick through the dust. My body aches from the morning's fight, from carrying my blade on my back once more, and I'm dirty all over. My mind needs some space.

I nearly cry when I spot the bathhouse—too perfect an answer to this day. Briefly, my promise to Liv to come and see the show resurfaces, but the Petrus inside me asks, who am I going to prioritize now?

A small booth fronts the bathhouse. A woman sits behind it, painting her friend's face with cosmetics. She's going a little heavy on the shadow, but it's definitely a look. "Just a bath," I say wearily.

She glances at me. "You need an oil down before you can come in our baths. Too much dust."

I inhale slowly, too weary to fight it. "Alright. Oil and strip, then a bath. Fair?"

"Five coppers."

My inner spendthrift wails—after paying for the mercenaries' medical care, I'm a little too tight for money, given I'm likely to need to get on the road again soon—but I count out the coins into the attendant's hand. She hands me a towel and waves me through. The bathhouse is divided into sections: men's and women's. I'd hated this when I dressed as a boy, and I know it's annoying for those who don't fit these neat categories the world is ordered by, but it's a relief to know I won't have to play the delicate feminine balancing act of dismissing interest and raising ire. It's not that I'm not good at it, just that it's work.

Inside, the bathhouse is dimly lit but clean. I duck under a curtain, and find a woman is waiting there. She has a piece of light cotton wrapped around her hips, but otherwise, she's naked. She rises when I enter and offers a curtsy. "It's alright, lass," I say, my voice graveled with weariness. "I'm an easy one tonight, just here for the clean." I tie the shaggy back of my hair off my neck.

She smiles faintly, and I undress, then settle onto a tall stool. Oil glistens from a bottle into her hands, the fragrance soothing as it rises into the air. She slicks it to warmth between her palms, then slips them all over my body. She's good at this, pressing through the tight points gently. Not quite a massage, which would've cost more, but it does help to loosen me up.

And after, it's the scrape that I love. She has a set of strigils in different sizes laid out, and she's efficient, scouring my skin clean and stripping away the dust and smell with the oil. Finishing with my face, she uses a different oil and scrubs it away with a rough cloth. She bows a little and gestures out of the cubicle. I smile at her vaguely as I leave, grateful.

The baths are steaming, clean and warm, and there's hardly anyone here. I sigh at the sight of them. It's always touch and go in these small towns, but this one is gorgeous, the wooden edging golden and warm. I ease down into the hot one and let myself float. Sounds are muted here under the water, and my breath slows. My muscles loosen, and peace steals me away to calm.

My mind replays the encounter with Armand. It's probably unsurprising I couldn't work the play after the day I've had, but if I've fucked it royally with the Rogue here in Valenta, it's not only that I won't get work here. Much as I might need it, money isn't the only thing that matters. If the Rogue is against me, it's not going to be safe to stay.

The goons will recover. They'll have a strange story to tell about me, one that will guarantee hordes turn out to take me down. After all, I killed one man and disarmed two others. Plus, if the Rogue knew those men were carrying the egg—if they knew it was more than some random trinket—chances are good they'll be searching me out. Those goons watched me scavenge the good stuff from their leader. They know I have it. They don't know I've hatched the dragon, which is probably just as well.

We should prepare to move on. Tonight would be best.

My eyes open, and I stare at the uneven, mosaicked roof. Of course. The wander from Kitchener's tavern to the bathhouse must have brought me back in range. *Can you leave me be?* I beg wearily. *I'm not going anywhere but to sleep tonight.*

We need to get to Calindrina, and you only want to stay because of that woman. The man in your head is right. I frown, then irritation crawls over me. Petrus. The last thing I need is another voice in my head telling me off. *You should stay as far from her as possible. It's a shame he's not here now, to help you resist her.*

My thought is a snap. *I don't need his help to resist her. I've spent years getting over her, and it worked! I'm over her! And as for Petrus, well, he made his choice...*

You didn't ask him to stay. He might have, but you didn't ask. I can see it right here in your memories. You let him go.

This stings, and my jaw tightens. *I don't have to explain myself to you, dragon.* Petrus had wanted more than I could offer—wanted me as a wife. Much as I loved him, he was my brother. I couldn't pretend to be more, not even to save us both the hurt. It would've been more of a betrayal to lie. I couldn't do that to him. Nor could I talk him out of his anger when he needed it to be able to walk away.

No, you don't have to explain yourself, it agrees equably, *but you know I'm correct about this. You let him walk away. Seems foolish to be as lonely as you are when there's someone out there who wants to be by your side.*

He wanted a damn sight more than that. More than I could ever give him. It made my heart ache to think of it again. He'd been my family, really. My family—more family than my mother had turned out to be. *And I'm fine alone. It's better this way.*

The dragon seems to contemplate this. *Mmm. Is that what you tell yourself about why you've never been back home, too?*

I splash upright, proper angry now. *You can shut your mouth about my mother. That wasn't in any way my fault. She kicked me out. The whole village did.*

I cannot work out why they would do such a thing, the dragon puzzles, like it's a riddle it can't make out. It makes the anger burn in my gut, fanning the embers of the old wound—both the injustice of it and that this tiny creature would treat it as a mere curiosity, an academic intrigue.

I'd been barely more than a child when they'd abandoned me, and it still ached. Picton—well, Liv and Picton, really—they'd saved me. A sixteen-year-old on my own, I'd never have survived, but they took me in ... and then I'd been caught in Liv's trap, unable to free myself, no matter how awful it had been. Until Petrus had helped me get away. Then Karina, and Besta...

My throat tightens. So much loss. I draw a deep breath to keep those age-old tears at bay. I've walked this path. Better not to think on it. *No child deserves such a thing*, I make myself reply. *And that's all I was.*

Well, obviously, mortal—the dragon is about as haughty as it's possible to be—*but you must be wrong about it merely being about what that woman has between her legs. No rational being could think that grounds for ostracizing a child.*

I let myself fall back into the water in frustration and helplessness. The very last thing I need to be thinking about right now is Liv's quim. Still, much as its arrogance grates, I am vaguely comforted by the fact it finds my mother's decision incomprehensible. *I need you to nick off out of my head, dragon. I need to be able to sleep, as soon as I get back. If you keep on at me about every error I've ever made, that'll never happen. Now, leave me be.*

The silence in my head feels almost too much for a moment, echoey and vast, but then I settle back into the water and close my eyes, letting myself drift, grateful for the peace. I need the dragon out of my head, and I need myself gone from Valenta. Despite my purses running dry, I'm going to have to leave. It's not safe—too many unknowns.

Calindrina—

No.

CHAPTER SIX

Morning has barely broken when I wake. The sight of the tiny dragon curled on the wooden crossbeam of the bedhead brings back the memories of yesterday in a remarkable flood. I groan, and there's a knock at the door. It sounds impatient this time—must've been the first that woke me—so I lever myself up and out of bed. I realize I'm naked and wrap myself in the sheet.

I open the door, but there's no one outside. The knock resounds again. *I believe it's the window,* the dragon tells me sardonically. *I don't know why you humans sleep at all if this is what it does to you.*

"Shouldn't you be hiding?" I demand. "Also, this is what *lack* of sleep does to humans."

I open the shutter to find a diminutive blond boy clinging to the frame outside. It takes me a moment to recall his name while he stares at me, wide-eyed. "Twisty? What are you doing here?"

"You need to know," he pants, breathless and utterly terrified.

I haul him through the window and push him into one of the chairs. "Alright, Twisty, it's alright." I pour him water into a cup. "What is it?" He swallows the whole cupful, and I hand him another one. "Did you run all the way here?" I ask. He nods.

I try to kick my mind into wakefulness. Something must be very wrong. I think about Armand last night, about the goons, about the dragon I've hatched. Too many options for why he's scared.

"Take your time, lad. Little we can do without breath," I say, injecting kindness and calm into my voice. Clothing. Clothing is helpful. As are weapons. I drop the sheet and start to clothe myself, weapons first.

I'm glad he averted his eyes as soon as the sheet disappeared; the number of blades I'm concealing about my person would not be a soothing sight. It's far from soothing for me either, but his anxiety is catching, and I'd rather be prepared. A sad farewell to the months I'd been without the vast array tucked into every crevice, but that encounter on the road had been too near a thing, and I'd prefer to avoid an encore. The kid's face seems to hover in the air before me, his mother's beside it. I don't like breaking oaths, even if they're only to myself.

That was so far from your fault. The dragon is matter-of-fact, not sympathetic.

My chin tightens. *It was my choice. I put him in charge.*

Finally, he speaks. "Your friends are dead."

Liv is dead? For a moment, I cannot breathe. Like I've jumped into a too-cold river; my lungs seize and refuse to allow air in. But wait—he knows nothing of Liv. Why would he?

"My friends?" I repeat, befuddled.

The mercenaries you saved, the dragon reminds me. I glance at the bedclothes where it's hiding, then back at Twisty.

My heartbeat kicks up. "Dead? At whose hand?"

This could be good for me, or so very bad. They won't be able to tell tales about me to the Rogue if they're dead. But if they're dead because someone wanted something from them—say, a dragon egg—I could be next.

Twisty shakes his head. "I know not, but..." He looks uncomfortable.

The moment at Kitchener's when Smit was ashamed. "But Smit told Armand about them. So it could have been the Roague," I surmise. Hmm.

Twisty frowns. This wasn't his first thought, obviously. "But I don't understand," he says. "Why would Armand torture them?"

"They were tortured?" I recall the cold desire for pain in Armand's eyes when he offered me his hand the night before, and I smile briefly. "Lad, you know the answer to that one."

Twisty purses his lips. "I don't know. Armand likes making pain, yes, but this didn't look like his work. And he would only give away the chance to hurt for a good reason."

"You saw?" I can't help the sorrow that strikes my face. I can only hope he's too bright for the pride his friends feel in being treated as adults.

"I saw." His grace is perfect, an acceptance of my sorrow mixed with a gentle refusal to disabuse me of my fantasy about the life he and his friends lead. Enough to break a heart, I swear. "It isn't his style."

I'm not sure I want to ask. "What is his style?"

"Narrow blades. Many cuts."

I raise a single brow. "Ah. This was...?"

"Blunt force. A club, I think."

"Beginning with the feet?"

He nods. His bare toes move restlessly, and I realize he's taking a considerable risk. I find a coin and push it into his hand. "My thanks, lad. Now go, and if Armand or any ask, you never met me, yes?"

Relief floods his face. It's touching—he clearly would have helped, had I asked. He pauses at the windowsill and seems to think too hard about something. "If you need me, I'll be at home. The farthest warehouse to the west, near the edge of town. We all live there." Can't help himself. He disappears back out the window, and I sigh.

Is this a problem? The dragon has crawled out from underneath the bedclothes, and its tone seems to inject disbelief. *Not that it matters, because we need to leave anyway. So, let's go.*

"I'm not going anywhere, not yet," I murmur, leaning my head into my hands. It's not just that I don't like being ordered around, though I really don't. The goons are dead. If whoever made them that way knows about me, or about the boys, we could be in big trouble. The kind you need a proper plan to outrun. *I need to know what is going on here.*

You need to get me to Calindrina, mortal. The dragon's words are precise, and it's not even command—too sure of authority to be that.

"Calindrina will have to wait, dragon," I say aloud.

Esquidamelion.

"Calindrina will have to wait, *Squid.*" Indignant waves come off the small animal, but I need maté. Then I need to find out what Rositus knows.

Downstairs, Indron nods a good morning, and at my desperate "Maté?" they almost grin, then hand me a large mug.

"You're an angel," I gush. They smile.

I take a seat near a front window so I can look out into the day. Some would say I'm not moving fast enough, given the news about torture, but it's a dicey thing. If I'm being watched, I need to not give away that I know.

The traffic is light in the early morning. No sign of trouble or spying eyes. The maté is excellent. I turn to ask for food, and a youngster stands uncertainly behind my shoulder, holding a roll filled with eggs and mushrooms, wrapped in paper, ready to go. "You're like an answer to a dream," I murmur as she offers it to me. She blushes, and I can't keep back a smirk as she scuttles away. I put a hand to my head, smoothing spiky bed hair into something more like order, but somehow, her response makes me feel momentarily better about Liv. *Liv, Liv, Liv.* I sigh.

I toss Indron too much silver for breakfast, and they nod, almost smiling again. That nut is just about cracked now.

Time to head to Rositus's. I eat as I walk, watching the patterns of the world as they pass me. The rhythms of the day are regular. Whatever went wrong last night at Rositus's, it hasn't been so big an issue that the whole of Valenta is concerned with it. Even as I weave through the streets to lose any possible tail, I can't make out anyone watching me.

The sky is clear above the dusty streets. I make my way past the main square, slowly filling with market stalls and those seeking food. No drama there either, which is a relief. I toss a coin to a lass for a hat. It's more country than I would usually choose, but it'll shade my face. As I head up the long Street of Flowers, where florists arrange their wares in wooden boxes in the shadow of brightly-colored stalls, something catches my attention.

Three young men, all a-horse and still red with dust from the road, dressed in the uniform of the King's Guard. They're an odd sight in a small town far from the capital. Indeed, I can't remember seeing the King's Guard anywhere except Pastira. That's odd. I keep my face turned away, pretending to be looking at daffodils as they meander past. They chatter to each other, but I can't hear them over the storekeeper's attempt to coerce me into buying.

"I'll have a think," I say hastily, and turn away from her disappointment to hurry along the street toward Rositus's.

The healer's door is open when I get there, which is a bad sign, and within is worse. Goods are spread everywhere. Everywhere. All the neat jars in rows on the wooden shelves are shattered across the floor. I back out swiftly and keep on up the street until I find a lane. Gotta be a back entrance.

Sure enough, a tall gate in a fence lets me into a small, neat herb garden with footprints stomped through the plants. I ease my way up the stairs toward the door, which sits ajar at the top, and loosen the blade over my shoulder.

I enter a small kitchen. Blood covers every surface, and I swallow my breakfast a second time at the sight. Twisty wasn't exaggerating. The two goons I'd injured then saved yesterday were definitely dead, and they had definitely been interrogated. Their corpses, tied to two chairs, bear injuries typical of a rough-and-ready but all too professional round of torture. Twisty hadn't missed his guess about them using a club. I ease my way further in, looking for Rositus. Twisty hadn't said anything about the healer.

I find him in the back room, where he used to mix his remedies, no doubt. He will mix no such thing again. He has no teeth left whole in his head. One of his hands—his left—is crushed, and he has been stabbed through the chest. I stare at the corpse for a long, long moment. This does not bode well for me.

The two goons' bodies were thoroughly, progressively broken. Either they'd not known anything, or they'd resisted more thoroughly than I'd have thought they would. Maybe they were more than mere goons. But Rositus... This body gave up some desired information far more quickly.

Fuck.

The goons are dead, and Rositus knew me. And like as not, told whoever tortured him about me.

I bite my lip, pull my sword, and make my way as quickly as I can back out into the laneway. Hearing footsteps, I hesitate, then duck through another gate, opposite Rositus's. Not a moment too soon.

A heavyset man and a thin man with a beard pause outside the gate. The thin man's eyes dart here and there, but when they turn toward my hiding place, I pull back in shock. His eyes are pale, paler than any I've ever seen. My skin crawls.

The larger man carries a club, and it's bloodied. Recently. I swallow. Looks like I've found the torturers. Fear fires through me.

"Careful now, Crainor," the thin man murmurs, and I strain to hear whether it's an accent coloring his speech. "If she's inside, she'll be alarmed, and we still need to know where the stone is. I wish we'd been able to leave a watch on this place." Stone? I gulp.

"We would have, 'cept that king just *had* to have his hearing first." The reply rumbles through a barrel chest, and Crainor's words are definitely accented. I sort through my players' catalog. Ascelin? They're a good long way from home out here. "Small towns are the worst for that. Useless as he was, I know working with their Sodality will help us find her, but what a waste of time."

"She'll turn up, don't you worry," the thin man says, stroking his beard for a moment. "She must. Ready?" He swings open the gate, and as if they'd never had the conversation about not alarming whatever woman they imagine might be inside, the heavyset man raises his club. My last glimpse of it is red-brown-stained wood. My heart beats in my throat.

I press against the brick of the fence, only now realizing I'm caught in another backyard and hoping beyond hope the owner doesn't spot me from the house.

I wait until both men ease through the gate, then I'm off, sprinting back down the laneway on light feet. I turn a quick right at the next corner, then the first left I can see, then pull myself up a downpipe and onto the roof. I need to escape, but I need to know who they are as well.

We need to go to Calindrina.

I don't even reply. They're after the egg. The dragon egg. And they think there's a "she" out there who knows where it is. My skin goes hot and then cold. They're after me. They have mercenaries arriving this morning. And I'm hanging about, wondering who they are.

I gulp and flatten myself against the roof. The two men reappear and make their way back down the laneway. I wriggle forward, trying to hear what they're saying. Anything, any hint about what they know about me, or about anything; but they're gone, murmuring too low for me to hear.

I turn over the brief conversation in my head. Is the king in town? They certainly seemed to have been presented to him, and there were the King's Guard soldiers I saw earlier. But if they were king's men, why the torture? Why not simply round the men up and send them into the dungeons? They'd have talked soon enough, I expect, with the promise of a pardon to the one that gave up the information first. And Ascelese? Surely king's men had to be Rescalin born and bred? Maybe just those in uniform?

I think of my four young friends, of Twisty's bravery in coming to see me. If Rositus gave me up—likely, since the two men knew they were looking for a woman, and his stabbing end probably signified the torture had been success-ful—he probably gave up the children as well.

I gulp hard, my mind dancing. If they know about the four thief lads, they might know where I'm staying. But that's unlikely since they didn't attack me in my sleep or make an appearance at breakfast. They'll be after the boys soon though, and they can't keep the secret. Indron's isn't safe anymore.

I slide to the ground and pause, torn. I can ensure my young friends are still hale, or I can head back to my tavern, to the dragon.

I narrow my eyes. If they're looking for a dragon egg, they're more likely to want Squid. And if they have my young friends, Squid would likely constitute the best trade. My hands turn clammy at the thought. Is it the idea of another kid dying on my watch? Or maybe it's just the thought of handing the tiny dragon over to those men with their bloodied club.

I draw a deep, deep breath. How the hell did this happen?

I set off for Indron's tavern at a dead run.

CHAPTER SEVEN

I duck behind Indron's tavern to check on Liza first. She is pleased to see me, which is sweet, but I'm brusque, saddling her with shaking fingers. How the hell did I get caught up in all of this? Kings and dragons and torture. Gods.

I scan the courtyard. Empty. I take Twisty's route up to my room, slipping a dagger between the shutters to unlatch the catch.

Nothing is disturbed inside. Squid is curled in the same spot on my bedhead. *Something wrong?* it asks, managing to sound unconcerned and annoyed at the same time. *We really do need to depart.* I brace the chair under the doorknob. It won't keep anyone at bay for long, but hopefully for long enough.

"Can't leave," I tell it, shoving my things into my pack with the ease of long practice. "Have to sort some things out first." I can't leave town without making sure the boys are alright. I'm not going to be responsible for another kid not making it to adulthood.

No. Have to leave. Cannot stay here.

"That kid—you know, the one from this morning? He might be in trouble, and it might be my fault." I keep my voice as low as I can in case the men looking for me are in the hallway. "And a bit your fault too, you know. Come on, you. Time to go."

I scoop Squid up into a leather pouch and pull the strings tight, then hook it around my neck. *Let me out. Now. I mean it.* The dragon sounds angry but not alarmed.

"Soon," I say, "but not yet. We've got to get out of here."

I pause, about to throw myself out the window. "No," I tell myself softly. "Slow down. Think... Better to leave enough of my stuff here that they think I haven't fled yet. Might buy me a moment to run once I've warned the boys. Plus, if they think I know they're coming after me, they'll bring those troops down hard. Better if I'm only facing a couple scouts."

I nod slowly, convincing myself. The other risk is Armand. He might not be involved, yet, but didn't like me nearly enough not to take money to kill me, no matter what the code says, and the code's cheerful words about not colluding with the Crown have been lip service for over a decade now. I don't want to take on the entirety of the Valentan Rogue *and* the king's men, not if I can avoid it. And if it's clear I've run, that's what would likely follow.

I pull open my bag and throw a few of the less essential elements of my pack around the room. Underwear, a hairbrush I haven't used since I cut my hair short, and a small dagger by the sink. I hope it's enough.

I stop again and bite my lip. Even once the kids are warned, I'm not free and clear. I'm low on coin, and there are only a few smaller settlements in reach before I wind up penniless. I kick myself for not stopping this morning to check whether Rositus had been robbed as well as killed. Coin. Fucksake. I gave him four gold only yesterday.

We need to leave, the dragon insists.

"We don't *need* to do anything," I hiss back, hauling open my pack again and pulling out a kirtle. No one in town has seen me in anything but trousers. It might be enough until I can get enough space to turn myself into a believable man. "I'm trying to work out what's going on here."

It's irrelevant.

"It might seem irrelevant to you," I snap back, "but it seems pretty significant to me. And to those boys, I'd warrant, being their lives and all!"

I can't leave them without warning them. Twisty warned me, at decent risk to himself. With any luck, they can lay low until everyone leaves town to chase after me. I'm not having their deaths on my conscience as well.

Deciding to ignore the little creature, I clamber out the window, slide down the roof and into the courtyard at speed, and tie my bags to Liza's saddle. I'm about to mount and ride out of the stables when a voice behind me sounds.

My sword is in my hand and angled at the person before I even register what was said.

"I'm sorry," Liv says, wide-eyed and hands raised. "I just wanted to talk to you."

I blink at her stupidly for a long moment, then slide the sword back into its scabbard. "You want to talk to me?" I repeat.

That's what she said, the petulant little voice says. *Isn't this the woman from yesterday,* and *from when your village rejected you?*

I close my eyes and inhale hard, narrowing my focus to Liv. "How did you even find me?"

"Some kids. I asked after you last night." My heart sinks, but I don't ask again. They've been telling more stories about me, and the gods know who *she's* told. My time in Valenta just got shorter. I'll be warning the boys and then heading for the nearest exit. She takes her chance when I don't reply. "I'm in trouble, Des. Big trouble. I need help as I've never needed it before."

I school everything—my thoughts, my face, my voice—even though all I want to do is run. Is she playing me? Could the torturers have got to her? Would they know she knows me? "You need my help? What on earth could you need my help for?" I can't keep a modicum of snark from my voice.

She presses her hands together, and her brows furrow. "I wanted to tell you last night, but you didn't..." She truly expected me to come and find her last night. The anger is a familiar burn in my gut. "But this morning, they were here, and I don't know what to do." A breath catches in her throat. "If they find me, they'll kill me."

I stare at her for a long moment. I really don't need this right now; I'm having a hard enough time working out how to take care of myself. But her eyes well with tears, the stress line between her brows is tighter than ever, and it sounds like honesty in her voice. She gulps, and I can't deny the satisfaction I feel at seeing how hard she has to work to swallow.

Liza snorts, and it jolts me out of the spell Liv manages to cast. Every. Fucking. Time. Torturers on my trail, and even now. "Liv, I don't have time for this."

"Des, please."

"I don't believe you, Liv," I say coldly, though in truth, the combination of her honesty and the fear in her eyes is getting to me.

She's still beautiful, even as bedraggled as she is. Those black curls are tangled, but somehow, they still shine, and despite being worn and sad, her green eyes are gorgeous in the frame of their lashes. I busy myself with retying the pack to Liza's back. Can't afford this today.

But if the King's Guard are after her too, she might know something about the dragon and the egg, and that could help me. Maybe I could hand the dragon over to someone who won't be so irritated by it. "You want my help? Then spill."

A wave of amusement emanates from the dragon in the pouch around my neck. I studiously ignore it.

"I... I'm not sure where to start." I can already hear the game unfolding.

"Liv, you play games with me, I will walk away. I might do it anyway. Don't push your luck." I revel in the chance to be aggressive. The mirth radiating from the little pouch deepens.

She looks shocked, which is a bit of a salve. "Alright, sheesh, you don't have to be so hostile." I limit my response to raised eyebrows, but it reins her in a little.

She bites her soft bottom lip. "I... I think it's because of Prince Shandor."

I don't say anything at all.

"So, about a year ago, we were playing in Pastira. Prince Shandor saw us, and, well, he took a shine to me." She looks almost coy, and I squash down the anger. "We... We had a fling. That's all it was, really."

"Did he think so?" I can't help myself.

Liv manages a look of mild shamefacedness, but it seems an effort. Unusual for a player of her talents. "I... I'm not sure. He was trying to impress me the night before we were leaving, trying to convince me to stay. He took me into this special vault. It was full of—you should have seen it, Des—full of gold. I've never seen so much gold in one place."

I can see where this is going. "You stole something."

"Des, I know you think I'm selfish." Liv shakes her head, but she only meets my eyes for a second. "Alright. I *am* selfish," she says softly, "but I wouldn't steal. Not from royalty. I'm not an idiot."

"So...?"

"He gave it to me," she says simply.

Dread flares, a prickle of goose bumps along my arms, but I don't let it show. "What? He gave you what?"

She raises one shoulder, shrugging out of the neck of her dress a little. "It wasn't anything precious. Just a little stone carving of an egg. I guess he figured no one would miss it."

Fuck. The king really *is* after the egg—and it's been stolen from him. Excellent. My mind is racing now, but as always, when things get dire, my playing skills kick up. I don't show anything. Does she know the egg isn't just a carving? Does she know about the mythic impossibility I'm carrying around my neck? "Except now they've decided they do?"

She makes a beautiful moue with her mouth. "Not quite. After I left, the prince sent word he'd made a terrible mistake and I should send it back with the next messenger." Liv scuffs a toe in the dirt, and I know she's playing, but the information is too important now. "I couldn't," she says, half sorrowful and half definitely not. "It was mine. I'd already given it away."

"You gave it away? To who?"

"I can't say." She gives me a glance from under her lashes.

"You'll find a way," I say bluntly, "or I'll leave you to sort this yourself."

"Fine." Her hands go to her hips, and she tosses her hair. "It's a lady, alright? She lives near the sea. So I told the prince I couldn't return it. I told him I'd lost it. And he sent another messenger, this one with—phew, with more gold than you've seen, Des, for serious. So I told him I'd try to find it."

"And?"

She'd sent messengers to this lady, messengers carrying swords, just in case, she tells me. The lady had handed the stone over to them, and Liv had arranged to meet them here in Valenta. She'd sent word to the prince to have someone come and collect it. Then, this morning, she'd heard men knocking at the doors of the caravans next to hers, asking after her. She slid out the hatch in the bottom of the van to escape and discovered as she fled that they were King's Guard. They busted in her door and searched the whole of her caravan.

Is that hatch the one she sent you out of in the early days, when you were concealing your relationship? Oh, and another memory here—you never caught anyone else climbing out it, but you thought about the possibility. A lot.

The dragon is right, and my gut curdles even further. That hatch had figured large in my jealous daydreams toward the end. I shake off the memory and focus on the story she's telling. "The King's Guard?" I narrow my eyes. Was I right before? Did the torturers work for the king? Have they got to her already, and this really is all a game? But she really does seem shocked they were there. Could she be sincere?

As if she knows what that means, I think bitterly.

"It was odd that it wasn't the regular army, now I come to think of it. The prince is the general, so I'd have thought he'd send them," she says. "I've never seen the King's Guard outside Pastira. Not without the king."

I draw a deep breath. King's Guard in Valenta. Torturers after the egg who've killed the goons who were carrying it. This makes a bit more sense of ... well, everything I'd seen this morning. Maybe I could hand the dragon over and be done with its whispering in my head.

Would they get me to Calindrina? The dragon sounds as taken with the idea as I am.

My gut twinges, though. Seems like overkill for the king to send torturers to take the egg back. Is this really what the Crown has come to? Hiring foreigners to do their dirty work against their own citizens? And the dragon is tiny—defenseless, really.

I'm a master of time, it says, almost wearily.

Does that stop a blade? I ask.

But I don't trust Liv, not as far as I could throw her. So, I play. "Where are these messengers you sent to this lady?" Did she know they were at Rositus's? Is she only here because she knew I knew them? Suspected me?

Her eyes go wide, and she spreads her hands. "I have absolutely no idea. They never showed up."

I nod slowly, buying time. She doesn't need to know I killed them. Killed them, stole an egg, somehow birthed a dragon. And that the witnesses had died, painfully, at the hands of a torturer who is either on her tail or mine.

I busy my hands with a bag to hide the realization that strikes me. The "she" that thin man with the creepy pale eyes mentioned could've been Liv. The King's Guard going through her caravan might mean they don't know about me yet. But does the king know the egg holds a dragon?

This is all irrelevant, the dragon tells me, bored. *We need to go to Calindrina.*

I raise my head. "What even is this, Liv?" I ask. "This carving? Why this reaction from all these powerful people? Doesn't it seem weird to you?"

"I have no idea. None." She throws her hands up and laughs, a sound that, somehow, even after all this, makes me want to smile. "That fucking gift is destroying my life, and I don't know how to stop it. A bloody stone carving of an egg! Could buy its like at any two-bit store."

"Alright. So, what were you doing at Rositus's store yesterday?"

She smiles at me, that same secret smile that makes my heart ache. "Finding you again," she says, eyes warm. Her hands curl into mine before I can react.

I can't help the half smile, but I take my hands back. "Yes, but you didn't know I was there, right?"

She clears her throat. "Oh, no. I was picking up some ... teas." She means teas to bring on menses and avoid pregnancy. Liv's never found without them. "Des, please. I'll pay you." She shakes a purse at her waist, coins clinking.

My eyelids flutter as I manage this pain.

Oh, says the familiar snarky voice in my head. *It was before you left with the boy who loved you, yes? Petrus? She had withdrawn her affection, and you offered to pay for it. She is callous.* It had been the ultimate humiliation when she'd said no.

I glance at her, and realization dawns in her face as she hears the echo too. "I was cruel," she murmurs, looking at her feet. "Please. You are a better person than I. Protect me."

I school my face and meet her green, green eyes for a moment. "I'm not sure who you think I am these days, but I certainly am not taking on the king for you. No way, no how. Especially when the prince is involved as well." I need to know if she knows the full extent of those after her or if she's playing me.

Her eyebrows pinch together. "Please, Des. You have friends here! Can't you find this egg? I'm scared. I thought it was nothing, but he's certainly not behaving that way."

She's mentioned my friends as if they're still alive, so she doesn't know about the murder scene at Rositus's, and she doesn't seem to know the egg held a dragon. I wish again I hadn't hatched it. "What makes you think I can do any kind of finding of anything? Or protecting you, for that matter?" I ask.

She glances at the floor, then up at me. Green eyes shine through those spiky black lashes. Trademark Liv. "Well, we saw Petrus, not so long ago," she murmurs quietly, and I hear the note in her voice that says she's done more than "see" Petrus. I barely flinch; my control is that good.

I understand she was mistreated as a youngling, but others have faced hardship without becoming this hurtful.

I can't disagree. Fuck. Anger and betrayal are like hot ice in my veins. Love is complicated, I get it, but still, Petrus...

"He told us that you'd trained, and I figured whoever you were traveling with probably had the same kind of training."

We have to leave, says Squid. *None of this matters. Only Calindrina matters.*

I pause, feeling the dragon shift slightly against my chest. I think of the boys, of the likely danger I've put them in. I think about Liv, about the pleading in her eyes, about the warmth her hands have left in mine, and about the King's Guard upending her van. I think about the danger I've managed to put myself in the middle of somehow, yet again. The first dragon in centuries, accidentally stolen from royalty, and now I've managed to hatch it. And the fact I have very little cash left after my misplaced generosity with the mercenaries, and any chance of making coin in Valenta dried up with Armand's ill humor.

But if I can work out how to play it right, there's the possibility of a big payday, depending on how grouchy the king might be about my accidental hatching ... but surely a dragon is a better prize than an egg. In the meantime, that jingle at her waist will be enough to get me someplace safer.

I remind myself sternly that this is not forgiveness, and it's not a prelude to a future together. It's that I don't need her dead. And I do need her money.

"Every coin, right now, and you have a deal," I tell her. "But I can't make promises. If this gets too hairy, I like my skin more than yours." I can't believe how cool my voice is. The Petrus inside me sighs, and I grimace once more at the pain over his betrayal. Liv will always bring me pain. And here I am, saying yes, again.

We pause near the back courtyard of Kitchener's tavern. Before we left the stable, we'd both changed. Liv wears my gray kirtle, plainer than the exceptionally memorable cascading white frills and deep green she'd been wearing, paired with the hat I'd bought that morning, which conceals her luxurious curls and hopefully the color of her eyes.

I'm back in my trousers, and my sword is strapped to my back. I need recognition for my next foolhardy rush at death. Liv's given me enough that I know there might be a king's ransom in the offing, or a torturer waiting for me. I'm operating in the dark here, and I need some light. Armand may not like me, but I need to know where he and his people stand, warn the boys, then find a stonemason. The sooner I have a replica of Squid's egg in my pocket, the better I'll feel.

"You stay here," I tell her. "Don't talk to anyone. I mean it, Liv. I don't know how safe it is here, but I don't know where else might be safer. Stay out of sight."

She tosses me a salute and a smile, and I scowl in return. "I'm serious. They might hand you over to whoever is hunting you."

Kitchener's tavern is quiet during the day. I enter through the back door. No one on guard, which is a little strange, but I figure this town is a bit of a backwater. Not much excitement. Bodes well for me. Two women are at work in the kitchen, but I slip past the door with no problems.

I turn to go up the stairs and find Smit's mouth a round O in his face. He starts to speak, and I leap up two steps to put a gentle finger to his lips. He follows me obediently into the cupboard under the stairs. "Lad, I wanted a word with Armand." It's half a lie, but it's the simplest way to cut to the chase.

He shakes his head, fear all through. "Not a good idea. He has a visitor."

"A visitor?" My blood runs a little cold.

"The prince," he says in a hushed whisper. I can barely see his face, but I can make out the fear on it.

"The prince?" My heartbeat kicks up into my throat, and I swallow. The noose is tightening. From Armand, it's a hop, skip, and a jump to me and Indron's tavern. He nods, baffled. The question hasn't turned his way yet. I swallow again, wondering if I need to protect Smit as well. "Any other visitors, lad?"

His gaze shutters. Clearly, I am not to be trusted. "Yes. Another out-of-town-er, actually. From another country, by his accent, but this one paid his dues. Creepiest eyes I've ever seen." I narrow my eyes. My mind reminds me of the mismatched pair leaving Rositus's this morning, the ones going on about a "she" they were after. Liv? Or me? Could they have been referring to Armand rather than the king this morning? Gods, how many players *are* there in this mess? The surprise on my face makes him pause, realizing he's said too much, no doubt. "But I'm not to speak of it."

I smile. "Ah, I'm still too much of an out-of-towner for you, even if I'm in the Rogue too?"

He stares at his feet and then his hands. "I have to get back upstairs."

"Thanks, lad," I say softly. "A lot."

He shakes his head, as if the thanks makes his generosity—and his lack of control over his tongue—uncomfortably real, and disappears upstairs. I pause a long moment, considering, but if he thinks it's not safe, he's probably right. I then decide to take his advice and head out the back.

I glance about for a moment in the courtyard. No sign of Liza or Liv. I frown, then peer out at the front of the tavern. Soldiers. I put two and two together. She's seen the risk, seen the soldiers in royal garb, and fled.

My heart plunges into my heels, and the ember of my fury at Liv flares to life. Like it wasn't enough to take me from my home, poison the troupe for me, and sleep with fucking Petrus, of all people.

"Fuck. Bitch stole my horse!"

CHAPTER EIGHT

I've been walking in circles for a good three hours through heat and dust, legs aching, cursing myself and Liv by turns. Clearly whatever protection she was claiming she wanted from me was bullshit. I got played, straight up. But does that mean she knew about the egg all along? That it's not a carving but actually held a dragon?

I mean, if she'd known that much, the dragon's original subterfuge as a fancy hairpiece would've counted for nothing except confirmation it was hatched. How many times will she manage to play me? My anger at Liv burns in my gut, just like it had when I first left Picton's.

I finally find my beloved Liza, tucked into a corner of town near the main square. A crowd of people surrounds her, some of whom appear to be grabbing for her reins. She's not having any of it, and she's heading toward attack. The crowd is laughing and dodging her teeth, but they won't stand much of a chance when she starts in with the hooves. Her horseshoes were specially made, and they're designed for damage.

I start singing the nonsense song I sing on the road as I jog toward her. Her ears prick, and I smile as I swoop in, slipping smoothly between folks in the crowd to place a gentle hand to her heaving sides. "Now, now, Liza, I'm sure these good people were trying to work out how to get you back to me," I say, keeping my tone calm but my voice loud. This is mostly for the crowd's sake.

"Who're you?" a broad-faced woman asks bluntly. "You are *not* the girl who was riding her."

"Trying to!" says one young man, and the crowd roars with laughter.

"That would be the thief that stole her from me." I scowl. "But my Liza's not like to take that kind of behavior, not for long!"

An older man grins. "She's a right smart animal, this one. Tossed that thief straight into the street. Went for her arm when she tried to clamber back up."

"Beautiful girl, but no grace."

"Warn't she the player from that troupe? Gorgeous. Shame to hear she's a thief."

"Often are, those traveling folks. Only way to make ends meet on the road."

"Not that they would've needed to! Best playin' I ever saw. Heard they performed for the king hisself, more'n once."

"The king, huh? I worked late last night, missed the show. They on again tonight?"

"Heard they split town earlier this morning," says another.

I hover to hear any further gossip, but none is forthcoming. I nod my thanks to all and sundry. "Thanks for looking out for 'er," I say. "Really. Kindhearted folks are lacking in this world, but not in this town!"

Having Liza back is utter relief. My hand tremors as I run it over her side, soothing both our trembling. One thing Liv hasn't succeeded in taking from me, but my fury is still hot. As I mount up, I realize that my bags, which I carefully strapped to Liza's back, are missing. Fuck. The rage makes my head pound. At least my sword is still strapped to my back. I want to put its edge to Liv's lily-white neck.

I climb into the saddle, rest a hand against Liza's neck, and then make the clicking noise with my tongue that asks her to walk. "Well done, Liza. You're such a smart beastie," I tell her softly. "So very smart." She blows air out her nostrils in disgust. "I know, I know. Liv's always trouble. Did you see where she went?"

She arches her neck and dances a couple of steps, demonstrating what she thinks of my obvious plan to pursue her. "I'm not gonna get back in with her,"

I say grimly. She snorts again. "No, really. Lesson learned. But, Liza ... I would like my bags back."

Liza hangs her head a little, as if ashamed. I pat her neck. "'Tis alright, girl. Liv's a slippery one. Always has been. But I'm not letting her slip off with all my gear. She's taken enough from me."

It's then that I realize it. I pat down my pockets, all my hidden crevices and corners, never minding the strange looks I earn. Fuck. I have a very light purse at my hip. And that's it. My coin—the coin Liv talked me into working for her with—was in the bag, shoved in as we changed in the stable. It's gone.

And so is the pouch. The one with the dragon and the two halves of the egg in it—the one with my other potential payday.

Gone.

I turn Liza toward where Twisty said the boys made their home. I cannot let them face this alone, just because of me. With the thought of the egg and the dragon in my head, I suddenly hear it. *Stupid girl! I will make my own way to Calindrina if you will not help me. You are a foolish human!* This *human may be callous and cruel, but she is far more intelligent than you.*

I close my eyes. Fucking Liv. She takes everything from me, why not this too? The voice is faint but there. I think at it deliberately. *She's not going to take you to Calindrina. She knows what you are. She knows people who want you. She's going to take you to the nearest one and sell you off for the highest price she can wrangle. And the closest I've come to those seeking the dragon egg broke every single one of a man's teeth out of his head.* A guilty twinge cuts through the heavy sludge of my rage. After all, hadn't handing the dragon over been my plan too?

I sense a vague wave of confusion mixed with revulsion at the image of the bodies at Rositus's shop. *I have to get to Calindrina.* For the first time, I can hear a note of uncertainty in its voice. *Are you sure she won't take me there?*

I take a deep breath and opt for honesty. *Dragon,* I say in my head, *I don't know what's going on. I don't know who Liv is working with, or whether she's run off with you because you're good leverage—the only leverage she knows of—with the prince. I don't know if the prince is working for the king. I don't know if there are other people involved. Armand? Maybe even those Ascelese who did the torturing last night. I don't know what's going on, but I do know they're after you.*

The thought strikes me abruptly. I have no clue how many of the stories I've heard about dragons bear any kind of semblance to the truth. I'd always dismissed them, put them down to silly stories for entertaining children by the fire, like the tales of giants and fairies also part of Picton troupe's repertoire of plays.

There were stories of dragons destroying whole continents, more or less, and only some at the behest of those trying to gain land or power or money. The Era of Storms, it was called—just about an apocalypse—but I recall only a vague sense of what it had involved. The story went that the dragons disappeared, all of them, and then we had peace for hundreds of years. I don't remember ever hearing about a real dragon being alive. Always about some mythic past. So where did this egg come from in the first place?

Squid, I think at it deliberately, *why does everyone want you?*

The response comes after a long pause, fainter than before. I have to strain to hear it, even though it's not in my ears. *I am a dragon,* it says. I hear a tinge of uncertainty, mixed with bucketloads of pride.

I roll my eyes. *Sure,* I think at it again, *but what does that mean? Do they want to have you for their menageries, or is there something else you can do?*

The uncertainty is growing. I can sense it. *I am a dragon. I came here to be born.*

From where, though?

From the Everlands, it says, and it's clear that it thinks I'm stupid. It's also clear that it's getting nervous. At least that makes it more helpful.

The Everlands? What is that?

There's no time, Squid says.

No time? Squid, I can't help if I don't know!

No, mortal, there's no time in the Everlands. That's why we come here to be born. Mortality is terrible and wonderful, and it's the only way we can live, or start to.

I shake my head. *You make no sense,* I think at it. *What do you mean? No, wait, never mind. Why would they want you? Or your egg? The king?*

Squid is arch. *I expect it is a great honor to birth a dragon, mortal. We are masters of time, after all.* A pause, and then faintly, very faintly, more people—overlapping people, like when I first blood-bonded to Squid—appear around me. *See? Time is mine.*

My gorge rises as I realize what the tiny thing means. Time. These ghostlike people are here because the dragon sees all of time, all at once. I can't grasp what it means, really; understanding keeps slipping away from me. I can't quite imagine what seeing layers of time could give you the power to do. Surely time just ... unfurls, like a road before us. What would there even be to master? As my mind begins to try to work out what this could mean—and what it could mean to royalty, especially—I shake my head. I wish I'd paid more attention to stories from the Era of Storms now. They'd probably tell me the exact risk of a dragon in royal hands. But it makes my skin tingle, thinking about that kind of power in the hands of people prepared to hire torturers just to get hold of the dragon.

Right, I send. *But three men were tortured and killed to try and find you. That doesn't seem to me like they're just doing it for the honor of, well, birthing you.*

When Squid speaks next, a faint embarrassment colours its tone. *I told you I need to get to Calindrina. It is your duty as my blood bonded to get me there.*

I frown. The sooner this blood bond is broken, the better. *Squid, honestly. Just tell me why they want you.*

Squid's reply is so faint I barely hear it. *I... This is why I need to get to Calindrina... I ... don't know.*

I close my eyes and sigh. *You don't know.*

Squid seems to hesitate, then a flood of thoughts, faint and wispy around the edges like fading dreams, fills my head. *I have to get to Calindrina. It's all I really know. I can't know everything yet. I know that I am made to know everything all at once, but I can't know it yet because of chained time. It's ridiculous, but that's how it is.* These thoughts are almost defensive. *I have to get to Calindrina because there is another dragon there. It has to die. Only one of us can be alive. I have to eat its brain.*

I make a face of disgust, and a passing vagabond gives me a funny look and then makes to avoid me. *Eat its brain?*

You mortals and your qualms. Honestly. You drank my blood and gave me yours, and this is too much?

Yes! It is!

Well, it is the only way. I don't know enough. All I know is that dragon—the dragon in Calindrina—it knows. And for me to know, to really know, to get the knowledge that has been passed down by the Guardians through the ages, I have to eat its brain.

I close my eyes and take a deep breath. Was it really only a day ago I was worried about my pretty silk jacket and whether I'd be able to mend a tear? This is really beyond me. I don't really want to go looking for Calindrina, wherever that is, and I don't understand why I should. I don't know anything about dragons. Maybe this is one of those cases I should leave to the experts. Let it go. Break the blood bond.

I do not think it is that simple.

But my fury at Liv is pricking me on, and I've been in risky situations often enough to know that not knowing what's going on is the surest way to wind up accidentally dead. Understanding these risks is what drew me to Rositus's this morning. It's what drew me to Kitchener's, despite knowing it might be me the two torturers were after. That, and the fact that I will not, *cannot*, leave those boys to face whatever dangers are coming their way alone.

I'm going to Calindrina, Squid tells me, *whether you help me—as is your* duty, *mortal—or not. Whether she helps me or not. I have to get there.*

I make a sound of frustrated irritation out loud, making a passing flower vendor look at me, startled, and Liza harrumph at me. *Alright, here's what's happening. I'm going to warn Twisty and his friends. Then I'm going to find my bags and fucking kill Liv. And then, and only then, will I make a plan about what the fuck I'm going to do with you.*

CHAPTER NINE

L iza snorts when I tell her we're not simply riding off into the sunset, but I can't leave town without at least letting the lads know they might be next in line for attention from our sovereign. The prince was at Armand's, and if he's the one hiring Ascelese mercenaries, the lads may be seriously at risk.

The warehouse I find is tall and dilapidated, sitting against the old stone wall that marked the edge of Valenta before it grew beyond its bounds. Despite her disapproving looks at my distrust, I tie Liza up and haul myself up the side of the building, all three floors. The window on the top floor is open, and I swing myself through it without hesitating, only to be brought to an abrupt stop.

The man inside has Twisty in a headlock, a dagger at his throat. Scarface and Kelt are against the opposite wall, scared but with weapons at the ready. My sword is drawn before I know it.

"Hello," I say, calm belying the pace of my heartbeat. "This doesn't look like a very fruitful conversation. Perhaps I can remedy that."

The man's dark eyes narrow, and a smirk mars his lips. My heart kicks up. He's the big torturer from this morning, the one who had been carrying the bloody club. Crainor. I glance about, wondering where his slender, pale-eyed compatriot is. "Well, by the goddess," he says. "It just took a fruitful turn."

All the confirmation I need—he's here after me. And Twisty, it would seem, was refusing to give me up. My heart gives a squeeze for the tiny man, but I don't let it show. "I take it you're after me, then. P'raps we should let these lads about their business and take our discussion elsewhere."

Crainor's mouth turns upward like I've been far more amusing than I have. He's broad and handsome, but his eyes have a wild edge in them. He snugs Twisty closer and traces the point of the blade gently against his neck. I'm meant to be horrified, and I can't keep all of my reaction down, so I distract us both by dipping my sword to the floor and twisting the tip against it, drawing up splinters.

"I think there might be some use they can be to me yet," he tells me, his Ascelese accent strong. "Well, not those two, most like." He nods at the others. "You wield your weapons well, lads. Off ye go."

Scarface glances at me, but Kelt is gone almost before he finishes talking. Scarface can see what Kelt's missing—that the man is trying to even any possible odds by getting them gone. The apologetic look he sends me as he turns for the stairs confirms it.

"At last, we have some privacy," I say, dancing my way around my sword so I can swing it up into readiness once more. "Why don't you let that boychild go, and us adults can have a proper conversation."

The smirk grows, but there's fury in his eyes as well. "Think you're smart, don't you, girlie?"

"Not overly," I say, keeping my voice even, "but smart enough to think involving a kid in whatever this mess is is unjustified." I pretend more warmth and tug at the neckline of my shirt, popping the top button to reveal a curve of breast. "Besides, we're grownups. I'm sure we can find a solution to this that doesn't involve blood being spilled."

He shakes his head a little. "I'm not interested, woman, so you can quit the games. My question is very simple. Where. Is. The. Egg?"

I blink at him, considering how dumb to play. "Egg? The egg is gone," I say.

The length of the blade eases closer to Twisty's neck, and those blue-green eyes, pinned to mine, widen in fear. "I don't believe you," Crainor almost sings. "Now tell me where it is."

I shrug. "I've no idea," I say, and it's true. Liv's gone the gods know where, and they're not talking.

His brown eyes meet mine, and now, they're cold as a snake's. "You play with me, I play with his life." He levers his dagger hand a little, and blood trickles down Twisty's neck. Astonishingly, the boy doesn't make a sound. I swallow hard as I realize Twisty is drawing downward, very slowly—too slowly to be noticed—toward his boot. If I can keep this killer occupied...

"Come now," I say, as saccharine as I can manage. Nothing will be more distracting than a blatant attempt at gameplay, I hope. "There's no need for that. I don't know where it is, but I know who had it last. At least, I think I do."

"Mmm-hmm. And who is that?"

"Some girl. She stole all my things. The egg was in a pouch." I carefully don't mention that it's broken in two.

Eyes narrow again. "Who is this girl, and where is she?"

I shrug. "Some player." I watch, and there's a spark of recognition in his eyes. Oh dear, Liv. Maybe these two *are* working for the prince. I dismiss the thought, my anger at her making it easy. The Petrus in my head approves. I have to force the words out, and I can't help that they still feel like betrayal. "She took my things and ran."

"Ran where?"

I half laugh, my sword still swinging loose in my grip. "Don't you think if I knew that, I might not be getting it back? How in the hell should I know? Wherever pretty players go when they've stolen all your stuff!"

Crainor's face doesn't change. "You think I'm stupid enough to take off on some wild goose chase after that green-eyed player bitch? On your say-so? No. More than like you're covering for her."

I swallow my reaction. Twisty's timing couldn't be better. The boy slides down, his whole weight against Crainor's arm. It tugs him out of alignment with the dagger, though it scrapes his skin hard enough to draw blood. I bound forward, but Crainor pulls a sword out to clash hard against mine.

"*Run!*" I yell at Twisty.

He slashes at Crainor's calves with his short knife.

Crainor roars, bringing the sword down hard, but Twisty's fast, rolling away from it. "Go!" I yell again, and this time, he follows my instruction, throwing himself down the stairs in the way only a kid can do. I leap for the window as soon as I see he's out of reach and toss myself through it.

I have two minor advantages on Crainor—one, I'm used to rooftop exits, and two, I came up this way. I slide down the brief span of roof tiles, landing heavy but hale on the next. Below me, I see Twisty appear in the back garden. "Liza," I call out, "he's with us! Twisty, the horse!"

Twisty slashes at the reins and glances back up above me. "Look out!" he calls.

I leap out and down, only just catching my footing on the next level of roofing, and throw myself back to keep from diving headfirst into the yard. I keep sliding, though, and land awkwardly on the hard ground. One ankle protests a little as I jump onto Liza's back. I haul the boy up in front of me, and Liza takes off without my urging.

Valenta is a speck on the horizon—a lonely speck on the horizon—before we slow. Farmland slowly carves into the desert, but the road itself is still red dust. Twisty bounces in front of me in the saddle. He seems both relieved to be changing pace and anxious about pursuit.

I am horribly mindful that I can't know the connections between any of the people who are after Liv and the dragon egg, which means I have no clue how many people might be brought out in pursuit. The two foreigners with a penchant for torture, the prince, and maybe the King's Guard. The Rogue. I glance over my shoulder, but there's no telltale cloud of dust rising in the distance.

"Alright, kid, we need to check to make sure that neck of yours has stopped bleeding," I tell the boy, letting my tone fill with pragmatism in the hope I don't scare him. He's been dripping blood the whole way, an obvious trail leading from that three-story building, through the western gate, and out onto the road. "Let's take a look."

I curse Liv beneath my breath as I tear away a shirt sleeve to press against the wound. I have proper bandages in my pack, but gods know where she's taken that. Liza, a little weary from the sprint, keeps us moving slowly away.

So you live yet, mortal, comes the haughty sound of the dragon's voice in my mind. *Are you far from us?*

I bite my lip, trying not to appear too distracted to Twist. *Shush a moment!* "Alright. It's a scratch. A nasty one, but only a scratch. You will heal up good as new..." I think of the bedroom where he and the other boys slept. "...so long as you keep it nice and clean."

Twisty is quiet, and I don't push for words. I press the cloth gently against the wound until it stops bleeding, then try a different tack. "Twisty, you probably need to have a think about what you want to do now." He blinks up at me, his blue eyes vague, and I feel for his hand. It's cold and clammy. He's in shock, and who can blame him? I smile at him tersely. "Alright, never mind. We need to keep moving for now, alright? But I've got you, so you can sleep." I tug my cloak away and wrap it around him, snugging him close against my torso. We have to keep moving, so I push away the guilt I feel at riding this lad farther from home and turn my attention elsewhere.

Alright, dragon, I think determinedly. *You wanted to talk?*

Where are you? Squid responds brusquely. *I don't know where this mortal is off to, but she's got a horse now. We've been riding for an age.*

I curse softly again. Bloody Liv. Definitely outside of Valenta, though. Same instinct as mine, which is just as well. Maybe I'll have half a chance of getting my bags back. *Are you heading toward the sun or away?*

The dragon is slow to reply. *Actually, I can't tell,* it says, with a note of shame in its tone. *I'm still inside a pouch. That one you put me in.*

I frown, a little guilty. *You mean she hasn't seen you?* Surely if Liv had planned to take the dragon, she'd have confirmed it was there?

She hasn't seen me. I'm still stuck in your pack, and she hasn't gone through it yet. I think she's scared of someone following her.

I blink, thinking quickly. In my fury at Liv fleeing, I had assumed she was doing me over in the worst conceivable way—that she knew everything and was playing me. But I frown, remembering the prince's men outside Armand's. It's possible—unlikely, maybe, but possible—that she'd just been scared to see him without the egg in hand, after the King's Guard destroying her van. I scowl. Guilt is like an irritating itch. I thought she'd stolen the dragon from me, ready to make her deal. And now I've put her in it with Crainor. My internal Petrus is the only thing between me and getting lost in the guilt.

Dragon, I think, as gently as I can manage.

Esquidamelion, it replies archly.

Squid, I compromise. *I think it may be better for you to ... not be seen by Liv. Do you think you can do that?*

I receive a blast of disdain mixed with confusion, but it settles quickly. *Why?* Squid finally asks.

Why, Squid, I'd be so pleased to explain my reasoning to you, I snark. I take a breath and exhale slowly. Twisty's breathing is soft and even. I'm fairly sure he's asleep. *Because right now, she may not know you exist. If that's the case, if she thought the egg was a carving and didn't know it had a dragon in it, it would be better for her to not know. If she sees you, she'll know you exist, and then, with no care for your wellbeing, she'll probably try to hand you over to those men.*

There's a ruminating pause. *What do you think she'll do when she finds the broken egg? Won't she know then?*

I shake my head, even though Squid is far, far away. *I doubt it. She'll just think it's broken. And with any luck, she'll try and get it fixed. Or get a copy. That'll get everyone off our backs.*

And then we can go to Calindrina.

I almost smile this time. It's repetitive, but that one almost sounded hopeful. *If you're really sure that's where you want to go,* I tease.

CHAPTER TEN

For a time, I let Liza take the lead, hoping it's enough of a break to recover from our galloping exit from Valenta.

Rain falls, and at first, it patters gently. As the sun sets, low across the red sand, it intensifies. All the dust becomes mud, wet enough to ping up a little with each droplet's strike. A rumble sounds, followed by lightning. I do my best to rouse myself, feeling the want of rest and food in my belly. I've done sleep deprivation on the road before. It's no fun, but at least I know I can do it.

I force myself to look back over my shoulder. My eyes glaze over a little from staring into the dusky light of sunset, but a slight movement catches my attention. Another flash of a lightning strike, and in that brief second, I see it. A horse with a rider, and they're headed this way.

It could go either way, with where we are, but it doesn't seem like a smart risk. People in Valenta seemed remarkably unhappy with me, in general. And I need to catch Liv before anyone else catches her so I can make sure Squid is safe. I think toward Squid for a moment, but there's no response. My belly flips disconsolately. At least there's the beginnings of bushland to the north of us. I turn Liza. It's the only place I can imagine losing them. A bit of a vain hope, maybe, since the trees are one of the few things marring the flat plain, but it's better than nothing.

I dismount and lead Liza under the trees, wondering if we might be able to hide in the shadows. She gives me a sidelong look. I take her a little further in amongst scrubby shrubs, then turn back to see how obvious our trail is.

Another crack of lightning, and I see him.

I don't know whether he's a second pursuer I missed seeing from the road, or he's moved quicker than I expected, but in the flash, I see him, and he sees me. He's ahorse, and the horse is weary and wet. Whoever sent him, he's bristling with weapons, and I do not want to wait to converse.

I gasp as fear jets through me.

In a split second, I'm back in the saddle behind Twisty and urging Liza on. He startles awake but stays coiled down against my belly. My hair, not so long but wet now from the rain, falls in my eyes.

She's a good horse—the best, really—and moments like these make me all the more grateful for her. She just takes over. The reins fall from my hands, and I curl forward over Twisty, gripping the pommel tight. Liza ducks and weaves between shrubs and eucalypts, graceful and quick. A thin branch whips at my cheek, opening a stinging cut before I tuck my head down again. She's remarkably fast.

Behind us, I make out the crash of not just one horse through the trees, but several. I glance back. Two. Another look, and my hands grip the pommel, white-knuckled. There's five. They're not in the red of the King's Guard, but they are definitely in uniform. I think it's gray, which would make it the Rescalin army, under the command of Prince Shandor, but it's hard to be sure through the rain and gold of sunset. And they all hold glimmering things in their hands. I imagine how sharp they would be and swallow hard.

"Alright, Liza, we've got to find a way out of here," I tell her. "They'll be winded soon if they've been searching for us this whole time. You've got the strength, you beautiful girl. You can keep up the pace long after they'll be failing."

Her neck strains forward as if she can understand me. "Stay down, Twist," I murmur in his ear. "You're lucky you're so light!"

I doubt he's thinking the same as he jounces around, pinned by my weight against the horse and with the pommel digging into his stomach, but it's better than the alternative. The trees thin abruptly, and we are out again, racing across red dust with no proper road in sight. I've not the first clue where I am. I pull up a little, giving Twisty more space.

The land is far too flat to stay out of sight easily, so we're relying on speed now. I urge Liza on, but she's already giving her all, so I pat her neck gently in thanks.

A whistling noise sounds to my right, and an arrow misses us by some distance. Liza's body is all tension and release now, her everything caught into each stride. Another whine, and I tuck myself down above Twisty again.

Another whistling noise, and pain resounds through my body from my right ear. "Bastards!" I hiss, wanting to grip where I've been struck. But if they've hit the ear once, the hand will only be a bigger target, so I lean low, squashing Twisty but more aerodynamic, and urge Liza on. Blood makes wet noises as it trickles into my ear.

The sound of the whistle doesn't quite reach us next, and then, when I risk a glance backward, I think we must be pulling away a little. The next arrow zooms past my left ear, but after that, I hear no more. Glancing back, I see that they're further away, slowing. One even seems to have stopped, and the next time I scan behind us, the horse is on the ground, its rider standing beside it. In the next lightning strike, I catch a reflected flash as the rider bends over the horse, and I am horrified at the thought that he's probably cutting its throat.

Liza sweats, and despite the cool rain, her sides heave, but I don't let her slow until the horizon's curve takes the riders out of sight. Her head is low with weariness as we reduce to a trot, and Twisty's thin arm points off to the right a little. A few thready green blades of grass push through the red mud, but a little beyond that, I see what he's pointing to.

A flood must have passed through here some time ago, or several, because there's a very narrow little stream. It's sunk between two much, much higher rocky banks, almost tall enough to be called cliffs. We gaze down at this brownish ribbon of water threading between green and grassy banks tucked away well below the level ground. Unless someone knows it's here, from the desert plain they won't even imagine we could be out of sight. It's a risk, of course—uniformed men are likely to have maps—but it's the best chance we've got right now.

I dismount to lead Liza down into the little ravine, hoping against hope it's not a trap. I shove a hand through my hair, accidentally knock my still-bleeding ear, and wince. Twisty forces a half grin, dripping curls tumbled all over his face. "Dampish, ain't it?"

We follow the brown stream for a while, heading east, Liza carrying both of us. I hope this will take us well and truly out of the path of the riders behind us, who, with some luck, will expect us to be still following the trail we set north. The ground beneath us is sticky, and after a while, it feels cruel to make Liza work that hard just to carry us a little further out of the way. I dismount into sucking mud and sigh. If my boots weren't already soaked, they certainly are now.

"Huh. Look at that." Twisty points again, and I feel silly that I haven't been keeping a better watch on what is around us. I follow the line of his finger and smile.

To either side of the river, the cliffs are rock made of layered sand—vermilion, ocher-red and turmeric compressed down into stone, only just visible in the low light. On this bend in the river, possibly during a flood, a swirl of water has carved out the beginnings of a cave—just the beginnings, but a definite overhang. Beneath it, the stone is pale and rosy—dry—edged by red and white darkness on either side, where the water cascades down from above. Not much more than a hollow, but it'll even let us have a small fire if we're lucky, given we're down below the level of the protection of the banks.

I laugh and then sigh, hanging on to the top of my boots as I pull my feet free of the mud and step up onto the rock. "C'mon then, you two," I say, and Liza snorts and shakes her head at me, a weary attempt at disapproval.

But I'm up in the nook and settling back against the rock in no time. It won't last long, with the sun gone, but it's warm against my back, and sitting feels like a blessing. Twisty settles next to me, pausing to cautiously shake out his hair like a dog before he rests back with me.

"Ah," he says, "this is the life!" He's working hard for his cheerfulness, and as he turns to grin at me, he winces a little and touches his neck. The cut the torturer had given him at his hidey-hole is bleeding again.

I half smile and reach out to press his shirt collar to the blood. "Twist? Can I ask you something? A few somethings, maybe?"

He looks at me askance. "Are you trying to distract me from the pain?"

I laugh. "Not a great nurse, am I? But no, I just need to work out about them as are following us, and I think it might have something to do with the murder you saw—well, the corpses. Who told you about them?"

He shrugs. "Well, look... Someone did come looking for you, like I said this morning. Green-eyed player girl, like that lout with the sword talked about, you know? She asked about you and about what you were doing here. We told her about the ... about your friends." I swallow. No wonder she ran off with all my stuff if she thought I had robbed her messengers. She plays me, I play her, she plays me harder. Gods. "And then, well ... Scarface had taken a fancy to her, so—we might have been drinking some—but we thought we'd go and see where she was, see if we could, you know, offer our services."

I try desperately not to laugh, but a snort escapes.

He rolls his eyes. "Not like that! We're not that stupid! But that's how we found them bodies."

"And did you see her there? Or any sign?" Has Liv added assassination to her array of tricks? Snuff has never been her style, but, well, she doesn't know me anymore either. Surely that had been Crainor's work. But if she'd seen them...

"No sign," Twisty says quickly. I narrow my eyes again, and he shrugs with a smile.

"Hmm." I shift the subject a little. "So, what do you think the Rogue's gonna do with all this, then? The King's Guard, the prince, whoever killed Rositus... Want to lay any bets?"

"I'm betting he's in trouble," Twisty says sensibly.

"Any word on why they're here? The King's Guard? The prince?"

Twist shrugs, then shivers a little. I wish I had blankets, but without my saddlebags, I'm straining for anything. "Alright. You lot stay here, and I'll get us wood for the fire." Standing patiently out of reach of the few red drips falling from above, Liza nods her head at me. I make a face. "Sorry, girl." I pat her as I pass. "First thing tomorrow, I'll feed you. And scrub you down."

I awake and am on my feet before I realize it, startled at a roar in my ears. I take a second to realize it's not really a roar. It's Squid, and it's not a happy dragon. *Where are you?* it bellows, over and over. I wince.

Settle, petal, I think at it, with the usual grumps of someone roused before they ought to have been. *What's going on?*

Where are you? the dragon asks. *You disappeared.* It almost sounds concerned amidst the anger.

I sigh and scrub a muddy hand across my face, looking out over the sunken riverbed we camped by last night. Where are we indeed. *No,* I say, as patiently as I can manage. *I think we were out of range. This... this... whatever it is... doesn't seem to work that well over long distances.* Somehow, it makes me feel vaguely nauseous. That or the hunger.

Unless I send really *hard,* the dragon amends.

Yes, unless you yell and scream like a two-year-old, I snark back. *Does this mean you and Liv are still traveling?*

Yes. She is very erratic, this woman you love and hate, it tells me matter-of-factly.

I cringe at the description. *I'm not—I don't*—and I recall abruptly that the dragon can hear everything I'm thinking. *Is she now?* I think more deliberately.

Yes. A smug note hovers behind the single word. *She keeps changing her mind about which way to go.*

She hasn't found you yet, though, right?

No. The dragon is smug about this too. *She searched your bags last night. Well, she tipped everything out. But I remain hidden from her.*

That's good, that's good. Well done, I say, an afterthought delivered with something less than perfect grace. A thought strikes me. *And your egg? The pieces?*

There's a moment of hesitation. *She saw those, but I am not sure she knows what they are. I had placed them back amongst your gold and silver in case.*

I frown a little. *Are... have you grown much, then?*

Oh yes, it agrees proudly.

How big are you now?

Oh, I would say that I am the same size as ... as Liza's hairbrush.

There's a currycomb in the pack. Squid's growing, and fast. Before long it'll be too big to stay hidden. I swallow hard. *Alright, well ...* I'm about to explain we will be headed toward them as soon as Twisty is ready when there's another howl through the ether. It cuts off quickly.

Squid? I try softly. *Are you alright?*

For a long moment, silence. It's enough to make me wonder whether I'd been crazy to think a dragon could talk to me, when finally, its voice sounds in my head again.

The woman you love and hate screamed. Loudly. It almost sounds like a whisper. *They're here.*

Who are—I cut off the thought. Risky for Squid to get caught. My heartbeat kicks up.

I think they're soldiers. I don't want to get out of this bag to find out. The last thought is almost shamefaced.

Don't worry, you're doing the right thing, I think hastily. *I'm going to try and come and find you, alright? I need you to keep making some kind of noise—well, thinking at me—so I can work out which direction you are in. Gods, I hope this works.* The fact the dragon roared at me earlier after being out of reach for so long overnight suggests it might be more complicated than that, but I have to try.

The dragon is in danger.

And so is Liv.

I squash the thought mercilessly. She's responsible for bringing that dragon into my life. Her mercenaries attacked me, and I had to kill one of them when I'd really hoped I wouldn't ever have to kill again. She's put the king and the prince and the Rogue and torturers on my tail and taken almost everything I own.

And now she's dragging the dragon away and leaving its voice resounding in my brain. I am not going to spend my life running from the hordes, with Squid sorting through my memories. No. Not going to happen. She's not getting her way this time.

I gently wake Twisty. "Time to go, kid," I say. "We've no food, so let's go find some."

He nods, yawning and stretching, and settles comfortably into Liza's saddle. We clamber carefully up to the red desert plain. I scan carefully, looking for enemies, but I can't see anyone. *And now, to look for a needle in a haystack,* I think.

A haystack? A magnet would help, the dragon says, less than helpfully. *Should I make a noise?*

Something even and steady so I can tell if it's getting louder.

Can you hear that? The low hum is almost out of reach of my hearing. Irritatingly so, but it will work.

That's great. Now hold tight, I tell it. And it feels quite strange, heading across the muddy soil toward it. It also feels right.

CHAPTER ELEVEN

The midday sun beats down on us before I feel like we're even starting to reach Squid. Every now and then, the hum is interspersed with commentary. *I think they've taken her prisoner, that woman,* it says perfunctorily. *Haven't found me, though. Might stick my head out, see what's going on.* I'm about to tell it I don't think that's wise, but I'm interrupted.

"Look!" Twisty says. I'm leading Liza as a compromise. Despite the grass she'd cheerfully torn up before we left the riverbank, she's hungry, and I haven't fed her properly. The least I can do is walk. But Twisty's barely heavy enough for her to recognize he's there, so he gets to ride. My feet ache. I wish I were smaller.

"What is it?" I ask, raising my head and shading my eyes. I curse Liv once more, this time for running off with my new hat. Well, add it to the list of betrayals. "The riders from yesterday?"

"I don't think so," he says, after a moment. I finally spot what he was pointing to on the horizon. "I think it's a camp?"

I am in a tent, Squid adds helpfully. *This one is white, but ... there are also red ones.*

That matches the white we can see—the red will blend into the dust. "It's a camp," I confirm, "but I'm not sure they're ... friendly."

Twisty sends me a quick look. He doesn't say it, but he doesn't have to. His expression says it for him: does everyone hate you?! The dragon chuckles. *Shush, you!*

I think ... yes! The dragon is exultant. *I have found the woman you love and hate! She is in a tent alone. Men with swords are standing around outside.*

That would figure, if she's their prisoner.

I will guide you, the dragon exclaims, *so that you can free us!*

I'm not sure I'm going to free her. The thought of Liv begging me again and me being able to coldly refuse feels like a salve. *And you'll have to show me where all my stuff is. Don't go looking, though! Someone might see you.*

I can make out the tents now, distantly, but we're likely about to be visible to anyone keeping watch. The scrubby trees behind the campsite and to the south won't provide much protection, but it'll be better than a bald-faced approach.

We circle around the camp at a safe distance, and I dismount in a greenish spot. Liza at least will appreciate the meal. "I'm going to go on alone," I tell Twisty and Liza, who both give me a look of such shared disdain and disappointment I have to swallow a giggle. "I'm just checking out who it is. A scout is quieter on their own. Besides, it's too dangerous. It might be too dangerous to even... Well, it's probably too dangerous," I conclude. Telling Twisty all the ins and outs of this complicated story seems less than smart. "Wait here. I'll come back and collect you."

I check all of my weapons are in place and then ease my way between the trees, slowing as I reach proximity to the campsite.

They will have lookouts, I figure, so I scout carefully. Four guards stand amongst the trees, all in some kind of uniform, but I don't recognize it. Dark green. I rack my brains for any leads about whose men they might be, but nothing appears.

Only one is doing any sort of patrol. The others sit around lazily, sharpening weapons or entertaining themselves with whittling. They don't seem too anxious about anyone trying to get into camp, which is all to the good.

You may want to hurry, Squid says. *A man left her tent. I'm going in.*

The idea of it makes me anxious, but I bind that feeling down tight. I can use the fear—it'll drive me to be fast and smart—but anxiety makes me stupid. I ease my way between the seated guards and duck down in the gap between two tents to take a measure of the camp itself.

We are in a red tent, the dragon adds, trying to be helpful.

I know. I try to keep from sounding testy. *Just let me work out where that is.*

I have an idea!

Before I can ask what the idea is, smoke rises from a tent not far from me. I blink at it stupidly for a long moment, then duck down again as three men run past me toward it, yelling at each other. *Dragon! Less than helpful!* I snap. Wait. What accent was that?

I didn't light the woman's tent, it tells me witheringly. *Only the one next to it.*

You mean the one you were in? The one with my stuff in it? I ask archly, but I can't quite keep the dismay at bay. Fuck. All my things!

I... Yes.

I huff a breath, saying a swift farewell to my pack and its carefully winnowed set of tools, clothing, and, well, everything a girl on the road with her horse could need. Including a pretty silk jacket, now stained, somewhat torn, and potentially burned.

A distinct commotion sounds further down the row of tents. I ignore the wise voice in my head screaming at me not to and race down the line until I reach the back of a red tent near the commotion. I duck beside it, draw a long dagger, and slice across the canvas.

I haul myself through the gap, expecting to find Liv in chains in a corner, potentially with a black eye, and with a definite gratitude to see me.

So it's something of a shock to find her reclining, sleep- and probably sex-tousled, amidst white sheets on a surprisingly non-camplike bed. She only starts to look concerned when she rouses enough to work out it's me who has disturbed her rest.

"Des?" she says in disbelief. "What the hell are you doing here?"

Something flies at my face before I can reply. I duck, but Squid catches hold of my shoulder, digging claws in to curl around to sit on it. It coos in my ear, clearly glad to see me. My anxiety settles at its proximity.

It rubs a scaly face against my cheekbone, which would almost be touching, except for the look of astonishment on Liv's face. "Gods, Des, what have you—" Her expression too quickly morphs into calculation, and from there, into her best game face.

Fuck. She didn't know 'til now, but now she's worked out the egg held a dragon. I cannot, *cannot*, leave her here. She'll definitely betray me again.

I leap across the distance between us, gripping the dagger tight. The dragon's claws dig into my shoulder as I curl my body around Liv's and press the blade against her throat. "Not a fucking word, ma'am," I whisper in her ear, my face pressed into the cloud of her dark hair, caught back in a silver clip. "Not a word. You're coming with us." I can't deny the flare of desire I feel with her body against me. This had been a game we'd played and perfected together—the kidnap—but no play this time.

"I'm not going with you, Des," she says, very clearly, loud enough to be heard outside, and I act without thinking, pushing her face down on the bed. My knee is in her back before I know it, and a hand wrapped around her mouth, fingers caught under her jaw to keep the mouth shut. No screams.

"You scream and I will fucking end you, Liv," I hiss. "This isn't a game, and your douse-word won't work this time. You stole my shit, my dragon, and my horse, and I will kill you as soon as not." It's hard to say, but I know without the harshness, she'll keep pushing. She has to believe it.

She makes a noise, and I press the dagger closer against her throat, just enough to let the blood free. Just enough to sell the play. Can't afford noise. There are crowds of unfriendly men outside the tent, ready to skewer me.

I tear the sheet while she's processing this, shove it into her mouth, then strap it in place with a belt—the belt I lent her!—that's sitting beside the bed. I slice another strip free, and as she starts wriggling beneath me, I lace her hands tightly together. I don't have to fake the anger I inject into tightening the knots. With one hand, I awkwardly bundle the remnants of the clothing I'd lent her yesterday morning in Valenta, shove it all in the center of a blanket, and toss in the fine wineskin, loaf, and cheese sitting on the silver platter beside the bed.

Some prisoner.

Out of sight, Squid, I tell the little dragon, and it burrows like a swift blue rabbit down into the pile of clothes. Liv makes a move like she's about to get up, so I shove her hard down against the bed. I bind the bundle to my back, pick up the dagger, and put it back at Liv's throat. "Now, up and march."

I haul her upright, roughly wrap another blanket from the bed around her naked body, and shove her toward the flapping tear I've made in the tent. It'll be touch and go, whether we'll get away. We're not inconspicuous.

I pause, shouldering her a little way behind me as I peer out from between the tents. The blaze in the next tent is out, but I can't go looking for my bags now. If they even survived the flames. Fortunately, there's so much commotion about the fire, it's the matter of a moment to yank Liv along behind me, blanket flapping, to the edge of the scrubby trees.

I pause for a long moment here, realizing that Liv, Twisty, and I will be far too much for Liza to carry. *Horses?* I ask the small blue dragon.

There's a scurrying movement against my back, and the tiny azure head with those bright sapphire eyes appears. The long nose stretches into the air. *South,* it says with utter certainty. Thank the gods one of us feels sure of something!

I head in the direction Squid indicated, yanking Liv down below the line of tents and pausing to listen for commotion. *What on earth did you do? They're taking forever to come back,* I say to Squid.

I lit the food. There were all kinds of things in there.

The first one goes off.

An almighty bang makes me jump, and smoke and even more yelling rise from the white tent. Liv attempts to scream behind her gag and throws herself toward me as if for protection. I shove her away from me, yanking firmly on the rag binding her hands. *Must've been some flour. Perhaps you're not just precious for your good looks.* I throw Squid a grin. *Alrighty, down you get now.* It burrows back into the bundle of clothes just as I'm coming up on the horses.

The bang has unsettled them, and another goes off, making them yank at their lead lines, but only a few have really pulled at their stakes. I narrow my eyes for a second, then grin to myself. If we can get away, chances are no one will be checking on Liv until they've sorted that fire. And even then, they don't need to know there was anyone else involved. But that will only work if the horses look like they've pulled themselves free.

I yank harder against two of the stakes, and thankfully, they pull out of the ground. I tug at half a dozen more, but only two more come free. I smack the rumps of two so they take off, but keep hold of the reins of the other two. This means, of course, that I've lucked out with the skittish horses.

They at least have reins, but neither carry saddles, and we don't have time to look for them. I catch up two half-empty nose bags hooked over a branch. Liza needs a proper feed. "Alright now, Liv, time to go," I say, almost sweet. "Let's do it!"

I try to get her up onto the back of a silver-gray mare, small and fine-limbed. Liv battles me for a long moment, making her body limp and heavy. The horse is uneasy, backing up and away.

I pause, and although I want to scream at her to do as I want, I know that only threats will work. So, I play it. "Liv, I will tie you across its back if you don't behave, and if that means you wind up dangling underneath... Or perhaps, really, it's easier to kill you here?"

Her body goes slack, and when I bend to brace her foot again, she is more biddable. I feel almost heartened, knowing she can't tell if I really would kill her. The rage inside me is pleased. Maybe my moving on really has been convincing. Maybe my playing has improved. I toss the blanket up to her to do whatever she can manage with her modesty and put the dagger in its sheath.

I clamber my way up onto the other horse, lead rope for the silver in my hand. The bay I've mounted snorts at me once as I turn it toward the trees, but my knees are tight in her ribs, and she knows not to fuck with me. We move at a slow walk.

I glance back, and Liv glares at me. My mouth goes tight. "Fine," I hiss, and urge the bay into a trot. Liv's gaze is a death stare now, but the sight of her, naked and jouncing, on the back of the silver, makes it almost worth it.

Twisty scrambles up from a seat leaning back against a tree, wide-eyed and astonished. "You... But... What... You know her?"

"I'll explain later," I say wearily, remembering that Liv and Twisty have met before. "But right now, we have to run."

"Again?" Twisty asks, a little plaintively.

"Again." I'm in no mood to deal with his disappointment.

"I need food."

I nod, and my belly grumbles in agreement. "I know." I twist the bundle around on my back and loosen it enough to let Squid out. Liv knows. Twisty may as well know. Maybe then he won't just believe I'm the most hated individual in all of Rescalin.

Think you can hang on to my shoulder, dragon? I ask, trying to be gentle. *I'm sure you're sick of hiding away.*

I can. Pride is in every line of Squid's body as it crawls out of the bundle. Then, with caution and some swaying, it clambers up and onto my shoulder.

Twisty looks on, agape. I glance at Liv. She's curious. Still angry, but curious too. "What ... what is *that*?" Twisty asks.

"That's Squid." I'm too tired and hungry for niceties as I lace the rough bundle of blankets and clothes onto the back of Liza's saddle. "My dragon."

I get a wave of intense indignation from Squid at the use of the possessive, but Twisty is so astonished he doesn't complain as I heave him into the saddle. And he forgets to demand answers to the other mystery: the mostly naked woman riding along behind us.

She's still ahorse, hands tied behind her back, breasts outthrust. She's beautiful, even when her green eyes are spitting fire. I pause beside the silver and tug the blanket free from her hands. It hadn't been much of a covering.

"Would you prefer the kirtle?" I ask her softly. "I can retie your hands in front if you'd like. It'd make riding easier." She sends me a fierce glare and turns her nose up.

"It's up to you," I say, "but we won't be under these trees all day, and that lily-white skin isn't like to cope so well with that."

Her mouth tightens—she hates giving way—but she nods, raises one leg over the horse's back—giving me a terrifyingly clear look at her sex—and turns sideways to slip off her steed. Of course, she lands gracefully before me, black curls bouncing around her shoulders.

"I'll do your hands."

She turns around. The tight knots are hard to untie, and it's not any easier with Liv's round butt sitting just beneath her hands. It's difficult to keep my focus. One of her hands comes free, and she spins away from me. I'm ready for this, though, and I tug her back, the fabric still wrapped around her other hand. "C'mon now, Liv," I say, aiming for sensible. "Let's not do this again."

Her green eyes meet mine, laughter in them as she wriggles against me suggestively.

"You *know* her?" Twisty breathes behind me, doubtless astonished at a woman so full of lust she'd turn it on her kidnapper. Liv's eyes rest on him, and they have a conniving gleam. How little he knows her. She probably used the same strategy with the men in the green uniforms. And really, I should've known she'd be able to manipulate her way into food and a bed, and probably more besides.

"Never you mind," I tell him, glaring at Liv. She's grinning at me behind the gag, and that, more than anything, warms me.

I tie her hands tight at the front, then yank the kirtle over her head. "Right. Ready?" She bats her eyelashes at me once more. "Up you go." I shove hard at her foot, then shift to pushing at her butt. She gasps a little, and so do I, as my hand slips a little too close for comfort. She's wet. That I did *not* need to know.

As I turn away without looking at her to mount my own steed, there's an "Mm-hmm," from behind me.

Twisty smirks at me, for all the world as if he knows exactly what's going on, and Squid is having complex thoughts of its own. *She smells ... interesting.*

I close my eyes as I settle into my seat, bareback on my bay mount, and catch hold of the silver's lead rope. How did this day get so gods-be-damned complicated? "Right," I say, my voice gravel. "Let's go."

I could swear there's a giggle behind me, but I can't tell whose it is.

CHAPTER TWELVE

It's evening before we happen on a small town. We're all exhausted, myself more than any, and I want to fill my belly. The loaf and cheese I'd taken from Liv's bedside in the camp had only really reminded me that I like real food, real regular.

We pause on a lightly grassed hillside outside the town. Gratitude swells my heart—even the promise of minor luxuries like bed, food, and bath makes me feel better. My oath to never deprive myself unnecessarily feels silly in this setting. I've fled three camps in the past two days, and I want to stay put for a bit.

Lamplight glows in the little town's streets. I send Twisty on to find us a decent place to stay while I remove Liv's gag and yank a dress over her head, glaring to keep her from talking to me. When Twisty reappears, he's already managed to feed himself. I'm so intensely jealous for a moment it's hard to return his smile. "Hello, lad. Looks like you've found us something good, I hope?"

He takes a deep breath, sighs out, and rubs his round belly. "Tav. Rooms. Next to the baths, and with a stew sitting on the fire that—"

I have to laugh. "Alright then, you. C'mon, less talk, more leading the way. And yes, you can have seconds." He grins.

Numerous eyes follow us as we make our way into town. Some pitying looks are directed Liv's way—probably sympathy for the armless girl with the beautiful face. She would hate that. I grin, and Squid's scaly little face rubs against the back of my neck. *Hold still,* I tell it. *You're a decoration on the pommel of my sword, remember?*

The tavern is practically the first in town. To my relief, it's small, probably about eight rooms. Double doors are thrown open to spill golden light into the night, and a few punters sit inside, nursing beer and sopping up the ends of stew with bread. We dismount, Liv grumpily, and I tie the two horses to the iron hoops designed for the purpose.

The woman behind the bar nods solemnly at Twisty and then at myself, granting him the respect of having been the original customer. "Evening, ma'am," I say, as courteously as I can manage. "I've two more beasts out the front, and I'd be much obliged if they could be cared for, fed, and housed, alongside the lad's mare. That doable?" I press coins to the bar.

She nods, smiles, and puts down a tankard of beer before a patron. We climb the stairs as she gestures a young girl over to her, who scurries off in the right direction.

Twisty opens the door to a large bedroom. At first, the sight of the lamplit, clean interior makes me smile, and then I turn a glare on him. "I said three beds, Twist. I remember being quite clear on that point, in fact." There's one large bed, designed for two, and a smaller bed, for one. This is not how I envisaged this.

He smirks. "Well, *I* can share with her, comes to that," he says.

Liv smiles at him winningly, and I can already see what will happen. "Nope, you can't," I say directly. "Gods, and here I was hoping for a proper night's sleep."

"I hope you don't think I will get in the way of that," Liv snarks, a sexy challenge in her eyes. "I'm really *quite* worn out."

I sigh. "Liv, I'm too tired for this." I settle onto a bed. Squid slithers away to curl up on the bedhead. It's bigger again than it had been at the soldiers' camp. Growing like a weed. I force myself to think about Liv. We need to have this conversation, especially as I'm not inclined to keep watch all night. "Right. We need to sort a deal. Twist, get us food, can you? This conversation can't be shared with the world, and I'm starving."

He makes a face, but he's a biddable lad and heads off downstairs, closing the door on his way out.

Liv stands before me, wrists still tied together under her dress. She looks bedraggled and smudged with dirt, but as ever, it doesn't matter. She still blazes in this place.

"Ah, Des, Des, Des," she says. "I don't know *what* you thought you were doing."

"I thought I was saving your life," I say bluntly, opening the bundle of clothing to keep myself from focusing on that smile, the warmth in her eyes. I can't help it. She's got a direct line to my cunt and she isn't afraid to use it. "You know? Saving you from torture, murder, all the rest." It's half a lie, but maintaining my fury at her when she's right there before me is harder.

She laughs again. "Ah, ye of little faith," she says softly, almost husky. "I can take care of myself, Des. You know that."

I nod and turn away to riffle through my pack. "Clearly. Which is why you hired me to protect you."

She sighs. "Alright, it's true. I was in danger in Valenta. But when you kidnapped me, well..."

"Well?" I'm snappy this time. Her gameplay is beyond me. My mind feels like sludge; I can't keep up. Probably not the wisest choice to have this conversation right now.

Agreed, says a voice in my head, half-irritating and half-comforting. *You should gag her again.*

The thought makes me smile as I turn back to face her, which sets her off balance. Gratification is like warmth in my gut. She hesitates a bare moment. "Des, it's simple. We need to give the dragon to a friend of mine, and then we'll be fine."

"Absolutely not!" The heat of protectiveness that floods me is astonishing, even for me. The dragon sends a sense of smugness my way, and I roll my eyes over both of them.

Will there ever be a time when those I care about won't try to hold that fact over me? I'm sharp, glancing sideways to glare at those sapphire points in the dim light. The gentle sense of meek apology is vaguely satisfying, even as I realize the little animal has goaded me into being more explicit about how I feel about it than I'd intended. In fact, I frown; I don't think I'd quite realized I did feel that way. I file the thought away for post-dinner, post-bath consideration.

"Alright," I say, after a long moment. "I can't have you running off, so what will it take for you to stay put?"

She smiles and settles beside me on the bed. "I won't run off," she says, sounding almost honest. "I swear I won't. I just need to understand. Explain it to me, and I'll stay with you until we sort out whatever this is."

I rub my face and huff out a breath. I can't trust her; I know this. But she knows about Squid now, and from the look she gave us back at the soldiers' camp, she knows the little carving the prince had given her was far from just a carving. Perhaps she knows more than I do. Perhaps something about who exactly is after me and what exactly they want. I'm hardly going to get answers unless she thinks my guard is dropped.

I rally my internal resources and school myself to play. I round out my shoulders, putting my elbows on my knees in weariness. For a moment, I rest there, and then I let out a sad little noise. Squid's head immediately comes up. *Shush, dragon, I'm alright. But I need to learn what she knows.* The little blue head drops back down, but the tiny sparkling eyes are attentive. My audience.

"I don't know what to do," I say, quiet and lost. "I don't understand what's going on. All these people are after me, and … I thought they were after you too, but … gods, I feel like such a fool. I'm sorry I kidnapped you, Liv. I truly am." I open my eyes wide and fix them on her green ones. "I just didn't know what to do. I couldn't *leave* you there!"

"Hush, lovely," Liv says, after a split second of calculation. She reaches out, rubbing a hand against my back in circles. I suppress the desire that fills me at her touch and focus on the performance. "I know. Shhh. It'll be alright. I'll tell you what I know, alright?"

I nod slowly, trying not to look too keen.

She takes a deep breath and stands. "What I told you in Valenta was part truth," she tells me, "but the prince hadn't explained everything to me. It was the prince's men you just kidnapped me from." I file this away. The green-clothed soldiers were the prince's? I could've sworn his troops dress in gray.

She pulls up a wooden chair opposite me and settles into it, leaning forward with her hands on her knees. "At first, I thought they were going to kill me, but, well ... we came to an arrangement, and the prince explained a few things to me." That I'd found her in that tent, asleep and well fed and in a proper bed, was probably evidence of her side of this "arrangement."

She takes a deep breath. "Basically, it's like this. That little carving ... I didn't realize it was an egg when he gave it to me. I genuinely thought it was just a carving. Anyways, it turns out the last king—King Aleshir's father—had stolen that egg from a tribe, far away and a long time ago. But for the better part of a year now, King Aleshir has been negotiating with the King of Ascelin, who is seeking land lost in some war, I think, in exchange for some trade arrangements. The egg was part of the deal.

"The prince didn't know any of that when he gave it to me, of course. After he'd given it to me, his father was meant to hand it over to King Tari of Ascelin. Because it disappeared so late in the peace, King Tari is taking personal insult." She takes a deep breath. "The king and the prince both thought it a myth that the egg was a dragon egg. Actually, they still think that. But they want it back to hand over to King Tari before he invades, like he invaded what was Seralin and is still trying for with Dagnon."

I nod, though my stomach drops to my feet. Squid's complicated enough without being at the center of some international royal intrigue, much as it explains the King's Guard being in Valenta and the glimpse of the gray-clothed Royal Army, not to mention the encampment of soldiers I'd stolen Liv back from. I swallow at the thought of the Ascelese torturers. Could they be working for King Tari? Gods. And what are all these royals going to make of the egg no longer being an egg? "He's threatening invasion?"

Liv's mouth goes tight. "He is. He calls himself Emperor. He's also said some wild things, really, like how he's going to order his troops to rape and then murder every person in their path, burn everything down, and salt the earth. He's threatening not to stop until the king and the prince themselves are dead. And that will only be after their families die. Painfully. In front of them." Her tone is pragmatic, but her distaste is obvious in her expression.

"Oh, gods, Liv..." I fix her with a startled gaze I'm not even faking. "I had no idea." And what the fuck am I going to do about this now? My gut roils. Up until now, the dragon had been an irritation, really, but now... I've always avoided personal guard work for aristocrats for this reason—I don't want to get tangled up in this kind of politics. Always seemed like a risky proposition, being expendable around diplomatic intrigue.

She raises a shoulder. "Nor did I, really. And it was only when that little thing appeared that I realized the egg must've hatched."

"So he wasn't trying to kill you back in Valenta?"

She laughs self-deprecatingly and spreads her hands. "It would seem not. I'm sorry, Des. I sincerely thought they were after me." I nod slowly, taking all of this in. "So?" She smiles at me winningly. "You've got my side of the story. Now it's time for yours. How ... how on earth did you wind up with a dragon following you around and doing your bidding?"

I don't even need to look to know Squid is betraying wild indignation. I cough to try to keep her attention away from it while I say, *Shush! Settle! She doesn't need to know you can understand us, you know!* It acquiesces grumpily, and I rub my face before meeting her eyes. I wonder how far to trust her. The prince's men wear gray, not green. I could almost swear it.

"It's a strange thing. I found it outside of Valenta, with the egg broken in two around it. It was in a pile of luggage that looked like it'd been abandoned after a fight. It's been growing a lot. Used to be easier to hide. But I just thought it was pretty."

Squid sends another wave of muted indignation, but I keep my gaze on Liv. I need to know if she understands anything about the blood bonding. Not that I understand it, but if she knows about it, she should ask something about whose blood birthed the dragon now. Liv's brows rise a little. "That'd be a surprise." Her smile gets affectionate. "Except I know you have a nose for trouble." Hmm. Not conclusive. She could be assuming one of the mercenaries hatched it.

I raise one brow, smiling in return, and pitch my voice low. "You are the best example of that, Liv."

She smiles broader at the half compliment, then seems to rouse herself. "Anyway. Do you see why we need to give the dragon to the prince now?" she says. "I mean, Ascelin is about to go to war with us over this weird little thing."

I nod slowly, tossing up the options. *Calindrina*, the dragon hisses in my mind. *I told you. I have to get to Calindrina.* "Let's sleep on it," I say softly. "I need to work out how we'd do that without them deciding to kill us all, especially if he thinks you've run off with me from that camp. And I don't even know why it's a dragon and not an egg anymore. They're not likely to be happy about that." The truth is I need to work out the risks of trusting Liv's story, but my head is like wool.

She shrugs. "I figure the dragon is even better, right? Really? Anyway..." She shakes her head, those satiny curls bouncing around her face. "You're right. We probably do need sleep before we come up with a plan." She smiles faintly. "I'm sorry about the bed thing, though."

I give her a tight smile. "It's alright. It was really for *your* comfort. Sharing a bed with an ex isn't ideal. But Twisty doesn't know anything about you, so..."

She smiles. "I figured. I can take the floor, though."

I laugh very softly and heave myself to standing. "It's alright. So long as you swear to keep your filthy, lady-lovin' hands to yourself." I wag a finger at her. It's hard to play this bit.

She quirks an eyebrow, grins, then replies, "So long as you swear the same, young lady."

I stick out a hand. "Deal?"

"Deal." She grins.

We shake, and it's almost just friendly. Or it would be but for the frisson that spirals from her touch. The dragon chortles in my head. "Anyway," I say brightly, taking my hand back and stepping for the door, "where *is* that boy? I need food!"

A few hours later, I float naked in warm water, my belly full almost to bursting, my head fuzzy with beer, and my skin alive, having been vigorously rubbed with oil and then scraped clean. This is practically heaven. I shake my head from side to side in the water, feeling the threads of my hair tug in different directions and imagining my head as a dandelion. Squid is atop my piled-up towel on the edge of the pool, having promised to stay out of sight, but it gleams in the steam, and the warmth seems to make its thoughts slower and more content. Like mine.

No, silly, that's you, it says, prying in on what would once have been private thoughts. *The way you feel; it's part of me. Just like the way I feel is part of you.*

I stare at the tiled ceiling. A fresco of a young god riding a goat. I wonder if the god is really small or the goat really large. Then I turn back to the quandary the dragon poses. *It's part of me? How?*

The little animal curls a glimmering claw against the towel. *I need to get to Calindrina,* it says, a little sadly.

I frown at the ceiling. *I know, Squid. But how are we part of each other?*

I ... I think it is to do with the blood we share now. Melancholy steals over me, and I glance over at it again.

Is that you? I ask. *Are you feeling sad?* The response isn't really a reply, just a sense of affirmation. I examine the ceiling some more. *So you think it's about the blood bonding, but you're not sure.*

I'm not sure, the dragon agrees, as if this is a monstrous concession.

I frown a little, then turn over and half wade, half swim to the edge where the little animal sits. I hesitantly reach out a damp finger and smooth across its little head. The sapphire eyes blink at me. *It's going to be alright,* I think, as gently as

I can manage. It nudges against my finger again, like a cat. *I don't expect you to know everything.*

It is astonishingly beautiful, this little thing, I realize, with the space to breathe and think. Scaled, like a snake rather than like a fish, with each scale blue and pearlescent. Almost like a long lizard with large folded wings, grown to the length of a small cat but far more slender. Its wings are batlike but cast in variegated blue scales. They sheen from the indigo of the sky after dusk at the line of each delicate bone, through the vivid depth of the sea and into a bright summer-blue sky. I catch the tiny claw at the end of the wing and stretch it out. I get a sense of shyness from the little dragon. I dip a fingertip in water, then let the droplet fall. It turns into a ball of quicksilver against the outstretched wing, like rain on nasturtium leaves. "Beautiful," I say aloud.

The dragon preens a little, darting its little head back and forth to demonstrate the sinuousness of its long, narrow neck. I smile down at it. *I'm sorry we haven't had a chance to get to know each other,* I say. *It's been a bit of a stressful time. I'm not always so ... grumpy.*

The dragon rears up on its back legs, spanning its wings—in grave breach of my strict rules about staying hidden—and slides its head along my jawline. *I know you're doing what you can,* it says, *and I know that you'll protect me.* Its thoughts are clear, but there's an underlying anxiety. It doesn't entirely trust me, and honestly, I don't blame it. But the thought is generous.

Liv's proposal that we hand over the dragon to the prince echoes in my head, but so does her claim that the green-clothed soldiers were the prince's men. I frown a little, staring at the dragon's broad wings. Even if I did want to make a deal, I'm not sure Liv would be the best middleman. I can't trust her, still.

I swallow. Would the prince even believe the carving was in fact an egg? That Squid had hatched from it? And if the disappearance of the egg had this self-declared emperor threatening invasion, what would happen if our dear sovereigns decided to keep Squid? Even the thought makes me uncomfortable, like I've a stone in my boot. I can't really countenance the thought of giving it away, despite knowing it's the most practical choice.

I am very pretty, the dragon puts in.

I grin and flick water at it. The little animal ducks and darts, and when I toss water at it again, it hisses out a little jet of flame, and the drops pop and evaporate in the air. I scoop my hands together and throw a handful of water. It ducks, but too slow, and in a second, it's saturated. It looks—and feels—startled at this, but as I laugh, it throws itself forward into the water, clearly expecting to be able to swim as I do.

But it can't.

It hits the water like a blue stone, sinking swiftly to the bottom. Panic jets through my body like fire, and for a second, I can't move. Sound deafens me, and my nose clogs with pungent smells. Naked bodies move around and through mine. Fear threads my veins.

But that panic is not entirely mine, and I scold myself. The layers of time haven't injured me yet. I shove the fear back, inhale hard, then duck down underwater, reaching down for my feet. Claws like pins dig into my arms as I lift the tiny thing back up out of the water and deposit it on my towel. "Breathe," I say as it chokes up water. It gives one final almighty splutter, water and fire flying out of its mouth. I back up quickly, and it settles down, sides heaving. *Don't scare me like that!*

Sorry, it says, shamefaced. *It looked easy.*

It tries to shake off the excess water but can't. I smile gently, patting it down with the towel and leaving it covered. *It's alright. I just hope no one saw us. Stay wrapped up for now, yeah? Clearly, dragons are not made for swimming. Good to know. See? Who needs Calindrina?* I only realize when I see the blood on the towel that I'm bleeding from both arms.

I'm sorry, it says again, horrified. *I didn't mean to.*

I know, I send back, patting down my new wounds with the towel. I wince as the loose threads catch on the cuts. Such guilt emanates from the dragon that I take pity on it. *So long as you've kept those claws nice and clean.* The sight of it examining its claws for cleanliness makes me laugh.

"My gods." Liv stands above me on the edge of the pool, shiny with massage oil. Her gleaming breasts are so perfect I nearly sigh aloud, despite, well, everything. Her nipples are pert, and for a split second, I'm back to where I was six years ago, jealousy like acid in my gut. What *has* that masseur been up to? "What the hell happened to your arms?"

I force down everything I'm feeling. Everything. "A misunderstanding," I say with a smile. I'm angling for friendly but without the promise of sex. I think. "How was the massage?"

"Oh, perfect," she replies, stretching up onto tiptoes, her arms above her head. It draws every line of her curves taut, her waist tight, and the arc of the line to her hips sweet and intoxicating all at once. "He wouldn't strigil me down, though."

I'm not entirely surprised. There's something impossibly seductive about her pale skin glowing with oil in the yellow lamplight. It's against the bathhouse rules, but I suspect that was far from a priority, with her before him. "Well, we need to get going soon," I say. "I was about to get out."

"No, wait!" she cries, running to where the stairs lead into the pool. "Wait for me!" She throws herself into the water.

I shove down at whatever this show is producing in me, refusing even to acknowledge it. "All pruney." I hold up my hands as proof. "Sorry. And there are these wounds I should probably look to."

"You're no fun," she says. The look she sends me is part pout, part smolder, and all trademark Liv, designed to rouse me against my best of intentions.

It makes my quim ache, but I grin at her. "Sorry, dollface. Time for bed for all of us, I think. Rinse yourself off and we'll get back to the tav."

She pouts once more, and I worry I'm pushing too hard, but she splashes happily while I catch up a second and less bloody towel from the hooks on the walls and dry myself down. I focus hard, trying not to see when she walks out of the water. I know the water will be forming droplets against her oily skin.

A movement catches my eye, and I see a young man behind a curtain. Probably her masseur, and this was probably the fruition of his plan. He's watching avidly, and she pretends not to notice. I look away, drying between every toe. *To avoid foot rot,* I explain to myself and the dragon, bent to my task. And then I feel one fingertip drop onto my head at the base of my skull.

It's a long, long line she traces slowly, over my shoulder and down my spine. She pauses at the crease of my buttocks, and it's barely enough of a break in the spell for me to yank myself together. "I'll wait outside," I manage to tell her, only just keeping my eyes on her face before turning to duck through the curtain, the towel-wrapped dragon in my arms. I run into the masseur, shove past him, yank my clothes on, and am out into the cool evening of the street. It's only then I feel like I can catch my breath.

When we return to the tav, clean and sweet-smelling, Twisty is already asleep in the single bed. I stare down at him for a moment, wondering what the fuck I'm going to do. Then I busy myself with packing, slowly.

Liv slides between the covers of the bed for two, wearing only her shirt. Somehow, I know this, despite not letting myself look, let alone think about it. *Her.* "Good night, Des," Liv murmurs. "Plenty of space over here."

I stand, tugging free a rope I've brought upstairs for this purpose. "Sorry, Liv, but can't have you running off on us in the middle of the night."

She doesn't answer, lashes shading her eyes as I tie the rope around her hands and to the bedhead, trying to ignore every memory it triggers. My breath comes short as I tie off her wrists. As I finish, those green eyes flash up at me, and I'm abruptly conscious of how warm I am. My nipples are sensitive, and I grasp after the lingering pain in my arms to try to break free. Her voice is low. Intimate. "I'm sorry things have been so complicated. But it really is nice to see you again. I worried that I'd driven you away forever."

I swallow and rake through my mind but can come up with nothing to say that isn't entirely unwise in the context. My iron will is the only thing keeping my eyes from drifting from her face down her body, and it's rusting fast. "It's good to see you too, Liv. Now, I'm exhausted. Sleep well, alright?"

Awkwardly, I slip between the covers, curling away from her and taking up as little space on the bed as possible. The more distance between us the better. I snug Squid close under the covers with me, its long blue neck snaking up to tuck under my chin.

And then, a little desperately, my mind occupies itself with arguing about whether I'd been sincere or playing when I told her it was good to see her again, so I don't contemplate the satin of her skin so close to mine, or the warmth of her breath, the soft curve of her lips... I squeeze my eyes shut, curse my own weakness, the desire heavy in my chest, and give up any chance of falling asleep that night.

CHAPTER THIRTEEN

A knock at the door wakes me in befuddlement. It's dark as dark, and I scowl, rolling over and clutching the blanket to me. "What is that?" Liv murmurs sleepily.

I open my eyes. "I'll get it," I groan, heaving myself to standing, and Squid clambers up my back to settle on my shoulder. I yank my trousers to my waist and grab a jerkin to cover the dragon, then open the door. Outside stands the young girl who'd taken care of the horses the previous day, a lantern clutched in her hand. "Yes?" I must be frowning, because she's speechless. I try to clear my expression. "Can I help you? Is something wrong?"

"Someone from the baths... They're downstairs... They say you forgot something..."

I squint at her again. "Forgot something?"

"Will you come?" She gestures down the hall with the lantern.

I scrub a hand through my hair, Squid shifting its head against my collarbone, and shrug. Following her downstairs and across the empty barroom in the dim light, my mind slowly comes back on deck. The front door of the tavern stands open, and a man is silhouetted against the very beginning of dawn. Great. I'll probably just get back to sleep and then have to wake up again, at this rate.

The girl gestures with the lantern. "Here she is."

"We forgot something?" I ask him, frowning. "We barely..." He mutely holds out a hair clip. Silver and twining. Liv's. I reach out a hand for it, blinking a little in confusion. "Thanks," I say, and then meet his eyes, the frown still lingering. "Why...?"

Fuck.

The realization is like a slap. I can see it in his eyes. Fucking Liv. I swear aloud, making them both recoil, and then throw myself back inside, bound up the dark stairs, and burst back into the room. Squid's talons dig into my shoulder as I slam to a stop.

The bed we shared is empty, the rope hanging from the bedhead.

She's gone, Squid says unnecessarily.

"Fuck!" I announce to the room at large. Twisty jerks awake as I throw open the window shutter. Skittering down the roof, I catch hold only at the last moment. My arms wrench, but I hit the ground gently enough and almost fall over my own feet before racing for the horses.

The doors to the stables are wide open. Liza is in her stall, eyeing me like the idiot I am, and the silver is beside her. But Liza has no saddle balanced over her stall door, and there's no other horse in the stable. She's gone.

I throw back my head to stare at the sky. "Fucking Liv. Fucking what the fuck."

Twisty appears behind me a moment later. "Des?"

"She's gone," I reply. "Gone and taken my saddle. I *liked* that saddle." Yet another loss to chalk up to Liv's presence in my life. Will they ever end?

I would not have made that error, Squid says.

I'm glad I was with it enough to take you with me. That bloody masseur. I've no doubt she'd have taken you, elsewise.

Twisty looks uncertain, and he swallows hard before saying, "So ... you're angry because she took your saddle?"

I close my eyes, taking a deep breath. "No, lad." I sag with the sense of failure. "I'm angry because..."

Fuck.

She knows. She knows about the dragon. She knows the egg is gone. She knows exactly where to guide the prince, or whoever it really was she was getting cozy with in that camp.

Fuck.

We stampede back upstairs to throw together the few things in my room we need to take with us. She knows far too much now. I'm furious with myself. I play her; she plays me.

"Fucking Liv," I swear as I shove clothing into blankets. I'd hoped to have time to buy new clothes today, to replace those lost—burned, probably—at the soldiers' camp. But now the priority has to be getting out of town. I have no doubt about Liv's intentions. The only thing I can try to make sure she *doesn't* know at this point is where we are. By running. I need enough space to work out what I'm going to do with the dragon, and we can't stay right where she promised the prince he'd find us.

"I'm sorry," Twisty says, guilt weighing his tone. "I fell asleep. I should've been the one sharing her bed. Then I would've known."

I pause for a moment, buckle the bag closed, and look at his dejected face. "Oh, lad." I tousle his hair. "It's so very far from your fault. I tied her hands, but apparently not well enough." I imagine her untying the knots with her teeth while I slept, as I had that first night with her. "And you're not the first and won't be the last that girl has slipped out on."

He nods without saying anything, clearly not buying my explanation that he's not to blame. I give him a weary smile. "See if you can get us some supplies from the kitchen, would you?" I say. "Show your sweet face and they won't be able to deny you anything." I smile and toss him a coin. "Well, your sweet face and the coin..."

He nods, grins, and heads downstairs ahead of me.

I bridle Liza and the silver that Liv left behind. Twisty reappears, cloth wrapped around food in hand, and I slip it inside the makeshift bag made of the blanket. Squid positions itself over the sword on my back, gripping tight to the leather straps.

I help the lad up onto the silver horse and then swear again as I clamber onto Liza's back. She's unimpressed with the lack of saddle too, but we know each other well enough. "Hold tight with your knees," I tell the lad. "Really tight. You'll fall a long way if you don't."

The bush here is easy riding, a broad path worn between the trees and little scrub between the eucalypts. We munch bread and cheese and a pork pie each, still in the saddle. The silver jerks in fear when a brown snake coils across our path, but Liza barely rears to stomp against it, breaking it in two. She's the best.

I guide us off the trail at midmorning, pausing to brush away the telltale signs of our horses' passage, and then continue between the trees until I find a stream. I refill the wineskin stolen from the soldiers' camp yesterday, and we walk in the shallows a while, erasing our scent. I've been chased before. I don't like it. I like it even less with so little food, drink, and bare necessities, like a saddle, but at least I'd got a bath and sleep before all this.

I sigh and shake my head. "Twist, I'm sorry. I thought it was safer to take you with me, back in Valenta, but everything just..."

He glances sideways at me, and I notice, amused, that his seat is becoming more relaxed. His poor thighs are probably aching, though he's got youth on his side. "You're protecting me," he says pragmatically. "I know that. I miss my friends, sure, and I don't quite know what's going on or why we're being chased or why you're chasing down that player ... or why she ran off, but..."

I meet his eyes, and my grin grows until I'm almost laughing. "Lad, come now. You're smart, and you're extraordinarily loyal, but really! Surely you've felt like you should be getting more answers? I mean, why would you even stick with us? Maybe you should've run off into that town we were in last night. Leave us, take my coin and disappear."

Now that I bother to think of it, it would've been safer for him if I'd told him to do precisely that. The guilt stings, but I'm also weary from feeling bad for other people. The echo of the guilt over the last kid is starting to remind me why I tend to travel alone. Well, at least since I put my sword away. Liza whickers as if to remind me that even alone has never been quite alone.

He blushes and smiles awkwardly. "Well, yes, but..." He gestures. "You wear a dragon on your back. It's like a story, like one of those hero stories..."

I glance sideways at him, trying not to smile. "Oh, Twist. This isn't a hero story, I can promise you that. Would a hero have let Liv escape? She played me! Twice! I'm not a hero, lad, and this seems to me very unlikely to come out anywhere near as well as one of your stories."

He stares straight ahead, his spine stiff. I've insulted him. I can't quite bring myself to be sorry about that, especially if it helps him recognize the reality. Eventually, he manages to say between stiff lips, "You saved me back in Valenta. You could have run. I'm not an idiot. Most would have. Even my friends—my brothers—even they ran."

I can't help the affection in my glance. "Well, I couldn't have let you die for me, but that doesn't make me a hero. That makes me selfish." He looks at me, finally, brows raised in query. "It would've broken me, that guilt," I tell him. "I've learned enough in my life to know that keeping my skin can't be the only priority."

He doesn't reply, only keeps his focus on the path through the trees. Then he seems to reach a decision. He shrugs, turns to me, grins, and says, "See? That's exactly why I'm staying." I can think of nothing to say to that, so I make myself smile in return, and we fall into companionable silence.

Magpies caroling in the trees in the distance are the only break in the quiet until Liza snorts at the sound of an animal in the undergrowth—a wombat, to judge from how noisy it is. It's almost pleasant, or would be, except for the pursuit that's likely behind us. Then Twist says, "But I wouldn't mind knowing a bit more."

I turn toward him and bite a lip. "It's not simple, lad, and it's risky. If you know more—"

"I'd never betray you! Not to them, not to anyone!" he says indignantly.

I raise a hand. "Peace, boyo! I'm not suggesting you would, but knowledge can be a dangerous thing."

He rolls his eyes. "I'm not some green boy, some innocent in from the country"—even his tone demonstrates how far from that he is—"so don't insult me. I've been part of the Rogue all my life. Secrets are what I've lived." He pauses. "You know, you don't know very much about me. My mother... She died when I was four. I didn't know why when it happened. My da was always away, and he'd told me he was a thief, but my mother didn't know."

He narrows his eyes. "My da double-crossed the wrong man, I guess? He came to my house an' cut my mother down in the kitchen while she was stirring the soup." There's pain vivid in the tension in his body, but you can't hear it in his voice. It makes my skin crawl. "I was there. When I heard the door crash open, I knew what had happened. I hid in a cupboard. I saw her die. She bled out, but it was slow. He searched for me, but he didn't find me. I didn't cry." He takes a breath. "My mother died because my da kept from her what could happen, so she was unprotected."

He stares at his hands on the reins. "I was furious with him when he came home and found her. He was sad, weeping, bent over her, and I beat him all over his back." His body betrays fury now, and the evenness of his tone becomes creepier by the second. "He said he wanted to protect her, but I knew the truth. He wanted to protect himself from her knowing he wasn't a good man. Knowing he was a thief."

My heart aches. The grief is familiar—I've lost several families, really—but watching your mother die because of your father... I nod slowly, and we keep on. Eventually, he continues. "So, I don't think not knowing things... Well, I don't see how it lets anyone be safe."

I nod again. "Very well. I'm deeply sorry about your mother, Twist. And I'll answer whatever questions you have."

It's a long conversation, and weirdly, I'm grateful for having someone I can share it all with without having to be careful about what threads I'm letting go of, as I was with Liv. He's bright, this lad, and he frowns as I add the little bits of information, especially the new but deeply questionable details Liv shared before she hoofed off into the sunrise. Eventually, I run out of anything more to add to the tale.

"So you have no idea why they all—the king, the prince, this emperor-king of Ascelin—why they all want the dragon?"

Squid's head rears back up off my shoulder as if in indignation. "Settle the ego, dragon." I smile. "I don't know, and it doesn't either, apparently."

Twisty nods his blond head slowly. "It's so weird that you can talk to it," he comments. "But... Well, is there any other magic it can do? Maybe that's why they want it?"

I think of the dizzying and nauseating experience of feeling every moment in time at once, and I shrug. "Well, the time thing is strange. Maybe it's connected to some kind of ability? Magic?" I can feel Squid listening closely and put up a fingertip to rub against its little head.

"Seeing every moment in time all at once doesn't seem that useful, though?" Twisty sounds dubious. "I mean, all I remember from the stories is the fire-breathing and flying. Maybe that's enough for kings to want them? Though," he glances at Squid, "I did heard they all went insane, and that's why they had to be killed off."

I nod. "Yes, but maybe there's something I don't know how to do yet. Maybe if Squid and I knew more, we'd be able to do things together?"

I need to get to Calindrina. Then I will know. Squid sounds almost ashamed, as if not knowing were against its nature.

"It's alright, Squid," I say, glancing at my shoulder and those sapphire-bright eyes. "We'll sort it out. We're just trying to work out what we know. Why you might be such a hot commodity for ... well, for all those following us."

Twisty's eyes narrow. "Didn't you say Squid gave you blood, and that's how you wound up connected?"

I nod, glancing sideways at him. "You think maybe that connection is what they wanted?" Squid tilts its head inquisitively. "You think it might work for anyone if Squid gives them its blood?" Twisty raises a shoulder. "Squid?"

I could...

Squid's talons tighten on my shoulder, and I cry out in pain. Wings flap desperately against my face, and I duck down. The tiny dragon maneuvers itself through the air, startling Twisty's mount, who throws her head back, trying to catch a glimpse of the flying terror. Twisty soothes her with a gentle pat, and Squid lands awkwardly on Twist's thigh. He winces as the talons grab tight, but he doesn't pull away.

Squid rears back on its hind legs and simply stares at the boy. Twisty stares back, going a little cross-eyed from the proximity, and then Squid inserts a talon between scales in its little claw and reaches it out toward Twisty's lips. Twisty almost recoils, but a moment later, he opens his mouth. A drop of Squid's pearlescent silver blood drips down a talon and onto Twisty's tongue.

We both tense, and I stupidly think we really should have thought about not doing this on horseback. I guide Liza closer, though she's unhappy about the proximity to the edgy silver horse, and watch Twisty closely.

His eyes are closed for a long moment, then he opens one, then the other, and grins at us both. "Nothing." Squid sags a little, and Twisty reaches out a tentative finger to stroke its head. "Not your fault, dragon," he says, smiling. "Probably just me. Not made for magic."

Squid raises its head and gazes for a long moment into Twisty's eyes. *I like this one,* it finally declares, then, with a swooshy movement, takes off to land awkwardly on my back again. Twisty winces and rubs his thigh where Squid's claws punctured his trousers. I send him a sympathetic grin.

"That probably means…" Twisty turns to look at me. "That probably doesn't mean good things for you, if you're the only one who Squid's blood works on."

He's right. If only one person can be affected by Squid's blood, then getting a dragon in place of an egg is probably going to be a problem. I gulp and shake my head. "Probably nothing." We both know I'm lying. "Besides, what can I do now?"

Twisty shrugs and smiles, but I can tell he's forcing it. "I wonder how we find out more about dragons. I mean, maybe if we knew more, we'd understand what the emperor wants with Squid. And maybe… Well, if we knew more, maybe we'd know how to keep you safe." His gaze slips sideways to the dragon's.

He means you might work out how to break the blood bond.

I know what he means, dragon. I frown a little. Why did the thought of that sting?

"A long time ago—back when I was leaving Picton's players' troupe—they were headed to some place just off the coast, I think. It was meant to be the best collection of old books from the time of the Era of Storms, at least outside of Pastira." I realize the scribe who'd transcribed every word of *The Slayer of Pastira* had probably come from this same archive. I strain after a name.

"Where was it?"

"I can't quite remember the name of the place ... but maybe if I saw a map?"

We need to get to Calindrina. The dragon sounds sad, almost like it doesn't want to say the words but feels like it has to.

Well, a map would help with that too, I say, somehow a little sad myself. Isn't breaking this bond what I'd wanted this whole time?

"We need food, anyway."

"And saddles," I say briskly. "Alright. We need to find a reasonable-sized town, without being seen by whoever Liv has run off to this time. Then we can make a plan."

CHAPTER FOURTEEN

O n the road a little later, I find a promise of a creek amongst the grass trees and ghost gums. We follow it until it joins a river, wade for long enough to conceal our scent and tracks, then ride along the banks for most of the morning. Blooming spots of wildflower are vivid amongst the leaf litter, and the breeze carries the heady scent of rain falling on hot earth. It's peaceful.

Until a sudden movement to our right breaks the false sense of security. I turn, and Liza responds to my tension, leaping away as I yell "Stay here!" to Twisty.

The scout—for that's what he is, I'm sure of it—rides hard, knowing no doubt how close his own men are. I yank a dagger from my waist, and then, crouching low over Liza's surging neck, I line up, grit teeth, and hurl it.

The shot isn't deadly, but it must hurt, lodged in his side like that, and it disturbs his steed so it swerves with a shrill whinny. Liza pushes harder. I weigh another dagger in my hand, shoving away the thought of another blade thrown, the guilt resonating like a plucked string.

He's a risk. Stopping him is the only way to ensure we have enough time to get to safety. I grab the tip of the weapon and throw. It strikes high, in the muscle between shoulder and neck. He bellows in pain this time, losing hold of the reins.

A second later, Squid, who I hadn't even noticed riding high on my shoulder, launches itself forward, a blue rocket speeding with wrapped wings toward the man. I catch a breath into lungs ill prepared, frightened for it, then yell, "Squid!"

The dragon's presence is too much. The horse dumps the man to the ground, and Squid is on him in a second, coughing out little jets of flame to keep him there until I slide off Liza beside the two of them. "Up," I say sternly to the blue dragon. With pride in every line of its body, Squid clambers up my shoulder and onto my back. I have my sword in hand already.

He's still wide-eyed, glancing between my face and the myth glaring at him from my shoulder. Whatever news this man's crew might have had about me, it's not the information Liv had to share—he wasn't expecting the dragon. If he doesn't know, that means there's likely at least two groups after me. I'd hoped it was just the prince using every tool at his disposal, with soldiers and torturers, but no.

Or perhaps I'm such a wonder he can't catch his breath, Squid responds, half snark and half serious, its little reptilian head beside my ear.

"Who is after us?" I ask, blade pointedly against his throat. "Who?"

"Not telling you nothing, bitch!" he declares.

I put on the toff voice Picton liked to use when correcting us, both in performance and outside it. "Not telling you anything, *ma'am*." I narrow my eyes, let my sword hand get lazy, and then run the tip through the gap in armor at his neck, dragging down to cut deep into his chest. I wince inside, but I need him to know I'm serious. He groans reluctantly. "I could kill you now. Figure it doesn't matter who you're working for if they don't know to come after me."

The man's eyes bulge as he tries to follow this line of thought through the pain across his chest. "Don't kill me," he manages to spit out. "I've got a little son and a wife at home."

"Then why aren't you there, hmm?" I ask, glaring down into his eyes.

He hesitates. "Because I work for the Rogue in Cylina." He makes the Rogues' sign. I ignore it.

"Are you doing the prince's bidding?"

"Prince? The Rogue of Cylina would never work for the prince," he says, but his eyes skitter sideways. He's lying. He may not be in the prince's gray, but he's no less the prince's man for that. Except that he's startled to see the dragon.

I frown, recalling a puzzle I hadn't solved yet. Liv's kidnappers hadn't been in gray. Could they have been the Rogue's men? In his trust? The prince had visited Armand in Valenta, but that green had been a uniform. Formal. Or are they the other players in this mess?

I force myself back to the task at hand. He needs to be dead. He needed to be dead as soon as he saw us.

"I'm sorry," I say softly, and his eyes grow even wider as I draw a straight line across his throat. I dodge the ooze of his blood, rising to my feet and wiping the blade clean on a nearby tree. I sigh, trying not to think about it. "Life, could you not be simple?" I ask the treetops.

Before I head back to Twisty, I ransack the mercenary's pockets to a pleasing jingle of coin. His horse has calmed a little, though her eyes roll as I approach. I put out a soothing hand and settle her further, then unsaddle her. It'll do for Twisty and help him keep his seat. Several saddlebags are attached, so I take those too. Then I give her a sharp spank to the backside, and she whinnies and takes off without a second glance.

I balance the saddle on Liza's back and lead her back to where I'd left Twisty. The lad leaps out from behind a tree at me, pulling out of the lunge in time for the blade in his hand to clear my shoulder, and the dragon on my sword hilt jutting over it. His chest is heaving, poor thing. Terrified. "Success!" I pretend not to notice and play at glee. "Found you a saddle!"

We riffle through the saddlebags and find dry bread, some dried meat, three apples, and a bit of cheese. Just a scout's daily rations, but it'll get us to the next town, I hope. I offer Squid a chunk carved from an apple, and it chews thoughtfully, then spits it out. *I don't need to eat, but it does taste interesting*, it offers.

He's not carrying any kind of map. I strain to recall the ragged scroll Petrus used to use to guide us around Rescalin. Useless. A map is a priority when we find that town.

A bare moment is all it takes to saddle the silver, and our pace improves immediately. Twisty even begins to hum softly as we wind our way along the riverbanks. The land is lush here, and the horses graze lightly when we're moving more slowly. The gurgle of the river is lulling, and I'm glad it's working for the boy. I'm still on edge. The mercenary's blood speckles the bottom of my trousers.

As I had figured would have to happen, a bridge appears in the distance. A road must run over that bridge, and that means a town, at least eventually. I sigh. It's midafternoon, the sun beginning to gold. We don't have long 'til evening, and I can't help but be worried that wherever we wind up, it'll be exactly where one of our pursuers will be. After all, everyone has to eat. My belly gurgles in agreement.

After a long moment standing still and silent below the bridge and straining my ears to listen for hoofbeats, I urge Liza up the steep incline and onto the road. "Twisty, I think you should stay here," I say finally, knowing the boy won't like it. "We're too recognizable together. You can stay here, safe and sound, and I'll bring back food, and blankets and clothes, and ... well, everything, really."

He's dubious. I take a moment to curse Liv's selfishness again and look at him seriously, before he can speak. "Listen. I need a lookout. I'll leave Squid with you. It understands you, and it can tell me if you need me or if anyone is coming after me. I don't want to get trapped in a town with mercenaries or soldiers. That sounds like a quick death. If you and Squid stay here, you'll be safe, and you can warn me if anyone passes over the bridge heading in the same direction."

Twisty watches me, and I can't work out whether he thinks I'm bullshitting so I can leave him behind or doing the hero thing. I wait. Finally, he says, "Alright. But if you're not here before dark, I'm coming after you."

I take a deep breath, hoping that's enough time, and nod. "Alright." I put a hand up for the dragon to clamber around. "Here."

It's quite a sight, this blue dragon, which is now approximately the length of my torso, curled around the full length of the blond boy's arm. Twisty looks a little anxious, but Squid sticks its nose out, against Twisty's, and makes the boy smile.

I nod. "Alright. Under the bridge so no one can see you. I'll see you in a few hours, with food."

I ride into town with an extra shirt wrapped around my head, concealing my hair and giving me something of the appearance of the Scondalese people from the south. Not a convincing disguise, but I figure we're far enough north that no one will be that familiar with the Scondalese, but far enough south that it won't be too remarkable. It's a delicate balance, and I can't be sure I'm right.

This is a smaller town than where we were last night, where Liv escaped. It'll do well for me; hopefully most of what I need will be limited to a few stalls in the marketplace and not scattered all over town. I ride into town, my neck feeling a little naked without a blue lizard decorating my sword hilt.

Few people pay me any heed, and I'm glad of it, trying to keep my eyes from darting to every potential threat. I pause at the first leatherworker's stall I see, clamber down, and tie Liza up outside. Inside, the smell of the tannery is terrible, but the products are good. I find a beautiful leather saddle that Liza will appreciate—she deserves something special after these past few days—and then add two large saddlebags and an ornate and complex belt to the mix.

The storekeep is happy to see the pile, and before long, we're haggling hard. I pretend to be about to leave, but in the end, we reach a cost that works for both of us, and he's happy enough that he helps me saddle Liza. She's weary, poor beastie, but pleased with her new accoutrements. The mason gets me for extra silver for quick work, but I'm willing enough to pay, even if it turns out to be a useless trinket in the end.

The next store has various clothes, and I purchase a range, swiftly and without much attention. Enough for Twisty and myself, and enough we can both dress as male or female, but with very little attention to anything as vain as fashion. Part of me is amused at how quickly I lose my vanity when under pressure. Then I turn to leave and pause, agape.

There, hanging against the rough wooden wall of the store, is a dress. Made of dark green velvet, it is cut deep in the neck and slinky fit to the hips, then flaring so it will drop straight to the floor. It's gorgeous, and my grubby mitts are stroking the fabric before I even think not to. Close up, silky embroidery traces patterns across the bodice and stretches in narrowing triangles down to the upper thighs. I sigh.

"Beautiful, is it not, ma'am?" the storekeep murmurs beside me. I can tell she's trying to work out whether I'd ever be able to afford such a thing. And that's enough. My pride is pricked.

"I'll take it," I say clearly, "but I'd like to wear it home, if I may."

Sometimes the best disguise for someone on the road is clothing that makes you look like you're not going further than the tavern on the corner. I slink out of the store, the image of myself in the mirror still hovering in my mind. I am not a natural beauty like Liv, but dress me right and I can steal a few breaths.

I smile and flirt my way into a few deals, at least, which makes the rest of my buying spree a little gentler on my purse than I'd been able to hope for. I'm still running low on coin by the time I finish, but the scout's savings have helped. And at least this way, I hope we'll have a bit more of a chance of staying ahead of whoever is chasing us. The swirl of the dress around my ankles as I walk is more reviving than I would have guessed.

Back by the leatherworker's store, I carefully pack everything into Liza's new packs and strap my sword across the back of the saddle so I don't have to wear it. Liza gives me a look intended to remind me of what happened last time I did that, but I shrug. My lovely green velvet disguise doesn't count for much if I'm obviously armed to the teeth. I'm not a fool, though, so the new belt I bought at the leatherworker's store settles easily about my hips without spoiling the line of the dress, with my longest dagger thrust through.

I run through the list in my head, making sure everything is crossed off. Bedrolls—two thereof—two extra blankets, clothes for Twisty, clothes for myself, a kit of crucial medicines and bandages, food enough for three days, some oats for the horses, that carving, and—the most important thing—the map. It tells me there's a road that runs parallel to the one I came in on, which seems like a safer bet for our departure given the earlier encounter with the scout.

Ready to leave, I settle my pretty dress about myself on Liza's back and ride back toward the road.

I don't get very far before I hear a ruckus by one of the tavs. I figure it's a mere bar fight, and I angle down a back alley to avoid getting caught up in it. But then someone—a manly someone—yells my name.

"Desta Mildue!"

My breath hitches.

CHAPTER FIFTEEN

I freeze for a long, long moment, the dark stretch of the alley before me. All I want is to ride Liza along it and find a way back out of town, but I think of Twisty and Squid, and suddenly, hiding under the bridge feels less safe than I'd hoped. I take a long, slow breath, reach behind me to loosen my sword from the blankets, and turn.

Men crowd around the entrance to a tavern, mostly on its veranda but also spilling out into the street. A number of them seem to be in the prince's gray, but they're interspersed with others. Rogues, perhaps, if the scout told true. They're all turned toward me now and are spreading to create flanks leading from me to a man silhouetted in the open double doors. The light behind him shadows his face, but he has a beard and is wearing a uniform.

And at his feet is Liv.

She's kneeling, his hand tangled in her hair. She is bruised, bloody, and broken. My gut lurches. Her white underdress, which is all she has on, is torn and dirty, and she sobs, not even looking at me.

My first thought is that no matter what happens, my pretty new dress will probably not make it to nightfall. My inner Petrus is impressed at how cold I am.

I turn Liza, straightening my back, but I don't pull out my sword. Not yet. If this can be resolved some other way, that's all to the better. There's a lot of men with blades between the man on the veranda and me.

I scan for possible exits and catch sight of them, then. They're well-hidden—tucked up on the roof in the shadow of the dormer window. Twisty, blond hair a little too bright for concealment, and, glinting in the low light beside him, Squid. Dread courses through me. I raise my head and school myself not to look at them, hoping that will be enough to keep any of this crowd of men from spotting them.

Don't move.

Squid's response isn't words, just a combination of indignation and determination. I resist the urge to gulp.

There's far too much riding on my brazen today, and I didn't even know it when I got up.

"I answer to that name," I announce, pitching my voice low, angling for authority.

"Your girl here has been telling us some mighty fine stories." The man holding Liv sneers. "Haven't you, Liv?"

Liv finally turns her face toward me, and I make out a split lip, a black eye, and a bruised cheek. It's hard not to react. "I'm sorry, Des," she cries, then falls back into silence.

Who is this man? Is he with the prince? Surely, Liv had just ridden back to that soldiers' camp I'd stolen her out of? They'd treated her well there. Surely, she'd told them about the dragon already being born and offered to lead them back to us. We weren't where she'd thought, but still. How could she have ended up so bloodied and beaten a bare handful of hours after she'd run?

"I'm not sure what you mean," I say, in a voice determined to be even. "What stories could a whore like that tell?" It's a deliberate play, but Liv flinches. My heart squeezes unexpectedly, even as her reaction lends credence to my attempt to reduce her value. If I have to pay to save her—and a decent part of me votes against this notion—it'll have to be less than I've got left in my pockets, which is almost nothing.

The man steps forward, and his face becomes clearer. He looks vaguely famil-iar, and my heart sinks as I realize where I recognize him from.

The back of a coin.

Fuck.

"She's been telling me tales of you carrying cargo you are far from fit to touch. Cargo that belongs to your betters."

The Crown Prince of Rescalin has addressed me by name, and he's beaten Liv in an attempt to find Squid. Or the egg, depending on what she gave up. I narrow my eyes. Liv's welcome seems to have run out. This could mean—well, it could mean almost anything. But it *could* mean she's not spilled every bit of her guts yet. She might have kept something back, to have earned such a beating. Or there's the other—potentially simpler—explanation: she's betrayed someone too high on the food chain this time...

"Cargo?" I spread my hands. "As you can see, good sir, I've no caravan in train. I'm not a trader." It's dicey, pretending not to know who he is, but most people will spill in anger what they won't share in calm.

It works. "I am your prince, you godless child of a whore"—he bites off every word—"and this playing at stupid does no one any favors."

I force my eyes into round astonishment and slip from Liza's back. She shuffles sideways, close enough still that I can grab my sword. I do love this horse. I settle my feet and spread my skirts, dropping into a curtsy and holding it like the best of his courtiers. My thighs ache after the bareback riding, but I've enough control to compensate. "Your Highness," I murmur softly. "Forgive me. I did not know you. How may your humble servant serve you?"

Liv's gaze on mine is appreciative of my art, and she's desperately trying to communicate something, but her gaze is less explicit than would be helpful. The prince's gloved hand draws back, and he hits her open-palmed across the cheek with enough force to throw her backward out of his grip, leaving strands of her hair in his other hand. Liv cowers against the floor, but I can see her playing it hard to keep out of his reach. I refuse to react.

Out of the corner of my eye, I see Squid easing down the rooftop toward the prince. *No. Stop.* That's all I can manage without it being evident on my face. My heart clutches. This feels like disaster about to land.

"I want my goods." The prince is blunt, his chin arrogant. "I want it now."

I don't know enough to know how to play it. If he wants the dragon, well, there's little I can do about that. But if—if, if—if Liv hasn't told him about the dragon, and he's still in search of the egg, well...

I let a shake enter my voice. "I ... Your Highness, I do not know that of which you speak. All the goods I have here ... well, most I have only just purchased. If I have purchased something you wanted, I'm sure I'd be more than happy to sell it to you." I pause, letting my voice trail off as I add, "Or I suppose I could make a gift of it..."

He stalks down the stairs, leaving Liv a sobbing wreck on the veranda. I keep my eyes on his so that, because he wants to dominate, he can't look away from me. It's small protection for the dragon, but it's all I have.

He stands over me, a head taller and using every inch. I drop my gaze as if overwhelmed, and he whispers, "I think you know what I'm seeking, wench. A singular item, round and stone and gray. Stolen from me by that whore back there. She says you did like and stole it from her."

I don't dare let show the flush of relief, and my eyes want desperately to dart back to Liv. He's after the egg. He thinks it's still whole. He doesn't know about the dragon. She didn't betray us, or, at any rate, she hasn't told him. That at least gives me space to play, and it might even let me save us all.

"Oh, you mean the carving?" I giggle a little. "I didn't steal it, Your Highness! I won it off her at cards. She *would* say I stole it, though. She hates to lose."

The prince's eyes are granite, and he doesn't respond. His jaw is tight with anger, and I don't dare to play it any further. Liv is messed up enough for the both of us. "Of course, you can have that, milord, if you want it! I'd not thought it to be so precious, nor that you were seeking it."

I'm babbling now as I approach Liza to make a show of searching through my packs, straining to keep his eyes on me. I am gladder than ever I'd thought to visit the stonemason this afternoon. There had been part of me lecturing it was a waste to bet on Liv not to betray me, but that part is silent now. "Let me see now, where did I put that little thing?" I can only hope I'm not overplaying that I believe the egg is worthless. My back prickles with the sense of the prince's hungry gaze on me. "Here it is!" I declare.

This is the moment.

I weigh the remade egg in my hand. It's cool.

I toss it to the prince before he can step closer. He glances at it resting solid in his hand, and my heart rises. His face is all relief—almost childlike.

Then it shifts.

Fuck.

I haul myself onto Liza's back, and she's moving before I press my heels to her.

Howls chorus as I ride directly for the tavern and men close in around us. Liza kicks out once before we hit the stairs, striking two soldiers and warning the rest to keep at bay, then she's up them. Liv is on her feet, and I grab her forearm, monkey-grip, our bodies still knowing the strength and balance needed for each other, and haul her up across the saddlebags.

"Go!" I yell, hoping to all the gods in heaven that Squid and Twisty are smart enough to be heading for the back to sneak out. *Do not let them see you!* Liv wriggles into place behind me as Liza leaps off the end of the veranda.

A harsh whistle sends us both hunkering down beside Liza's neck, dodging the arrow. There's another two, but both miss. Liza's at a gallop, careening down the wide town street despite her heavy load. I hear a low, puzzling roar, pitched like thunder, then sounds of astonishment and horror behind us. I risk turning to look.

Several men in the crowd around the tavern beat at flames running along their arms. Squid roars, a roar that sounds too low and fierce to come from so small an animal. It's in the air, darting back and forth across the tops of the crowd, bellowing flame.

Whoa.

The little being really *is* a dragon. I'm caught between astonishment and horror. There's no way the prince doesn't know now. Whatever Liv paid to keep back the truth is done. Not a bloody chance of getting out of town without being chased, and they know the exact shape of us all.

Squid looks like it's running low on fire. It swoops once more, only managing a cough of flame and a few sparks, then soars up into the night sky. Arrows follow, but thankfully, the prince bellows to his men to hold their fire, and after a moment, Squid can no longer be seen against the black.

Liza has slowed, feeling my distraction. I hear another galloping horse and urge her on, hunkering low.

A low whistle sounds, and Liv cries out in pain, her grip on me loosening. "Hold on!" I cry. "Liv! Just hold on!"

Her hands on my waist tighten, but she sways alarmingly, making both our seats uncertain. We ride hard, Liza straining, out the gate and down the road, into the forest. Soldiers will be behind us in next to no time. I swerve onto a smaller path, heading deeper in the bush. Whoever is behind me follows.

I risk a glance back, and relief fills me. It's Twisty, riding hard on the back of the silver. No sign of Squid, though.

At the thought, Squid says in my head, *I am unharmed. I'll find you once I've put these soldiers off.* I glance back again and notice lights behind us in the forest. *Not lights*, says Squid, a little smug. *And you can express the depths of your gratitude to me later.*

I grin. The dragon may be low on fire, but it has enough to set the bush ablaze.

When the river appears, I guide Liza down the bank, and we splash along its edges. It gets suddenly deeper, but it's never higher than Liza's belly, so at least she doesn't have to swim. I urge Twisty up alongside. "Thank all the gods you're alright," I tell him, annoyance clear in my tone. "What the hell were you thinking?"

"I was thinking you were taking an awful long time," he says, looking unimpressed, "and that it was stupid to stay under the bridge waiting for you when

I could help." His little jaw juts in the low light. "Besides, I told Squid to tell you."

I sigh and roll my eyes. "You two!" I shake my head. "Liv? How're we doing?"

"Apart from the arrow?" She manages the caustic words, but her tone is worn. "I think I could do with a rest."

I glance over my shoulder, where she's curled up against my back, unable to hold her own weight up. "Oh, Liv," I say, and I can't quite keep a hint of disappointed tenderness out of my voice. "What on earth...?"

She's sliding sideways, so I urge Liza out of the water and onto a bank in the dark. I can only hope we have enough of a head start—and enough dragon-lit fires—to keep our pursuers behind us. I slip awkwardly to the ground, Liv following a moment later, her limbs floppy, and I realize as I lay her down gently that she's passed out.

"Not good, Liv," I murmur, inspecting the arrow that has passed through her upper arm. Twisty slides to the ground from his silver.

Moving quickly to take advantage of her unconsciousness, I turn her onto her side, grab the arrow in two hands, and snap off the feathered end as close to her body as possible, doing my best to keep from worsening the wound. Rolling her back onto her front, I wrap the leather of my nearly-empty purse around my hand, then grab the narrow, bloody shaft between the arrowhead and flesh. I wince at the feel of the blood oozing through the white fabric of her underclothes and against my fingers. "We need gauze and bandages, lad," I say, forcing my voice to be even. "They're in the medic's pack, in the front left saddlebag on Liza."

Liza stays still while he roots around in the pack on her back. I take a deep, deep breath, then, knee pinning Liv's arm to the ground and the other hand pressing against her shoulder, I yank up as hard as I can. Liv bursts back into consciousness with a scream of pain, then falls back in a faint. "Sorry, love, so sorry," I murmur. Twisty hands me the pack, eyes wide. "She'll be alright, lad," I promise softly. "She just needs time and rest."

I press the gauze against the wound and begin wrapping the bandage around it. "But ... they're behind us, and ... well ... why did you save her?" he asks, finally, struggling to keep his anger in check. "Again? Didn't she ... she betrayed us!"

I slow, focus narrowing to the correct overlap of each new wrap of bandage as I consider his words. "Well ... it's a long story, lad. But she didn't betray us."

"Hell she didn't," he says. "She told the prince your *name*. How is that not a betrayal?"

I smile faintly and brush a tangled curl from Liv's face. My mind maintains a critical stance. I hope. "It's complicated. She told him less than she could have to save my life, and while she was trying to save her own. Look at her and tell me she wasn't tortured this day. She held out, and it cost her—almost cost her life. That has to count a little, lad." I shoot a glance, and his gaze is still disbelieving. I couldn't leave her there to be tortured and killed. Maybe it's what she's earned, but I couldn't.

I shrug. "Alright. Doesn't matter now. We have to ride on. Can you balance her if I strap her to the saddle, lad? Liza's done her dash for today, I think, carrying the two of us."

Twisty's mouth is tight. Liv is an affront to his sense of loyalty, and Liza's disgusted whicker expresses the same. But he nods.

Squid? I call. *We're heading on. Are you alright?* I figure the little dragon probably is since I've felt nothing but glee from it for a while now.

Yes, yes, yes, comes the reply. *I'll join you once I'm sure they're not following. This flying thing—like, proper flying, in the sky—is fun!*

I smile to myself, shifting Liv's dead weight in the saddle. The silver moves uneasily under her, but I soothe her with a gentle pat. "You're a lovely girl," I whisper to her as I strap Liv's legs to the saddle. "We should really name you."

Twisty, helping me tie Liv into place, says, "I already have. I think we should call her Quicksilver. She's a bit skittish, but she's nimble too."

I grin again and help him up into the saddle. "Apt," I say as he balances Liv. Her arms dangle down amongst Quicksilver's mane, and she'll wake to pain in her neck, but at least we'll be alive and away from those who want to kill us, I figure. "Thank you, lad. You're a better ally than I deserve."

He blushes instantly to bright red and grins. I smile back and pat him on the leg. "Alright. Let me know if she starts sliding, and we'll stop again. But I'd like to get a head start tonight, and the soldiers are like to wait until morning, relying on their numbers in the light."

He nods. "And we know where we're going now, right?"

I smile a reply. "Twisty, I made such good purchases today. We have a map, *and* you'll have new clothes. Once we can stop and light a lantern, we'll know where we are, where we're headed, and you'll be properly dressed. How's that sound for a deal?"

I sound more resolved than I feel. I've not much clue where we can flee to, now we've managed to stir the wasp nests of the Rogues *and* our sovereigns. All I can hope is if we can get sufficiently clear of the prince and the Rogue's men, the map will help me chart our next course.

Calindrina? Squid sounds far away.

Hopefully it's marked, I reply. I realize I'm no longer even contemplating handing the dragon over now. I can't tell if it's because the blood bond is feeling more fact and less imposition or because the nature of those looking for it has been made so clear, but I do wish we knew more about dragons. Then I might know how to play these odds, to find a way to keep us all alive.

Twist grins back at me, and I force a smile, my heart squeezing a little. It's hard, talking him out of his doubts about me and about Liv, and knowing all those doubts are not only justified but also probably the instincts that have kept him alive this long in the Rogue. They'd likely do me some good too. I step up into Liza's saddle and start into the dark of the trees, angling north and a little west. This will keep us amongst the trees, off the plains, and hopefully, at some point before dawn, we can find some shelter.

CHAPTER SIXTEEN

By some luck, we get a clear run away from the little town through the night. Twisty droops with weariness by the time we stop, midmorning, at an A-frame shepherd's hut under the trees on the edge of an open paddock. A snake, copper and lithe, slips silently into the grass as we dismount.

I hand Twist a little bag of cooked dumplings gone a bit dense, another of sticky rice wrapped in leaves, and a bread roll and some blue cheese to munch on while I settle Liv into my bedroll. She's sleeping now, rather than unconscious, and her eyes open briefly. She even manages a smile as I check her bandage. A little blood shows through, but it's dry, which hopefully means it's not bleeding anymore.

I roll out Twisty's bedroll beside her, and when he appears at the entrance of the little hut, I smile. "C'mon, lad, time for bed."

At the sight of the roll, he grins broader than I've yet seen and throws himself down on it with a kind of sleepy enthusiasm. "Ah!" he exclaims. "Better than a mattress!"

I laugh, tousle his hair, and stand up, leaning on my knees to aid my weary muscles.

Quicksilver and Liza, both tired, wander slowly out into the field to munch great mouthfuls of yellowing grass. Once they're both unsaddled, I search through the packs for the new currycomb and give them both a halfhearted brush. My arms are weak with fatigue and aching, but I figure a bit of a brush is better than none.

With their nosebags filled with oats, I settle myself on a well-placed stump, stripping a eucalyptus leaf while I try to keep watch. Twist's asleep, and all I have are my thoughts. What are we going to do now? I need somewhere to run to. A refuge. Somewhere to hide. A plan. Home's never been any good. Petrus would once have been the only thought I had to have, but not anymore, and everywhere else I can think of, I've been a faceless sellsword amongst a crowd. No one I can rely on to protect us. Loneliness has been a more constant friend than anyone, really.

Squid? I ask the ether. *Are you going to join us at some point?*

A long pause of silence makes me a little anxious, then glee starts to fill me. Faint to begin with, and, as a blue streak crosses the cloudy sky above, it's fierce. I can't help but smile, tired though I am, as Squid loops the loop in front of me and then barrel rolls through an earthward dive. *So I guess you're enjoying the flying,* I say.

You could say that, it replies, proper still, but the emotion that comes with it makes me grin again. *I shouldn't have ever ridden on your back.*

Take it easy, I caution far too late, as I realize the small dragon—well, small but swiftly growing dragon—has only really been in the world for about a week and has never properly flown until now. *Someone could see you. It's light now, and there's clouds above you.*

But I'm getting so good! The response comes with an upward streak and then a downward spiral, growing tighter and tighter as the ground grows closer.

You are, I acknowledge, admiring the flash of sun against those blue wings, even as my heart clutches. I try not to let my fear affect Squid's joy. *You look amazing.*

A moment of preening brings distraction and an almighty crash into a low-hanging branch, and the dragon tumbles, blue and sparkling, through the long yellowed grasses. I convulse with weary laughter, my head in my hands, and then peer up to see an almost shamefaced Squid making its way toward me. On foot, like an injured cat. *Well, you did,* I correct myself, grinning.

Mortal, replies Squid, an acknowledgment with an uncanny precision of tone, conveying both snark and a tinge of embarrassment.

No need to be embarrassed, dragon, I say. *I'm sure everyone crash-lands at some point when learning to fly.*

Squid's disapproval shows in every line of its body, for all the world like a cat who knows it is being laughed at. I giggle until I'm too tired to keep it up and then settle with my head in my hands, still sitting on the stump.

Maybe you should sleep, Squid observes. *You look exhausted.*

Maybe, I respond, *but someone needs to keep watch. If the soldiers come, we will have to run.* I sigh and rise to pull out the map to decide on something of a route for when we head off.

I can keep watch, the dragon says, caught between a prideful grump and uncertainty. *I'm not sleepy. And I can sleep on your back while we ride, when we leave?*

As tempting as it is to comment on how quickly it has given up the flying, I restrain myself. I stare at the map, trying to get my recalcitrant mind to work out where we are, where we should be, and how risky each of the paths out of here are. I put a fingertip against a town near a river. Cylina, where we must have been the evening prior. Fortunately, there are no direct roads between here and there. They all go directly north and then head east around the top of the forest to join up with the main road running north–south. The villages east are accessible by road only by going around the forest. That means moving a great squadron of soldiers is likely laborious and time-consuming if they try to beat their way through the bush.

I narrow my eyes, though, trying to think of where we should be going. *Calindrina,* the dragon reminds me, its tone gentler than it has been about this matter so far.

I know, dragon, I say, weary. *I'm just trying to find it.*

An apologetic feeling emanates from the dragon, who has clambered up a nearby tree and settled on a limb. I spend a long time scanning the map, but there's no Calindrina to be found. *Do you have any clue about where it is?* I finally ask Squid. *Is it east? South?*

I think north, maybe? Squid replies, but it's uncertain and unhappy about it.

I stare at the top of the map, and something strikes me. It's the same as every map—where the map ends, there's always a mark. And there, scrawled within a decorative depiction of—yes—a dragon, is the phrase, "Here be dragons." I stare at it for a long time. It's tradition, I'd always thought, but now I scowl. Perhaps the tradition started somewhere? I'm not the world's biggest fan of a wild goose chase, and the leap from a map-marking to a goose feels too easy.

I need to go to Calindrina, Squid repeats, almost miserably.

I know it, small one. I think you might be right with the thought it's north.

I gaze at the long, dark line of the Great North Road. Even the length of it makes me feel tired, and Calindrina might not even be there. Plus, it's a major thoroughfare, and I know from caravan work that traversing it without being spotted will be tough, if not impossible. It's one of the few roads under the king's protection.

I sigh. It would also mean we'd probably have to go west and north, both directions not great for avoiding whatever small army the prince is bringing against us. I almost laugh aloud at the ridiculousness of that thought. How on earth can I have gone from a faceless nobody to facing down the prince in a matter of days? I wish I understood more about what was going on—more about why they want the dragon and how much I might have cocked up their plans, what with the hatching and the blood bonding.

I look up at Squid, curled elegantly along the length of the branch, and shake my head. So few options.

"Alright, li'l beastie," I say affectionately. "Wake me if anyone comes this way, or at sunset, whichever comes earlier. And don't fall asleep. Tonight, we head north."

The sun is still up when the dragon wakes me. It's gentle this time, a rough tongue to my cheek. I'm squeezed in between Liv and Twisty, falling mainly into the gap between their bedrolls in my pretty green dress, but at least it's been warm.

I startle upright, pulling my arm from across Liv's body, but the dragon soothes. *No one has come close, but the sun has set. I'll go and see if I can find where those soldiers are in case they're close.*

I nod, shuffling my hands through my hair to remove the twigs I earned with my rough pillow. *Thanks.*

Gently, I shake Twisty awake, smiling so that he knows nothing is wrong as he wakes up. He still has dark circles under his eyes, and I feel badly for the lad.

On my other side, Liv sleeps on. She's angelic when she's asleep, but I make myself shake her awake. "How are you feeling?" I ask softly, as she wades back into wakefulness. It's visibly hard work, and she looks awful. The black eye is still purpling, her lip is still at least twice the size it should be, and her cheek is bruised and bears a split from the slap the prince gave her while I mouthed off at him.

She struggles to upright, wincing despite not using the arm with the arrow wound in it. "Terrible," she replies, and her voice is gravelly, her tone too exhausted for play—unless that's a play in itself, of course. "Des, if we want to survive, that dragon has to go to someone. You can choose who: the King of Ascelin or Prince Shandor or King Aleshir—I can make any of them happen—but we won't survive unless you do."

I sigh. "Liv, I just saved your life."

She shakes her head vehemently, then touches a hand to it, in pain. "No, lovely, *I* saved *yours.*"

I swallow. So she really did hold back the truth about Squid, and under torture. It makes me cranky, to feel humbled after she's played me so many times. And to think that risk to her life, keeping back the truth about the dragon like that, has barely earned us our freedom. That moment on Liza's back, with the army arrayed behind us... She's lucky it was only an arrow to the shoulder she caught. By rights, we should be dead.

"I need to look at your wound," I say, changing the subject. She acquiesces, and I unwind the bandage. It's stiff with blood and will need a good washing. Twisty pokes his head back into the shelter. "New bandage?" I ask him.

Halfway through unwinding, I can't keep it in anymore. "I don't understand you, Liv. First, you leave me to join up with the prince, then you do it again, only this time, he beats you silly. And then I save you, and all you want to do is go back to him? What kind of a hold does he have on you?"

She shakes her head, looking down at her hands. "The first lot of soldiers, at that camp ... they weren't the prince's." She swallows and looks up at me. I don't even feel satisfied to have that suspicion confirmed, really. "They belonged to the King—well, he calls himself Emperor now—of Ascelin. He was there, in Valenta. He wants the egg—the dragon. He wants it enough to go to war with Rescalin; I didn't lie about that. And he has and will kill for it again." Dread uncurls low in my belly. Twisty silently hands me the medic pack.

I blink at her slowly. A few more unexplained elements from the conversation between Crainor and the thin man with the pale eyes, way back in Valenta, fall into place. Had they been in the camp too? I imagine what would have happened if we'd been seen in that ludicrous escape, with my dagger to the naked Liv's neck, and nausea courses through me.

The wound is a bit moist, but otherwise clear. I concentrate on blotting it with antiseptic, ignoring her flinch. "Alright. So first, the prince gave you the egg. You gave it to someone else. You got it back, and you were going to give it to the prince."

She licks her lips and raises her chin. "I got a better offer."

I blink at her again, disbelieving. "You—you got *a better offer*? I'm not sure if you noticed, Liv, but you're now lucky to be alive. And this is all because there was a better deal on the table?" I shake my head. "You've never been so stupid before."

She gulps, and oddly for Liv, doesn't respond to the insult. "It's too late to lay blame. If we want to live, we need protection. We need to pick a side."

I shake my head. "Can't do that, Liv." I know the certainty is at least partly borrowed from Squid, but fuck, if I feel it, I feel it. Liv doesn't get to decide, not again. "Besides, where were you headed? I'm guessing if the prince tortured you, it's not like you brought him information he wanted."

She moves her shoulders uncertainly, wincing at the pain. "No." She trembles even at the memory. I'd feel guilty, but I need the clarity. "I was trying to extricate myself from the whole thing. Lay low for a while." I raise my brows. She swallows hard and meets my gaze for a second before looking away again. "The lady. Remember the lady who had the egg? I thought she might protect me, so I was riding there when the prince caught me. He was angry because I hadn't come straight to him." She swallows again as if against bile. "He was angry because he thought I was playing both sides."

"Which you were," I say, more for confirmation than to make her feel guilty, but her body curls further in on itself, and I know it stings.

She squares her shoulders momentarily. "But it's too late for that, and they're too near," she explains, eyes wide. My breath comes short. "We have to pick a side, hand the dragon over, and then let them fight it out. It's our only way. And honestly, the Emperor of Ascelin scares me more than the fucker that did this to my face. His eyes are so ... they're so pale. White. I've never seen anything like them. And he's..." She shudders. "I can't see how he'll ever stop."

I sigh. My belly flops over. None of this is good. "Liv, I can't. I need to know more about the dragon, about what it means. I can't just hand it over. They'd kill me outright, like as not." I narrow my eyes at her. "This lady... Why did you think she could protect you?"

She wipes her eyes, flinching with pain as she touches the bruised one. "Because... Well, because she's a duchess."

My eyes narrow further. "A duchess?"

She nods, weary and without rancor. "By the sea. She lives alone with her books. Well, she has a household, you know, but she doesn't like court. You never met her. We only went there after you left the troupe."

Dots connect in my mind. Books. An aristocrat by the sea. She could've sent the scribe to copy down *The Slayer of Pastira*, then sent a request to Picton to bring the troupe to perform for her. She could well hold the collection about the Era of Storms. I swallow, wondering if there's a way to get Liv to confirm my suspicions. I lick my lips. It's a risk, but it's not as big a risk as trying to get north from where we are, with king's men keeping peace on the only road that'd get us there, and to a place that may or may not exist. I don't like our options at all, but this...

Calindrina exists.

I just have no idea where, Squid. Its response is quiet sadness mixed with a tinge of shame. I send it warmth. *We will find it, but this could give us the answer, and it's safer.* Unless she decides to hand us over to the king anyway, of course, but surely we can get some answers first. *A bit safer.*

I get up and fetch the map from Liza's saddlebags. "Where?" I demand.

CHAPTER SEVENTEEN

B y the time we're on the road, having all eaten our fill, I have half a plan in mind. Liv doesn't like it, but she doesn't have to. She's not going to run while she's recovering, and with any luck, by the time she's well enough, we'll be at the duchess's house. Castle. Palace. Fort. Whatever. Hopefully, with some more options before us.

Squid is not entirely happy about the change of plans, but it agrees more quickly than I'd expected. Scyless Castle, where the duchess lives, lies on the west coast, north of where we currently are, and I suspect it heard all the uncertain thoughts I'd had about trusting a mark on a map for the location of Calindrina.

The plan for avoiding the immediate threat from the prince is simple—perhaps too simple. We head a little way north, far enough to miss the town of Cylina when we turn west through the forest, but not so far as to be on a road. The forest will slow us, but I figure the prince will expect us to put as much distance between himself and us as possible. That hopefully means he expects to find us on the roads. And, with a little luck, that means he will have left only a small squad in Cylina to maintain a presence; most of his army will have moved out.

I hope, too, that our disguises work. My chest is bound as flat as I can get it these days, and I'm dressed as a moderately convincing man. Twisty looked at me with wide, impressed eyes when I left the hut where I'd changed, and that was near enough for me. Liv wears the new kirtle I'd bought for myself in town over a white underdress. I'm only a little jealous of how it looks on her. And Twisty—poor Twisty.

He's dressed as a girl. Both Liv and I had to restrain laughter when he left the tent. The skirt of the dress was about right, hitting him just below the knee. He protested as I put his hair into curling pigtails to either side, but now, glancing sideways at him astride Quicksilver, arms around Liv, I'm glad I insisted on it. We can almost pass as a family, and appearing as a new sex is the best disguise, in my experience.

Squid coils on my back, and I'm a little surprised at the weight of it. I tickle its head now to wake it. *Squid, would you mind checking again? We're getting close to Cylina, and I have no desire to face down those soldiers. You did a great job on them last time, but without the element of surprise...*

With a warm acquiescence, it takes off, wending between the branches of the trees and out of sight. I glance sideways at Liv. She's weary, slumped down in her saddle, but her color is a little better than it has been. We won't be able to make good time with her, but with any luck, once we're clear of Cylina, that won't matter.

"You're sure you didn't say anything about where either of us was headed?" I check with her again. "If the prince or the King of Rescalin knows, that's the direction they'll be headed in."

She shakes her head. "I didn't dare put Elouise in it, and as I said, I didn't even know where you were headed. I told them you tended to head home when things were bad." I frown at her, stung, and she shrugs. "Seemed like one of those likely sounding lies, you know? And besides, when they..." She falls quiet, and I know she's thinking about the torture again. She trembles, and Twisty shoots me an anxious look.

"I won't let it happen again, Liv," I promise her softly. "I swear."

She gives me a sharp look. "If you meant that, you'd turn around right now and hand that fucking beast over."

There's no reply to that, so I don't offer one, just urge Liza on so we don't have to speak to each other. I get that it makes no sense to her, but I also can't argue with her, especially when she looks so battered.

Squid lands on my shoulder. *All clear,* it announces, then falls abruptly back to sleep. I feel bad for waking the dragon. Clearly, all the flying has taken it out of the poor wee thing.

As the afternoon wears on, rain drips through the leaves, and the leaf litter sends up earthy menthol scents. Grass trees offer limited cover, but we see no one. So far, so good.

We hit the western edge of the forest before I expect us to and pause for a long moment. The sun is setting, casting golden light and long, dark shadows that stretch toward us across plains of yellow. The rain has eased, but I don't like the look of the clouds overhead. We could be in for a wet night.

Rain begins to fall before it's fully dark, and I call a halt when Liv starts shivering. Her face is a carving in stoic bad humor. Twisty and I do most of the work of setting up camp: unsaddling horses, setting up a rough cover, laying down another to keep the damp from soaking up toward us, and unrolling the bedrolls and blankets. I light the little lantern I bought—I hadn't dared the night before—and by its flickering, I check Liv's shoulder.

I have to let some pus drain and then clear it out with the precious alcohol. Liv sets her jaw to tolerate the pain, but blame emanates from her. I force myself to be cheerful. "There we go! You lie down and keep warm, and I'll organize some food." She nods without looking at me and obediently takes one of the bedrolls.

As the cold sets in, the three of us squeeze under the canvas shelter and curl up under the bedrolls together. It's the work of a moment to polish off the food, and then the other two are asleep.

Squid soon joins us, flapping wings and shaking the rough canvas cover. I smile faintly. *Too weary to watch?* I ask. It offers a humble and slightly shamefaced agreement, and so I pull myself out of the warm little pile, letting the dragon climb in instead, and settle myself on a log nearby. It's not like I don't have enough worries to keep me from sleep. Beginning with the reception we can expect in Scyless.

I wish I knew more about politics; maybe then I'd be able to find a way to play this duchess against the king. I find my sharpening stone, unsheathe my sword, and, listening to the drip of the rain, work my way through all of my blades until they glisten, sharp enough to cut flesh like butter.

Riding across these endless plains of long golden grass is incredibly tedious, a disquieting counterpoint to the tension that keeps me glancing over my shoulder at the horizon. It reminds me of when Petrus and I accepted a job guiding a caravan—but for a wine merchant called Brossus.

We'd had to ride across these same monotonous plains alone first, and then back with the train of travelers and oaken barrels. At least then we could sing. Now, it seems unwise. We stand out like an aristocrat in a two-bit tav—definitely not mistakable for the bounding wallabies and kangaroos that are the largest animals in this landscape. They won't need to get close to spot us. My head aches. I keep blinking to try and clear my blurring vision and keep a proper watch.

Squid, grown around the belly to the size of a large house cat but much longer, now habitually spends much of its time hovering above us, learning how to catch the breeze and hold steady like a bird of prey. Its coloring helps me relax. Even with our connection, I find it hard to spot against an empty sky. The problems will come when the bright sky covers in cloud—the blue will be too vivid to be missed—but this spring has proven itself low on rain, and so I haven't been forced to play killjoy to the dragon as yet.

Of us all, Squid is probably in the best condition. Everyone is utterly exhausted. Only Squid rides Liza's saddle, between flights, as I walk alongside to try to spare her. A day ago, a pursuer caught her flank with an arrow as we fled.

I've already cleaned her wound, but it oozes slightly. Twisty is walking too, with nervy Quicksilver on a lead, her head hanging low.

Liv's bruises have yellowed and grown even more unpleasant, and there was a rough moment when I had to press a red-hot dagger to her suppurating wound, but she can walk without pain now. We're all kept to Liv's pace, really, so throughout the day, she rides until her shoulder won't let her be jolted around any longer. The back of my neck keeps prickling. I can only hope Squid was right to say we left the men with the bows and arrows far behind.

Almost as much as I think about what's behind us, I worry about what's ahead. I turn over possibilities in my mind, trying to untangle the threads, to find a safer, better way. But over and again, despite the fact it's Liv's way out we're borrowing and I still can't fully trust her, I decide that the duchess—and more to the point, her archive—offers us more possibilities than anything else I can come up with. A possibility to understand what the dragon actually represents to these sovereigns; a chance to work out how to negotiate. An opportunity to find Calindrina.

It doesn't stop my thoughts from churning over and over the same terrain. After all, the duchess is related to the king. In my head, I practice speeches designed to get her on our side, to convince her to let us see her repository. I even practice greetings—a curtsy and a bow—trying to decide what's more courteous when you're a woman dressed as a man. I turn over whether it's better to send Liv in ahead, but this would leave us entirely at the mercy of the story Liv wants to tell the duchess, and she's made her position on the dragon all too clear. I decide finally that I'll have to ask Squid to stay behind, flying above the sea, until I've had the chance to give the duchess our story.

Every night, we watch kangaroos nibble at the grass while we eat our lackluster rations. We settle the horses and set up a makeshift tent under a tree to help keep us warm, and then I pull out the little lantern and examine the map using a very shuttered light. Most nights, Liv and Twisty curl up in the bedrolls, Squid with them. The mark Liv left on the map with her unhappy bloody fingertip is still visible. I gaze at it, wondering when the land will shift from the long, yellowed grass to the sandy greenery that promises the sea.

Finally, on the tenth day since we ran from the river, the land changes. The ground loses its flatness first, and the grass turns green. The trees thicken, and I relax a little at the extra coverage. The earth is soft and damp, lush ferns between giant, snake-rooted figs. Twisty is taken with the size of the goannas, and chitters back at the monkeys we occasionally disturb. I swat irritably at mosquitoes.

We crest three rises and then one definite hill. The rainforest thins here, giving way to the beginnings of sand. And, for the first time in what feels like eons, we can see where we're going. To the south of us, we can now make out the silver ribbon of the river we left behind turned north again to find us, wending its way between low green hills.

I track the line of it, narrowing my eyes against the setting sun to try to see where it spiderwebs out toward the sea. Eventually, the delta should appear, if we've traveled the right way, but I'm probably too hopeful as yet. The river mouth is likely concealed beyond these fertile green hills, and there's still a distance to travel. Still yet more time in which to wonder whether I'm sending us all to our deaths. I glance sideways at Liv, queasy as I wonder, yet again, how I can win her to our side so she doesn't hand us—and Squid—over to the duchess.

CHAPTER EIGHTEEN

O n the seventh day, we reach a crest that gives way to the broad, shining spread of the delta. It's a majestic sight, but as we stand there, gaping, Squid speaks inside my head. *People on the approach. They do not look friendly.*

"Time to go," I say to the other two. "Let's move." *And you, dragon, come join us. The skies are too gray for you to hide properly today.*

A few minutes later, as we're crossing another hill, there's a swooping sound, and the dragon dives between the horses, startling Quicksilver. This dive has become a gleeful habit, but the silver doesn't seem to be adjusting. Squid sweeps in a broad circle and comes to land before me on the pommel of Liza's saddle. Its little sides heave as I grin down at it. "Will that ever get old?" I ask aloud.

Squid's bright eyes meet mine, and that's when it happens.

Three men, dressed in leather that's seen better days, run out of a thicket to our right, wielding swords. I haul my own out of the scabbard on my back. "Liv, *run!*" I scream, turning my mount to face them down. Squid takes off with an enormous flap of its wings, scraping past my shoulder as it heads skyward. Liza gives a loud whinny of anger.

They obviously hadn't expected me to turn to face them, because now, they slow. I narrow my eyes. They expected me to ride on. "Liv! Not that way! Head to the sea!" I yell. "It's a trap!"

She glances back over her shoulder as I glance back over mine. A spark of something shoots between us, something I wouldn't know how to put into words, and then I'm in the fight.

One man races at me, axe up, but Liza rears back and brings her sharp hooves down, crunching into bone and flesh. Another with a sword, clearly attempting to flank me, approaches my left side, but I toss my sword to that hand and swipe at him. He dodges away.

The battle fever floods my body now, and I guide Liza with my knees to avoid the flanking maneuver. They're both ahead of me, and both carry swords, which I'm almost grateful for—a balance of reach on each side—but there's still two of them.

I glance from one to the other, trying to work out which to tackle first, when a bright blue streak chooses for me. Squid flies directly at the head of the one to the left, so I swing right and raise my blade. The first clash is enough to yank me out of the saddle, and I curl into an acrobat's tumble and rise to my feet, yelling to Liza to get clear.

I turn back, shoving hair and sweat out of my eyes. "Ye're no lad!" the man exclaims.

"Eyes like an eagle, this one," I reply, then feint high, and again low, only to swing in from the left. He's not that adept a fighter, and he's down in a second. I stab clear through his heart, then turn to Squid's enemy. Squid has set his hair on fire, but to his credit, he's still swinging—ugly, graceless swipes—at the blue dragon.

Clear, Squid. I've got this. Squid spirals upward, out of reach entirely, and the man's sword is raised too high to block my cut in time. He's dead in a second. *Not that skilled,* I tell the dragon. *Are the others clear? Where are they?*

The dragon disappears above the trees and then says, *They're being pursued, but they have a good lead. Almost on the beach.*

The beach? I suddenly realize how close we are and call for Liza. "C'mon! Let's go, girl." I leap for the saddle and spin west, but it feels like it's taking forever. Liv is no fighter, and Twisty, brave and loyal as he is, is basically defenseless too. With the sea hemming them in, their only hope is that they're close enough—and that the duchess lets them in.

My throat is one big lump. I'd imagined this as a slow, civilized approach, with time to develop an argument, an appeal for why the duchess should help us, and to finally win Liv to using whatever coin she might have with this noblewoman to save our skins and avoid handing Squid over. Now we'll be lucky to make it to her gate. It's a bad plan, but options are thin. I gulp.

Can you harry their pursuers? I ask Squid in desperation. *Safely?*

Cries sound to the west and south of me, and I guide Liza away from them, fiercely urging her on. After long minutes, I catch sight of two men still trying to put out the fires on their clothing and saddlebags. I draw my sword, and as we ride past at speed, I slash the girth of their saddles clear. They won't be following us anytime soon.

"C'mon, Liza," I repeat softly, probably too softly for her to hear. She is all stretch and release, her entire being in the gallop.

We burst clear of the trees and ride swiftly across sandy soil and pale green grasses, then we're down a dune and on the beach proper, wind whipping hair into my eyes. I brush it clear and narrow them, assessing.

The sand is flat and dry. The tide has been out for some time. In the distance, I can make out a hill against the seashore with towers rising out of it. The duchess's home. I'd seen it marked so often on a map but never bothered to wonder how exactly a castle could sit on a seashore.

Quicksilver has a good start, but there are four men still in pursuit. As I watch, Squid swoops in and sets another horse's mane alight. It swerves in panic and takes out another. The remaining two gain on the silver and her two riders—the poor mare doesn't have the stamina for this.

I pass the pursuers a moment later, but they're beyond my sword's reach. *Squid, please. Just one more.*

It soars in without reply and huffs fire across the line of the other two. One swerves away in time, but the other raises a bow and shoots at terrifyingly close range. Squid lets out a squawk as the arrow hits one of its wings, puncturing it clear through.

It weaves, trying to stay in the air, then begins to spiral. I gape, pain rippling through me. I'm caught both underwater and above for a long moment, breathing air and inhaling water simultaneously. I spasm, a cough that can't catch on anything wrenching my body. Bile burns the back of my throat. Then Squid hits the ground, and time snaps back to singular. The dragon is a pitiful little blue pile in the sand.

The man is gleeful, turning about to scoop the dragon up. I yell to get his attention and urge Liza on, sword in hand, but he's focused on the dragon. He hasn't even turned toward me when I slash hard across his chest, carving through leather and into flesh. He won't be following us.

The dragon raises its head as I pass, time blurs back into the multiple, and I grit my teeth. I can't make out the dragon amid the layers of history, so I'm operating by memory of where it hit the sand.

I reach down, foot hooked dangerously in the stirrup and almost losing my balance, but I manage to catch it up. Pain resounds through me, but it's Squid's, and somehow that pain is more intimate than the pin-sharp talons dug into my wrist.

I shove back the pain as fiercely as I can. Every now and then, the vomit-inducing time layers reappear, leaving me gasping for air, shadowed by pain I can feel but can't make sense of—I don't have a wing. But in a moment of the dragon's unconsciousness, I raise my head, and my heart sings as I realize all of us now have a clear run to the castle. More men appear out of the dunes, but they are south of us now.

We may not die today.

I yell "Woohoo!" in glee and see Liv's head turn toward me, but I've spoken too soon. I've almost caught them up when a good five hundred men pour out of the trees to the right like angry fire ants out of a nest, some in green and some in plain leather.

I can't... Squid warns me as if I might ask it to take them on. Time doubles, trebles, and I force myself to breathe as usual despite the sensation of inhaling water that flickers in and out of existence. It's nauseating. *I can't...*

No, I reply fiercely. *No. No. You'll be alright, Squid. We just have to get inside.*

In another moment, I've pulled alongside Liv and Twisty. "Will she let us in?" I yell.

"She doesn't even know we're coming!" Liv bellows back, and I know she's furious. "And she will hate being put in a position like this. We have to give them the dragon!"

"No!" I roar. "She has to let us in!"

We're near enough now that I can see the duchess's castle more clearly. The island it's on is just offshore, connected to the mainland by a causeway. As I watch, the first wave crashes over the narrow rocky bridge. Tide's been out, but it's coming in now—one of the best natural defenses I've ever seen on a castle—but it gives us precious little time to make it inside the enormous gates.

"Go!" I scream at Liv.

"You can't make it once the water is over," she shouts back. "No one can. They told me never to try. We have to turn back."

"We'll make it," I yell, and lead the way, Liza's galloping hooves clicking neatly on the rock of the causeway.

"Fuck you, Des!" Liv cries behind me, but she follows.

Terror swamps me, and it's not helped by Squid swimming in and out of consciousness. Riding pell-mell across wet and slippery rocks while waves crash around and on us numbs my mind with fear, and being not quite clear about whether it's really happening makes it even worse. Half the time, I inhale water that disappears in the next split second, just as I begin to cough. Fortunately, part way across, Squid's little head sinks down onto my wrist, and it's out.

The current reality, undiluted, is no less terrifying. Waves crash up and onto the rocky bridge, startling Liza and making me pray for my life. My hair whips back from my face, and we move at such a speed that I know if Liza falls, we're both goners.

I glance back over my shoulder. On the shore, some soldiers hold back, waiting, clearly thinking we will founder ourselves with no help from them, but many are still in pursuit, right behind Quicksilver. "C'mon, Liv!" I yell. "We have to make it inside!"

It's a long moment of riding, riding, riding, with waves crashing over the causeway, threatening to engulf us at any moment. The water is rising, and I'm saturated from Liza's kickback. I gaze directly ahead and see the closed gates of the castle. This bit, this bit...

I haven't thought this bit through.

We skitter to a halt before them, and Liv dismounts alongside me. "Elouise! Elouise, please! Let me in! Please! I need your help. Elouise!" Liv pounds on the gate with a fist, gasping, then stops and falls to her knees with a sob.

The waves crash closer and the green-clad men ride nearer. Despair catches up with me and takes hold.

Then, with a grind and a groan, the gates—like a miracle—begin to open. We squeeze our way in as soon as there's space enough, with the men behind us about to reach us, and I yell desperately to the gatekeeper to close it again. He nods firmly but calmly, refusing my fear, and spins the wheel in the opposite direction.

The gates close, inexorable, and, like a miracle, we are safe.

We slip from our saddles, and guards step forward to take our reins. Out of breath and wary, we climb the stairs to enormous wooden doors which, again, are open just enough to allow us through and close as soon as we enter. Here, we enter an expansive courtyard, all pale sand and white marble. I register half a dozen guards with drawn blades, two maids with their washing baskets set down before them, and a hostler leaning against a stable door, along with another dozen, at least, and every person standing in it watches us.

Then they disappear. For a moment, bare rocks and sea lions and seabirds' cries mix with the hustle and bustle of a castle, deafening and disorienting. I reel and stagger, dizzy, my gorge rising. Then the dragon, still in my arms, again loses consciousness, and I'm shoved back into my own time.

Opposite us, a long marble staircase leads down from the castle proper, silver and moonstone gates behind it. There's something comforting about the promise of having three sets of gates between the soldiers and us, but right now, it's one more hurdle.

A white-haired woman in a pale blue gown stands at the head of the staircase, her hands clasped together at her waist. At the sight of her, Liv sobs in the back of her throat and races clumsily forward. Twisty and I follow more sedately. Liv throws herself down and wraps her arms around the woman's legs, weeping and begging forgiveness. I've never seen her like this. It's more than a little disconcerting.

We reach the point where it would be rude not to acknowledge the lady who as yet has not responded to Liv's display. I bow low, matching my attire, awkwardly still holding Squid like a reptilian baby in my arms, and murmur, "Your Grace, my most profound thanks." All my careful plans for how this conversation might play out—gone.

Fuck. I really didn't want to be putting Squid in her hands like this.

The woman is not yet old, but she's no longer young—around forty-five, I would say—but with hair gone unusually white for her age. She is graceful, slim, and completely in control. Her slender silver-gray eyes take in everything in the space of a moment. Despite the sobbing woman at her feet, she smiles graciously in welcome to both myself and Twisty, spreading her hands. "Welcome to my home, travelers. I do hope you were not accosted on the road." A spark of humor lights her eyes, and I like her already. It's enough to raise my wariness a notch.

She bends and gently helps Liv to her feet. "Livinia. That's enough now, my dear. You've quite lost your head. Anyone would think I'd refused to aid you, the way you're carrying on."

And with that, without even asking our names, she turns, the enormous silver-white doors behind her clang open, and she leads us into her home.

CHAPTER NINETEEN

After all our time on the road, Scyless is the most incredible luxury, but it's not enough to soothe my anxieties. I'm horribly aware I've put all of us in the hands of a woman I don't know from a bar of soap.

Elouise is a gracious host, demanding nothing, not even answers, of us. Indeed, for a few days, we don't even see her—remarkable, given the hordes of armed men we all know are gathering on the shore—but she arranges everything from afar. Food and wine, her avian veterinarian for Squid's wing, a medic to look over the humans, her best hostler to care for Liza and Quicksilver (who revel in the attention), new clothes, a suite of apartments overlooking the sea, and, glory of all glory, a bath set into the floor within—all are provided to us.

But she's no fool. Guards—they call themselves escorts—stand at the door of the suite we occupy. When I emerge, rested and freshly washed, from our rooms, they offer to take me to visit Squid's veterinarian. "Oh, I like to wander a new place," I say cheerfully.

"We can't have you getting lost," the gray-eyed soldier says, with a smile that doesn't reach his eyes.

I acquiesce with the best grace I can manage, but it's clear we're prisoners. Soldiers patrol the garden beneath our balcony as well, with a regular watch set along the castle battlements visible from our rooms. Even Twisty, who might be able to get away with the indulgence that some offer youth, can't shake our kind, implacable guard. He keeps trying, regardless.

Liv disappears, not even returning to her room at night. I figure she's spending time with the duchess she calls by her first name. The thought of her explaining Squid and Twisty and me to the woman who now holds our lives in the palm of her hand makes me sleepless, but when I request an audience, the same gray-eyed soldier tells me the duchess will send for me when she is ready. I spend half the night turning over how to respond to the questions we're likely to confront after Liv's story has been told.

On the second day, I am escorted through the castle to the veterinarian's quarters. I blink at the sight of Liv leaning over Squid, gently pasting into place a piece of fabric over the puncture in its wing using a viscous golden fluid from a bowl. The dragon's sapphire gaze meets mine, and a slow warmth burgeons inside me. *Morning*, I send, smiling at its pleasure. For a moment, I want to walk away before Liv sees me; the scene is that intimate.

Liv looks away when she sees it's me. "Oh. The master left me to do this. He gave Squid an antipyretic for its fever earlier—though he wasn't sure what its normal temperature is. Anyway, we're patching the puncture so it doesn't lose all its wing strength while it heals. He said it was time to do it and explained to me what to do. I'm being careful, I swear. He couldn't stay, but this formulation only stays good for a short while. Apparently one of the hunting eagles was shot down above the castle, and he left to see if there was anything he could do."

Is this Liv on the defensive? Her expression is disconcerting. All the slow-burning anger and resentment she carried as we made our way to Scyless is gone, and she's ... quiet. Fragile, somehow.

I hesitate, wondering if I should leave. "What are you doing?" I ask, finally. "Is that..."

"It's silk," she replies, bending back over her work, dark curls shielding her face from view. "The master says it should let it fly while the wing still heals."

I nod, settling down beside her. "It's been longing to fly again. Like it's been weeks instead of a couple of days."

If I could fly, I could help work out a way to make sure we're safe.

We're safe, Squid. It might just be more temporary than we'd like.

"I can understand. If you could fly, imagine how hard it would be to not ..."

For a while, I watch her work. She's gentle and delicate in how she touches Squid. It's almost a shock, after how willing she's been this whole time to hand it over to any of the violent sovereigns on our tail. Finally, I can't bear not asking. "Liv..."

"I never wanted to hurt anyone. Or anything," she murmurs, her gaze still fixed on Squid's wing. "And this little beastie is... It's very beautiful, Des." She glances up, a flash of green, and then away. "Anyway. There's something I should say." I watch her shoulders hunch a little. "Des, I'm sorry about Petrus."

My mind reels, and I gape silently, but she's so focused on Squid's wing she doesn't notice. Is she sorry for sleeping with him? Sorry he's so far away? Sorry he fell for me? Or what? "Well, I'm sorry for a lot of things about Petrus," I say, "and most of them have nothing to do with you." It's true. Some days I miss his presence at my side so intensely I wonder if I could've been happy playing at being the woman he wanted.

She meets my eyes and shakes her head. "Yes, but, Des, I'm sorry that I slept with him." She's so direct I have to look away, my breath stolen. "I really only did it to get back at you, and if there's anything that's been made clear over the past ... well, since Valenta ... it's that that you didn't deserve it." She stands, walking over to a table to pour the remainder of the adhesive into a brown glass vial.

I stay quiet. "I don't know what to say," I tell her eventually. "I mean, sure, that stung. But Petrus was angry with me, and, well ... it's not like it's really out of character for you." I feel almost cruel saying the words, even though they're true.

When I had been with Liv, I'd had a long list of the people she had slept with while we were together crowded in my head. I hadn't wanted to, but my mind had kept track. Some were utterly random, but more than a few were those I might have been close to—or rather, those I might have become close to—had she not slept with them.

Liv stands by a small basin, washing the paintbrush she'd used to mend Squid's wing. She nods silently, accepting all of this. Eventually, she sighs and turns around. Her green gaze meets mine, and I almost flinch from the honesty there. "I am sorry. I'm not a fool; I'm not asking for or expecting forgiveness. But I am sorry."

Then she walks away, her practical trousers hugging her backside as her hips sway. I shake my head at myself and then run my hands through my hair, tugging hard. *The woman you love and hate is very complicated,* Squid comments.

Indeed. Would you mind leaving me alone with my thoughts for a moment, Squid? I try to keep my thoughts calm, but I know it feels the anger in them.

I do not pretend to understand the desire for privacy, Squid says, *but, if it helps, even I cannot see how to resolve this relationship between you. It is complex and intense. I know you wish to leave it behind you, and sometimes not. But I cannot see how it will go away.*

I close my eyes for a long moment, then pick up the pillow with Squid on it. *Let's get you back to the suite. Our escort is just outside.*

On the fourth day, Twisty and I sit on the gracious, sweeping balcony outside our suite, overlooking the sea beyond the battlements. I play at being unconcerned, in a filmy dress and silver beaded sandals. We eat breakfast and covertly watch the shore, where the scurrying green figures slowly construct a large machine. Most likely Ascelin preparing to attack.

"They just won't let me," he says again, frustrated. "Every time I try, there's some smiling soldier blocking the way."

I shake my head. "It's not your fault, lad. The duchess has made her decision about how we're to be treated, and there's not much to be done about it." My words are comforting, but my gut sinks as I say them aloud. She's a *duchess*. Sworn to the king. How did I ever imagine we might find a way to the truth about Calindrina? The anxiety in my belly draws so tight I'm almost breathless.

"But we need to do *something*," Twisty says.

"We can't afford to annoy the only person who might—"

A knock at the door interrupts, and we turn to look as a graceful older woman appears. Somehow, her curtsy manages to be centered beautifully in the framing of the doorway. "Her Grace requests the pleasure of your company," she says formally. "She wonders if you might join her for lunch."

Twisty blinks at me, clearly overcome, so I smile, nod, and say, "We would be most pleased. We have been waiting for the opportunity to thank Her Grace for her generosity."

The woman nods. "She will send an escort to fetch you."

By silent accord, we wait until we hear the door inside latch shut before we speak. "Does this mean trouble?" Twisty is well out of his depth, and it makes him anxious.

I grin because he's getting worried just as I see the first hint of an opportunity, even if it is one that makes my gut tighten fiercely. It'll take all my playing skills to find a way out for us. But right now, I need Twist calm. If Twist is his gregarious self with the duchess, I'll get to watch her, try to find what makes her tick. "Lad, if there's one thing in all my time I've learned about these fancy people, it's that they're just people. Busy, lazy, filthy rich, appallingly powerful people, but people nonetheless. If she had wanted to make trouble, there were far more efficient ways for her to do so. Like leaving us out on that causeway."

Twisty shudders. "I couldn't believe it when you started riding out there. You know I can't swim, right?"

I shake my head. "I can't swim either, but it was ride or die, so I chose..."

A sound like a gale sweeps out of our apartments, a moment of silence, and then Squid stalks out. The familiar sound of another attempt at taking off. It is not happy about being unable to fly, though the veterinarian visited again and promised yesterday that it would only be another few days. "He said it wouldn't be long, Squid," I say aloud for Twisty's sake, "but that you should give it a rest."

But I hate it! Squid whines in my head.

"I know it's hard. But you want that wing nice and strong."

To get to Calindrina.

"Yes. To get to Calindrina." I hand down a strawberry. It doesn't really eat, but it likes to try new flavors.

A yell echoes from below the balcony.

I automatically reach under my skirts for the long blade strapped to my thigh. Twisty grabs a dagger from his boot, and we're against the balustrade in a split second.

Below, there's a large man, dressed in green and bristling with blades. He's being hauled out of the thick brush against the garden wall by three broad guardsmen dressed in the pale blue of the duchess's troops.

I swallow. They have it under control, but it adds another unknown to the whirling inside my head—that whatever the duchess's plans for us, the men in green might not even give us the space to see them through.

"I think they have it, lad," I say to Twisty, who nods and sheaths his dagger. Useful to know he isn't one to let his guard down easily. Though that's unsurprising, being raised by the Rogue headed by Armand.

"Will they check, though? For other…"

"Intruders?"

"Well, yes."

"I expect so," I say, a little too calmly for his taste.

"I guess we can check at lunch, right?"

I force a smile and carve away a slice of the soft cheese, smooshing it down into the bread. "I guess we can."

He seems troubled still. "So, do we know what she will want?"

"The duchess?" I spear a chunk of mango and munch it down, thinking. "Well, I've barely seen Liv. Chances are she's been spending her time with the duchess." Saying it out loud stings a little more, but it's hard to be properly jealous. "That means she probably knows a fair bit about us and our business. Whatever we've told Liv, I'd guess."

Twisty nods slowly. "Do you think she'll help us, then?"

I tilt my head at him. "She already has, lad."

Twisty stares at the floor. "Yes, but…"

I sigh and stop playing stupid. Trying to save people the worry doesn't always work. "You mean, what if she decides to hand us over?"

"Well, I just want to know if she will."

I sigh and let the light fabric of my dress dance over my palm. "She may," I say bluntly. "It's entirely possible, even probable. I'm not exactly sure who those men who chased us here worked for—most seemed like mercenaries or Rogues, but the others were in green. That *might* make them the King of Ascelin's men. If that's so, well, I suspect our king will have something to say about them even being in this country. That doesn't bode particularly well for us—she *is* a relative of the king's, after all, and no doubt sworn to him. That said, it seems like a lot of work, taking care of all of us, if all she wanted to do was hand over the dragon. She could've done that when we arrived."

Twisty takes this in. "Alright. I just wanted to know."

I smile at him and sip at my cup of maté. "Lad, if I had more answers, I'd be sharing them. But since we're both in the dark, I refuse to borrow trouble." I wonder if he's going to comment on the shadows under my eyes betraying my sleeplessness, but Twisty smiles slowly.

"Can you borrow trouble in the dark?" he asks.

I grin. "I'd have thought it was easier!"

When the escort comes to take us to lunch, though, I've sharpened my wits as much as I might. I'm still in the floaty dress, but I've concealed another narrow blade inside my belt. The man in green made me edgy, even though it looked like he'd been caught just as he made it over the wall. I don't know the politics of anything, and there's always the risk that it'd be easier to let us die and be rid of a problem.

CHAPTER TWENTY

T he young boy who comes to collect us has a cheeky grin, and it broadens at the sight of Twisty. They're of an age. Twisty smiles back, but a little hesitantly, like any good child of the city.

"I'm Timble," he tells us, with a bow too quick to even be perfunctory. "Shall we go?" It's only as we nod that he pauses, tearing his gaze away from Twisty and toward me. "She asked—I mean, Her Grace requests that the dragon attend also."

I nod graciously, covering Twisty's tension. *Sorry, Squid, looks like you're with us for lunch.* The dragon doesn't reply in words but sends a sense of sorrow at losing its comfy bed as I scoop it up off the pillow. *You could walk, you know,* I tell it.

I miss your scabbard, it responds. It's bigger still than it had been—its chest now the size of a small dog, but from nose to tail, it's as long as Twisty now, probably.

You're likely too big for that now! I get a wave of wan gratitude and sappiness. It's not coping at all with a sore wing. Carrying it is awkward, but eventually, I get it arranged.

"This way!" Timble hurries off. He's fast, and Twisty automatically speeds up to keep up with him, forcing me to huff and puff my way through the halls with the dragon, barely keeping them in sight. I wonder if this is the duchess's game to put us on a back foot.

Though, as we hurry into a long, open room with filmy white curtains billowing inwards from a balcony, the duchess rises to her feet at the head of the table, a look of dismay on her face.

"Oh, Timble," she says, and the note of disappointment in her voice makes the lad wilt. "I asked you to escort them, not race them."

"I'm sorry!" he cries, and he does sound sorry. "But they brought the dragon, and I know you wanted to see it, and so I wanted to hurry, and..."

She turns to us, then, her silver eyes soft. "My apologies for your escort, Mistress Mildue, Master Rogers. I had hoped that perhaps you and Timble might enjoy one another's company, Master Rogers, but it seems you've barely had breath even to work that out!"

I shake my head and then curtsy. It's not easy, holding the dragon, but I manage the proper depth and hold it for a second longer than is necessary. Her gaze on me is approving, and that is surprisingly warming. My own reaction makes me edgy. "Your Grace, you are far too thoughtful," I say. "You have taken such great care of us. It is wonderful to meet you properly, especially given our unceremonious arrival. And Timble made a very gracious escort—and a nimble one."

We all smile at my tiny rhyme, and the tension in the room eases. The duchess gestures us into seats near her own. I settle Squid into the seat beside me, and it sits upright, narrow head poking over the edge of the table. The duchess's maid pours us each a glass of fruit juice. At least I don't need to fight the effects of alcohol. The maid leaves the room as soon as she's done.

I wonder for a moment where Liv is, but, as if she can read my mind, the duchess explains. "Livinia and I were playing orlan this morning, and she felt quite wearied by it. Her wound has quite taken a toll on her, poor lass, though it is healing well now. I hope you don't mind if she joins us later?"

I smile, avoiding meeting Twisty's anxious look. "Of course not, Your Grace. I have been quite concerned about Liv—Livinia's well-being myself. But she seems to have healed remarkably, thanks to your kindness. You have been extraordinarily generous, and I thank you."

Unlike most nobles I have known, she does not make a show of receiving thanks but simply inclines her head and continues the conversation. "I hope that you both are recovered also. Although I, of course, wanted to hear all you would tell of your journey here—for it seems to have been quite an exciting one!—I thought it best to wait."

She's creating an opening, but it's up to us whether we step into it. I weigh the two, then decide our openness may be all we can offer with so little to trade ourselves. But that doesn't mean telling her everything. "I must thank you again, Your Grace, for opening the gates when you did. We were ... well, rather pressed." A ghost of a smile crosses her face. "Though, to be frank, I am not completely clear whose army that was—or were they simply mercenaries?"

"And did they die? Did you kill them? Or did the waves? There was a lot!" Twisty's restraint, it would seem, is reduced by the presence of the duchess's immaculate control. I'm glad of it.

She turns to him and leans on her elbow toward him in a friendly echo of his excitement. "Some did! Some were swept away by waves behind you on the causeway. I suspect you missed seeing that! Swept right into the sea. But most of them are camped on the beach currently. I have not decided their fate as yet, though they occasionally try the gate when the tide is low. But my captain of the guard has some *very* particular ideas for how to deal with those. I suspect you two might get along smashingly."

I smile at Twisty's befuddlement at being taken so seriously by a noble and am taken aback as she turns toward me. "They're Ascelese, but their ranks are filled with mercenaries. It seems the rest of the Ascelese army is busy pressing the capital. From what we've heard, it isn't a siege yet, but rather a 'trade negotiation.' One with most of an army encamped on the hills around Pastira." The duchess sips from her glass, eyes still on me. "I've sent word to the king but haven't heard back from him. I gather he's rather busy."

I want to swallow under her gaze—I feel pinned by it, like a butterfly laid out for examination—but I refuse to. I know what she is asking. It's all about the potential war over this land and trade deal that included the dragon egg. Liv has clearly shared with her my recalcitrance when it comes to handing the dragon over. My heart sinks. It looks like my fears about the duchess handing us over to the king are to be fulfilled. I'm not sure what to say, so I keep my mouth shut, and after a moment, with the grace I'm beginning to notice is characteristic, she turns her gaze to Squid.

"I didn't want to ask as soon as we were together," she explains quietly, her eyes glimmering with excitement. "After all, you are my guests, and I wanted to welcome you. But can I ask now? The dragon?"

I smile indulgently, though inside, I'm wary. "Of course, Your Grace! What would you like to know?"

Squid pulls itself up onto the table, delicately avoiding the place settings and glasses and wending its way, glimmering in the light with tail held high, toward the duchess. *I want to know more about her. She seems much more intelligent than most of the humans I've encountered.*

The duchess is mesmerized and reaches out a pale fingertip. Squid bumps its head up under it like a cat, but she doesn't seem startled. She slides the finger along Squid's azure head and then tucks it under its chin. Squid's eyes narrow as if in pleasure.

"Warmer than I'd thought," she murmurs. "Lit from within."

"It breathes flame," Twisty blurts out. "So, I figure there's fire in its belly."

She glances at him, nodding in thanks, and goes back to stroking Squid. "Does it have a name? Or is it a he? A she?"

I smile. "A name, yes. Sq—" I'm interrupted in my head by Squid's correction. "I'm sorry. Esquidamelion. And as for a sex..." I ask Squid the question, wondering that I've never thought of it before. "It does not seem to have one, Your Grace."

"Fascinating," the duchess murmurs. "I wonder how they reproduce."

I just decide to make an egg, and it comes through, Squid tells me, helpful and confusing. *At least, I think so. I might learn more in Calindrina.*

I shake my head, though the question sets me on edge. "Not a clue, I'm afraid." I'm suddenly loath to let her know how we are connected, of the blood bond. "I just wound up taking care of it."

The duchess meets my eyes, not fooled an iota. But she lets me keep that secret, at least for now. She claps her hands as if the topic is done, and the maid reappears, followed by a trail of servants bearing food. I swallow as soon as her gaze moves from me. The servants enter through double doors opposite those we entered through, but it's the only other exit except for the the the balcony. I wish Squid could fly properly.

"Let's eat! And perhaps, Master Rogers, you can tell me about Valenta? Or, Mistress Mildue, mayhap you'd be willing to share with me the story of your travels after you left the players' troupe you were in with Livinia?"

"You never told me that!" Twisty exclaims, and we all laugh.

We eat and drink and tell our tales. She, in turn, shares stories—somewhat censored, I suspect—of meeting Liv and how she nearly fell off the causeway when she was a child. Twisty is enchanted. His guard drops entirely. Mine does not. She plays her games exceptionally well, but I don't trust her. Not yet. But I share my stories, making her laugh and angling for an appearance of openness, and I scan the potential exits repeatedly, wondering if it would be best to simply run. Then again ... we're on an island.

The duchess ends a burst of laughter over one of Twisty's stories from the Rogue's circle in Valenta with a sigh. "Ah, I believe I've eaten enough. Mistress Mildue, I wonder if you might join me for a game of orlan? Master Rogers—"

"Just Twisty, ma'am, for sure," he says.

"Twisty, then." She smiles. "Twisty, would you like me to fetch Timble back, and he can introduce you to my captain of the guard? I'm sure he could use your perspective on the best way to tackle the armies waiting on the beach..."

It's perfectly pitched to appeal to him, delivered with the right level of seriousness to make Twisty feel she's not simply indulging him, and he's sufficiently at ease that he only glances at me once to check in. I nod, and he looks relieved.

I wish briefly we'd seen this coming, come up with a plan. He'd be in a much better position to have a man-to-man conversation with the guards about security on the island. The maid reappears with Timble in train in a moment, and the boys run off, ready to make mischief. I turn back to the duchess with a smile, covering my rising anxiety. "That was kind, Your Grace."

"I need some time to speak with you," she replies, rising from her seat. I follow suit, Squid curling up my arm to settle on my shoulder. It's a comfort, given the duchess's candor. "I can see he's loyal and protective, but he also cannot—nor should he have to—grapple with the magnitude of the difficulties that lie before us."

My defensiveness rises, though she's not entirely wrong. *She wastes no time, does she?* Squid observes. She at least offers me the generosity of turning toward the open doors so I don't feel observed as I take this in.

I take a deep breath, following her toward the balcony. "We are in agreement on that, Your Grace. You are very generous, once more."

The view outside is to the north, with the line of the shore to the right. The bulk of the army of mercenaries is visible from here. They look like a colony of ants. A sobering sight.

The duchess settles into a chair beside a table and gestures at the one opposite it for me. She begins, with all too efficient fingers, to lay out the game. "Your Grace." I settle into my chair, Squid on my shoulder. "I fear you may be far more than my match. It's been years since I've played."

She pauses, glancing up at me. "Mistress Mildue," she says, nothing but kindliness in her tone. "If you wish not to play, I have no objection. It was merely an adult ruse to let the boy spend some time elsewhere."

"Oh, I appreciate it!" I reply with a smile. "I just wanted to let you know."

But she sets down the counters anyway. Her gray eyes settle on mine. "Mistress Mildue, I wish to be candid with you. I can see you can play the games of diplomacy well enough, and I appreciate watching those with skill engaging it, but I do not think that we have time for such." She pours us both glasses of water from a jug with mint and lime floating in it. "As you are likely aware, I have known Livinia for some time, and she trusts me. She has had quite a tale to tell."

I turn the glass in my fingers, not meeting her eyes. "You are close, then," I comment.

The duchess smiles faintly. "We both know she has been my lover."

"We both know you have not been her only one." I bite my tongue, literally, to keep from saying anything more. I look up, and her eyes, resting on me, are calm. She's not amused, nor is she angry. "Your Grace, I apologize; that was rude."

"Nonsense, my dear girl," she replies, and her tone is so matter of fact it almost stings. "It was truth. But I am sorry; she had not told me you and she had been... She can be selective with her disclosures. In fact, I think she has told me many stories of you, but with a false name. It does explain some of the more extraordinary parts of her tale."

I raise a brow in query.

"That you would work so hard to save her."

I go still at this comment, and then smile. "I was very young when I fell in love with her. Young and foolish. But it's as they say—you never forget your first love."

The duchess smiles even more broadly at this. "Indeed. I find I never forget any love, but it has been my experience that this is ... uncommon." I return the smile, and she sighs. "Well, Livinia seems very clear on one thing. That the dragon must be handed over."

I conceal my gritted teeth, heart beating fast. Is her decision made, then? "She has been repetitive on that point, yes."

The duchess leans forward suddenly and takes my hand. "Mistress Mildue. I do not wish to overstep, and I know that I may seem ... distant or reserved. I understand that you may find it difficult to trust me, and, well, thanks to Livinia, I can hardly blame you. Had I known we had both ... supped from that honeypot, shall we say..." Her smile takes a wicked edge for a moment, and I can see why Liv is so caught in her spell. I swallow a giggle.

"If I'd known," she continues, "I would have been more open and certainly more careful to not sound dismissive. But we both know this situation has little to do with Livinia now. She rarely gets herself into trouble this serious, and now that she has, she cannot think about it with any kind of clarity. She's panicking, and it's driving her decisions. And if there is one thing we must not do when the situation is this serious, it is panic."

Relief floods through me, chased by surprise. The duchess rises, releasing my hand, and walks over to the balcony's edge to lean on the low balustrade. "Since you arrived, I have had my archivist and his librarians search my library for any tale about dragons. I have many—I have made a point of collecting stories about the Era of Storms, but I asked for more details. For the real dragons, behind the myth. At first, they refused to take me seriously, but once my veterinarian verified that the animal you carried could only be described as a dragon, they took to their research with a will."

Squid barely shifts on my shoulder, but I am tense. "Oh?" I force my tone to be casual. "And what have they found?"

She turns toward me, her face, beautiful still, grave. "I am afraid what they have found suggests this dragon is far, far more than merely a sweetener in the trade deal, if it could ever have been just that. It is not for nothing the King of Ascelin has already sent mercenaries into Rescalin. That is almost a declaration of war, and we are supposed to believe it is all because our king, that sweet, foolish man, told him that he couldn't find it?"

She shakes her head. "But it's more complicated than that. I... I am not sure, because of course the stories are legends, melodramatic, excessive, made greater, more magical and more terrible than could be real ... but as I have read further, I have come to fear that either the King of Ascelin has been taking fairytales too seriously and is prepared to go to war over them, or that this dragon—and whose hands it is in—has the potential to radically change the course of ... well, of the entire country, at least, and potentially the history of our relations with Ascelin. Perhaps of the entire world."

I blink at her a little dumbly for a moment and then laugh, hard. It's a harsh sound. "Come now, Your Grace. Let's be serious. I understand dragons were thought to be gone from this world. I know the lengths that royalty will go to to have the singular precious thing. And I do not doubt that Ascelin has a wonderful royal menagerie or something that simply *must* have a dragon in it. But surely ... it *must* be that the Ascelin king is in love with the mythology!"

Am I not special enough? Squid asks a little sardonically.

It's not that... It's just—

I told you we are masters of time, Squid says, without rancor. *You seem to forget.* For a brief moment, it shares a disorienting overlap of time that leaves me hanging in midair with nothing beneath me before the castle reappears.

Squid! Hardly the moment.

The duchess shakes her head. "I know it sounds ridiculous, but we have so little to go on, and what there is..." She purses her lips. "If it is true—has any chance of being true—it is not power I would put in the hands of an enemy king, at least not without significant thought."

All I can do is look at her, my mind churning. "I... Your Grace, I'm sorry. Did you say you *don't* want to hand Squid over?"

She smiles faintly. "My dear, I think ... Squid ... may be the first dragon in five hundred years to even exist. If it can be used as the stories suggest, then handing Squid over is like to gift a king with the power to kill off thousands, if not hundreds of thousands, or even millions. Do you understand? Entire countries, perhaps even continents. And that man came from nowhere, overthrew the rightful sovereigns, has annexed Seralin, and calls himself an emperor. Does that sound like a safe man to entrust with such power?"

Squid shifts on my shoulder. *I'm not sure what she's talking about,* it admits. *It does sound bad, though.*

I agree in my head and then nod slowly. "I had better see some of this research, don't you think?"

CHAPTER TWENTY-ONE

The library is more enormous than any I've seen before. I don't spend much time in libraries, but I've seen a few, and this is definitely bigger. Every rumor I've heard about Scyless is true.

We enter through a small door. Bar the large, uncovered windows that face the sea, every wall is covered in dark wooden bookshelves. More jut out at regular intervals from the wall toward the center of the room, where four large desks have been pushed together to create an enormous single table. Books, maps, even scrolls cover the surface. And I catch sight of a wooden box, its cover slid back to reveal a small collection of blades.

Four heads are bent over the table, but they all look up to greet us. I note that the three younger people—I'm assuming the librarians—don't rise to greet the duchess but simply nod acknowledgment and get back to what looks like feverish work. These people are very much her people.

The archivist, however, rushes to his feet, bows, kisses the duchess's hand, and announces, "Very little more progress, Your Grace, but a little."

"Thank you, Master Redney. Master, may I present Mistress Mildue? She is visiting, and as you can see, she has brought us the guest who has had you and your staff in such a to-do."

He doesn't respond to her words, for he's staring at Squid. *Should he be looking at me like that?* Squid asks. *He seems terrified or fascinated or... Are all humans like this?* It sounds delighted at the prospect.

He's probably both, and don't expect me to start drooling whenever I look at you!

"May I, Mistress?" Redney finally asks. "May I ... touch it?"

I shrug and raise a hand to help Squid down onto the table. *Please play nice, Squid.* I get a wave of indignant dismissal in return. I almost smile as Squid plays to their fascination. The librarians have realized what is happening now, and they're more attentive. They begin to *ooh* and *aah* over Squid, and I surreptitiously glance at a piece of paper to my left.

We had all thought the dragon was our greatest ally, the paper reads, in a scrawled, hasty hand, *but at the moment of our greatest need, when we were pressed from all sides, it simply turned and breathed fire over the entire battleground. Friend and foe alike died screaming. The champion, riding on the dragon's back, tried without success to turn the beast away. Finally, he was forced to draw his sword and hack through the scarlet scales of its neck, though he sacrificed his own life to do so. The dragon spiraled out of the sky, and the crater left by its impact will not soon heal. May it stand as a reminder of that dreadful day, enough that no one ever in the future shall trust in that terrible race again.*

Heat chases cold across my skin.

Squid is distracted, and it's just as well. It adores the attention and shoots me more than one comment to the effect that I should do more of this kind of thing. I give up the pretense and take advantage of its preoccupation read more thoroughly, scanning the various pages, the maps, the notes, becoming feverish.

As I do, my belly drops into my feet, and my ears roar. It is hard to see Squid in any of these stories of devastation and destruction, but it's too easy to see that, for people focused on power, my small companion is very likely to be worth going to war over.

The duchess peers over my shoulder. Her proximity is distracting, then I'm caught back into the text. "You see?" she asks, pointing a long finger.

The Era of Storms had always been so long ago, buried in the fog of legend. A terrible time when dragons began attacking humans. I'd never really paid much attention. But as I read, my heart pounds in my ears. I realize this period had entirely rewritten the map of the whole continent of Eliar. Rescalin and Ascelin had come into being only after this point, and they replaced countries that had existed for millennia. People had been driven from their homes and fled thousands of miles across the continent in search of safety. Even the common tongue, an awkward conglomeration of languages from across the continent, had its origins in the chaos.

No one fully understood the origin of the unrest. One theory said the dragons went insane and started attacking humans. The other said kings and warlords competed more and more violently for the power a dragon gave them, destroying each other's forces in order to acquire yet more land. The latter strikes me as more plausible, but I glance up at Squid, still playing for attention from the librarians and distracted from how disturbed I am.

Those seeking power would lure an enemy close, then send the dragon in to incinerate the whole field of soldiers. Field after field after field of soldiers. The death toll was awful. Sometimes, the dragons would even slaughter their own side's soldiers, turning around—so the stories ran—in the middle of the battle, killing off everyone.

There were more stories too—stories of dragons who helped a leader conquer other countries, other nations. Some fought other dragons. There were even stories of empires that rose and fell at the fiery breath of a dragon. All dust now.

Whether dragon insanity or human greed was the cause, the stories told of dragons burning and tearing down castle after castle, village after village, town after town. The destruction was total. No corner of the continent was left untouched.

I raise my head, heartbeat in my throat, to find the duchess watching me. "I see."

"And I think this point we need to ponder also..." She shuffles through a sheaf of papers until she finds the right one. "Here."

As I read, my heart sinks. Dragons, part of a massive battle that saw three hundred thousand soldiers confront each other, left only twelve survivors. Those survivors fled to Scylethe, an island, with their stories. This island.

I stare out at the sea, unseeing. Squid could be a weapon—a more serious weapon than I'd ever thought. A weapon that could reshape the world.

After hours spent poring over maps and notes and myths and drawings and even a long, ancient blade and an enormous rolled painting, I'm convinced. The little dragon whose egg I cracked open with a drop of my blood is powerful and extraordinarily dangerous. And if Squid's appearance signals the return of dragons to this world, we simply cannot let this be the return of the Era of Storms. That must be avoided at almost any cost. So much death. It makes me feel a little ill.

When evening comes, the duchess invites me into her luxurious, dimly-lit chambers to discuss the matter, and apart from maids, who have lit the fire and poured us wine, we are left alone. Part of me that wonders whether Liv might be jealous—if she even knows—then I reprimand myself for being frivolous.

"I'm going to assume from the fact you're sitting there sipping your wine that you're convinced of Esquidamelion's..."

I raise a brow. "Potential? Threat? Risk? Value?" I sigh and lean forward. "I'm convinced. A little confused, still, but convinced."

The duchess leans back in her chair, the most relaxed posture I've seen her in yet. "Well, we're definitely on the same page there." She pauses, then meets my eyes. "Here's the thing, Mistress Mildue."

"Des," I correct her.

"Des. I'm not sure if you're aware of this, but the king? He's my cousin."

I inhale slowly. "I ... assumed there was some connection," I reply. It's a lie; I'd known they were related, but I'd hoped... Well, I guess that's that. Family blood is thicker than water. And thicker than dragon blood too, I'd guess.

She nods and turns the wine glass by the stem. "Some—and I do not doubt he is one of this crowd—would think that might mean I am honor-bound to hand you over: you, Livinia, Esquidamelion, and even the poor young lad you've dragged with you from his hometown."

I open my mouth to defend myself, then realize what she's saying. "Some?"

"Some," she confirms, examining her wine. "And that creates some difficulty for us. However, I know the king. I grew up with him. We fought. We played. We shared a first love." She quirks an eyebrow. "I don't think he ever recovered."

I nearly choke on my wine. "Did *she?*"

This wrings a wicked smile from her. "If recovery is going back ... then no. But the point is, I know the man. I know him well. I saw Aleshir grow into his vices and his virtues. He's quite a good king. He's more or less just, most of the time, though he could be a little more ... adventurous. His advisers are working on him, but he is often determined to take people at their word. It's unfortunate, in a king."

I can't quite believe I'm sitting in a duchess's sitting room while she assesses the performance of our sovereign, so I sip my wine some more.

"He's a good king," she repeats, "and he's far too straightforward for this trade deal with Ascelin." She leans forward. "I don't trust Tari—the King of Ascelin—as far as I can throw him. He's wily, and alongside our good, honest, and barely smart enough king? It's a disaster waiting to happen. I suspect he is still imagining Ascelin is solely invading because Tari's in a fit of pique about not getting the egg. It probably hasn't even occurred to him that there might be something else at stake."

She eyes me briefly. "Don't get me wrong; the king has some excellent advisers. It may well be they have spotted the disproportionate reaction over a trade deal going awry. But trying to work out what might warrant such a reaction... Well, they're unlikely to have much of a clue where to even begin with working that out. And when things don't make sense to him like that, Aleshir gets frustrated and is a little too quick to simplify."

I nod. "Alright," I say, mostly to fill in the gap.

"But ... and I ask you not to repeat this, though, of course, I cannot stop you if you wish to share it ... our king, our just and virtuous king"—she sighs heavily—"he would not have the first clue what the dragon represents. He, in fact, is unlikely to see the dragon as anything more than the potential resolution of this disaster in foreign affairs."

I nod slowly, settling forward to watch the flames. "And you think there's more at stake."

"Do you not?" she asks softly.

I sigh out a breath. "You think the King of Ascelin has, well, a better sense of Squid's powers?"

She smiles a little. "Squid. I so like that you've nipped that extravagant name down to such a sweet little one. And yes. In fact, I would be shocked if he didn't. Did you know there was a central point for everything ... dragon-related, at one time? A small place called Calindrina." Even at this distance—it's snugged up in my bed—there's a mental roar from Squid. I school my face, but something must have slipped because an eyebrow quirks. Thankfully, the question doesn't follow. She continues with her lesson instead.

"Calindrina used to fall within Ascelin. It was a little odd, as my archivist pointed out, that when the trade deal the egg was part of was drawn up, the agreement was that Tari would receive almost all of the land Rescalin acquired in the War of the Shivering Waters, a border dispute some half century ago. Almost all—except for that stretch of mountains."

She tugs a side table into place between us and rises to unfurl a map across it. First, she points to a clearly marked spot: Calindrina. For a second, I can't look away. It's real. An actual place, marked on a map. I shake my head and focus. "The border?"

I can see what she means when she draws a finger along the proposed re-drawn borders between the two countries. "I think everyone thought that was some useless bit of the land we won off them in a war, which makes sense." She points to a river. "There's fertile land here and here, and that gives them access to trade routes across to the sea... and that stretch of the mountains doesn't seem that special."

"But you think they were trying to conceal an interest in Calindrina?"

She nods, silver eyes sparkling as they meet mine. I warm with her approval. "Yes. Or at least keeping King Aleshir from paying too much attention to what was there." She pauses. "Does Squid know anything about Calindrina?" Her voice is cool, but it makes me tense. I sigh.

"Yes. Not much, but it knows it needs to go there. It's been begging me to take it. Since it was... Since I found it, originally."

She nods, kindly letting me have my slip—Liv has probably told her about the blood bond anyway, or it might even be written about in her library. "And have you ever asked Squid what is in Calindrina?"

Part of my mind notes she has clearly assumed Squid can speak with me, but it's enchanting, being drawn into her mind's clever spirals. "The old dragon," I say. "It has to... Well, it's only by going there that Squid will learn everything it thinks it needs to know."

She ponders this. "Des, I think part of what is in Calindrina... Well, I think one of the things Tari is interested in, and interested in concealing his interest in, is an old tribe."

"Tribe?"

She nods, excited now. "There's a tribe who lives there. Our librarians found records of a blade from them, which should have been in the archives we are going through, but there's no sign of it so far. We will keep looking. Anyway, no one remembers them very well, and I think it's partly because no one has heard from them since the dragons stopped slaughtering humans by the thousands." She quirks a brow at her own description. "Before, they dedicated themselves to honoring the dragons, the story goes. They were the only humans who had any kind of information about the dragons. The tale runs that they were the ones who stopped the dragons from killing us."

I shiver, remembering the notes I'd read that evening. I hadn't dared to check with Squid about them—and what more would it know, anyway, without the insights it would gain from the old dragon at Calindrina? "So, this tribe ... who are they?"

She settles back in her seat, her cheeks pink. "They, my dear, are the Quenchers."

"Quenchers?"

"Quenchers of the Great Fire, they were called—that's where their name comes from, though they have their own name for themselves, I expect." She smiles. "Actually, it's not so extraordinary. There are lots of different stories about their origins, but one says that following the dragon attacks and the various disasters we are both now far too familiar with, the Quenchers intervened. They offered to serve the dragons far from humans. They did so for many hundreds of years, if my records are correct, until eventually, the number of dragons fell—they disappeared, or so the story went. And so did the Quenchers."

"You think they're still there? In Calindrina?"

"Des, my dear..." She pauses and meets my gaze. "I certainly hope so. Because if they are not, we are stuck with my research—which is not nearly enough—and a dragon who is at the center of some international... well..."

I nod slowly. "So... Your Grace..."

"Elouise, please," she says, with a small warm smile.

"Elouise," I repeat carefully, and I can't stop the little thrill that goes through me as I do. Oh gods. "What do you think we ought to be doing?"

She settles back in her chair and doesn't speak for a long moment. "Des, I think that we cannot hand this dragon over to Aleshir. If he does anything, he will hand it over to Ascelin. And if Tari gets hold of it ... I hate to think what he could do. Those stories, those old myths. I know they're not all true, but some of them are."

I nod slowly. "So ... what do we do?"

"I think we're out of options, my dear." She offers a small laugh. "I think you have to do as Squid commands and take it to Calindrina. Seek the Quenchers and the old dragon. Find out... Well, find out what it is that we don't know we don't know." She smiles as she says this as if she knows how ludicrous it is. I toss the glass from hand to hand, thinking. "I'd forgotten you were a juggler," she murmurs. "You're so different to Livinia. I forget you worked with her."

My smile is a little terse. "There are days I wish I could do the same." That subject is not safe, so I veer to more solid ground. "Very well, Elouise. You have convinced me." I take a deep breath. "I'm not really the person for this—and it would help if I knew *why* I was headed to Calindrina, what we're like to find there—but I trust you know the king, and I think you're right about the King of Ascelin." I catch the glass and meet her eyes. "I wish there was another way, but you're right."

She nods. "It will be hard; I don't doubt it. But I cannot see any other option. For the moment, the King of Ascelin is at bay. Our beloved sovereign will be riding to my rescue ... and when he gets here, and when he saves me, well, I know what price he will expect me to pay." She smiles a very tight smile. "And I fear we'd risk the world with it."

I raise a brow. She alone will carry the risk of a king's fury. "Don't let's be too clear about the risks, hmm?" I say. "I'm not sure I can handle the world riding on my shoulders. And remember, we don't even know what I'd be learning in Calindrina."

"Oh, I know," she confirms hurriedly. "My apologies, my dear. I have a tendency for the dramatic, occasionally."

I grin. "Well, it does make me want to play at hero for you," I say, and then blush momentously as regret envelops me.

She smiles, and there's only a corner of wickedness in it, but it's enough. That particular option would be profoundly unwise, and I've not drunk nearly enough for it—just enough to make my will weak. I force myself to stand. "Your Grace, I must beg my leave. If we are to depart soon, I will need every minute I can spend in an actual bed." She quirks a brow, and I curse my turn of phrase, hurriedly adding, "Sleeping!" but she nods a regal acquiescence, and I make my escape.

I pause outside the door to catch my breath. Gods. No wonder Liv is smitten. And there is no way that could not get too complicated for my poor head. Bed is safer. Much safer.

CHAPTER TWENTY-TWO

The castle is quiet as I walk back to our shared apartments along long corridors carpeted with rugs. The guards who had been on our door are gone. A sign of a change in Elouise's regard?

I'm a little buzzy from the alcohol, enough to make me entertain all the terrible, beautiful thoughts I'd managed to keep at bay while I was talking to the duchess. I linger in the corridor outside our suite, enjoying the languor. I sigh sweetly to myself, leaning against the cool stone wall and sliding one hand across my neck and down past my collarbones.

A loud "boom!" from somewhere far away startles me from my thoughts. I only know it's the sound of a catapult's load crashing against the castle wall because I fought at the Battle of Semila. I swallow and force myself to breathe slowly. It's far away. The castle is strong.

A scream sounds.

The walls are thick enough it's unlikely anyone else has heard it. I recognize it in half an instant as Liv's, and the next fear shoots through me. I am through the door in a heartbeat, my short blade ringing free of its sheath under my skirts as I leap into her room.

Des?

Not right now. Find Twist. Keep both of you safe.

I shake my head to clear it.

There's no intruder in the room. Liv is on the far side of the bed, in her night-gown, and her face is carved in fury. "He jumped," she says simply, pointing to the open balcony door. I race across to peer down into the darkness, but there's nothing there—nothing, nothing, nothing.

A moment later, guards pour into the room. I point out the window mutely, trying to clear my head and having to work hard at sheathing my dagger. I hasten over to Liv's side. "Are you alright?" I ask, ducking my head to meet her eyes.

She shoves a hand through her hair. "I'm fine. He didn't get the dragon, right?"

I shake my head but call out to Squid to be sure.

Are you sure *I can't come in?* it asks plaintively.

I imagine the reaction of the guards, and it acquiesces grumpily. A small blond head appears around the door. Twisty's face is all fear. I smile to reassure him and wave him over to us. "It's all alright, Twist," I promise softly. "Every-one's safe and sound, aren't they, Liv?"

Incredibly, Liv pulls herself together to offer more calm than I managed and nods. "Scary for a minute there, though. Sorry if I frightened you, lad." She winces as she ruffles a hand through his hair. Her shoulder still pains her.

I strive for calm as I turn to Twisty. "Can you stay with her?" I ask softly, trying not to feel the urgency I do. "I need to check on Squid."

As if the thought has activated something, I hear the roar like thunder that Squid makes whenever it is going to breathe fire.

Attack!

Fear sets me racing. I shove my way through the crowd of bemused guards and into my bedroom. A figure in black stands over the azure dragon. It looks so tiny and defenseless, and the fury that floods my veins is like a bucket of iced water thrown over me, but hot—blazing hot. Without thinking, I grab for my sword slung across the back of a chair and yank the blade from its scabbard. Then I roar, just as Squid is, and leap forward, cutting down.

Halfway through the jump, I realize who I'm facing. The big torturer from Valenta—Crainor. The club he holds is new and unbloodied. It catches my blade for a split second, breaking the momentum. I whip it back. He swings it at me, and there's no doubt he's a master with his weapons. I dodge the first time, but it's a feint, and he's already swinging at my shoulder. I swipe at him anyway, and he clocks me hard on the ear with a fist. If it had been the club, my head would've caved.

A small figure dashes in the door, and as it draws its dagger I realize it's Twist. I open my mouth to yell to him to get back, but it's too late.

The torturer raises the club, not terribly high, trying to respond to this newest threat, and as I swing my blade, it comes crashing down.

Twist screams, horrifyingly shrill, and I slice in against the torturer's shoulder as the blond head drops to the floor. I roar, fierce and wordless, stepping forward to put myself between the crumpled heap of Twist and that club. Not this time. No. Never again.

Then Squid roars an echo of mine, fury blazes through me, and this time, flame spurts straight toward the man's backside. He squeals, then yells distractedly, turning to face down the fierce little lizard. And from behind him, I swing the blade high and then down again, an arc carving deep through his collarbone and into his spine. He drops like gold in water. I pull the blade free and chuck it on the bed, ignoring the men who have finally—finally—come through the door, and I reach for Squid.

It tugs itself into my arms, talons puncturing my skin, but I don't mind. It curls its long neck around mine and settles its head against my cheek. My breath heaves in and out of me, but the calm that settles over me is instantaneous.

You're alright, you're alright, you're alright. The words echo in my head, but I can't even tell whose they are anymore. Time concertinas, just a little.

When we are both breathing evenly again, its head stirs against my shoulder. *You recognized him?*

I suddenly realize Liv is kneeling in front of me, blood beneath her slippers, supporting Twist's head. He's pale and bleeding. She reaches out to touch my knee. "Des, lovely, back you come," she says softly. "Come back to us, Des. It's safe now."

I raise my head. "We're fine, Liv. Are you alright?"

She smiles, strain around her eyes. "Phew. You were unresponsive for a good half a minute there. Don't scare us like that! The guards had no clue what to do."

Guilt flows through me. "Twist?"

"He passed out, poor lad. Physic's on the way."

We look up at a stomping and clanging of armor. Guards are forming up.

In the doorway, Elouise stands. She's dressed, astonishingly, in a white leather tunic designed for practicality, aside from the color. On one side, she wears full armor, and in her right hand is a slender blade. A page stands beside her, clearly wanting to attach the remaining pieces of armor she holds. A physic slips through the crowd to kneel at Twist's side. Elouise takes in the scene in a moment.

"Des, Liv, Twisty, Squid—to my quarters, now. Master Korel, you will go with them and tend to the lad. Whatever he needs. Elba, Kinsella, Shelain, Bestan, Carbard, Staven, Pilar, and Evart, escort them, please." I'm mildly impressed, amongst everything, that she knows the names of her soldiers. "Check the quarters thoroughly for intruders, then set a guard. I will be with you all shortly." She turns away. "Corfin, send a runner to the gate. I need a report on the situation there as soon as may be."

I realize abruptly that the quiet of night is broken. The sound of battle comes from the beachfront side of the castle. I swallow, realizing how lucky we were to have guards even respond during an attack. Corfin nods once and disappears. Elouise turns back to the remaining soldiers. "Captain Velon, report, please."

As we shuffle out, Squid still wrapped around me and the bloody blade in my hand, the captain offers a brief report of what he has seen. From what I hear, it leaves out a fair few elements, but I'm not particularly concerned about that right now. The escort is well-trained, clearly; two forward, two to the back, and four intersperse themselves amongst us. Their blades are all drawn, bar the soldier carrying Twist, and I am relieved I don't need to ready myself for danger any more than instinct already encourages me to. There's an enormous boom, and I flinch. Looks like the war machines are getting a workout ahead of what will doubtless be a dawn sally.

It's still dark when I hear the duchess outside the door to her sitting room, where Liv and Twisty and I have somehow managed to sleep. I rise slowly, still holding Squid, open the door sleepily, and she's there, bright-eyed as I cannot be. "I am sorry, my dear," she says briskly, but no less sincerely for that. "I should have expected some kind of bid, especially when I received the report that the war machines were being moved into position—perfect distraction, of course, for their assassins—but we don't have time to consider the merits of prior decisions. Will you join me in my chamber of war?"

The name of it makes me gulp, but I nod, set Squid down on my seat, catch up my blade and sheath it, then ease the door closed behind me. I catch brief sight of two tousled heads as I do: Twist and Liv sleep on. Squid gazes at me unblinkingly from where its chin rests on the arm of the couch. *I will watch them.*

I am relieved to see the eight who escorted us still standing with drawn blades in the hallway. I try not to notice Twist's blood on the armor of the one who carried him. Captain Velon has fallen in behind his mistress, his stride long and purposeful, his movements the pragmatic form of a man whose body has been given over to strength.

I follow Elouise and her captain up a long flight of stairs. At the top, we open a wooden door out onto a garden that faces out to sea, cross it swiftly, then make our way through another, heavier wooden door and up a stone spiral staircase with archers' niches cut into the stone.

The stairs open out into a round room with a large circular wooden table at the center. A fire is lit in a grate, with a series of comfortable chairs set around it. Three doors open out onto the terrace that encircles the room. Once the captain has inspected the room and balcony, Elouise asks him to wait at the base of the stairs and leads me out into the chill of the night. He nods once, his brusque, dark eyes hooded. I gaze back longingly at the golden light of the room, but she's determined.

I've spent so much time in our apartments that I don't fully understand the castle's layout, so this dizzying view under the moonlight gives me an astonishing sense of the scale of the place. Scyless, the duchess's castle, is built on an island, and it has taken over almost every inch of it. The only trees that grow here grow within courtyards, small gardens like the one we crossed to reach the tower, or the long, central gardens of the place. Tall battlements hem in the rest of the castle, made of walls that drive up from the uneven, rocky shores. In some spots, the sea crashes directly against the wall; in others, the waves break upon a tumble of smaller rocks, lipping the edge of the wall only at the highest tides.

The duchess stands with hands resting atop the battlements, her white hair whipping out of its pins. Speckles of light are scattered across the shore, and the whine and whistle of rock sent flying against the battlements is clear, each crash echoing in the night air.

She turns to acknowledge me. "I am sorry, Des," she says, her voice pitched to carry in the wind. Her use of my first name feels a little too intimate, somehow, and I regret having asked her to use it—giving myself away. "First this attack—well, both attacks—and now..." She points to dim lights far back from the shore, barely visible behind the shadowed rows of catapults. They're far away, in the hills behind the dunes, but there are many of them. "I received a bird," she tells me. "It would seem that my cousin is concerned for my welfare. They will arrive, fully, within two days."

I take a deep breath. Another resounding crash shatters the silence. I can't tell if I'm imagining feeling the battlements shake beneath my feet. Whatever peace we've earned over the past few days is gone.

Elouise turns back to me. "Des, I'm not sure if you know who the man you killed is."

I shake my head sadly. "I wish I knew who he was. His name is Crainor, and that's pretty much all I know. I've fought him before, in Valenta. And he tortured... Well, it doesn't matter. But I don't know who he works for."

She nods. "I feel like I know that name but can't recall where from. It's by the by, in the end. Ascelin have made their attempt. The king is on his way. The time for you to leave is coming swiftly. I have a plan to ensure that you and Squid get away. You will leave before sunup; it's safest that way." My belly sinks, even though I know she's right. She pauses. "Twisty will stay here with me. He is a child—or he ought to be—and I'll not have you take him into such unknowns, especially when his arm needs to heal." The half a reprimand in there stings, but I nod. What else can I do? "Livinia…"

I sigh. "Liv should stay." I try not to feel like a martyr.

Elouise turns to look at me, her silver eyes clear and glimmering in the moonlight, and I'm almost anxious about how much she sees. "I don't think she should," she says softly. "She's begging to. Has been since she arrived. I suppose you've noticed she's avoiding you."

I aim for half a smile. "That's alright," I say, possibly a little too bravely. "I'm hardly her favorite person." Apart from that strange interlude when she apologized to me, I've barely seen her. "And we had ourselves some quality time tonight."

Elouise tilts her head a little and smiles. "You two have a complicated history, I think. Usually, I can trust her to at least be honest with me—I've earned that much trust from her. But with you, I get the story in half-truths. Livinia is all too good at running away from the complexity she makes." She shakes her head. "It would be good for her to confront it, but that's not really why. She's not safe here. If I haven't missed my guess—and I rarely do where that girl is concerned—she tried to play the two sides off against each other, and neither are people who enjoy being trifled with. At some point, I will have to open my gates to someone. And whoever that is, Livinia is unlikely to be in their favor. No, Livinia will be safest very far from here." She pauses, a hint of villainy in her grin. "Besides, it seems quite clear to me that Livinia has a lot to learn, and I'm almost certain this journey will be the best teacher."

I gaze toward the shore, where the moonlight catches on the froth and churn as the waves crash. "I don't much like being Liv's teacher. And she hates it. I don't think it's a good idea."

"I've made my decision," she says, quiet but implacable, and I can see how she's royalty. Something in me arcs up at the tone, but I force myself to shrug. I can always let Liv go once I'm out of this woman's sights. The duchess might have control here, but not elsewhere.

She sighs. She reaches out a finger, places it against the edge of my jaw, and turns my head toward her. "Des, the story of you and Liv is not yet played out. She has betrayed you more than twice, and yet you saved her. And her most recent betrayal, from what I gather, was not quite as total as it could have been. She didn't announce the dragon to them. She's tried to convince you to do as she thinks is wise, but she hasn't turned on you when you refused. That's fairly remarkable for Livinia. She dislikes not getting her way. You may turn away from the significance of that if you like—I can hardly make you face it—but it will still be there."

"You're probably right," I confirm a little sullenly, wanting to let this whole conversation go. "Does she know?"

Elouise smiles. "She's not as against the idea as you seem to assume, my dear. She has begged to stay, but she has seen what is coming, and she has seen what you will do for her. And she knows that for me, things are not quite so simple. I suspect she knows you may be a better option in all of this."

"Any port in a storm," I say sardonically. The Petrus inside me won't let me say anything else.

Elouise shakes her head but is silent for a long moment. "Livinia is a lovely girl. She's beautiful and clever and funny. And inventive when it comes to sex." She meets my gaze for a moment with half a smile. "She's also complex. She has a perverse streak, likely born of too much disappointment and abandonment, which demands that she not care too much, and when she does, she will hurt herself to ensure that others cannot."

"You sound very certain of her." I can't help the frost that comes into my tone.

Elouise turns to me and takes both of my hands. The intimacy sets me afire and sets my teeth on edge. It's all too much. "She and I have been close," she affirms. "But it is seeing her speak of you, and you of her, this time, that has helped me to see her as she is."

I pull my hands away with less grace than I would have hoped for. "You seem to be under the impression—the mistaken impression—that I want her back," I say, and I regret the harshness of my tone even as the words come out. "I don't think there's anything to be sorted between her and me."

"I've overstepped," she says, her face still and impassive once more. "I apologize. I never assumed that you necessarily wanted her back. Only that there are unresolved things between the two of you."

"Not everything can be resolved," I say, and though I'm aiming for gentle, it sounds hard. I shake my head. "I'm sorry. It's been a difficult night. I spent a long time getting over Liv, and I'd done a pretty good job of it."

She quirks me a smile. "I know, my dear," she replies warmly. "You did an excellent job of it."

It's an answer that begs for more conversation, but I don't fully trust this woman—or myself with more intimacy with her—so I shake my whole body as if rousing myself. "So, anyway." I narrow my eyes at the point where the causeway from the island hits the sand. It's still covered in water right now. "I figure you have the tides sorted. Have you planned how we might make our escape? I guess you have your guards, but we'll have to move quickly if you only want to appear to be attacking Ascelese men. Taking on your own cousin is probably not a good idea."

She grins. "I'm not imagining we should be taking on anyone."

Downstairs, the duchess sends me two assistants, Caryl and Ilien, to help me pack up both my own and Liv's things. They bring almost-full oilcloth shoulder packs with them and manage—only just—to not stare at Squid, still coiled comfortingly around me. The guards check through the suite once more before I'm given free rein to pack anything from the wardrobes in my room. I spend some time longingly caressing the gorgeous fabrics of the dresses, and then finally, with Caryl's gentle guidance, dress back in the practical clothes I'd bought for myself in Cylina. I don't even ask what Ilien has put in Liv's pack.

The night seems to go on forever. Once I'm packed, Caryl and two of the guards from outside our suite lead me back through the castle and into the duchess's quarters. The duchess scribbles a signature on a piece of paper, and her manservant bows and leaves us, taking it with him. "Welcome, Des, and of course, the lovely Esquidamelion," she says, soft enough not to wake the others. "I had hoped to be able to have something of a more formal dinner before we all parted, but it will have to wait for another time."

I bow, and Squid, losing its balance a little, takes off from my shoulder and lands on the back of one of the armchairs near the duchess. "Hello, you lovely creature." Elouise slips a long finger down the length of Squid's body.

I'm going to miss her, Squid tells me.

"It's going to miss you," I repeat. "I think it feels like this place has been the worthiest of its noble heritage." This last is half a dig at Squid, but all I get back is amusement.

"I'm glad," the duchess murmurs, trailing a delicate finger along the edge of a wing. Squid stretches it out—the injured wing, nearly healed and growing in strength—to allow her to appreciate it even more fully.

"Are those packs? Can we eat?" Twisty asks, barely awake and plaintive. He gazes with big eyes in his pale, wan face at the small table, which is bowed under the weight of the food on it. I almost smile. I suspect this is as close to guilt as the duchess ever gets. "I'm hungry, and it seems likely that wherever we are going, we won't get food like this again."

My heart squeezes in my chest. Liv hasn't moved from her spot on the couch, but I realize now that her green eyes are open, and she watches wakefully. There's a potent pause. I could let the duchess tell Twisty—the gods know she was the one who made the decision—but I know this needs to be played differently.

I take a step toward him. "You're needed here," I say bluntly. "The duchess needs your help."

"I do," the duchess affirms, following my lead. "Des was gracious enough to allow me to borrow you for the coming fight."

It's a little overplayed, and for a moment, the warring emotions in Twisty are on full display: part fury and part sadness. The latter wins out, and it's turned on me. "You don't want me to go with you?" he asks, and his eyes fill with tears. My brave little man, who didn't weep even when wounded, who has shown nothing but valiant courage, loyalty, and smarts, is about to cry.

Impulsively, I step close and wrap my arms around him, careful to avoid his bandaged, splinted arm. I still feel the thrill of tension from pain through his body. His face is buried in my ribs, and we hold still for a moment. My eyes prickle, but I will the tears away. Squid clambers down the armchair onto the ground and slides across the floor to rear up, its front claws against the boy's hip. Twisty takes his good hand from around me and places it against Squid's head. We hold together like this for a long, long moment.

Twisty doesn't look at me but bends down to Squid. Squid stares into the lad's eyes, then flicks out a snaky tongue to taste Twisty's damp cheeks, then repeats it until his face is dry. Somehow, this gesture is unspeakably tender, and Twisty is left smiling by the end. Squid clambers up the boy, wary of his broken arm, and coils across his shoulders like a lady's scarf, tail and head on his chest. Twisty grins up at me. "That'd be right. Ignores me the whole trip here, and then when you're about to leave me behind, it gets affectionate."

I grin back, thankful for the forgiveness in his tone, and ruffle his hair. "The ways of the dragon are mysterious, lad."

"Mysterious and stupid," Liv puts in, and shockingly, she's almost smiling.

Squid raises its head in indignation, and we all laugh.

The duchess pours us all juice from a tall glass carafe. "To mystery and stupidity," she toasts. We raise glasses, and I drink deep.

CHAPTER TWENTY-THREE

B arely an hour later, Liv and I clamber out across slippery rocks in the dark to a small boat pulled up amidst the craggy coast behind the island. In silence, we row out to a larger shadow. One of the sailors reaches down to steady me by the arm as I climb up the rope ladder and onto the ship's deck. I can only imagine how they have got Liza aboard.

I glance back at the well-lit castle. The duchess has ordered lanterns be lit along the battlements. It's designed to look like preparedness to fight—mostlike the dawn will bring the first real sally in this battle—and welcome for her kin, but it also helps sink the sea around the island into darkness.

I turn to help Liv up as she reaches the deck. There is one lantern, and the side that faces the beach is shaded. I hope it's enough. I also wonder what the duchess is doing, having associations with smugglers—because that's what they must be.

"Take a seat, girlies, and keep your mouths shut," one of the four grizzled, bearded sailors tells us both, and Liv and I obediently take our seats, set back against the wooden wall of the pomp.

The sails snap to full, and we flee at extraordinary speed across the water. I'm accustomed to sailors yelling at each other, from my few trips by sea. This crew are silent, yet seem to know precisely what is required at any moment. It's an impressive feat.

Liv and I maintain our silence until the captain appears before us, wearing a truly amazing hat decorated with feathers of purple, green, and blue. It reminds me of the hat Liv had swept off her head the night I first met her. "Welcome aboard, mistresses," he says, grinning. "Her Grace told us you might be willful girls, but thus far, you've been remarkably obedient."

I grin back. "I was taught the best seacraft for a landlubber was to sit still and shut the fuck up," I tell him, and he guffaws, head thrown back. "Besides, doesn't the story go that noise travels easy over water at night?"

"That's true," he acknowledges.

"I've never been on a boat before," Liv announces, and I realize that, even in the dim light of the shaded lantern, she looks a little green.

"Ah dear," the captain says. "Well, if you need to heave your guts, I'd thank you to be doing it into the sea."

"*You'd* thank her?" calls the first mate from where he's checking one of the sheets. "You're not the one who'd be cleaning it up." He glances at Liv's face. "But yes, please, mistress. If you're ill, the sea's the best place for it."

All the talk of vomiting is making it an inevitability. "I shouldn't have eaten so much," she murmurs to me. "What was I thinking?"

I grin. "That we'll likely starve to death before we reach Calindrina?"

She manages a weak smile. "I might go and have a look over here." She gestures toward the gunwale to port, staggers over to it, and promptly does, indeed, heave her guts into the sea.

"That's the way, mistress," the first mate calls encouragingly. "If you've aught else in your belly, best to stay right where you are."

Liv vomits again, and I roll my eyes. A keg of fresh water stands open on the deck, so I grab a wooden cup off the hook above it, thankful my sea legs are back in action already. I carry it to poor Liv, who sucks it down greedily while I warn her to take it easy. She vomits that up as well.

"I'm sorry, Liv," I say. "I know it's horrible. But if it's any consolation, it'll settle down in a bit."

She grips the side of the boat tight, the hairpin the duchess had given her thankfully keeping her abundant curls out of the way. "Consolation? Not really." Her eyes glimmer with annoyance. "Just get me another cupful, will you?"

After restocking her supply, I head downstairs into the belly of the ship. Squid has been providing me with silent commentary since it was loaded onto the boat. All our packs, including the oilcloth shoulder bags I'd packed in the middle of the night, are in a pile on a pallet with some extras, and beside them is a large wooden crate. The duchess considered it wise to hide Squid from the sailors. "Let's not give them anything to wonder about," she'd told me. "You're secret couriers for me. Let's leave it at that."

Squid pokes a narrow reptilian snout out of one of the handholds of the crate. *You are meant to be a secret, Squid,* I tell it.

I know, Squid says, caught between nonchalance and guilt, *but this is boring. It was exciting at first, but I don't like boxes. And besides, from what you're sharing, I think I want to be up on deck.*

I grin and stroke what I can see of the snout. *It won't be long, I promise.*

In the very center of the ship's hold, where the movement will be the least, rough wooden shelters have been put up. Inside are Quicksilver and Liza. They're quiet, and I peer through a crack between the planks. The two shift from hoof to hoof with the movement of the ship. I can tell they're anxious—Quicksilver is sweating—but there's little to be done. Better not to distract them by speaking to them, so I clamber back up the steep stairs and onto the deck.

One of the sailors—grizzled like the rest—offers me a cup as I appear. He grins and nods, and I sniff at the cup as I take it. Alcohol. Some kind of rum, mostlike, but the scent of it is so fierce it's hard to work it out. I lean against the edge of the gunwale, staring out at the little I can see of the waves, and swallow it down.

It burns a fiery line to my belly and steals my breath, but it makes me grin fiercely too. It feels almost foolish—this brave, reckless feeling—like maybe it's cockiness gone a step too far, but the past few weeks have been filled with so much desperation, exhaustion, and fear that I haven't felt quite myself. It's a relief to know that fierceness isn't gone altogether, even if it's mostly courage earned through drink.

Liv appears beside me. I steel myself for the conversation, but I've got no clue how to begin it, so I start with what I feel most worried about. "It was her decision. The duchess. Not me."

"I know," she says softly. Her eyes glimmer a little in the low lantern light. "She was clear enough about that." She dips her head away, and I realize I've misplayed.

"I am glad to have you along." It's awkward because we can both hear it's not quite true. I try again. "Company is good."

Liv's smile deepens, a dimple punctuating her cheek, and irritation blossoms in my chest like I've been played, but she didn't even need to do anything. I played myself. "Company *is* good." Her voice is soft and a bit too warm.

"Feeling better, then?" I ask, over-cheerful. "I threw my guts up for six hours first time I was at sea."

She wrinkles her nose, and Squid comments, *Nothing like discussing disgusting things to end awkwardness, right?*

"It was with Petrus," I say finally, to have something to speak of. "We were acting as contract couriers for a merchant with delusions of grandeur and all the attendant paranoias. Petrus laughed at me nonstop, all the way out to sea. It felt like I was going to turn myself inside out and slip over the edge into the abyss."

Liv looks a little green, and guilt twinges, so I give in and try to change the subject again. "Better than the desert, though, if you ask me. Although ... there is the jungle too, I guess. Not the biggest fan of snakes—and spiders as big as your hand... That's something I could take or leave, with a clear preference on the latter." I'm babbling, so I stop, more for my sake than for hers. Why should I be trying to make her feel comfortable, anyway?

Liv sighs, meets my eyes, and slumps her shoulders. "Alright, I can't do it," she says ruefully. "What did you think of the duchess?"

I can't work out what I think about this topic of conversation, so I shrug. "She's nice," I say noncommittally.

"Nice?"

I smile a little. "Yes. Nice. She's also far too smart for her own good."

"True enough," Liv says wryly. "I've always had a weakness." She pauses. "You don't think she's beautiful?"

I remember the crawl of desire from that late-night, wine-fueled chat, and let my smile show it. "She definitely has her charms," I say.

"Did you sleep with her?" Liv asks, with a tense note that isn't quite jealousy.

"No," I say, then pause. "I don't have to sleep with everyone that comes in view to prove something."

Liv grins at me, weakly but sincerely, and wrinkles her nose. "Are you trying to hurt me, Des? Because I'd have thought you knew by now that I'm never going to apologize for sleeping with people. And I don't think you should either."

"You apologized to me for sleeping with Petrus," I tell her bluntly. "So, you know..."

She sighs. "Des, I'm sorry because I didn't do that just for desire. Petrus is nice and all, but you could've trained him better." This has a note of snark in it, and I open my mouth to say I'd never slept with him but close it with a snap. Is she playing me? "I did it because I wanted to... Well, I wanted to get back at you for leaving me."

I wish this line of conversation had never started. "Yep."

Liv sighs. "Don't be like that, Des. Anyway, we were talking about Elouise. I have been trying to work her out."

"Work her out?" I play at stupid.

"Yeah. Why she has such a hold on me." She flutters her lashes melodramatically in the dim light. "I sound sarcastic, I know, but I actually mean it. I don't understand. As soon as she's around, it's like I lose any capacity to ... well, to take any control."

I eye her, sidelong. "She is definitely always in control," I offer, stingy.

Liv narrows her eyes and eases herself down to the deck, settling back against a coil of rope. "That might be it. I guess I'm used to getting my way."

I lower myself down beside her. "It's not quite control," I finally say, feeling like I'm giving something away. "It's authority. She just has it." I hesitate, trying to work out the wisdom of recounting any of the conversation between me and Elouise, then shrug. "When she says a thing, it simply is and will be the case." I narrow my eyes. "But it's different from you. You get control because you manipulate." She gives me a glance that is half-amused and half-exasperated. "What? It's true! But she doesn't manipulate, and she is honest."

"Alright, alright, I've no right to compare myself to that paragon of virtue."

I grin. "That wasn't quite what I meant, Liv, but it's true you've no right. She's a noble, and you and I... Well, we're two-bit players."

"I'm at *least* a five-bit player," she rejoins, also grinning. After a moment of silence, she frowns a little, and half smiles. "I feel so ... well, so not in control around Elouise. I love it when I'm there. It feels like relief. But when I leave, I look back on it and I feel like a completely different person. And like I've been... like I've shared too much of me."

I smile. "Somehow, I told her more truth than I would've imagined I'd trust anyone with," I admit. "She's pretty extraordinary."

Liv grins. "And you didn't even sleep with her." She shakes her head. "Seriously. I didn't think anyone could teach me anything more about sex. Honestly. I've slept with courtesans and royalty and farm boys. I thought I'd seen it all; thought I knew everything anyone could make this body do..." She shrugs. "But I was wrong."

I almost smile. She's like a cat, voluptuous in her enjoyment of her own body. I'd always known that, but it's one of the nicer things to revisit. "Sometimes it's good to be wrong, I guess."

She chuckles, one arm cushioning behind her head, eyes closed. "Indeed it is. If we survive this and make it back there, you should definitely find a way into her bed."

I frown a bit. "You wouldn't be jealous?"

She smirks, eyes still closed. "Oh, Des. We're not together. Besides, I know you don't understand this at all, but I really think you should see what pleasures she can wring from a body. It's kind of amazing. Like an art form."

I shake myself, realizing I'd somehow wound up talking about sex with Liv. Again. And she's relaxed, reclining back as if we were at ease with each other once more. I sigh. "I've never understood you, Liv," I say, angling for light and playful, but somehow winding up with some angst in there.

"I know," she grins, opening one eye a crack. "But that's half the fun."

"Half your fun," I retort. "I'm not that huge a fan."

Liv opens both eyes. "Honestly, Des. If you were drawn to simple and easily understood, you wouldn't have abandoned Petrus. He was absolutely, totally, and completely head over heels for you, and he was simple as sunshine. And you left him. If that doesn't tell you something, I don't know what does."

Her description of my leaving Petrus is a tad overwrought, but I bite my tongue against the defensiveness. "Are you telling me I'm destined to always be trying desperately to understand people I'm destined never to understand?"

She smiles and leans toward me. "Des ... there are worse things than that, believe me."

Her smile is warm, and that curve of her lips luscious. A tingle runs from my breasts to the warmth of my sex, and my body feels defined by this triangle. All I want to do is lean forward—it wouldn't take much—and lose myself in the warmth and softness of her mouth. I can almost hear the dragon chuckling in my head, but it's not enough to quash the longing.

"I loved you, Liv," I say, as if this explains something.

"I know you did, lovely," she says, her smile traced with sadness. "And I loved you too. But I barely understand myself. I don't know why you ever expected to understand me."

I'm caught, longing and desire and frustration tied together. Then I scrabble upright, out of the intimacy we've somehow made between us on this deck. I sigh, staring out at the dark seas, and don't reply.

I've barely slept on my pile of ropes when the dawn stretches rosy fingers above the horizon. As I raise my head, the captain, catching the movement, nods a good morning and says, "I'm thinking this delivery might be slightly more complicated than expected, mistress."

I frown and heave my stiff body upright. As soon as I clear the railing on the deck, my heart sinks. There, on the horizon, arrayed only a short distance from the shoreline, is an armada of ships, all flying the Ascelese flag. They're round bellied with enormous battened sails on multiple masts. Designed to disgorge the maximum number of soldiers onto foreign shores. Fuck.

"Where did the duchess suggest you let us disembark?"

He points. "In behind that promontory there's a town called Hathway. They have a decent jetty, so it would make a good place to make sure the horses and your package can be unloaded."

I nod. "But to get to Hathway, we have to sail past that lot, right?"

He nods. "I don't know what might be going on with Ascelin. We usually have a good relationship with them, but if I don't miss my guess, there were Ascelese soldiers amongst those mercenaries on the beach at Scyless." He cocks his head, and his gaze is considering. "Nothing to do with you, right? Ascelin flags both at Scyless and here?"

I shrug carefully, playing for nonchalance. "Might be, might not be. I'm not clear what they were doing at Scyless, and I'm not so far in Her Grace's favor that she shared that information with me." I lie easily, my mind racing. Unlikely that there are any simple connections between the soldiers at Scyless and the armada here. If there were, the fleet would probably be heading south to bolster the attack on Scyless rather than hanging about further north. I frown and shield my eyes from the sun. "Wait. Shit. Are they ... *moving?*" It's as if they heard my thoughts.

The captain pulls the telescope from the belt at his waist and peers through it. "They are. This way," he says brusquely. "Time for us to get the hell outta the way."

"How're we going to do that?" I ask, eyes wide. "We need to go north!'"

"We can go north. After those warships have passed us by on whatever business they're pursuing." He gives me a steely look. "The duchess paid us well for your transport—well enough I knew this wasn't a contract to be asking questions about—but if her tight lips and yours sink my bloody ship, I'll haunt the both of yez."

I swallow hard. "So we'll sail for the coast? As agreed?"

The man nods only once, and it's clear enough he's pissed. I nod back and head out of sight down below, looking for Liv.

I find her swinging in a hammock, fast asleep. She always looks so innocent when she's sleeping. I force myself not to wait, not to gaze on her like I would have once, not to take the opportunity to consider her beauty, and instead put a gentle hand on her shoulder.

She awakens slowly—she's always awakened slowly—and smiles sleepily at me. "Good morning, lovely," she murmurs, and the greeting—a long habit from when we were together—makes my heart squeeze up in some mysterious way. I can't tell if it hurts or not.

"Good morning," I say, my tone not quite as cool as I might have wished for. "Time to rise and shine."

She snaps to alert. "Something wrong?"

"Something might be. Best to be prepared."

She nods and throws back the blankets. She's in her shift, and I look aside, but not quickly enough to miss her nipples peaking the fabric over her chest. A bandage is still wrapped around her shoulder. "I'll be up in five."

"We might be best to stay down here," I tell her in response, after barely a moment's preoccupied hesitation.

As if in confirmation, one of the grizzled old sailors ducks his head down the stairs and peers at us. "Best you stay down below, lassies," he tells us both, then pauses, distracted at the sight of Liv in her shift. Liv smiles and stretches while he watches. I roll my eyes. He finds his words after a moment of catching flies, mouth ajar. "Not sure if they're friendly or not, and we're hoping they're friendly enough to let us pass."

His head disappears, and a moment later, the ship rolls abruptly, and I can tell we're heading—very swiftly—for the shore.

I do not like being in here when we might be in danger, Squid announces in my head. *I do not like it at all.*

I know, I say. *I get that. But the last thing we want is these sailors deciding the simpler solution to this is handing you over.*

A grumpy concession. I take a deep breath. The packs are all ready to go so we can leave at a moment's notice. The only thing we need now is some food and we'll be good to disappear once the ship makes land. I sigh, dreaming briefly of warm porridge or scrambled eggs, and settle myself down on a coil of rope to root through our packs to find us breakfast.

When breakfast is done, I poke my head out on deck. "How're we doing?" I ask the same sailor who told us to stay below.

"We're not the booty they're after, it would seem," he says, gimlet eyes bright, "but the captain wants you gone quick as may be. And he'd best not see you up here before he's ready for you. I don't know what you did, but he's mighty unhappy with you *and* Her Grace right now."

I swallow and nod once, then head below again.

CHAPTER TWENTY-FOUR

"**O**n deck now, passengers!" The bellow is designed to be rousing, and Liv and I scurry upward.

The sight that greets us on deck—the jetty of Hathway—makes my heart buoy for all of a moment before I realize the full gravity of the situation. Behind us, further out to sea, is the whole Ascelese armada. They're sailing south, away from us. "Thank the blessed heavens," I say to the captain.

"Indeed," he replies, his brows beetling. He seems unimpressed with this latest cargo.

I stare out toward the Ascelese ships again, and then narrow my eyes. "What's that?"

The captain's gaze swings to follow my arm, and he swears fulsomely. One smaller junk bobs between us and the flotilla—the only one that is headed this way. A scout.

The captain's fierce eyebrows take on a life of their own, and his face reddens with anger. "We have no time. We need to unload right this second, and you need to flee. That junk is a scout, nothing more and nothing less, but at the barest signal from them, we'll be facing down all of that." He waves his arm eloquently at the forest of masts out at sea. "And that is *not* survivable."

I draw a deep breath and focus on the jetty. "So why are we not at the jetty yet, then?"

"Because of that." He gestures to a flag flying above a stone building—the flag of Ascelin. I scan the waterfront of the little town and realize it is eerily quiet.

I swallow, but Liv asks the question. "What does that mean?"

The first mate joins the conversation. "Farked if I know, but it looks like the Ascelese army has decided this is their first foothold in Rescalin. Can't know what you'll be facing onshore."

I swallow again, wondering if I should plead with them to drop us elsewhere. Even Tyrasene can't be far from here. But another glance at the captain's beetling brow puts paid to that notion. "Alright. So we need to be ready to go as soon as we hit the jetty. I'll prepare the horses."

"And your package," the captain puts in, and his eyes hold mine, unrelenting. "How are you going to transport it without a cart?"

I blow out my breath between pouting lips, thinking. "I'll repack it in our packs," I say. "It'll be fine. So long as Liv and I and the horses are delivered safe onto the jetty, you'll be paid."

The first mate eyes me sideways. "Let's hope Her Grace agrees with you," he says, then strides away, yelling orders.

"Something about this is fishy," the captain says, his voice rough with suppressed fury, "and I've not the time nor inclination to investigate. But you had best not be leading me astray, girlie, or my first cut will be for you, duchess or no." He pats his cutlass meaningfully, and I swallow, nod, and hasten away.

Liv follows me downstairs. "I don't like this." Her brow is furrowed. "This is much more dangerous than Elouise could have known. I don't think it's safe."

I offer her something between a wince and smile. "It's not safe. It was never going to be safe." I lick my lips. "We were always going to have to deal with this at some point or another. Once we're out of Hathway, I think we'll be fine." We can both hear the lie, I have no doubt, but we both need to focus on this problem, not the thousands awaiting us on the way to Calindrina. "Let's saddle the horses. We're not going to have time for them to be anxious when we're disembarking, so you need to take a deep breath and calm yourself. Quicksilver's an antsy enough beast as it is; she doesn't need your anxiety too."

Liv glares at me but nods, twisting her hair back into a tight bun. I grab Liza's saddle and an apple from our packs and ease my way into her stall. She's glad to see me, but I can see the whites of her eyes. This is going to be tough. If Liza's nervy, Quicksilver will spot it.

"Hello, beautiful girl." I pat her neck gently, forcing myself to take the time. A minute here might save us going into the water between the ship and the jetty. "I'm sorry, I know you hate being at sea." Liza eyes me sidelong, and I smile at her. "Here you go." I let her snuffle at the apple in my hand and throw the saddle over her back.

"We're going to be off soon, Liza," I say, hoping to all the gods her preternatural ability to understand me doesn't give out, "and it's going to be dicey. We will have to get to the jetty and then fly out onto that road into the mountains. No time to stop in town. In fact, we might have some not very friendly types in town, so we're going to need to leave quick smart."

I should help with that, Squid adds.

I know you'd love to, and I'd love you to, but it's safer if we look like we don't have you with us. If they see you, they will follow.

They'll probably follow anyway, Squid says, a little grumpily. *And if this is about my wing, it's healed. I can fly. It doesn't even hurt now.*

I smile a little as I lace the girth through the buckle. The dragon is restless after being trapped inside the crate, and who could blame it? *They might,* I allow, *but they might leave us be, and that would be better. So, let's try my way first, hmm?*

Very well, mortal. I will allow you to make your mistakes. Squid is haughty, hearkening back to its ways of communicating from when we were first blood bonded.

I echo its tone. *You are very generous, dragon.* It responds with a hint of amusement, but only a hint.

I tie the packs to Liza's saddle, whispering to her about how strong she is. Liv is doing the same next door, telling Quicksilver she's brave and smart. I can only hope Quicksilver will follow Liza's lead.

"I'll be back in a moment, girl," I tell the horse, and head back out into the open area where the wooden crate containing Squid is.

"Alright, dragon," I say aloud. "Time to pack you up."

I lever up the top of the crate, prying nails out of the wood. The second the lid is loose, Squid is pressing against it. *I didn't know you were so unhappy in there,* I say sarcastically as it bursts out into the small space, spreading its ever-growing wings. *No, no, don't fly! You'll scare the horses.*

Humph. I almost grin but manage to restrain myself. It settles down, fixing me with a sapphire eye. *Alright, human. How are we going to do this?*

I unfurl my bedroll. *Not many options, I'm afraid.*

You have to be joking, the dragon says, dropping the fancy talk. *I can't go in there.*

You need to be hidden. I grasp after patience even as I'm bracing for the impact of the ship against the jetty at any moment. *We can't afford for you to be seen.*

The dragon's tone is unamused. *So let me get this right. You want me to be rolled up in your bedroll and laced to the back of the horse...*

"That's the plan," I say aloud. "That is, indeed, the plan."

With a mighty glare, the dragon cautiously clambers onto the blanket. *I'll be interested to see how you manage this.*

Like ... so. I tuck the blanket around it and swiftly roll it up, like usual. Alarm and anxiety mixed with a little dizziness emanates from the dragon, but it's quickly done. I buckle the bedroll to itself and, staggering, carry the bundle into Liza's stall.

The horse eyes me sideways, almost amused, as if she understands exactly what happened, and holds extra still while I tie the bedroll to the back of the saddle.

Alright, dragon? I aim for perfunctory, but probably let slip a note of amusement.

The dragon's response feels almost muffled. *Fine.*

Good. Now make sure you coil your tail in, won't you? I tug on the narrow tip sticking out of the bedroll. It disappears up into the blanket. *Can't have the sailors wondering what it is we have in here and thinking better of putting us ashore.*

"Good to go, Liv?" I call.

"She's anxious," the reply comes, "but she's ready."

I pat Liza. "Hopefully, she'll play follow-the-leader. Because you'll be fine, right, girl?" Liza blows air out of her nostrils as if to say it'll be a piece of cake. I can only hope.

A moment later, the ship connects with the dock. "Now!" comes the bellow from upstairs. I take off, scrambling up the stairs holding Liza's reins. She follows, the gorgeous beast, brave as ever. On deck, Liza staggers a little sideways with the movement of the ship.

"Here, here!" yells the first mate. "Get you gone, girlies!"

I jump into Liza's saddle, and she staggers again a little, but we head for the first mate. The gangplank crashes into place, and before it's even fully secured, I urge Liza down onto the jetty.

She moves too slowly for my jangling nerves, and we're high above the deep water, but she makes it. Once she hits the jetty, she settles, the tension dropping out of her as she shakes her head and whinnies. I turn her about, hoping against hope Liv is behind me. She's not—of course, she's not—and Quicksilver is at the top of the gangplank, ignoring her rider. Liv's eyes meet mine, and she looks terrified.

"Wait here," I tell Liza, and scramble out of the saddle and up the gangplank. Every nerve in my body wants to haul against the reins, tugging Quicksilver down, but I know that will only make her dig in her heels.

"Hello, beautiful." I greet her trembling with a gentle hand to the velvet nose. "I know it's scary, but the ground is right there. We're going to take it easy."

I take hold of the reins, ignoring Liv and my desire to glance over my shoulder toward the town, and walk backward down the quivering gangplank. It's much worse doing this slowly, but I school myself to calm and whisper nothings to Quicksilver. She follows, cautious and anxious, but with eyes on me. That's the best I could hope for.

As she puts her first hoof onto the jetty, the first arrow spears through the air, striking the side of the ship. Another follows, slamming into the wood of the mast, and another into the gangplank. Quicksilver tosses her head back. Liv screams.

I lose grip on the reins, dodging sideways just in time as she takes off, a silver streak heading straight—too straight to avoid the arrows—toward the shore and the stone-paved docks that line it.

Like some kind of miracle, Liv keeps her seat. "Fuck!" The cry blows back toward me, barely audible.

Swearing, I haul myself into Liza's saddle, ducking low, and take off. Arrows whistle overhead.

"Des!" Liv cries, and I can see her yanking hand over hand on the reins, desperate to regain some control of her steed. "Which way?'"

"Right! Head right!" I scream back, and thank all the gods, Quicksilver finally responds to her rider as they hit the end of the jetty, and skittering sideways on the stone, they head right along the waterfront.

I finally make out the green-clothed archers concealed in the upper windows of the double-story warehouses that line the docks. If we stay, we'll be sitting ducks.

"Left!" I bellow. "Liv, into the town!"

As we hit the end of the jetty, I yank right and then left on Liza's reins, and she weaves gracefully, heading directly into a roadway going north. I had been hoping the warehouses would give way to wide streets and cover, but instead Hathway is cramped, double-story buildings leaning in toward each other over cobbled streets. At least this way, we're out of range of the archers. I hope. I guide her right at the first opportunity, hoping against hope to find Liv.

Green-clothed soldiers appear on foot before me, and I dodge left. They run after me a short way but give up quickly. I lead Liza to the right again, and an arrow strikes sparks off the stone where my head was a moment ago. Liza lunges forward, pushing for more speed.

I hear hoofbeats before I see them. Liv is wild-eyed, and Quicksilver is little better, but Liza is alert enough to slow a little as she joins them, enough to keep Quicksilver from panicking.

"We have to get out of here," I yell to Liv. "This place is overrun."

Liza takes the lead, and thank all the gods she does, because, we're confronted with a square full of soldiers, all afoot. I guide Liza right, aiming for the shortest route out of the enclosed space and toward the road east. A soldier steps to the left of our path, clearly angling to cut the girth, and I swear as I tug Liza left and she runs him down. I grip tight to the pommel and swing out from the saddle to cut down another soldier in green.

Liv, displaying better riding than I've seen from her yet, manages to keep Quicksilver directly behind us, out of the action but following in our path.

There are too many behind us, though, racing into the narrow streets around the square like floodwaters. They're going to be blocking the way out; that much is clear. We don't have long before the vise closes. Fuck.

Let me out, Squid says, something between pleading and command in its tone.

No. The risk will be greater if they see you. I'm almost yelling in my own head, but it's hard dodging enemies and talking at the same time.

The risk is we all die, Squid tells me matter-of-factly. *Wouldn't it be better to at least get out of town? This is a death trap!*

"Des!" Liv screams, and when I glance back, she's pointing ahead at a crowd of green-clothed soldiers. Fuck.

Let me out, Squid whispers.

I dodge right, then left again, but there is another crowd of soldiers at the end of the street. I duck into an alleyway to the right, and it's thankfully empty. But then we follow it around a corner, and confront a small squad waiting for us in the T-intersection, two abreast in the narrow space.

It's too late to pull back, so Liza slows enough that when we reach them, she rears back and brings her hooves down fiercely, taking out the first row. I swing my sword like a cudgel, taking out the two to the right and then dodging left as Liza takes out the other two. She whinnies shrilly, and I know she's been cut. I can only hope it's not too bad a wound. The girth at least seems to still be in place. I guide her right, and we gallop off into the empty alley.

Quicksilver whinnies high in pain, but she follows us like a bat out of hell. "She's fine, just a shallow cut," Liv yells, "but we need to get out of here, Des!"

I turn left at the first junction I hit and urge Liza on at the sight of the blessedly empty street. Quicksilver's hooves are fast behind us, and abruptly, we are spat out of the dense buildings and paved streets and onto a narrow, uneven roadway of dusty yellow cutting through bare earth. It's clearly not the road we're after—a major trade thoroughfare which must be further north—but it's something. We don't slacken off but rather go even faster.

"Des!" Liv's tone bears a warning, and I glance over my shoulder. Panic threatens, and I haul in a breath to settle it. A horde of green-clothed soldiers pours out of the town and into our wake. I swear a long string of nonsensical curses as I frantically catalog our options.

Set me free, the dragon whispers, and I bite my cheek hard. The pain clears my head. There are too few choices left. Whatever inexplicable reluctance I'm feeling about turning a dragon against humans is so much vanity right now.

As you wish. Any chance of sneaking out of Hathway without suspicion is definitively gone anyway.

"Do not slow," I yell to Liv. "We have to keep going."

She nods, eyes wide.

I yank the dagger from my waist, turn about, and cut at the leather buckling my bedroll to itself.

As it unfurls, the dragon spirals in a barrel roll out of it. For a long moment, it seems to spin in midair behind Liza's fluttering tail, a long blue lizard, its wings bound in tight. Then Squid spreads its wings and soars upward, back toward the soldiers.

I stare over my shoulder as it spears toward them. It dives, wings clamped to its sides—clearly a lesson learned from the arrow that punctured its wing—and then spews flame like a tumble of coals falling from a too-full fire over the first line.

The screams reach us, and I realize this is our only chance to escape. "On!" I scream to Liv. *I'm trusting you, dragon*, I say.

There's no response but a fierce, angry glee. I am desperately glad the dragon is on our side, but I can't deny the curl of dread in my gut. Elouise's books have made me wary.

The horses stretch out even further. The narrow road we're on soon joins up with a main road, like a straight line between Hathway behind us and the mountains ahead and to the north. There's a short plain bisected by the road, but my eyes can't make out what happens to it when it hits the mountains. I can only hope we find cover there. And a road.

CHAPTER TWENTY-FIVE

We ride hard, and the horses are starting to wilt as we reach the foothills. The mountains, craggy and jungled and wild, loom above us, blocking much of the afternoon sun.

With the sun setting behind us, the road thankfully begins to wind, which will give us at least some cover from the spying eyes that are doubtless going to be following us from behind. No matter what the dragon has managed to pull off, someone's still in charge back there, and they will send scouts, especially now they'll have had reports of a blue dragon breathing fire.

They knew anyway, Squid says. It's unnervingly comforting to know it's still close and still alive. *Or they would have found out. At least this way, they'll be a bit wary of following us.* In its tone is a kind of glee—a pride, different to the performance of pride it has shared with me since its first days. A pride born of action.

And, I can't help but notice, of killing. I try to keep my mixed feelings about it to myself, but I've not yet found a way to regain that privacy.

As we hit the foothills, jungle springs up on either side and the road curves right, tucking into darkness behind a small crest. Small, but enough. I drop back to a trot, and Liza's head begins to hang in weariness. Quicksilver still looks a little wild-eyed, but she slows too, and Liv speaks softly to her, stroking her neck and praising her.

"Think we're safe?" Liv asks after a moment.

My laugh is rough. "Well, no ... not in the least. But Squid has kept them from being right on our tail, and that will help if we can find some cover somewhere in these mountains."

She's silent for a moment, and I glance sideways at her. "They're just so ... big," she comments, gazing up. A rare moment of awe.

I glance up. She's right. The mountains seem to appear out of nowhere. We're in the foothills, but even here, the trees are narrow and pole-like, tall, and garbed in vine. In short order, the foothills give way to karst, abrupt limestone towers thrusting toward the skies, some with alarmingly sheer sides. They are covered in dark green trees, plants, and vines, with gold, white, and gray stone showing through where the sides are simply too vertical for anything to grow.

It's hard to imagine any paths through a place like this—ways that we don't have to carve out ourselves with machetes. The trees ahead of us seem even taller. I gaze up, trying to track a potential trail through the giant, precipitous karsts. Between them, I hope, because over would involve abandoning our mounts immediately and climbing sheer rock faces. I regret not playing a bigger part in our packing arrangements. I hope Elouise knew what she was doing and that we have some proper clothing for these conditions, not to mention something machete-like. I'd rather not blunt my blade. I slap at a mosquito.

"Yep, huge." I sigh. "The map said there was a trade route, which will get us at least as far as... I can't remember the name of the town, but it's only a few miles into these mountains. But, any way we go, there's no way we're getting over them unless we have a chance to rest the horses. They're worn out."

Liv nods slowly, and I can almost feel her reconciling herself to the reality before us. "So, really, we need somewhere safe to rest."

I laugh again, a rough, humorless sound. "Well, safer. I doubt we're going to find another Elouise here."

Liv bites her lip and falls silent. I wonder idly how long it will be before she tries to run.

I glance to my right. A gleaming blue streak heads for the mountains, and I watch as it shoots ahead of us, weaving as it hits the crags.

Any chance of some cover, Squid? I ask hopefully. *We all need to rest, and I'm afraid it's not safe on the road.*

The blue streak spirals in dizzying circles, and my gaze follows until I can't make it out. It's searching, but we wait a long time for a reply. The golden light of the sun disappears, concealed by the crest behind us, leaving us in shadow. Beneath the heavy foliage, it was already dim, but now it's almost dark. I slap another mosquito, too late to avoid the itch. I'm starting to get anxious when the dragon finally reappears, flying low.

I've found some shelter, Squid announces, *over the next ridge. A cave.*

Misgivings make me edgy—most of the caves I've ever found have already been inhabited—but they're overwhelmed by a sense of gratitude. We might even have a place to rest for the night. Then I sigh, looking up at what Squid described as a "ridge," and angle south with the road. Sometimes going around is the better option.

It is, of course, harder to reach the cave even than I had imagined, and Liv and I are breathless and weary by the time we gain the mouth. The path off the main road is narrow and grows narrower, and goes from steep to steeper, until we have to dismount and climb, the horses struggling along behind us.

The cave itself doesn't quite live up to promise. It looks like another fold in the rock—a crack that's wider at the bottom and narrows at the top—but behind it, a tunnel extends back. We enter uneasily, stopping as soon as we are covered by shadow from prying eyes, and wait for our eyes to adjust to the twilight inside.

The cave walls are covered with alarming formations that look like long pointy teeth stretching down to the ground from rounded upper jaws, concealing gods know what inside these stony jowls. The rock is rough and sandy-looking. At least the uneven walls are good for hiding us, if someone comes looking.

The sun is low now, casting the crags in rose gold and shadow. I lean on my knees for a moment, half catching my breath and half stretching out my back. It's been a long, rough day. I think of the sailors on the ship and hope they found their way to safety after letting us land.

Liv is, of course, already dismounted and settled back against a rock. She looks exhausted, though inevitably no less beautiful for that. I open my mouth to tell her we need to make sure the cave is safe, care for the horses, unpack, and prepare food and all, but I stop myself. We need to check the cave, that much is true, but if we need to move on and find somewhere else to sleep, a moment of rest won't have done her any harm.

"Alright, you can have a rest," I say. "But if we can stay here, we're going to need a fire at some point." I direct a pointed glance her way, but her eyes are already closed.

As I'm fumbling with the feedbags for both horses, Squid soars low into the cave opening. "I hope they didn't see you," I say aloud in greeting.

Of course not. The tiny creature's pride has only grown. *I was careful.*

"You're also blue and bright and flashy." Liv gives me a sidelong look, rousing to wonder if I'm talking to her. I busy myself once more. The horses munch, and the smell of chaff fills the small space. *It's time.*

We could stay here, where we know it's safe, Squid observes.

I do not want to waken in the night to company. Especially not company with big teeth and claws. Better to know now.

"I'm going to check out the rest of the cave," I tell Liv. "You stay here. Don't unsaddle the horses. If we need to get out of here in a hurry…"

She nods and then goes back to snoozing. At least she's got that much of life on the road covered. You snatch sleep at any possibility; it's a rule. I try not to resent her.

Fatigue makes my limbs feel like lead, but I force myself to sort through the saddlebags on Liza's back. Elouise knew her business—or hired someone who did—because everything I could possibly have hoped might be there is there, folded, coiled, and tucked neatly into pockets. It's vaguely heartening. I don't think I've ever been so prepared for a trip, and certainly not when I was in charge of it! Eventually, I find a box of tinder and flint, a coil of waxen rope, and a small bag of dried pine resin. Clearly, someone thought we might wind up in caves. Somehow it's comforting to think that the stories Elouise and Twisty might be telling each other about our journey might even be vaguely accurate ... if they're not too busy with the siege.

I find a branch on the ground at the lip of the cave, incise the end, insert a piece of pine resin, and wind the waxen rope around one end, cutting it from the coil and tucking the end in. Behind one of the stony mouth formations to block the light from prying eyes, I kneel to light it with the flint. It takes a minute, and I let the wax drip a little before I sigh, grit my teeth, and stand.

I could've lit that, you know, Squid observes.

Now you tell me, I respond, forcing a smile. *I'm off. Are you coming to defend me?*

The little dragon—who is now almost as long as Liza, I realize abruptly, from snout to spiked tail-tip—is coiled up beside Liv. *How about you call me if you get into trouble?*

I raise a brow and shrug. *As you wish. But any prey is mine.*

The dragon sends me a chuckle—because, of course, it doesn't eat food like us—and settles its head down. I stare into the blackness at the back of the cave and try to rally myself. Eventually, I pull my sword out and set off.

I stumble on my way back. The torch is little more than glowing ember when the dimming sunlight from outside finally becomes visible. I swallow again against a too-dry throat and try to slow my breathing, which had gotten tight and short in the small spaces. Between the dark and what I eventually discovered were bats, I'm not too proud to admit I'd been scared.

"Anything?" Liv asks. She is, amazingly, sitting on a cushion before a small fire she has lit behind a large formation near the front of the cave. The light will be blocked, at least for the most part, and the little nook will hold the heat better than the open space of the ledge at the cave mouth. It's practical beyond what I would have expected of her.

"Some bats," I say. "Nice fire."

She smiles and pats a second cushion beside her. She's folded the bedroll to protect against the cold of the cave floor. "Thanks. I figured if you could venture into the dark on your own like that, the least I could do is set a fire and collect some wood." Astonishingly, beside a pile of wood, she's even set a few dampish logs to face the fire. They're steaming sweetly, as is the little copper kettle she's placed over the embers.

Squid is settled opposite us, snugged between the rock and the fire. I can almost see the single raised brow. The dragon is not sure about Liv either. "My goodness." I let myself smile. "It's almost like home."

Liv smiles back, and there's something behind it. "I know I don't really do rough, at least not as you do, but I know how to make a bit of a home out of not very much. That, I have a lot of practice with. And I figure since you're going to have to take care of the rough parts, I should at least take care of the slightly less rough bits."

I narrow my eyes a little—more game?—but she's bending to pour the boiling water over some dried meat and vegetables mixed with salt and some herbs, and the scent is like heaven.

The curve of her waist into her hip also seems very clear, and I try to keep myself from running my eyes along that line. It's hard, especially when she's just been telling me that I know how to do rough better than her. The memory of that first night in her caravan is sharp and clear in my mind. I bite my tongue against the half-flirtatious lines that want to be said and cast about for something else to think about.

She saves me. "Do you think we're safe here?"

"Not really," I say. "We'll have to bank the fire soon to keep the light from drawing anyone too near. But we're also a fair way off the road, and the sun isn't quite down yet, so that counts in our favor. And the climb up here is pretty steep. We'd likely hear them coming, at least if there's more than two."

She nods and stirs the pot. "So we'll need to take turns with the watching, then?"

I narrow my eyes. "You're playing it a bit hard, aren't you, Liv?"

She frowns at me, finally meeting my eyes. "What do you mean?"

"All of, well, *this*?" I spread a hand, gesturing to the fire and the food and the carefully folded bedrolls.

She sighs. "Des, listen. I don't know quite how to start with this. I know it was me who made you as suspicious as you are. I know it. And I feel badly for that, because now... Well ... Elouise and I ...We talked. Quite a lot on this visit. Usually, there's not so much talking, but I guess with the wound in my arm and throwing ourselves on her mercy, she wasn't as interested in the sexy stuff. I mean, we did have sex, and it was as mind blowing as it ever is, but ... we also talked."

I close my eyes, already irritated.

"Wait, no, that's not it," she cries. "It's not about Elouise. It's about me. She told me I have a lot to learn. She... Well, she wasn't very nice to me." It could sound almost petulant, but as she stirs the pot again, I can see the tightness of her mouth and throat. Elouise got to her. "When I eventually told her the story of how we came to Scyless, she told me I was selfish. Selfish and extraordinarily lucky."

She swallows hard—visibly, which is unusual for such a consummate player. Unless she's playing. "She told me I was lucky because of you." I stare at the ground, biting my lip. "I need to thank you," Liv manages to spit out, painfully. "You saved my life. You saved my life a lot, actually. I owe you."

I shake my head. "It wasn't about you," I say, and I can't tell if I say it because I want to be cruel or because it's true, or both. "It was the best out. That's it. You don't owe me anything."

She almost smiles as if the barb were a mere confirmation. "Elouise said you'd say that." She stirs the pot again and nods. "This is ready."

We carefully pour the soup into two bowls with handles, and an uneasy silence reigns while we eat. At least, it's uneasy for me. I've got my Liv-handling skills perfected thanks to years of Petrus's snarky comments, but this leaves me on uncertain footing. She's introspective, thoughtful, and weirdly, apparently being honest.

So, of course, it turns me into a petulant child. "These bedrolls aren't that comfortable, are they? At least not when used to sit on. They could have packed us some little camping stools, right? And the soup was alright, but it could have used some more salt."

A smile quirks the corner of Liv's mouth. "Oh, really? More salt?"

I frown. "Yes, more salt."

"Anything else Her Grace would like with dinner?"

I half smile back, catching the humor. "We-ell!" I begin, and I'm all over-the-top noble, like the Lady Kestrel I played in the performance of *Kestrel's Flight*. "I do think that it could have been let cool a tad more. And this silverware leaves a lot to be desired. But of course, that is doubtless acceptable for a lady of my lowly standing." I flutter my lashes, and Liv chuckles.

"You're hilarious," she says. "I'd forgotten how good you are at that."

And somehow, in this cave mouth in the jungle, with hordes on our tail, we find our way to humor. It's silliness and old in-jokes from our Picton days, and as Liv's sad edges begin to fade, I am drawn into the game of making her laugh over and over again. Then she snorts, and I almost shout with laughter at the sound, and I'm helpless as I realize she's literally inhaled her soup.

I open my mouth to try to crack another joke, but I can barely get the words out. "No indeed, Mrs. Ingleblot, I do not wish to correct an inferior—"

"Inferior!"

I try to reply, but I can't hold character, and we're both lost to helpless laughter again, the stress of the chase coming out in a rush of release. This time, though, we're closer, and Liv leans against me to hold herself up.

Would you two work out how you feel about each other and let it go? This change and change about is hard to keep track of.

The snarky comment comes just as Liv leans toward me, and I'm in a tumult of mixed emotions as her lips touch mine. And all that tumult abruptly clears.

It's beyond a lightning bolt.

Every nerve snaps to attention as they never have, and never could, with anyone I'd kissed in the intervening years. I moan as my mouth opens helplessly to hers, swept up and into the warmth of her. My hands catch her to me, one lost in a cloud of dark curls and the other pulling tight at her nipped-in waist. She kisses me back, artless for once, fiercely covering my face in between capturing my mouth.

It is everything like I remember, and nothing at all.

We both inhale together, barely inches apart, drawing the same air. Then she yanks both my shirt and her shirt free, and we're tumbling, giggling, kissing and all hands, into a pile on the bedrolls.

I slide my weight atop her, a thigh between hers, and she arches toward me, pressing the hot, wet center of her sex hard against me. Breathless and gasping in each other's breath, we move against one another. She arches back again, and I capture one of those impossibly perfect nipples between my lips, sucking and then battering the hardened nub with my tongue.

I work my way up to her neck, biting and suckling until she moans in my ear, warm and deep, and arousal floods my quim.

"Take them off, take them off," she whispers urgently, pulling at her own trousers and mine by turns until we both manage to wriggle out of them a little.

At the sight of her almost naked—her trousers still caught on her ankles by her boots—I gasp a little. "Gods, Liv, you are unbelievably gorgeous." My voice is thick with naked desire, and there's half a second of fear or caution or something where I wonder if *this* is the moment she turns the tables back.

But no. She smiles and grabs me to catch a nipple with her mouth for a bare moment. The feeling is too much, threading from my breasts to heat my sex until it throbs. I'll come in a second if I let her have her way, and I'm not like to do that, so I kiss my way down that satiny belly to the cluster of tighter curls. I pause a moment, inhaling her scent, remembering her, remembering this, and I can feel the tension building in her body. "Please," she whispers, and desire cascades through me. I need no more urging than that.

I bury my mouth against her clit and suckle gently, stroking with my tongue and moving against her. My mouth knows precisely how to mold to her flesh, the soft and wet slick against my tongue. A memory built into the very makeup of my body; a knowledge I could never articulate but cannot unknow.

She moans, loud this time, and I slip one finger, then two, deep inside her. She's hot and silky-wet, and feels like nothing so much as heaven. Arching hard against my hand, her moans become regular as my tongue and mouth take on a rhythm.

My fingers match it, and I'm lost. My mouth is not mine, and her cunt is not hers. The two are conjoined, making something that—my gods—I cannot recollect being so heightened before. I can't help it—I tuck a hand between my legs, reaching for my own saturated sex, and urge us both onwards.

I hear the shivery half yell, half moan of her coming just as the heat soars through me, and I am blind to the world. Somehow, as she bends, clutching me close, I keep my mouth moving against her clit, my fingers hard inside her, pressing her toward bliss as pleasure sparkles through all my nerves, throbbing through my sex.

Her breathing slowly settles. I rest my head against her belly, not daring yet to see her eyes. I can't help it. Dread sinks my stomach. I slide my fingers gently from her warmth.

The Petrus in my mind shakes his head at me. I sigh out a breath, quietly, ragged. What am I even doing? Why, gods, why did Elouise send her with me?

Well goodness, says Squid in my head, a study in contrasts with a matter-of-fact tone. *I didn't know it was like* that. *I can almost understand what all the fuss is about.*

I start to try to formulate a reply, an agony of regret in my chest, but the gorgeous warmth of Liv against me is too much. So instead, I dismiss rational thought, yank the second bedroll over the two of us, and we snuggle in together, wordless, until we fall asleep.

CHAPTER TWENTY-SIX

T he night is the darkest it gets, and the embers of the fire are barely alight when I awake. My wakefulness is total, but I'm not sure what dragged me out of sleep. Liv's arm is still thrown over me. She was always a cuddler in bed.

It was me, Squid says, and from the tone, it has tried to speak to me several times now. *There's a boy in the cave.*

Fuck.

I don't move but lie very, very still, letting my eyes adjust. I've not the first idea where my sword is—or my dagger, for that matter. My shirt is gone, and my trousers are still caught around my ankles. Literally caught with my pants down. I'm cursing myself for a fool, and not just for sleeping with Liv. It's been a good long time since I've been in a position like this. I hope I don't pay for it with life or limb. I hope we don't.

He's not really ... moving. Just watching.

Me?

Yes, you. And me. He's sitting on a rock, watching us all.

Creepy.

I suppose it could be understood as creepy. The dragon sounds like it doesn't want to admit feeling creeped out because it might be beneath it, but it clearly is.

Hmm. I wish I had my sword.

I could burn him.

But he might be harmless.

He might not be.

That's true.

But... he didn't come up the path. So I don't think he's with the soldiers.

Unless the soldiers have a strangely thorough knowledge of this area, which they could. Story goes this bit of land used to belong to Ascelin.

Could be. But he doesn't feel like a soldier to me. He's eating a mango. And he doesn't have any weapons.

No weapons?!

Not that I can see. None.

That's decisive. I shoot to my feet, yanking my trousers up at the same time, and lunge for my sword, which is still in the scabbard and shoulder rig leaned against a rock. Liv is thrown back, startling awake with a cry, and I stride across to where the boy sits in the shadows.

I level the sword point at his neck. He's barely two years older than Twisty. It makes me guilty, but I snap, "Who are you and what is your business here?"

His eyes look up at mine, mild and unconcerned. They're also unnervingly pale, and in the dim light they look like he has no iris, just a pupil tiny in the center of whites, but I know that can't be right. He chews slowly on a piece of fruit. "I am Iradine," he says calmly, so calm he makes me feel slightly out of control. "I have come to take the dragonet to Calindrina."

He what?

Let me handle this, Squid.

I cast around for the right question. "What do you know of Calindrina?" I ask.

You really are a master, Squid says in my mind, sarcastic but amused.

"I live there," he replies, sucking the last of the mango off the stone.

"You live there?" I repeat.

Peerless.

"Yes." This conversation feels like it's dragging through mud.

"But what do you want with the dragon?" Liv appears at my side, fully clothed, reminding me I'm still standing topless with my sword leveled at this kid's throat. I want desperately to go and pull my shirt on, but I can't lose face.

Oh, you've got face to lose, don't worry, Squid says, the sarcasm perfect.

When did you get so snarky, anyway?!

Must've spent too long with you.

"The dragonet must come to Calindrina. The dragon commands it."

I frown my confusion. "What dragon? This dragon?"

"No. Elimanesion. The Guardian Dragon of Calindrina."

He knows the old dragon?! Squid crosses the distance from the fireside to the boy in a heartbeat and rears up on hind legs, pressing clawed feet against the boy's shoulders.

"Squid!" I exclaim. "What are you doing?"

We have to go with him. Now. The dragon turns sapphire eyes toward me. *Right now.* The boy strokes a single finger along the dragon's nose.

"We don't even know who he is!"

"I am Iradine," the boy repeats. "And you are birth-bonded? You are deeply honored, my lady. As the dragonet's chosen, I too honor the choice. You have my allegiance." It sounds like a ritual, but I don't know the response.

"Allegiance?" Liv almost laughs. "What in the blessed heavens is going on?"

We have to go!

"Squid, hold on a minute. I want to know who this boy is."

"A dragon's chosen is not often slow of wit, but it is in the stories," the boy announces. "And the blood bond is the real choice, in any case." Is that a note of excitement in his voice?

"Slow of wit?" I repeat, then I'm annoyed for confirming the assessment. I drop the sword, feeling stupid beyond measure. "I need to put on my shirt." Squid, as if it suddenly realizes we are not going to up and follow the boy, settles back down onto the ground.

"Of course, my lady."

I stump over to where my clothes lie scattered on the ground. At least this way, I'm unlikely to have to deal with the fallout from Liv and my misconceived rekindling of our relationship last night. But as I pull my shirt over my head, I hear Liv announce to the boy that she is my lover. Nice of her to share that with me before she goes sharing it with strangers. I'm too tired and grumpy to even try to sort through whether it is a play or real.

By the time I'm laced into my shirt and jacket, I'm in a black mood. I've also reconciled myself to the fact this boy is probably a gift horse, and he also seems to have very nice teeth. Even if I'm edgy about it, there are gods know how many soldiers behind us, and this boy has already shown us he knows far more about our situation than we do. I take a deep breath, shove a hand through my hair, and straighten my jacket. Right.

"My apologies, lad," I say as I approach, playing at so relaxed I hope it looks like casual mastery. "You caught me asleep and unaware. I'm sorry my questions weren't as clear as they could have been. I am Desta Mildue. This is Liv—Livinia Equitor. And the dragon is Esquidamelion. We are birth bonded, as you guessed, and blood bonded also. We have been traveling for some time, and yes, we are heading for Calindrina."

The boy hesitates, taking this in, a flickering of the eyes against something—sadness or hurt, perhaps?—then he nods, and I can feel Liv's eyes on me. I resist the urge to turn and find out whether she's laughing at me or impressed. "Good. I have been sent to guide you."

"We could use a guide," Liv adds.

"But we need to know a little more about you," I temporize. "So perhaps we could offer you a cup of tea and we can discuss the matter?" I glance at Liv, and she gives me a quick and somewhat amused grin but drops me a wink as well. It makes me smile. It's disconcerting but lovely to have us both playing on the same team again.

"Very well," Iradine says, and it could be my imagination, but he seems a trifle cooler than he had been. "But we cannot spend long. We need to be away before daylight. There are soldiers below us. They have stopped for the night, but at dawn, they will be on us, and that will complicate the situation."

"Complicate is one word for it," Liv murmurs, stoking up the fire and filling the kettle with water.

Iradine sits gracefully, cross-legged on the ground. I find the tea amongst our things. "So, Iradine. Tell us about your family." My careful question is designed to affirm or reject a theory that has just started developing in my sluggish morning brain. Elouise's research may yet prove helpful.

"I am a child of a long heritage, a clan who have always lived in the mountains. We are mostly unknown in the world now, but a few remember our name. Others call us—"

"Quenchers," I finish for him. Liv gives me a sharp look.

His pale eyes meet mine with more respect, though it's clear he's not my biggest fan. "Indeed, my lady. Quenchers. We are grown small now—many of our clan's children leave Calindrina—but we persist."

"So does your memory," I say, with a small smile. I need this boy onside. I don't quite trust him, but he is who we need. "Not in all places, but when dragons come up, so do you."

He smiles in return, open and honest, or playing at it well. "Yes, dragons. Esquidamelion is a beauty. Elimanesion will be pleased, I imagine."

"What is Elimanesion like?" I ask, as the little kettle begins to whistle.

Iradine smiles a little sadly. "Old. As old as one can be without dying."

I blink at him. "What do you mean?"

"Elimanesion is Esquidamelion's parent. Dragons do not need two to reproduce; they are both male and female in one, or transcending the two, if you prefer—they are unclear on this point. But Elimanesion laid the one egg it may lay in its lifetime a long, long time ago. Hundreds of years. It had despaired of ever finding its egg after it was stolen. We searched, we Quenchers, but could find no trace."

Until I was born, Squid comments to me alone.

"That happened many years ago. Generations ago. So Elimanesion is old. It is worn, weak, tired, and old. It deserves to die, deserves the rest and solace of it, but it cannot. It is hanging onto a thread of life to pass the torch of time to the next dragon, else the line will be broken."

That's me, Squid remarks, and it sounds caught between pride and fear.

I pour hot water into two cups with the leaves and hand one silently to Liv and another to Iradine. Liv's fingers graze mine—deliberately, I've no doubt—and she meets my eyes, a strange combination of warmth and warning. "So you've come in search of Squid, then?"

Iradine looks unimpressed—almost disapproving—at the nickname. "We Quenchers were sent to all corners of the country when Elimanesion sensed the blood birth of its child. We have been searching for some weeks."

I nod slowly, wondering whether Iradine has any clue of how many other people are after Squid. "I see. Iradine, you do seem to know a lot about dragons. I want to believe you. I want to trust you, because honestly, with the number of soldiers behind us, any luck would be good luck. We seem to be stuck between a rock—a ginormous rock in the form of a mountain—and a hard place. A hard, pointy place with people who want to kill us. We need an out, but I need to know I can trust you. And what you're telling me you could have learned from anywhere. From books." The boy frowns, confused. I sigh. "Iradine, do you have any proof that you are as you say you are? A Quencher?"

The boy scowls in earnest. I've injured his integrity. "I have never had anyone question my honor—or my family's honor!—before. This is grave insult."

My sigh is audible, my irritation showing. Liv glances from the boy to me and back again but doesn't speak. "Iradine, as I said, I do not wish to insult you. I wish to trust you. But we are pursued. All of those soldiers down there, they seek us. We have few options. I do not want to choose wrong." Iradine's face is stiff. I'm not helping, clearly, so I lapse into silence.

"Iradine, isn't it?" Liv's tone is sweet—player-sweet. I narrow my eyes at her, but her entire gaze is pinned on the boy. "I'm sorry. Des is frightened, and when she's frightened, she is abrasive and rude, oftentimes." I bite my tongue. "She fears for the dragonet. She wishes only for its safety. We were pursued from the sea into these mountains only yesterday, and we only escaped because Esquidamelion chose to protect us. It is truly a noble animal, and it will be a long time before I see a sight to rival it bellowing fire down on those troops. It has great things before it, truly, and I for one wish to be alive to see them."

Iradine shakes his head. "Dragons no longer participate in the lives of mortals, except those of we Quenchers. The Accord has been honored for three dragon generations now—even if Elimanesion's lifetime was longer than most—and it gave us our clan name and our unending task. This is an agreement that all blood bonded must honor as much as dragon. Without it, the world will fall. Esquidamelion ought not to be encouraged."

I frown, glancing at Squid, but it only registers confusion, mixed with the indignation I expect. *How dare he tell me what I may or may not choose to do? A mortal seeking to place his judgment above my own? I am a master of time!*

Squid, I know he's annoying, but let's try and listen. He obviously knows the ways through these mountains, and keeping off the road may be all that can keep us alive. Who knows what's out there? I don't, but he probably does.

It offers a grumbly acquiescence.

"I can understand that," Liv murmurs sweetly. "The Quenchers have knowledge we could all use. It is amazing and terrible that they have fallen from the memory of this land, and that should be rectified." Iradine opens his mouth, but Liv speaks first. "But Iradine, living so far away, in the mountains... You may not know. The world has become a hard, hard place. We know this better than many."

She swallows hard—a consummate performer, I think—but as she says the next words, I wonder if it's truth. "I myself have been tortured by those seeking the dragon. Des does not wish to say it, but she does not fear for herself alone. She would give her life to save mine, and nearly has, not a fortnight ago. Those seeking the dragon... Well, they have played us false before. Our mistrust has been hard earned, and these lessons hard learned. She only wishes to protect the dragon. And me." She reaches out, takes my hand, and kisses it, first on the back, then on the palm. Iradine is riveted, his eyes glued to her mouth, and I wonder what Quencher lore says about women loving women.

Liv gazes at me as if in adoration, so I smile and dip my eyes as if ashamed and overtaken by my love of her. Damn her.

Iradine leans forward. "My lady, my apologies. I understand why you would be cautious, with such a wondrous beautiful and gentle heart in your keeping.

Unfortunately, if I do not mistake my guess, all of your knowledge of the Quenchers comes from ... well, from books, does it not? And if you could have learned it from books, so too could your enemy. What knowledge could I offer that might prove I am who I say I am?" In my sleep- and embarrassment-sozzled state, this entirely accurate observation feels like the boy is getting one over on me.

He looks for a long moment at Squid, then turns back to me, eyes cool. "But the dragon could. This spot is the furthest I have ever come. I have only visited it once before, with my father and Elimanesion. If you are truly blood bonded, Esquidamelion may do you the honor of the Traverse." He pronounces the word with weight and significance.

For a long moment, I can't work out what he's talking about and am trying to find a way to ask without giving ground, when suddenly, half a breath before I dive into the layers of history, I know.

Squid draws me into the impossible world where everything—or rather, *every time*—is layered, one on top of the other. I grab at a rocky outcrop for balance, but it disappears. I'm steadied by something, but I'm so lost in the haze of changing colors, seasons, and vistas, and overwhelmed by the intense scents of sea and green and smoke, I can't even tell what it is.

Limestone outcrops are both there and not there, the green both sapling and ancient tree tumbled in a storm. The mineral growths inside the cave are both absent and present and growing. The smells are less unbearable than they are in a town, and interestingly, I feel less nauseous than our previous journeys into the layers of time, but they are still intense: growth, decay, and earth after rain, all at once. Then, abruptly, the haze generated by trees and rocks layered over each other simplifies—clarifies. I sigh in relief, expecting to see Iradine and Liv.

Instead, a young boy of about eight stands before me on a rocky outcrop, staring out at the crystal-blue sea, mouth agape as his father stands with hands on his shoulders. Both have their backs to me. "This is the furthest you will ever likely see, Iradine, if you make the choice to stay with us and remain a Quencher. We must hold the line. The world can never know the sacrifice, and will never need to. That is how it must be. We protect them."

Then, abruptly, from the ledge above the cave, a dragon the size of three houses together lurches out into the air, sweeping enormous wings down and buffeting all of us in its wake. It glitters purple and silver in the sunshine. I shade my eyes and realize this is what Squid will become. At the rate it's growing, in not so very long.

The younger Iradine watches, rapt. "But if I stay, I may be blood bonded, like you are with Elimanesion. Is it not so, Father?"

His father smiles sadly down at him. "Perhaps, lad, but we cannot know. You must not rely on it. And it is not a simple matter." He turns the boy, then kneels so he can look him direct in the eye. "You call me father, but out there, in the world, many children only have one father—the man whose seed let a woman give them birth."

Iradine frowns. "But I have many fathers—Father Joi, Father Kabri, Father Limini, and you, Father Riibi. You are all my fathers."

Riibi smiles again. "Yes. Amongst Quenchers, this is our way. The man whose seed let your mother give you birth is far away from here, seeking the lost egg. But, Iradine, I have seen children born and grow into men and die. Many of them. I saw the man who gave your mother seed grow from a baby, and his mother, and her mother before that."

Iradine's face changes, caught between a scowl and something that almost looks like fear. "But ... that would mean you are older than Grandpappy Genia. But you are only a little gray."

Riibi sighs, eyes turned toward the distant sea. "Child, I was birth bonded and blood bonded to Elimanesion many, many years ago. Over a century ago, if I may tell you true. To those who are dragon bonded, a strange thing happens. Our fate becomes so entangled with the fate of the dragon that until it dies, we cannot. And when it does, we must. We are honored to be Burned by the child of our bonded after the Incorporation."

Iradine's eyes are wide, and he gapes wordlessly. I don't know what to say either, but anxiety expands in my chest. Live for as long as Squid does?

I didn't know, Squid tells me softly, rearing back to settle its chin on my shoulder. Even its presence feels comforting at this moment.

I know what Riibi is going to say next, even if young Iradine does not, and my gut is in knots. I know because my thoughts have taken this one truth, and like quicksilver dropped onto a hard surface, they are scattering, tracking the consequences, my breath coming short. "I have loved more people than you are likely to know in your entire life, lad, and I have grieved most of them. My life now is a string of sadness, always awaiting the next sorrow. I take joy yet, but it is hard. It has four lifetimes' worth of loss to weigh against, and that is not a fair fight."

He stares out to sea now, and I can understand how his eyes acquired their depth and melancholy. I swallow, terrified, and blink.

I think it is enough to prove he is who he says he is, Squid says, almost gentle in my mind. *I am sorry, Des. I did not know.* It hesitates. *It is unbearable, knowing so little. And feeling your hurt and fear.* It says it softer this time. *Let us get to Calindrina as soon as we may, so I can learn it all. Perhaps there is a way to ensure that you live only your own mortality so that you may share it with the woman you love and hate without grieving her loss for centuries. If there is, we will find it. Now, school yourself, and we will Traverse back.*

Absurd anger and tears rise in my throat, and I have to swallow both. It is a comfort and a pain to have my fears and my desires named so clearly. *Have they been able to see us while we were away?*

They have seen you but have not heard anything. You did not speak aloud, except for some cries at the beginning. I am sorry I have not yet perfected sorting through time to find the right moment. The dragon sounds almost embarrassed. *You vomited.*

It's all too much, so I think of Iradine and our need to pack and try to guide myself through the list of things I need to make sure are in place before we leave. Almost like a meditation, except in reverse. Filling my head with stuff so it overwhelms the hard bits.

I close my eyes, and the next I open them, I'm on the ground, and Liv is fanning my face with her hand, green eyes all worry. "Oh, thank all the gods, Des! I thought you were having a fit!"

"Something like that," I reply as coolly as I can manage, which is not very cool, given the wave of longing that has cascaded through me at the sight of her face. I swallow hard against it. Possessiveness is not a good thing when it comes to Liv. I curse whatever fate bound me to become bonded to the dragon. And to Liv.

I am sorry, the dragon says, contrition personified. *I truly am.*

I know.

"I'm alright, though," I tell her. "I'm sorry if I scared you."

"Not half," she says, unimpressed, and rises to stand. "So, what now?"

I meet Iradine's eyes. His expression is calm, but I can read it a little better now. He knew precisely the significance of the moment he suggested. I can't work out if it was malice borne of jealousy, pragmatism, or perhaps even a misplaced desire to give me access to a truth he knew and I might not. I don't trust him, not entirely, but he can get us where we need to go. And the sky is already graying. Sunrise isn't far off. "Now we go. The lad is who he says he is." I can't help how brusque my voice sounds.

"You're sure?" Liv can hear the too-much in my tone, and it sets her on edge. She watches Iradine, uncertain now.

"Positive," I say, forcing a smile. "C'mon, let's pack up this mess."

"We will have to leave the beasts," Iradine says calmly. "They cannot go where we go."

"And where exactly is that?" Liv's friendliness has dissipated. I've scared her.

"Through the mountains," Iradine says. "Bring only what you need and warm clothes. It is chill down there."

Liv shoots him a look of disbelief—the air has been warm and thick since we arrived in the mountains—but after a quick glance at me, she begins sorting through the packs.

The idea of leaving Liza behind and heading into the darkness that nearly stopped me breathing when I explored the night before makes my palms dampen. "The soldiers won't find us in there," I manage to Liv. "I'll set the horses on their way. You pack."

Liza eyes me sideways as I approach with an apple in hand and another two in my pocket. "I am sorry, girl," I murmur to her, stroking her long, strong neck as I lead her and Quicksilver down the steep hill. Will she even be safe? I can't take her with us, but gods, how can I leave her? My most loyal friend. "I wish it could be otherwise, but without us, you're much safer, and we are safer in the caves." I can only hope this is true. Liza is dubious enough to make me doubt it. If she rides back to Hathway, perhaps an Ascelese soldier will find his way to caring for her? Probably a better outcome for her than what could happen in the jungle without me.

Tears fill my eyes, and, I sob into her mane. Liza. Brave and true. My weeping sets her on edge, dancing sideways a little, and Quicksilver's eyes roll, so I take a few shuddering breaths and press down the sense of impending loss. I feed her another apple. "We will see each other again, I'm sure of it," I tell her. "I will find you. Now, off you go!" I smack her rump, hard enough for her to know I'm serious, and she takes off, pausing as she reaches the tree line to send me a reproachful glance. "Off, you lovely damn beast," I say.

Liv's silver makes quick work of the apple I offer, happy to follow Liza into the trees. I raise my hand at them both as if in farewell, then, before I can think on this—or anything else—anymore, I clamber back up to the cavern.

Liv and Iradine have a pack each, and another is at Liv's feet. Squid coils up the wall like a blue lizard but turns its head to stare at me. Liv has prepared and lit a torch, and three more are laced to the side of her pack. Every time I underestimate her, I am astonished. Except where fidelity is concerned, my internal Petrus reminds me.

"We must away," Iradine says, and his strange eyes almost glow in the dark.

"Off then," I say briskly, shouldering my pack. "Lead on."

CHAPTER TWENTY-SEVEN

I radine leads us more swiftly than I had moved through the terrain last night, and at the first fork, chooses the path I hadn't explored. Even less well formed, we dodge large rocks and crevices threatening ankles. Iradine moves as if he were born to it, silent and nimble. Liv and I do our best to mimic him, but we're breathless and clumsy. He glares at any noise, even tumble of pebbles dislodged by our passage. He's lost his calm somewhere. Probably with the evidence of my blood bonding with Squid, I think, remembering the longing in his boyish voice during the Traverse.

Squid is creepily fast, speeding across the formations against the wall like a spider or a lizard. Liv is quite taken with the dusty, chalky cascades and towers made of stone, but they can't rouse my interest. I'm still trying to get my head around my potential extended lifespan. Does that mean if Squid is killed, I die too? What was the talk of burning? I swallow. It sounds awful. And the thought of Liza, wandering with Quicksilver through the jungle, makes my gut clench. How could I leave her?

After a while, Liv thrusts the torch at me, and I accept it, aiming simply to keep the boy's back in view. I focus on one foot in front of the other, treating the solving of the problem of the route through these caves as if it were enough to suck up all my attention. It's not, really, but I do a decent job of making out I'm not thinking of anything else. I'm almost convinced.

Abruptly, the boy stops. I reluctantly catch him up. "We go down," he says, pointing to a large and rather black hole in the floor.

"Down? You're sure?" Liv asks. She sounds uncertain and suspicious. I can't tell if it's a play or not, but either way, Iradine seems unmoved. He is already tying a length of rope to a rock.

I gaze at him evenly. *Squid, what happens if a dragon's blood bonded dies? Does the dragon bond again?*

Squid's reply is shamefaced. *I'm afraid that is a question that I can only answer ... uh ... later.*

I nod slowly, watching the boy closely. The vertical passage is small and dark, but at least we don't have to go far. I let him go first, and he goes down hand over hand, barely using his feet at all. Liv is slower, anxiously winding the rope between her feet. Finally, I clamber down, the torch wedged under my chin. I hurry, mainly going hand over hand and limiting the use of my legs, to minimize the chances of Iradine using this moment to take me out of the picture. It pulls the muscles in my shoulders, but they'll recover sooner than I would from a fall. I hit the ground with a bit of a shock, and I swallow. Well, at least Iradine doesn't want to kill me yet. Or is working harder to lower my guard.

Squid follows me down, flapping noisily in the dark. The torchlight barely pierces the black, creating a bare halo around us. It flickers low, and in the dim light, Liv looks alarmed. I echo it. I don't want to be down here in the dark, and we've already used up all three torches she had made before we left.

"It is safe to stop here and take a break," Iradine says, yanking at the rope so it slithers alarmingly down toward him. I only just used that rope and had thought it firmly tied! "And I think perhaps we can shift to using the Quenchers' light source. I do not think the soldiers will venture this far into the dark places."

Sitting on a nearby rock, he searches through his pockets and pulls out a thin, black, shiny length. I frown as he presses the end to the guttering torch, and not a moment too soon—it putters out as the substance flares into astonishingly bright, warm golden light. "I would not look directly at it," Iradine warns. "Your eyes will have grown accustomed to the low light of the torch, and it could damage them."

I look away immediately, and Liv grabs my arm in a viselike grip. I glance at her briefly, then follow her wide-eyed gaze, and my mouth drops open in astonishment.

Glittering refractions of light bounce back at me, startling my eyes. I narrow them and stare about me. I find myself on my feet, taking two quick steps forward and turning around and around in astonishment. Liv joins me.

The cave is enormous, stretching down at a gentle slope from where we are and off into the distance. Squid takes flight, shooting off at speed and banking as a speck near the far wall. The entire cavern is clustered with formations—glittery and waxy versions of the rough teeth-and-jaw shapes I'd found in the entrance to the cave, along with tall columns formed of repetitions of the same thing. Long icicles drip from the ceiling, alongside broad swathes of glittering white curtains sitting ready to be swept aside. It is like stumbling into a wonderland, and I turn and turn, taking it in.

Below the hole through which we descended is a large block of fallen rock, and beside that is a broad white waxy substance that looks like a viscous liquid in very slow flow across the ground. I slide my hand across it. The entire surface is damp but solid, and my hand comes away wet and gritty. Above is a cluster of whitened hay, sprouting from the wall like plants pushing their way out between bricks.

I glance at Liv's face, which is pure astonishment. She touches everything she can, intrigued and unable to quite compass the beauty. A narrow straw breaks off in her fingers, and she looks so chagrined I almost laugh.

It is beautiful, but soon my skin begins to crawl. It looks unreal, and in the golden light, it feels too pretty, like a trap. *Squid? Are you alright?* I ask, staring off into the shadowed crevices at the far end of the cave.

It's safe, it says, replying more to my concern than the question itself. *There's not much even alive down here.*

That doesn't make me feel better, I send back. *Alive is good.*

Squid chortles, then zooms out of the dim light, a blue blur heading for us. I dodge at the last minute, and it catches hold of the strap on my pack to land on my shoulder and curl its nose into my ear. It warms me more than I want to acknowledge. Today has been hard so far, and any care from either of my other two companions would just hurt. This feels easy, somehow. *I miss Liza,* I tell Squid.

Me too, Squid agrees, and I smile at it and snuggle my head against its flank. *You're actually not that light anymore, you know.*

I can feel Squid's smile in my head. *Just making up for all the times when you'll be riding me when I get big.*

Riding you? My eyes go wide. *Are you serious?*

Squid laughs at me again in my head and takes off for another shadowed corner, leaving me lurching.

Iradine's gaze is on me, and a glance tells me it's pure jealousy. I file that away. Liv scans my face and smiles, heading into safer territory. "So amazing, isn't it, Des?" she says, all delight. "I've never seen anything so beautiful."

I grin at her. "Ain't seen much, then, hmm?" I play.

She laughs and turns back to wondering at the white cave. Iradine watches this exchange in silence. "Thank you for the light," she says shyly to him, after a long moment of simply taking in the sight. "Will it all be like this?"

Iradine is drawn into the conversation with her, and she plays it out while we drink water and swallow down some nuts and traveling biscuit. I am grateful to her for doing what I cannot. Today has already been too hard. I simply gaze at the glitter on the stones until we are on our way again.

"We are not far off now." Iradine smiles at Liv. "Soon, you will meet everyone. There's not that many of us. The whole clan is less than fifty people, but almost everyone is friendly."

This is the turn it's taken over the past few days—if they are even days down here. Iradine is friendly and open with Liv, and cool, bordering on cold, with me. It doesn't bother me too much. Perhaps it should—him having his guard down would probably have been of more use—but I am weary of playing, my mind too full of trying to compass the weird semi-immortality I wandered into with that original happenstance of blood-birthing Squid.

The dragon is bigger but still narrow enough to lie across the top of my pack, its tail dangling below my waist on one side, neck wrapped around mine, and head tucked in across my clavicle. It won't be able to do it for much longer, but I appreciate it now. It's comforting—both the physical comfort of Squid's warm belly against the back of my neck and the emotional comfort the dragon silently sends me.

From the white crystal cavern, Iradine has led us in a circuitous path, passing through varied tunnels and caves. Some have been smaller versions of the white crystal cavern, but with more colors threaded through the decorative formations. Some stretches have stunk badly, and others had breezes fresh enough to riffle our hair. Vast, broad caverns with ceilings dipping low enough to make us crawl are matched by narrow paths that seem to be mere cracks in the rock, catching at our toes.

Occasionally, a roar has filled our ears so slowly that we only realize it when we catch a glimpse of rushing blue-green water in the distance or far down a terrifying cliff. And always the warm, golden light that Iradine bears makes these alien spaces feel too friendly. They still make my skin crawl. The knowledge that if I wanted to flee now, I would have zero hope of reaching the surface alive without Iradine doesn't better my mood. Even Squid's assurances that it would be able to find the way back out have lost their certainty as we've continued.

Of a night, Liv and I have taken to sleeping with our bedrolls together, and I'm not sure if we're merely playing out the story of being lovers. She cuddles into me at night more than might be strictly necessary to keep up a pretense. She smiles at me now, across the pot she is stirring, crowned by a spray of white straws fixed to the wall behind her.

Liv, Liv, Liv.

"What are their names?" I ask Iradine, trying to make an effort.

Iradine starts out chilly, but as he begins listing all the individuals in his little clan, he can't help but soften. Then he chokes with laughter and tells us a story of them. "One of the young ones, Elitta, was learning some of our lore. We all have to learn it by heart, and we're taught by our various parents—the adults of the tribe. Elitta was only young, I think about four at this point, but she'd been struggling to remember things by heart, and all Quenchers are taught to learn from only one recital.

"So, it was a kind of a test—Jonna and Urissa had recited a short passage of the Accord, and Elitta was meant to recite it to the whole tribe around the fire." He begins to chuckle. "She started, and she made only a few errors, and then she reaches the end of that clause, which finishes, *And so hereafter shall the world be thus shaped.* But she went on unexpectedly, adding, *But Kribin's arms are incomparable, to tell you truth, and all he has to do is flex them. I almost dare you, or even one of the young girls, to watch the daily warriors' practice without comment!*"

Liv laughs. "I take it Kribin's arms are not the subject of much comment in the Accord?"

Iradine giggles. "No, indeed. Little mention is made of them in the Accord. Though Urissa seemed to think them worthy!"

Much of what he tells us suggests the Quenchers have built the entirety of the clan's life around Elimanesion and Riibi, the blood bonded. He recounts long nights spent curled by the fire, listening to stories about dragons and planning who would polish Elimanesion's scales the next day.

I wonder uneasily what they think will happen once Squid reaches the old dragon. Do they think I will join them? Is it even possible to join a tribe like this? My heart sinks. I am not sure I'm made for cleaning scales.

I am a master of time, Squid reminds me. *None of these puny mortals will be able to make me do what I don't want to. Besides, you would make a terrible scale cleaner. You don't have the patience. I would insist someone else do it.* Squid has been making an effort to joke with me gently the past few days, as if it knows the best way for me to be tugged out of my melancholy is through humor. Which, of course, it is, and so, it does know.

I smile and focus on unpacking the bowls and spoons. *Well, that's a relief, anyway,* I tell it in my head. *I just hope whatever you want to do kind of aligns with what I want to do!*

Squid flaps out of the cave behind us and flicks its tail precisely through my too-long fringe as it passes. *We'll see,* it says complacently, a consummate tease, then, relenting, adds, *You haven't noticed, have you? We are too close to be able to bear each other's suffering easily now. You might regret the blood bond, but it does make you ... unusual to me.*

I hesitate, staring for too long into the tumbled depths of a pack. *You think I regret it?* Somehow, it feels a long time since I've regretted the bond.

Squid coughs out loud, a tiny bit of flame pooching from its mouth. *I know you well enough now that I understand how you can regret and not regret, all at the same time. See what I mean about unusual? How else could an eminently rational being such as myself bear such contradiction?* It's arch, characteristically, but it's playful now.

I smile at the barb. *Some benefits, I guess...* I bring the bowls and spoons to Liv, who grins her thanks up at me. "So, when do you think we'll arrive?" I ask Iradine, trying to sound excited. "I mean, it's hard to even think in days down here, but do you have any sense?"

Iradine's face shutters as he replies. "Because much of our lives are spent in the caves, we are very good at keeping track of long periods of time. We have been traveling for six days, and we will travel for one more. So, as I said, not long now."

"Indeed," I say, with a smile, pushing through his unwillingness. "I am glad of it. This wonderland you have shown us is cool and astonishing in its shades and colors, and the drip-drip-drip you say builds these formations ... amazing. But it is damp, and I wouldn't mind breathing fresh air."

Iradine almost frowns, but Liv laughs. "I wouldn't mind a breath—and some sun on my face!"

Iradine smiles at her. "I miss the sun too. The air will change after midday tomorrow—you will be able to taste the difference. The gritty feel of it will ease, and you might even be able to scent the green."

Liv's eyes are knowing at the gratitude I send her with my glance. I swallow a little. Being with her is both new and ancient, like fresh rain filling a dry creek bed. All unsettling and comfortable at once. Somehow, the unfamiliarity of these dark places allows the contradiction, lets me tolerate them. Part of me can't help but wish we had more time down here. The emergence into the bright of day feels like it will draw a line under the ambiguous terrain we've traveled together and demand some kind of reckoning, and that's aside from the dragon and the Quenchers.

Too much. I shove the thought away and slurp my soup.

CHAPTER TWENTY-EIGHT

I radine's prediction proves almost exactly accurate. At midday the next day, we do indeed smell something that came from the surface, but it is not green. It is not green at all.

Smoke.

With the first scent of it, Iradine frowns, puzzled. "You smell that?" he asks.

I smell smoke. Big smoke, Squid tells me.

"Smoke?" I hazard. "Could it be from a campfire?"

He frowns again, not so much puzzled this time as concerned. "I don't know," he admits. "I've never smelled smoke this deep in the caves before, and the clan always has a fire going."

Liv doesn't say anything, but as he lifts his pack a little higher on his back and strides off, bearing the light with him, she shoots me an anxious look. I loosen my sword in its scabbard, just in case.

I hope that the scent will waft away, that it will turn out to be some quirk of the movement of air through the long tunnels we have been following. But as we clamber slowly up an opening that Iradine calls a "chimney," the smell only grows stronger. There's no mistaking it. Wood fire.

Once we're all safely on the level, Iradine coils the rope while walking, then speeds to almost a run. "I don't understand," he keeps muttering to himself. "What is going on here?"

Liv glances at me, her brows furrowed in concern. I smile as bravely as I can. "It'll be alright, Liv."

She smiles a little wanly. "I hope you're right. There's not much that's been alright on this journey." It stings a little, and she knows me well enough to see the tells. "Not that, lovely Des," she says softly. "That I do not regret one iota. But if you and I are killed before we work out what, precisely, we think this might be this time around... Well, that will most definitely not be alright by me."

I can't help the quaver of my brows. "You think there might be a something."

Liv sighs. "I know you've not quite bothered to notice, but since we left Elouise's, I have been working hard—and it is very hard work, you know, for me!—to be absolutely honest with you."

I look at her, wishing there were a way to discern when she spoke the truth, and I'm a little taken aback by the intensity in her eyes. "I... Alright, I have no clue what to do with an honest Liv."

She grins, obviously pleased by this. "Elouise said that would be it. You'd dealt with all of me except the honest, non-player version. She said if I wanted to floor you, that's what I had to try."

I blink at her, pausing in my tracks. "You wanted to floor me?"

Liv smiles, almost sadly. "Des, I've always wanted to floor you. I just never thought I could do that without playing."

My face takes on a weird, unfamiliar expression of bemusement, concern, and bashful happiness. "Liv..."

She shakes her head. "Oh no. No, no, no. Not right now, Des, my dear. Right now, we need to focus on making sure we both have a future in which to have that conversation you're itching to have right now." I glance at the floor and nod, hoisting my pack higher. Her cool finger curls across my cheek and under my chin, raising it so I meet her eyes as she adds, very softly but with a gaze more brave and vulnerable than I've ever seen on her, "But I swear to you—honestly, on my life—that if we survive whatever happens next, we will have that conversation." Her smile is small. "It might be hard, and I might hate it, but we will have it."

I blink at her again and then smile hesitantly. "I... I can't promise anything, Liv. It's been... I wasn't playing at being hurt, you know."

She smiles, and there's just enough heartache in it to soothe something in me. "I know, Des. No promises but a conversation—the one I've been dodging for eight years. That much I will swear to you." She puts one hand over her heart, the other over mine, and nods, green eyes serious, then turns to follow Iradine up the steep slope.

I pause for a long moment, baffled.

Well, that's a change, Squid comments coolly, appearing on the wall beside me.

I blink again, walking slowly in Liv's footsteps. *I... I don't know what to make of it. Maybe Elouise was right when she said Liv would hurt herself before others could. Maybe she's finally... Do you think she's finally willing to let herself feel it?*

Squid almost laughs at me. *You're asking me, a dragon, to assess the likelihood of the woman you love and hate being sincere? I have no idea. But maybe she wants to make up for what she's done ... all she's done.*

My thoughts are like a cascade, each rushing on the other's heels, barely catching hold of what Squid is saying. *Maybe... Maybe she's finally willing to feel it, to admit it, to not run from it. Doesn't mean it'd work. Doesn't mean she wouldn't flinch away again when the fear gets to be too much, or try to hurt me again. But maybe... Do you think that's what she means?*

I do not know what it all means, Squid says, *but it probably does mean something. She is realizing this now and realizing that what she had thought was courage and wisdom was cowardice and stupidity, so she wants to try to make up for it.*

It's growing dark, so I pick up the pace. *Make up for it? You think so?*

I do. The dragon gives a mental shrug. *But what do I know? As she says, I'm just an overgrown lizard, really.*

I hear Iradine's cry and race past Liv to catch up to him. The smell of smoke has been growing stronger, and a haze now hangs from the ceiling. As I follow the curve around the bend, I see the source.

Calindrina—or at least, what was once the Quenchers' home inside the caves at Calindrina—is burning.

Before me is a long, broad cave. Flames lick black onto the wall in one corner, but all along the long edge are the charred remains of something wooden. Iradine is silent, still, in the center of the cave. His face bears an expression I've not seen on it before.

"Iradine?" I say. "What is going on?"

"Our stores. These were our stores. They've burned our stores."

He sprints off, leaving Liv and me in the darkness lit only by the sullen fire. If they've burned the Quenchers' stores, the gods only know what they've done to the people themselves. After a brief moment, Liv whispers, "Who are 'they?'" We share a look of consternation and follow Iradine.

When we find him again, Liv gasps, her hands flying to her mouth. He kneels on the floor beside four small bodies, keening and plucking helplessly at the clothing of one. Blood is everywhere. Sprayed across walls, pooling on the floor, congealing amidst the fragments of scrolls, and sizzling in the corner where a pile of cushions has had flame put to them. I swallow bile and take a breath against the buzz of adrenaline.

For a long moment, we stand in shock and silence. The corpses are of children, and they did not die quickly. As I reach out to touch Iradine's shoulder, he rises and takes off again, leaving me with a hand in the air. This time, Squid is hot on his heels.

Squid, for fuck's sake! We can't know who is there! I cry, beating a too-slow path in its wake. I loosen my sword in its scabbard, fighting against every instinct that says that running after them, following them outside, is likely the road to a swift death. I grit my teeth and force myself to speed up.

I burst suddenly into light, barely able to make out what lies before me. The sun is overhead, and once my watering eyes recover, it leaves absolutely nothing in uncertainty.

There has been a massacre here.

The Quenchers' village is on a small, bare hilltop surrounded by thick jungle, hazy in the heat and humidity. It lies in the shadow of a taller mountain, which thrusts upward as if it's seeking to touch the sun.

But at this moment, this astonishing sight is barely noticeable for the devastation of the village itself. The remains of small wooden homes burn, sending up thick black smoke. The fire in the fire pit has been stoked higher than it should be, the remnants of long, low bench seating jutting from it. Slender rollers are all that remains of more scrolls.

And blood. So much blood. Less than in the cave, but enough to make Iradine wild-eyed and desperate, casting about in every direction. My too-clinical mercenary eyes tell me it's probably about ten dead.

Plus the four young ones inside makes about a quarter of his clan, Squid reminds me. The dragon is glinting and bright in the sunlight, but as if it half acknowledges my plea to stay safe, it has crawled up a nearby tree. The tree is leafless and scorched, and does little to hide the dragon's coloring, but it's a compromise.

The poor lad.

He keeps taking a step as if to do something, initiate some action, then rethinking that plan. Tears run nonstop down his face. Every few seconds, he wails, low and soft, grief too profound to know what to do. I approach him hesitantly, scanning the bare hillside, especially where it runs down into the tree line.

"Iradine?" I ask, my sword somehow in hand. "I don't think we should be in the open for too long." He looks at me vacantly, as if he doesn't know me, and then nods. When he doesn't say anything, I say, "Iradine? I'm sorry, but ... is there anywhere that might be safe? Somewhere that's not the caves or the..." I cast around for a word, then gesture silently at the burning village around us.

He's still slow to respond, but eventually nods as if he's remembering how. "Follow me," he says, as if from a great distance.

Liv still stands at the cave's entrance, wordless and gaping. He heads toward her. I nod at her to follow, and she obediently turns back inside, followed by a swift-moving Squid. I pause in the cave's mouth to look out across the burning and burned remains of the village.

What happened here that prompted such a severe response? And why would someone burn everything? I understand anger, but that burns hot and swift. This was methodical. This was planned.

I scowl and scan the skyline once more. Two birds of prey circle above. I bite my lip, sword still in hand, and scour my gaze slowly along the tree line again. The mercenary within me knows how this is played. If you kill and burn in order to root out an enemy, you don't leave the area unsurveilled.

And there it is—just a glimmer, but it's there nonetheless. High in a vine-covered tree is the glint of armor over green cloth—a shade too dark for full concealment. Green again. I think of the crowds of mercenaries on the beach at Scyless. Could this be the emperor's forces? A scout left to keep an eye on the devastation? The sight sends fear coasting through me, and I force myself to exhale slowly, to still the impulse to flee.

I pretend I haven't seen him as I scour back and forth. If I were sure I could catch him without leaving everyone else unprotected, I would be sprinting across the charred remains of the Quenchers' village. But I am not. Besides, there might be other scouts I can't see in the trees—it's what I'd do—and that might leave me dead, and Liv, Iradine, and Squid without a sword. My bare blade, between all of us and whoever produced this devastation. My heart beats hard in my throat.

The presence of a scout here likely means there's at least some posted within the caves. We might even have stampeded past them.

I cannot smell anyone, Squid says, its thoughts tinged with chagrin at my original anxiety being proved right. *I do not think there's anyone in here with us.*

Mmm. I doubt you could smell them over all this smoke. Or could you?

I don't know.

I take a deep breath, then catch it as a bird spirals up from the undergrowth. It pauses, then speeds toward the mountain that towers over the village. I watch for a long moment, knowing this likely spells our doom and wishing I had a bow and arrow and a serious proficiency with them.

I could cook it in the air, Squid offers, a little too casually, *then go straight to Elimanesion. You'd be safe then, right?*

I keep my eyes steady, scanning, but my skin crawls, and I remember Iradine's concern about Squid killing. I let my mind skitter away from the thought as I back toward the cave, knowing Squid is listening in. *No. It's too risky,* I say. *Remember what happened to your wing that time? We don't have time to let you heal—and we don't have the experts to take care of you either.*

Alright, Squid acquiesces, uncharacteristically short.

Clearly, it can hear my thoughts about it killing. I consider apologizing, then sigh, figuring Squid's heard all of these thoughts as well. *You know, it's awfully hard to play with someone who is already in your head. I don't even get to work out what I think about anything before you know it.*

Squid is almost amused. I feel guilty for doubting the dragon. Of anyone, it knows me best.

Eventually, just as the cool shadow of the cave mouth swallows me up, it sends a reply which isn't quite words but somehow manages to encompass hurt, understanding, and a sense of being in the complexity of our situation together. It's more tender and intimate than anything I've felt, even with Liv, and an intense rush of gratitude makes tears prickle my eyes. I blink back over my shoulder at the sunlight so it can't see them, though of course, it knows.

I swallow hard and turn toward the dim of the cave.

My eyes take a minute to adjust even enough to make out Liv and Iradine pressed against one of the walls around the first corner. Iradine has slid down the wall, forehead pressed to his knees, but if he sobs, it's silent. "Thank fuck," Liv breathes, as I meet her wide eyes. She comes toward me, hugs me briefly, and presses a firm kiss to my lips. "What do you think is going on?"

"They know we're here," I say briskly, "and I think wherever Iradine was hoping to take us, he should hurry up and do it." I feel heartless, but urgency makes me snippy. "Iradine, I'm serious. I think we probably have ten minutes to get somewhere safe. I'm not even sure heading back into these caves was a good plan. We don't know whether someone saw us come out of the cave system you led us through, but we have to imagine they did. Is there anywhere else that could be safe?"

Iradine looks up at me, and now there's undisguised hatred in his eyes, which takes me aback. I know I'm not his favorite person, and I understand the jealousy over my bond with the dragon, but hatred?

He holds a hand out to Liv to help him up, then he sets off without a word into the dark. He knows these caves well enough to manage them without light. Liv and I hurry along behind him, making our way behind him mostly based on sound. We're slow and clumsy by comparison, and we fall behind. "Iradine?" Liv calls hesitantly. "We can't see, and we don't know this place as well as you do. Can we light something?"

"Not safe," the reply comes back. "Our light is too bright."

"We need it," I confirm.

Iradine stops and stares at me. Squid climbs up me, coiling around my shoulder and sliding its narrow head against my cheek to level his bright gaze at the boy. Iradine is incandescent with repressed rage, but a moment later, he lights a strip of bright light. He doesn't move, just keeps his angry glance on me.

Liv stares at us all for a moment, then shakes her head. "It doesn't matter. We have no time. Let's go," she says tersely, and Iradine's hateful gaze breaks from mine. "Angry," Liv comments to me.

"Yep," I say.

Liv shrugs. "He's grieving. That's probably enough explanation for all of this."

I nod slowly. It might be true, but I'm not so sure it explains his reaction. I swallow hard, my mouth sour. Why does it feel like, at any moment, he's going to become untrustworthy?

Did you do something, Squid? I ask. *He's angry with me, and I've got no idea what I did.* I can't rein my mind back from thinking about the dragons killing so many people all that time ago. It's hard to feel this distrust of my connection with Squid, and Iradine's anger, and not understand why. What does he know that I don't?

I'm a dragon, Des. A master of time, it tells me. *We can talk about it later. And I'm sorry that you are scared and Iradine is angry, but I cannot be other than I am. Am I not keeping you safe?*

Too many questions crowd my mind, so I set the whole thing aside. *You are. And thank you.*

Then I focus on following Iradine's back.

CHAPTER TWENTY-NINE

For a short while, the tunnels we follow are carpeted with long rugs woven in rich dark colors, with shelves and chairs and tables scattered along it. Furnishings are torn, scorched, burnt, bloody, or broken, but it's clear this was a warm, comfortable space before the violence. Iradine leads us into a bigger room, a bedroom carved from the rock with pick marks still in the walls. He walks across to a large wardrobe that bears the marks of attempts to kindle it to flame, opens the enormous door, and then pulls back a trap door in the floor. Silently, he uncoils a rope for us.

We descend once more into darkness. The tunnels under here are bare and cool and dark. We twist and turn until I am quite lost. The caves are still and silent, except for our movements and huffing breaths. I tell myself I'd hear anyone coming before they got to us. Eventually, I put my sword away.

And so, when I find a spear to my throat, I have nothing to push back with.

Liv gasps beside me, but my attention is narrowed to the point of the blade. The man glaring down the weapon at me has a bloodied forehead, but he is clothed much as Iradine is, in cotton clothes wrapped about his body. His eyes, fixed and wide, are pale, like Iradine's. Another Quencher, face is haggard and fierce. I swallow hard, realizing that right now the Quenchers could be as much of a threat as whoever attacked them.

"This is the blood bonded," Iradine says, and he sounds almost unhappy about being forced to share this with the man. The spear drops, and the man falls to one knee. I glance at Iradine, embarrassed. The hatred might be less naked than before, but he's fine with my discomfort.

"My apologies, my lady," the man says, his head still bent. "I was unaware. You bring the dragonet?"

Squid crawls down the wall and into the man's line of sight. His eyes widen, then he dips his head even lower, practically touching the floor.

Are all the Quenchers going to react like this? I ask Squid. *Because I'm not going to be able to keep a straight face if they do.*

Squid is arch. *They are only responding as befits a master of time. Just because you don't know how to respond to greatness on earth...* I can barely keep my laughter to a quiet snicker. Iradine, of course, interprets this as laughter at the Quencher's expense and glares yet more fiercely.

I clear my throat. "Rise, sir," I say, stepping forward to help the man up. "The dragonet is pleased with your welcome but concerned that we may yet be pursued. Where did you appear from? May it constitute our own safety?"

The man nods twice, then heads off down the narrowing tunnels leading the way, Iradine beside him in a moment. They speak in low voices, their heads bent to avoid the low ceiling. The man puts an arm around Iradine's shoulders, and a little of the tension the lad has been carrying empties out of his body. I am glad for him that we are amongst his own again. Grief is hard anyway, but it's almost impossible alone.

Liv grins at me. "Nice gracious lady, Desta Mildue," she says as she passes. "They'll be singing your praises for seasons yet."

It's the classic compliment between players. I grin at her. The Petrus in my head is unimpressed, faint but strong enough to prompt me. "We still have a conversation to have, Liv," I say quietly to her back as I follow.

She smirks over her shoulder at me. "We do, but you are aware that was a complete non sequitur, right?" I don't know what to say. She glances back at me again, the smile ghosting on her lips. "But nice to know where you're at."

I sigh. "I wish I wasn't so easy to read."

Dark curls bounce around her shoulders as her smile broadens. "You're not that easy. Not to everyone. But you're written in my language."

I smile at her back, feeling warm.

This woman you love and hate is complex, the dragon comments, *and has an interesting sense of timing.*

We clamber down and then up, further along, and then down again. The chimneys here are passable without rope by bracing ourselves between the walls, but it takes it out of us, climbing them. The caves are growing paler and sandier and the passages more difficult, with rocks strewn everywhere. Although I know it will make following us slower and more complicated for any potential pursuers, my legs ache.

Then we follow the two Quenchers around a corner and into a room full of the bright Quencher light. It's a small cave, and at first glance, it seems full of people. Low wooden benches covered in cushions are arrayed in one corner, and a series of sling beds are lined up against two walls. All six beds are full. Some of their occupants are injured, with bandages wrapped around limbs and marked with blood. A few are unconscious or sleeping. Others, also looking wan, are propped up against the cave wall.

The cushioned benches hold only a few wide-eyed children gathered around a woman. Another moves back and forth amongst the injured, caring for them. But one glance tells me almost everything I need to know. This is the wounded, the old and infirm, and the young. There are only a handful of able, young-but-not-too-young warriors amongst them. This is scarcely a force that could stand against the armies we face.

It was never really going to be, I remind myself against despair. I always knew the tribe was small. Surely, I couldn't have been imagining that the tribe were going to be our protection against two nations' worth of soldiers, mercenaries, and assassins? My heart sinks anyway.

At the sight of the dragon trailing into the cave behind me, the Quenchers fall to their knees. The children move first, and it is a little chilling to see them so still and silent with respect. Even those having their injuries treated seek to give honor. I take a deep breath, step forward, and raise my head. Time to play.

"Greetings, Quenchers," I announce, pitching my voice so it fills the cavern. "Please, we beg you to rise. Esquidamelion and I, the blood bonded, thank you for your welcome and extend our gratitude to Iradine, whose bravery has kept us safe this long. We regret the pain and loss you have recently suffered. We know little of what has befallen you but would listen with avid ears to your tale. Do you know who caused such devastation to your village?"

Voices clamor, and I hear "the emperor" echoing amongst the cacophony. My heart sinks. A man with old eyes—with a jolt, I recognize him as an older version of the man Iradine had called his father during the Traverse—rises, and everyone quiets. "Welcome, Esquidamelion. Welcome, blood bonded, and to your companion. You find us in a state of grief, but nonetheless, you have both been long awaited and keenly sought. Your coming, though we may grieve it as late, is yet gladdening." He places his hand over his heart and bows at me and the dragon coiled about my shoulders.

"My name is Riibi. As leader of this small clan, I extend all hospitality we can offer, little though it may be. As you have witnessed, we have lost much in the destruction of our small village. You must be weary, hungry, and in need of ablutions. We will provide whatever we may." He gazes about him. "My family, please, would you make ready what food and drink we can for our honored guests?"

A young woman rises smoothly and rounds up three boys barely entering puberty, and they move out of the room through another tunnel. The old man smiles a sad smile that doesn't reach his eyes. It is so old a smile it makes my skin crawl. I can't help but see him as a future self I can't quite grasp I could be. Squid shifts lightly against the back of my neck, reminding me I am not alone.

"I fear it may be some few minutes for them to prepare for you." The old man is apologetic. "In the meantime, my lady, I think you and I and the dragonet should speak together. There are matters of some urgency that my lord Elimanesion wishes me to convey to the young one. And to you, of course, my lady. But in the next room, you will find water and towels to cleanse yourselves. May I await your presence in my sitting rooms to discuss once you have refreshed yourselves?"

The Quenchers hush as if waiting to hear my answer. Iradine's eyes are poison. I give the man a deep nod—somewhere between a bow and a nod, really—and a small child leads Liv and me through a low, narrow hall and into another, yet smaller, room.

Liv and I make quick work of cleaning up. Liv scrubs at ingrained dirt on her cheek. "Do you think we'll be safe here? From...?"

I swallow. "No idea. Any guess about who that might be?" It's a trifle too close to asking about her earlier betrayals of me, so my voice is hesitant.

She shakes her head. "No clue."

I nod, dipping the edge of a cloth into the water and scraping at my face. I wonder what she's really thinking. The Quenchers seem to think it's the Emperor of Ascelin and I realize I've been assuming the same. But that's only because of the invasion we saw at Hathway, the green-clothed sentry outside the village, the enemies on the beach at Scyless, and Elouise's guess, based on the details of a trade deal. They're good signs, but I also know that too many assumptions will be trouble.

"Do you trust them?" she asks, in a low but conversational voice.

I blink. "I don't know. Do you?"

She stares at herself in the mirror, scrubbing at her neck inside the collar of her shirt. "Well, I don't know if I trust Iradine, at least with you"—she sends me a rueful half smile—"but that old man seems..."

"Old," I finish.

Squid sends me a thread of emotion that is amusement and eye roll mixed together. *I don't know what you mean. Of course we trust him. How can we not?*

"Well, yes, but also ... somehow it feels like he's waited all this time ... for you?"

I nod. "On the one hand, unlikely to cause us harm. On the other, it feels like they've been waiting for something or someone very particular. Which may be only what we need, but..." I shift gears, testing waters I should be leaving well enough alone. "I mean, the gods only know what expectations *you* could come up with for me if you had decades to prepare!"

She swats at me with a damp cloth, letting me change the subject. "Oh, Des, you have no idea!"

I grin at her in the mirror, but I can't quite match her laugh. My gut sinks. We'd aimed for this place, but now I'm here I wish I understood more about, well, everything. I wish I'd had more time to read Elouise's archives. The Traverse revealed life-changing information. What else do I not know?

We make quick work of the rest of our washing up, and when we poke our head out into the corridor, we find a wide-eyed child standing beside the door, looking almost awkward. She glances down at her maroon boots, then leads us away down the hall. She knocks three times with her little fist on another poorly-fitting wooden door, then, without waiting for an answer, opens it. I make myself take a deep breath, pulling myself together. This is where we'd been trying to get to. Now I just need to work my way through whatever the Quenchers bring.

CHAPTER THIRTY

The room is small but more graciously appointed than the sparse bathroom. It is filled with cushions. Riibi sits cross-legged upon them, with three tough-looking warriors behind him. Two have blood marking their leather armor. He half nods, half bows to us and gestures for us to sit. The low table between us is set with fine colored glassware and a teapot.

I step inside, and Liv makes as if to follow, but the child pipes up. "You are welcome with us, lady," she says. Liv looks from Riibi to me to the child.

I nod, though I swallow fear to do it. Her mouth twists in unhappiness, but she kisses me once, brusquely but on the lips, making my face flame, and follows the child back down the hall. I enter and close the door behind me.

We settle ourselves around the table, Squid's head tucked onto my leg. Riibi pours me tea. He's slow and methodical, until I'm impatient waiting for him to talk. He sips the tea, so I do the same, indicating acceptance of his hospitality. It's smokier than any I've had before, like fumes in my nostrils. He smiles, again that sad smile that doesn't reach his pale eyes.

"My name is Riibi," he repeats. "Welcome to Calindrina. Esquidamelion, it is an honor to meet you at last. You have been long awaited and longed for. Elimanesion wishes me to convey its gratitude that you have arrived and its hope that you will be ... together, soon."

He is avoiding saying that we will become one through me eating the old one, Squid says, for all the world like a jade in company unable to keep from telling tales of her trade.

Yes, thank you, Squid; I figured that one out, I respond. *I seem to recall you led with that detail about eating another dragon alive, back when you were a tiny baby.*

Squid sends a rush of indignation, followed by amusement as it realizes it's fallen for my teasing.

"Forgive me for being blunt, but time is of the essence," Riibi continues. "The enemy have Elimanesion captured, and we have experienced the most sustained attack this last night that we Quenchers have ever had."

"Do you know who it was?" I ask.

Riibi's pale eyes go chilly for a moment, and I blink, then they turn sad again. "I have a thought about that," he replies. "And I would speak of it to you, but we are the blood bonded, and we have other priorities that must come first. I am not sure how much you know, either of you, of our history or the history of dragons. We do not have much time—not nearly enough!—but there is some that I must tell you.

"We Quenchers, a long time ago now, created the Accord that bound the dragons—stopped them from interfering in humanity's history. And the Accord has given us many centuries of peace." I hear an echo of something Iradine said. I get the feeling Riibi is reciting pieces from a dozen stories told over and over again. He sighs, still speaking more slowly than my nerves are happy with. "We had not expected that the Accord would or could ever be broken. For the dragons, once a thing is, it cannot be otherwise, so once the Accord was struck, it is solid, unchanging—even more so than stone or mountain. It became a law, like the law that up is up and down is down. Or so we thought."

He pauses, swallowing hard. "Perhaps we Quenchers were too close to the dragons in this matter. That was self-aggrandizement, on our part, a forgetting of the distance between our kinds. We told ourselves our own story as if we had written the laws of this earth itself, dictated the very terms of existence. We persisted in thinking it was dragons that were the risk. It is perhaps unsurprising, given their extraordinary power. We dressed it up as honoring them, and believed that if the dragons were ... managed, the conflict between dragons and humans would be as naught." He sighs.

"But the dragons were only ever half of the Accord—*are*, if we can keep it held. Only Quenchers were the blood bonded, and we understood the risks, were raised to know them. We were raised to that sacrifice. We thought it the best control of the other half of the Accord—and we protected the rest of humanity through ignorance. By disappearing from the world and keeping the blood bond to those raised to it, we believed it would be enough to preserve the hard-earned peace from humanity's greed.

"And for a time, it was. The Accord held. We drifted from the world's knowledge, even from its stories. We became legend, and then myth, and so did the dragons. Our grand rewriting of the world worked for such a long time. We kept the precious knowledge." He bows his head in grief. "But I see now that in keeping ourselves cut off, we have left ourselves vulnerable. The control we fantasized of is the source of our weakness. Our archives burn, and I fear the Accord hangs by a thread. By the slender thread of you, Esquidamelion."

The dragon's attention narrows to the man's face. I swallow.

Elimanesion and I must become one, Squid reminds me. I feel like I am being carefully handled from two sides. *We do not know how long Elimanesion will be kept alive. If our enemies wish to destroy all knowledge of dragons, they will kill Elimanesion before we can become one. I don't even know what Elimanesion knows, and what I will only come to know through Incorporation.*

But ... why would they not already have killed it if that is their plan?

Squid's sapphire eyes glint at me, and it hesitates a moment. *Because they want me; they know that as long as Elimanesion is alive, I will try to get to it.*

"You mean it's a trap!" I say aloud, already heated. "A trap you think we should all walk into."

Riibi's face is serious. Somehow, he's put together the conversation between Squid and me. But I guess it's obvious to them both what needs to happen. "It *is* a trap, but we do have surprise on our side. They think we are all dead. We will

be able to get in. And afterward, Esquidamelion will be able to fly out, after it
has Incorporated Elimanesion. Dragons grow swiftly during Incorporation."

I look helplessly between the two. They're focusing on the wrong thing,
surely? The protection of the twenty-four people still living here is more important than Squid eating an old dragon from the inside out. Surely. "But the
Quenchers! All that knowledge! Your people!"

Riibi shakes his head. "My people and their history exist for one purpose: to
support the Accord. They have no other. If Esquidamelion does not become
one with the line of guardians, the Accord will be undone. The Era of Storms
will return, and we—all of us, all of humanity—will be destroyed. Slowly, but
inevitably."

He hesitates, spreading his hands before himself and examining the lines on
them. "The Accord is maintained only by each new guardian dragon becoming
one with the line; through Incorporation, the dragon becomes both itself *and*
its line. Incorporation makes the Accord law for each new dragon. It holds it to
the Accord, prevents it from turning destructive."

I feel a little like I'm hallucinating. "By eating its brain," I say, trying to bring
pragmatism to a conversation that feels untethered from reality.

"Not only its brain," Riibi says calmly, steadfastly looking into my eyes.
"There is a pattern of innards that Esquidamelion must consume in order to
be both itself and its line. The brain is the beginning. The eyes are second."

I feel ill.

Knowledge is not only in the brain, Squid says, as if this explains everything.

"The Accord is the guarantee," Riibi says again. "It is all that stands between
the peace we have maintained for five hundred years and the Era of Storms it
ended. Without the Accord, and without the Incorporation of the guardian,
dragons would flood into this world and devastate the land."

He says it like we'd manage that on our own, Squid adds, caustic and confusing.

I swallow hard, staring at the ceiling, and try to school my thoughts. It is like
herding cats. "Alright. Alright." I give up trying to convince the clan leader that
he must prioritize his people for a moment. That argument can wait. Let me

give way on something first, and then he may give way on another. "So you have a plan to get Squid to Elimanesion?"

Riibi nods thoughtfully. "Elimanesion is in the heart of the enemy camp. We think it is the Emperor of Ascelin, but..." He hesitates. "That discussion will have to wait," he says cryptically, then goes on. "They have put up fences around it. They would be useless if it had even a quarter of the strength it once had, but it is as near to death as it can be without dying, and it is weak. We must bring Esquidamelion to it. We have already made the plan. They will likely be expecting Esquidamelion to arrive by air—it is the dragon's way—so we will go underground."

He takes up a rock and draws two concentric circles in the sand of the cave floor and points to the smaller circle. "Elimanesion is located here, within a small crater carved out by long centuries of dragons. This"—he indicates the larger circle—"is the volcano's crater." I must look alarmed because he smiles faintly and shakes his head. "It is long dead, my lady. Now, the crater's edge is forest, and many archers have been stationed in those trees. Far more, in fact, than the guards of the inner crater. They expect Esquidamelion to arrive by air."

I nod as if willing, my mind racing. "Alright, so ... how?"

Riibi's gaze is serious. "It has been kept secret, knowledge only given from one blood bonded to another. The cave system has been extended to ensure a direct line to the guardian for the blood bonded. They will get us close. Nonetheless, there will be guards around Elimanesion. It will take three of our warriors and myself to break through the lines."

"And me," I say firmly.

Riibi looks a little cagey. "My lady, the rules of the ritual are clear. The blood bonded must be present for Incorporation. It would be safer if you remained in the caves, out of sight. We have warriors who can take Esquidamelion down to Incorporate."

My face is ugly disbelief; I can feel it. "You will take Esquidamelion nowhere without me. This is the condition."

Spoken like a true blood bonded, Squid says, both pride and amusement coming off the dragon in waves.

Don't play it like you know, Squid, I respond, almost nasty. I hesitate. *Sorry. This is not how things were meant to go down.* I can feel acknowledgment from the dragon—and no less amusement.

Riibi stills. "I cannot guarantee your safety, my lady."

I narrow my eyes. "What happens if a blood bonded is killed? Does the dragon bond again?"

Riibi makes a funny movement with his mouth. "It is not simple, and it is not good for the dragon either."

"So the dragon can bond again if I die," I say, aiming for blunt clarity. "Is that correct?"

"It can," Riibi says, "but there are consequences."

I raise my brows. He sighs—this is clearly not something he wanted to share—but adds, "It has been a long time since there was such an occurrence, and it was only prior to the Accord. But it is thought to make a dragon less ... sound of mind."

I blink. "Oh." That sounds not good.

"Yes."

But there's still something inside me that hesitates. *I don't know about you going in without me,* I say to Squid.

I don't know either, says Squid, and its uncertainty makes my heart hurt.

I think I trust him, I reply uneasily. *Do you?*

He knows more than anyone else we've found. He's a Quencher. He's in Calindrina. But I wish I knew more about all of them. I need to Incorporate so I can tell.

I swallow. I can hear the urgency in its thoughts. Its goal is almost in reach. *I don't know.* I think of Iradine, of his jealousy and his desire for the bond. Is Riibi trying to get me out of the way so another Quencher can bond, even if it risks Squid's sanity? Could he be trying to keep me out of the way so I'm easier to get rid of?

But I need to Incorporate; I know that much. That's not from a Quencher, that's from within me.

It will happen, I reply, holding my uncertainties on a tight leash. *Whatever I wind up having to do.* "I will see whether I wait in the cave or not. If it is safer for

Squid, perhaps I should." I aim to sound as open as possible, despite my doubts and hesitations. I want to trust this sad old man. It would be so much safer to have allies.

"I wish it were not necessary to have you present, but this Incorporation must work, and we have never attempted one without a blood bonded present. I do not know what impact it might have, and we cannot risk the Accord. We will do our best to keep you safe. It must happen tonight if we are to be successful. Otherwise, they will come for us."

I nod, though everything feels like it's moving too quickly. "Very well. We should make a plan to ensure that you are safe also. I will not ask you not to go—I know what the blood bond is—but ... afterward."

Riibi hesitates, then acquiesces, but his eyes are hooded. I don't trust him. *Squid?* Squid feels strangely like it's keeping itself apart from me. I swallow against the fear that I'm missing something key.

He knows I must Burn him. It is how it is done.

Alarm cascades through me. I raise my head. "But we cannot leave your clan here to die. After the four of you leave, there are only, what, twenty left? Most are children and old folks. I still think we should send whoever we can spare through to the sea. It will be safer than here." A thought strikes me. "In fact, if you could convince the other Quenchers, there is a place they could be safe, and their knowledge too. A place where there are scholars who would be pleased to assist with scribing the knowledge they carry." I take a deep breath. "But only if they take Livinia, my ... companion ... with them." I know Liv is going to kill me for sending her back to Elouise, but I cannot have her in danger. She will only distract me.

Riibi takes a long moment, nods, and strokes his beard. "Very well, my lady. If you, as blood bonded, give your word that this place you wish to send us to will be safe, the remaining Quenchers will leave Calindrina for the first time since the Accord, in the hope we can safeguard what remains of our knowledge."

"I give my word," I say firmly, hoping against hope Elouise will step up. Surely Liv will make sure she does.

"Good." Riibi rises. "We must hurry, though. There's much doing to be done before sundown if we want to ensure both these plans succeed."

He doesn't sound very hopeful, Squid comments.

I know. Do you think I did the right thing?

Doing something is better than doing nothing. I need to be one with Elimanesion. That is essential, and everything else must come after it. And this is a better plan than none. I must get to Elimanesion.

I know, I know. You've only been telling me that since we bonded, I say, as the dragon clambers up my leg and back to coil around my shoulders. *I guess we'd better get on with it, then.*

CHAPTER THIRTY-ONE

When we return to the cave full of Quenchers, Riibi announces what we have agreed, and the uninjured clan folk disperse to pack and make further plans. Liv approaches me, and I smile, hold out an arm to her, and guide her to a corner. It's the nearest we'll get to privacy. She leans against me, and I hug her close, planting a kiss against her temple.

"What's going on?" she asks in a small voice. "You haven't been this easily affectionate with me since... Well, since before." She meets my eyes, and her green ones are wary. "Wait..."

"Liv, listen." I take both her hands in my own and gaze into her eyes, injecting all the honesty and sincerity I can muster into my voice and shoving the anxiety I feel back. "I have to do something, and it's dangerous. It is. They are sneaking Squid into the enemy camp. There is no other way; it must be done. And they have a good plan, a way to keep us safe." It's not quite true, but I can't have her worrying about that.

She swallows visibly. "Alright," she says finally, nodding. "If we have to."

My mouth tightens. "Not you, lovely," I make myself say. My throat is so tight it's hard to get the words out. "I need you to take the survivors out. I need you far away from here, safe. I cannot have you here, not when there is so much danger." I force myself to say the words, even though I know they will hurt her.

"But I can help," she says, her voice still small. "If it's the prince, or the king, or the emperor... I know these people, remember? I can intervene."

I sigh, pressing my lips together. "It's beyond that now, Liv. It was beyond that when they burned the Quenchers' village and tried to kill them all. There's no negotiating, not anymore. We need to be sneaky. They will expect Squid to fly in, so we must go underground, then over land, but that means confronting scouts, soldiers, everything...

"It's dangerous, and I'm not sure your history with these people would keep you safe. We think it's the emperor, and he... Well, you fled his camp and wound up in the prince's hands. Fuck knows what they'd do to you. No, I need you to take the survivors. Get them to Elouise. She will be able to protect them. And you."

This stings her pride. "So this is my punishment for being so foolish back then? Why can you not forgive me?" She barely meets my eyes—just glimmers of green through black lashes. Playing me.

It's hard to keep the unfurling anger at bay. Hot and fierce, it burns in my gut and reminds me of everything that is left unresolved between us—but reminds me of the promise of it too. "Liv. Honesty, remember?" My tone is hard, and I force my expression to match.

She inhales, and I can see her fighting back anger at the position I've put her in, battling to stay honest when she's scared. It near breaks my heart. It feels more akin to commitment than anything I've ever had from her, than anything I've ever thought I could want from her. It feels like fidelity, and that was something that even in my flightiest dreams, I'd never imagined.

"Alright. Honesty." She pulls her hands away and tosses her dark hair. "I am hurt. I cannot believe that after all of this, that after all these weeks and all my work—because it is hard for me, Des, you know how hard it is for me—to be honest, to give you only what I know I can, but to give that as freely as I can... And after all of working to be with you, to work alongside, to be more than just rescued..."

I blink, unable to take it in. Liv is crying, and these are not stage tears but actual sobs, wrenching and deep. My heart fills until it feels like it must overflow.

"Liv. Liv. Liv, no, don't cry, love," I say, and pull her into my arms. "This is not a punishment. It's a promise, the same promise. We will be together again. We have a conversation that we have to have."

"Then have it with me!" she cries, pulling away. "How can you risk that? How can you risk us? And on a chance that's so... Des, their whole tribe nearly died, and you want to go to war with their conqueror?"

I shake my head as I look at her, so beautiful despite the red-rimmed eyes. "Liv," I say, my heart squeezing. "This is something I must do because I am me. Just as..." I take a deep breath and shove my internal Petrus back, swallowing hard and pitching for honest. Honest is hard. I can't help it—I've worked so hard to make this a lie. "Just as I must love you, because I am me, and because you are you."

I smile, swallowing tears. "Liv, you've been honest, now I have to be. I have loved you forever, and I will love you 'til then too. We will be together again, I swear it. As I live, I cannot be without you. I have tried, and it is half a life." It's true, though the drama of it feels unfamiliar. Warmth fills me. I've denied myself that kind of big emotion for too long—distrusted it after it was put to the lie.

She softens into smiles as I speak, but at the last, she hardens again. "Corpses can't keep vows," she says, and her voice is stony.

I nod my agreement. "They cannot. Which is why I will be remaining very much alive."

She swallows. "But all those dead..."

"Do you truly have so little faith in my swordplay?" I ask, teasing now to try to lighten the mood. "Truly? Remember, I've saved you how many times now?"

She hesitates for a long moment, meeting my eyes, then shakes her head, spreads her hands, and smiles. "Alright. I give in."

I squeeze her hands once more. "Don't get too used to submission, lovely. I've missed our gameplay."

She grins, sexy as fuck, and I grin back. "That's a promise, you know," she tells me.

"It is," I say, hoping against hope I have even the vaguest capacity to fulfill it.

"My lady?" Iradine interrupts, not meeting my eyes. "Livinia is coming with us?"

"So it would seem," Liv says, with half a smile. She kisses me, passionate enough to make my head reel, and then she is gone, a cloud of ebony curls disappearing around a corner into the dark. It feels too quick, this farewell—there's so much left to say.

You two are extremely complicated, Squid observes.

"They're leaving already?" I feel a little bereft. I look around, and all are gone, in fact, except Riibi, the three stern warriors, and a dragon. It all feels like it's happening too fast. I take a deep breath. "Alright. Let's do this, then."

Riibi takes the lead, bearing the bright light, and I scurry to keep up with the three burly warriors he has selected to accompany us. They introduce themselves, bowing perfunctorily, as Lemna, Jonna, and Kribin. They make me feel a little inexperienced, somehow, despite my long years joining merc companies made up of people just like them.

Besides, you're my blood bonded, Squid says.

I send amusement to it. *Yes, but that only means something to them, really. Doesn't make me a better fighter, does it?*

It might yet, Squid comments, a little enigmatically. *Which is another reason I have to get to Elimanesion.*

Looks like I'll get more practice today anyway, I respond grimly.

After a while, the tunnels change. The caves allow single file only, and Squid, traveling on the wall near the ceiling, has to dig its claws into stone in order to keep out of the way of heads and shoulders. At first, the levels are flat, but after a little while, they head abruptly uphill, with small niches carved into the deeply sloped floor of the tunnel. It's almost a chimney, almost stairs, but not quite either.

The warriors barely lose their breath, and Riibi is remarkably fit for a man of his age. I'm hardly unfit—being on the run will help with that—but after a while of bending double and somehow still walking uphill, I'm a little breathless.

Riibi drops back to walk just behind me so I can hear his voice. "There is something I must share with you. The others will go on ahead a little. The rest of the clan do not know what I suspect, but I share it with you because I do not know when I may die. Especially once you and Elimanesion become one, and I am gone." He addresses this to Squid, and I bite my lip, my own death an echo in his words. I'm grateful he can't see my expression.

"Of course, Elimanesion will know this, but it is so old and frail that it and I both fear perhaps the Incorporation will no longer work as it once did. Dragons are not made for mortality, yet nor are they made for the strange immortality they live here amidst what they call time's chains. It is the oldest, we think, that has ever been. We do not know the effects of extended mortal time on dragons, and nor do any of the records we have. And the records..." He meets the questions in my gaze, interprets them as only one. "The ransacking burned all the archives."

I inhale sharply. "Wait, the entire history of the Quenchers?"

"I believe so, other than those we fled with. The talespinner is injured, but she may recover yet. But it is this destruction that makes me fear I am right in my guess." He takes a deep breath. "Forgive me telling this as a story, but that is all it is, now. We have buried knowledge of it—it was the elders who made the decision, and all those who knew the tale amongst this clan are dead now, except for me and the current talespinner.

"We Quenchers are a small clan, and we do not keep our children here against their will. If they wish to leave, we allow them to. Many do. It is a quiet and thankless life, here in the mountains, cut off from the rest of humanity. But one of our children, long ago, we sent away. We did not do this lightly.

"The boy was fascinated with Elimanesion. This is not unusual—indeed, it is usually the reason that our children stay, if they do—but this fascination was obsessive. The boy learned to read faster and better than any of the other children. We discovered that, for months, he had been sneaking bright light from the stores and spending entire nights in our archives—the secret ones, the ones that no one but our elders knew existed. This had been going on for months before we learned of it.

"But we only found out because Elimanesion called to me one night. The lad had crept from his bed—all of eleven he was at this point—and up the mountain to the dragon itself. The dragon was not slumbering, but Elimanesion had lived a life of peace and did not expect harm to come from a Quencher, especially one so small. But the lad had crept close, beneath Elimanesion's front leg, and with a small knife we use for cutting meat, he punctured the skin beneath the joint, where the scales are rubbed thin by wear."

There's a small noise, and I turn slightly to look. Riibi weeps, silent tears tracking down his face, but he doesn't look up at me. I hesitate a moment and keep climbing through the cave. "You must understand. Since the Accord, no human has had any reason to do any dragon harm. Since the Accord, no human had. Indeed, that was part of why the dragons agreed to it—they who hate death more than we do. It is why the Accord must be preserved—peace is guaranteed by it—else we risk a return to the Era of Storms. Elimanesion, thankfully, recognized a foolish boy's desire to see a dragon's blood must not jeopardize the long peace, and it reined in its anger.

"We ejected the boy from the clan. Not harshly—we do not have it in our nature to be harsh—but we sent him to live in the world. We had thought that was the end of it."

He pauses. Dread sweeps over me like fever, my mind connecting disparate pieces of information. How many times had I heard people speak of the emperor's pale, unsettling eyes, so like Iradine's and Riibi's and the rest of the clan's? And the duchess told me the emperor had appeared as if from nowhere to take Ascelin from its former king. The green of the scout in the tree by Calindrina. I gulp, skin prickling. "You think he's back," I say.

Riibi meets my eyes. "I do. We called our child Tariij, and that emperor is Tari—almost as if the Ascelese took his Quencher name and made it their own. I think this attack, this capture of Elimanesion, and the destruction of our village... It could only have been planned by one who knew our layout. The soldiers knew precisely how thorough to be. They torched our entire archive, and..."

He thinks they all are doomed, Squid finishes as he trails off. *He thinks it only a matter of time before he sends more after them.*

"You think this is genocide?" I finally manage. "You think he destroyed everything? *Deliberately?*"

"Can it be a genocide of so few?" he asks sadly. "This loss, as marked and re-markable as it is to us, as devastating as it is to humanity's continued survival..." I glance back at his pause, and he shakes his head. "We let ourselves become few, become small. When I was a lad, all those years ago, the Quencher clan was thousands strong. Now ... after last night, we number barely four-and-twenty, and I do not like our chances. With an enemy who knows our caves as well as we do..." I can hear the submission in his voice. This is a man who has already given up. He sounds so tired.

I exhale slowly, stepping into the role. There has to be a voice of hope some-where, and it looks like I have to be it today. "Riibi, I know that it is hard, but you cannot give up." I stop moving and turn toward him, meeting his gaze.

He smiles small and sad. "I am not giving up, my lady," he says softly, "but I cannot see a way out either."

And he is old. He does not want a way out, Squid opines in my head. *He knows he must abandon his people. I will Burn him after Incorporation, and he will no longer have to worry about this tribe he has led to nothing.*

My gut roils at the dragon's ease with the idea of killing this man, old beyond old though he is. *Careful, Squid. He's an old man, and he has lost a lot this past day. Let us be kind.* There's no response, but I can feel the dragon's dismissal.

"There are always ways." I smile as gently and as optimistically as I can manage. "The way through to the sea is clear, or it was when Iradine led us back. It may not be now, but the tunnels are narrow, much of the time, and any skirmishes that might be necessary will be on their terms. They will make it. You could go back—join them."

Riibi looks at me, and his eyes are gentle. "You are very kind, my lady, but my duty lies here, with you. All our duties do. I thought you should know the story, understand who the enemy is. It may prove important." I can see that he thinks none of us will survive, and my breath comes short. He nods once, then steps past me and continues on, leaving me to stare at his back before I follow.

Without him speaking, it's quiet in the caves. It makes too much space in my head. I've always made sure that anytime I had to face down enemies, the half hour before was spent doing something busy—talking to people, playing royals... anything to keep the space at bay. And now I remember why. As I trot along behind them all, my uncertainties well up. I didn't have much choice, but nonetheless, I've managed to put myself and Squid in the hands of a man I met barely three hours ago.

Three hours or ten years ago, Squid comments.

I guess, I reply, recalling Riibi's words to Iradine in the Traverse, and Iradine's jealousy and anger at me. I don't like making enemies, especially amongst those who are almost my friends. I don't particularly dislike the boy. Watching his sorrow and grief felt somehow awfully intimate, and it's hard to feel much but pity for him. Thinking of Iradine makes me wonder, again, whether Riibi's steadfast loyalty to the Accord would include killing me so that I might be replaced in the blood bond. He'd been so clear it was meant to be a Quencher holding up the human side of the agreement.

They could have easily overwhelmed us earlier, Squid observes. *Even Iradine, that first morning by the cave. You and Liv were asleep. It was only me as guard.*

I don't know, I say. *It's hard to know who to trust. But you're right; they've had many opportunities.* And besides, perhaps this is Riibi's belated attempt to grow the Quenchers, learning from what he sees as their mistakes.

I think I would prefer you by my side, Squid says hesitantly. *I don't like the idea of you being left behind in these caves alone.*

I don't either, I reply, *and the fact that Riibi wants me close but not with you... If his plan is to take me out and replace me with one of these Quencher warriors*—I glance forward at Jonna's broad, muscled back—*perhaps the easiest way to foil that plan is to be alongside all of you in the fight...*

I can't help but think of Liv following back through the tunnels to the coast, leading the small tribe to Scyless and Elouise. I couldn't have expected the sense of peace I have from having told her—once more, after all this time—that I love her. It's odd that honesty can do that. I think of all the years I spent shoving that truth away, mocking my own love, with Petrus to help... And I think of that kiss, that final kiss, and I smile a little in the dark. It's so uncertain. I can't know what she wants. I barely understand what I want. But a conversation. A promise to keep.

Then I school my thoughts—scattered never made for a good fight—and focus on walking and keeping thoughts of that conversation with Liv at bay.

The tunnel goes even more vertical. I take a breath, gather my strength, and push myself into clambering up the tall chimney. Shallow dips for hand- and footholds are carved to either side, but they're rough and slippery. Kribin, climbing behind me, catches my foot back into a foothold at one point. I thank him breathlessly, trying hard not to imagine what might have happened. What a stupid end that would have been.

The tunnel exits into a small cavern. Riibi comes up last, and he extinguishes the bright light before he does. It makes me grateful I'd had the light as the darkness cascades in.

We pause here, just a series of breaths in the dark. I breathe deeply to keep my reaction to absolute black at bay. My legs are shaking with effort.

"I will be with you all," I tell Riibi in a firm voice.

His pale eyes glimmer in the darkness, but he nods once, an affirmation. "We are just within the perimeter of the camp," Riibi whispers to me. "Lemna scouted earlier, and the sentry line should be just behind us. We need to check and make sure we don't catch them while they move to the next post, which they do approximately every quarter hour."

I nod. "And then?"

"Then we have only a little stretch of forest before it gives way to the crater proper, and it won't be too thick. Taller trees and a strong canopy mean there's less growth down here on the ground."

"The crater proper?" I repeat, even though he's been through this before. As if being sure of the lay of the land guaranteed the outcome.

"We will come out within the bowl of the old volcano," Riibi says, patient. "The jungle that surrounds it has gradually encroached on the edges, and that's where we will exit the tunnel. We will have a bit of cover for a while, but only for a while. The trees and vines peter out after a few hundred feet. The approach to the dragon's crater at the center is bare—very limited protection, and they'll likely be at us with arrows. We will each carry a shield, but that must protect the dragonet most of all. Once we reach the dragon's crater at the center, the fence line is around the top of the crater."

"The fence line?" I repeat and try to breathe through the panic.

"Yes. They've put a line of pikes around the dragon crater." He pauses. "There are only a few guards in the center, we think, and we will be able to fight them, but there are many archers on the trees around the edge of the bowl. Once we reach the fence line, we will be beyond the reach of their arrows, so we will be exposed from the edge of the rainforest to the edge of the central crater."

"Where the fence line is?" I repeat, trying to get the image clear in my head.

Riibi nods—I can feel the movement in the dark. He hesitates for a long moment, then adds, "But, my lady, I must be honest. It is perilous. It is a long and rocky sprint across the bare ground to the dragon crater at the center. They will send guards in as soon as the alarm is raised. We can only hope to buy Esquidamelion enough time to complete the Incorporation." I can almost feel his gaze in the dark. "Perhaps you should remain here. It is a risk, and you are the blood bonded. You are as much a target as the dragonet, perhaps more so. Perhaps, if we make it back, we can all flee through the tunnels together, and then you will not be putting yourself at risk."

I swallow in the dark, half-annoyed he's revisiting including me. He has no intention of returning alive—I know this. He expects to be Burned by Squid after the Incorporation, if he even survives that long. Is he really trying to protect me, or is this all just manipulation to have me left behind here so an assassin can come up behind me in the dark?

I know odds, and the odds of this sally succeeding are not good. I can't leave Squid to face that alone, after everything. I swallow once more, hard. "This is our best shot, though, right?"

I feel rather than see Riibi's nod. "It is, my lady."

This is riskier than I thought, Squid comments, sounding as if it wishes it didn't have to say it. *After all we've done to get here ... I don't like that you are in such danger.*

Nor do I, I say, *but that's what we signed up for, right?*

Well, I did, by getting born, but I'm not so sure about you. I can hear the dragon's guilt for foisting immortality on me.

Too late for doubts, I send back firmly. *Get ready.*

CHAPTER THIRTY-TWO

L emna returns a moment later, and with a gentle push, sends us all out of the dark tunnel. The opening is narrow and covered with spiderwebs and jungly growth. I slither out into a night muggy, warm, and full of insects. The slope is steep and covered in tall trees, but unlike on the mountainside where we met Iradine, and even different to the Quencher's village, vines don't rope between the trees as much, and the way before us is not clogged with growth. Rainforest rather than jungle. I can barely see, but a few spikes of moonlight make it through the growth.

Jonna, a burly woman with arms twice the size of mine, leads the way through, hacking as quietly as possible at the few ferns and vines in our path, and clambering spryly over fallen tree trunks.

I follow, Squid beside me. I'm noisier than any of the Quenchers, and the jungle catches at my everything, seeking to stop me getting through. I savagely settle such superstition, but still, I feel singularly ill-equipped for this particular escapade. "Give me thugs in a city street any day," I murmur to myself, earning a glare from Riibi.

Movement sounds off in the rainforest to our right, and we still, listening hard. All I can hear is my heart hammering in my ears. After what feels like an eternity, Jonna signals us on.

Finally, we reach the edge of the rainforest, pausing in the last stretch of its shadow. I swallow, hoping there are no archers concealed in the trees above us. The bare section between the edge of the rainforest and the pikes around the rim of the dragon's crater—the distance that Riibi had described as "long"—looks like it goes forever from here.

We won't be able to follow the rough path to our right as it leaves the trees in case the guards see us, but we will join it eventually. It heads down a slope and then out across ground so uneven it promises at least one of us will break an ankle. Squid clambers up to coil around my shoulders. It's comforting, but it reminds me of how big it is. It won't be able to do that for much longer. If we survive.

I swallow again, shoving at dread.

"Ready yourself, my lady," Lemna says to me softly. "We don't have long. And if the alert has been raised, we will have even less time to make our way to the center. We cannot wait."

I have to get there, Squid tells me, sounding a little desperate.

I know, I send back.

But it's more dangerous than I thought it would be.

I know that too.

I should go alone.

That's very noble, I reply, *but we talked about this. I don't fully trust these Quenchers not to be trying to take you from me in the name of their bloody Accord by separating us now. Also, I know how to use a sword. I'm going with you.*

The warriors form their shields into a big rectangle, bracing the four together into a rough shelter. *You're meant to go under there,* I tell Squid. *This is a better chance. The best chance.* All I can hope is the alarm takes a long time to be raised.

Are you sure? Squid sounds dubious. *Better than me against the night sky?*

The moon is out. I point to the orb hanging over the edge of the bowl and silvering everything. *You'd be seen in a second.*

And you?

As if in answer to Squid's question, Jonna hands me a shield. "You will need to protect yourself, my lady," she tells me softly. "We will be too busy protecting the dragonet to help."

This just gets better and better, Squid sends me, sounding almost panicky. *Who came up with this plan, anyway?*

Not so long ago, you were all in! Deep breath, dragon, I say softly. *We are almost to where we have been aiming to be for months now. This is not the moment to lose your nerve.*

Lose my nerve! Squid sounds indignant, which is precisely what I was aiming for. As if to prove how courageous it is, it slips down from my shoulders to the ground.

"We all run at Riibi's pace, or this won't work," Lemna whispers. "Ready all?" Jonna and Kribin murmur agreement.

"Now!" Jonna hisses, and the large shield, made up of the four smaller shields, moves forward.

They emerge from the trees, with Squid keeping pace beneath, slithering like a goanna across the uneven ground. With the same quiet agility Iradine had displayed in the caves, they run full pelt while awkwardly shielding the dragonet. Squid races away from me faster than I could have expected. Panic shoots through my veins. I resist it for a bare second.

Then I force myself to take a deep breath, lift the shield above my head, and follow, sprinting as hard as I possibly can.

All I can hear is my own heart and feet, both pounding. A yell behind me sounds, the alert being called between the sentries. I hunch my shoulders, expecting an arrow in the back at any moment, but there is nothing, not for a long, long moment.

Then a whistle sounds behind me and a thunk as the arrow strikes the ground to my right. I'm in range. Another flush of fear kicks everything into gear, and I'm racing, following the ludicrous dragon shield and keeping my eyes on Squid's blue tail, swishing back and forth as it matches pace with the warriors and Riibi.

Another whistle and another thunk off to the side, then another, and another, and another. Pain like a lightning flash scores my ankle, and I nearly stumble.

Squid sends me anxiety and fear, and in response, I master the pain in a split second, still running. *If I'm running, I'm not injured*, I point out brusquely, then focus again on the sound of arrows. Getting closer one second, it feels like, then the next, like we're almost out of reach. One second, the fence is only a step away. The next, like the distance is endless.

My breath scissors in my lungs.

Abruptly, we hit the line of pikes. Squid slithers easily between the stakes set in the ground. As I haul myself forward and squeeze between the stakes, I see a truly astonishing sight.

I have seen Elimanesion before, as it was only a few years ago. This dragon is a little older, significantly weaker, and is clearly weary. It is also the most massive animal I have ever seen. Easily the size of a large mansion, with fronds curling back from beside its enormous jaws, it is a faded blue-purple, with pearly white along the folds in its neck. As Squid slides on its belly down the dark crater toward it, Elimanesion sighs the biggest, softest sound I have heard, and then the immense jaws part to form a deadly cave. A welcome.

But between Squid and the old dragon is a line of guards. Eight, I somehow know, and I throw myself forward, free of the pikes as Squid hesitates, roaring like a thunderclap. No. No.

No one is going to get between my dragon and the old one.

At the first clash of sword against unfamiliar shield, I realize how stupid these odds are. My heart leaps into my throat. A roar matches mine, and the four Quenchers join me in the fray. The odds are still stupid. My arm reverberates as I block a heavy blow that would have almost cut me in half. I bite my tongue. The shock shakes my bones.

Then, my swordplay player steps in, and I am calmly, calmly, center-of-storm, blocking and dodging. I stab through, spearing first through the shoulder, then deftly, quickly, pulling the sword free and plunging the point of my blade through the gap in the armor at the neck. My opponent falls.

I turn, swinging my sword ahead of me, and just in time too because another sword aims at my neck. My blade twists, but I hold fast, trying to take in what is happening behind me.

Jonna is still going strong, but Lemna is down. I block the swing at my thigh, then shove my shield toward the grim-faced guard, hoping to shove her off balance. I glance again, and Kribin is on one knee, thigh bleeding black in the moonlight. But we're down to four opponents, and Riibi is surprisingly fast for an old man, slicing in with double blades to bring another down. As he turns away, he falls.

But there's a path. A path through the battle. It blazes in the moonlight as if a beam of sunlight lit it.

"SQUID!" I scream, my voice barely more than a croak. "NOW!"

I slash savagely at my opponent and go back-to-back with Jonna, defending ourselves against the three who still stand.

And Squid—a blue-black serpentine line in the moonlight—scurries forward, clambers up and over those enormous white teeth, and into the mouth. The colossal jaws begin to close.

Terror, a fear of loss unlike anything I've ever felt, floods me, nearly sending me to the ground.

I open my mouth to cry to it. *Oh, Squid,* I settle for sending. *Good luck! Good luck! Come back to me!*

And so it begins.

I swing a wild blade at my opponent's head, then reverse to cut deep into her thigh. She falls, and I stab hard through her neck.

I turn, catching a glimpse as the old dragon first moans, then groans deep. It slides over to its side, and its narrow claws begin to twitch in the air. It is so clearly in enormous pain, and even more clearly fixed to tolerate it. There's something both admirable and utterly alien about its calm.

I dodge and swing, then push back with my shield, and this guard trips, falling down. I raise my blade, slash across his neck, and turn, breathing hard, to assist Jonna against the final two.

My mind explodes.

Time layers, like in the Traverse but moving in and out of focus. Not only is the when in flux this time, but the where as well. I'm no longer in the dark, moonlit crater. I hover high above a colony of ants glimmering in a sunlight so bright it makes my eyes ache. And then I realize, just as my fire descends upon them, that they're not ants at all.

It's an army, and the faint cries of hundreds and hundreds of soldiers burning to a crisp as their armor begins to melt sounds troublingly like discordant music. It's just a glimpse, then it's gone.

I am in a tall stone hall, and a queen, recognizable by the crown on her head and the scepter in her hand, is on one knee before me, genuflecting before her own throne.

An animal like a wombat careers down a hillside towards me, a human carrying twin hatchets balanced on its back. Then a horse, also bearing a human, races towards me, and I reach out one long leg to pull myself towards the pair, and then another long, hard claw to carve through the horse's backside.

I roar flame down across an undulating hillside, taking out crops and animals and small village buildings as if they were all the same. Because they are all the same. Rage swallows me up, and I could not say why.

And then sorrow, bone deep, and I sail over a fray. Blood has coagulated with mud, and horses are up to their knees in it and struggling to move. A sob catches in my throat—the waste of it all—and I bellow up flame like vomit, taking them out of the world that causes such devastation. My tears sizzle as they drip to earth.

Calm, broad satisfaction fills me. I sail through the air, spiraling down through cloud toward a mountain peak, the sun gleaming, my wings soaking up its rays.

Then anguish swoops through me, such as I have never known. An anguish of exile and loss, of the unbearable knowledge that life will end, of knowing that life need not have beginnings and endings as this, of knowing that I am condemned to this injustice. It is the most profound grief, like I can no longer find myself.

I curl through hot sand, burrowing deeper beneath it until I am cool on my belly and warmed above and my blood slows languid and joyous in my veins.

Then my world is circumscribed, a small crater within a crater, where I am curled up, soaking up sun and warmth from the volcano beneath, but old and melancholy and longing for a death I also abhor.

The flashes speed up, and I am overwhelmed by sound and smell and taste and touch and thoughts and words and people and emotions like a dam bursting, and through it all, the unbearable, unending loneliness of being the only, of knowing others only as shadows, as part of me, never as fully another. Except for these small, incomprehensibly short-lived mortals, too minute but to be fixated on their own lives and concerns...

And then black.

CHAPTER THIRTY-THREE

I come to, aching and blurry, and the world looks starkly different. Darkness still. Flaming torches held beside swords surround and blind me, and a tall, handsome man stands barely two feet away. He is speaking, but as much as I strain, my mind cannot understand what he is saying. I blink. Is he blinded? Why are his eyes so pale? My memory nudges at me.

Squid?

Hush, lass, the dragon sends back.

Gladness floods me. *Lass?* I think. *Since when do you call me lass?*

Hush now. Do not speak aloud. They will kill you if they suspect you are my blood bonded.

I blink at the sky for a long moment, trying to take this in. Everything—even my eyes—hurts. I try to rally whatever resources are left, but there is almost none. It takes all my strength to raise my head.

A corpse smokes not far from me. Riibi's neck is cut and almost severed, his wide, pale eyes staring at me out of a face blackened by flame. My gorge rises. Beside him, I make out the other three Quencher warriors. They are all dead. Even Jonna, brave Jonna, who must have defended me as I lost myself in the dragon's chaotic transformation. Tears spring to my eyes.

Between the soldiers' legs, I make out the remains of Elimanesion's corpse—mostly patches of skin and bone, with some fat and sinew beside it. I roll sideways and vomit in the dirt.

As I do, I spot Squid. They have put it in a cage made of thick metal with large holes punctured in it. Not even a cage, really, more of a large box. The blue eyes glimmer at me. It looks so different but still the same. Bigger.

They have you? I say, almost plaintive in my disbelief. *No, Squid! No! We made it so far!*

Do not focus on me or they will know, Squid sends me calmly. *They cannot know.*

But you're in a cage.

They will kill you if they know. This is serious, lass. Life or death. Fear floods me, sparking all of my nerves in spite of the bone-breaking exhaustion that fills my body.

"The survivor!" the handsome man comments as I haul myself upright. I blink at him and realize that what I'd thought was blindness was the same pale Quencher eyes as Iradine and Riibi and all the others. Is this Tariij? As Riibi said? But I know him too. I frown, trying to work out where from. My vomit reeks, and I have to swallow hard to keep from heaving again. "Fainted with fear, did you?"

And then, horribly, I see who is standing beside him, smiling up at him, green eyes rimmed in kohl, pink skirts prettily arranged, and her hair cascading around her pale, bare shoulders. She holds a fan as a concession to the humidity, and with a laugh, she playfully waves it at the handsome man.

Liv.

A spear thrusts through my heart. Disbelief is like a blow, then bile rises in my throat again, and hatred of an intensity I have never, ever known fills me. It burns until there is nothing left, until I am nothing but hate.

She may be our only chance now, Squid reminds me. *Play nice. Remember, he cannot know you are my blood bonded. You must not hesitate when you walk away. He cannot have you. Must not. Des. He must not. Everything hangs on this.*

"You see, your majesty?" Liv says to him. "As I said. The one weak link. This is it."

With an effort that feels like it might send me cascading back into unconsciousness, I school my everything and turn my face toward the handsome man. Stupid seems safest. I don't have the blade to back the brazen. And so, I play. Weak link. "It was so dark! So scary! And there were arrows everywhere. I was so scared!"

"You're all so *scary*," the handsome man says to his soldiers, his accent clear, and they all laugh.

Liv smiles along with it, adding wryly, "Though to be fair, this one would probably find a monkey terrifying." The soldiers laugh harder.

The man's voice changes to granite. "Pull her up. Let's see just how scary she finds us." Two soldiers haul me up by the arms. I stumble to my feet and then freeze at a prick to my neck—a sword against my throat. I glance at Liv. She's still, the small smile yet on her lips. She doesn't even react. Hatred boils inside me.

"Not quite a Quencher, then, are you?" the handsome man says snidely. Suddenly, I recognize him. Walking beside Crainor—the brute I killed in Scyless—in that laneway in Valenta. The one seeking the gem. The torturer. I think of the ruined corpses of the two goons. Of Rositus.

I swallow my gorge. Fuck.

Fear crashes like ice water over me. "N-n-no, m-my lord," I quaver, venturing a guess at rank to seek the clarification. Liv had said, "majesty" ...

He laughs. "Not a *lord*, girl. Your new *emperor*! To the empire!" he adds to his audience, and the soldiers roar a cheer. The blade at my throat wavers away to point at the ground, and I remember how to breathe.

My knees tremble. I feel like I have been beaten six ways then left out in the sun to bake in my own juices. "Y-y-your I-imperial M-majesty?" I try again, and it's not hard to make my curtsy awkward, with my body aching as it is. "What is going on?"

"You see, Emperor Tari," Liv says, smoothly but carelessly, with one hand resting on the man's forearm and her breast pressing against his upper arm.

Watching her play makes my nausea rise. "Weak. Doctor Phelian is not made for battle nor for intrigue. From what I learned of traveling with her, she is a gentle soul, a scholar really, but without the rigor to feel at home in the hierarchy at the king's college. Getting caught up in these events has left her befuddled."

She bends and plucks at my sleeve, and fury stops the breath in my chest. "Look, her shirt is far too fine to be a mercenary's, and she's obviously not of that weird little tribe. Her eyes are too dark. She cannot be the one you seek. Perhaps it was one of these—that blood-bonded one you sought?" She looks around at the Quencher corpses, nonchalant. "The good doctor was just my ride, my best chance for recapturing the dragon, as I promised. I knew whoever stole it would be driven north, and she knew this area from her studies." He glares down at me with the casual gaze of a cruel child deciding whether to pluck the wings from a fly. Liv pauses a moment, then goes on. "As you see fit, of course, Your Glorious Momentousness."

Her excessive epithet makes him glance at her to see if she mocks him, and I can breathe the moment he looks away. The expression on her face is perfectly calculated—enough wickedness to betray that she sought to play, but not so much she sought to make him a fool.

The bile rises in my throat, my blood roiling, as she goes on. "But in my estimation, Phelian knows nothing of the Quenchers' attempts to circumvent your plans. She was drawn to care for the remnants of the tribe after the attack, that's all. It would be of most benefit to leave her here when we head back to Ascelin. She will make an excellent propagandist for your cause, what with a scholar's commitment to truth, connections to the king's college, and her evident intimidation and overwhelm at Your Imperiousness."

I gape at her, but she ignores me utterly. Her tone is precise, clinical. She might be giving me an out, but it can't change the fact that she's handed Squid over to him and, in exchange, has obviously won herself significant standing in the court, and probably more besides. The earth feels like it moves beneath me. Has she been playing me all along? All for this? All that honesty I thought I'd won from her... I think of her apology over Petrus, of her prizing open the space between us by that cave above Hathway. Of her promises. The bile rises again, and I spit it onto the ground. She's won, again. And I didn't even think it a fight.

The emperor wrinkles his nose. "An herbalist she called you, Doctor," he says to me, his eyes wary and cautious. "Madam Livinia thinks you would be best left behind, but perhaps ... You cared for the few who escaped our attack on the Quenchers? Are you skilled in nursing the injured?"

I have a split second in which to make this decision, and Squid is very clear. *No. You must flee. There is no other option. Free, you can help me. Captured, we are both done for.* I draw up every shred of player skill I can find and shake my head sadly. "I fear not, Your Majesty. I am not made for blood, as you can see." I spread my hands helplessly and indicate the pile of vomit I left on the ground behind me. "I have specialized in respiratory illnesses. I helped those whose lungs burned in the fire. Someone else had to deal with the wounds, for I..." I pretend to gag at the recollection. "But few survived, despite my assistance, and those that did will mostlike die within days." It's a desperate lie, and I can only hope Liv hasn't sold out the surviving Quenchers as well. She's made clear she'd sell her own grandmother, though, so I don't like our chances.

The emperor's eyes narrow. "And you wound up in Calindrina, caught up in this mess because..."

This is the moment, lass. She gave you the space, whatever else she's stolen from you. Take the lie, and make it work. Play it.

I had thought the adrenaline was done, but it spikes through me, damping down the pain and speeding up my thoughts. I lie as quickly as I can, my mind dancing through the options. "I had heard, Your Majesty, that some time ago now—twenty years, perhaps..."—long enough to be a story, not truth, but not so long that this Tari would have known it before he was banished from the Quencher village—"a great medicine woman with an exceptional knowledge of fevers and coughs had returned from the mountains near Calindrina with a rare rainforest plant which had the power to break a fever within a day, clear the lungs, and support the body in healing. If it is true, then this is an extraordinary finding."

I let scholarly excitement fill my voice. "It would save so many lives, especially amongst the old and the young, and the poor, who so often die simply because their bodies cannot bear the ravages of their illness and they are too poor to afford warmth when they need it. It would transform medicine, I believe, to be able to administer so reliable an antipyretic, and one which would promote healing also. Transform it! Well, it would have if I had found it..."

The emperor is bored already, which is precisely what I was aiming for. "Yes? And you wound up in this crater with these treasonous cowards?" He gestures at Riibi's dead body.

I swallow fury, banking it in my bones. I have an opportunity here, if I can spin it right. "I... I saw the fire, Your Majesty, and made toward it. I helped these few survivors, as my art demands, Your Majesty. They were all that was left. They said coming down into this crater was safer than fleeing alone, and my companion, Livinia, had disappeared, so I joined them.

"I only realized when we were coming down here that they meant to attack, but it was too late, and I didn't know where I was, so I couldn't leave. But, Your Majesty, I didn't know they were traitors!" I aim for innocent and shocked. "Had I known..." I let tears fill my eyes. "Oh, Your Majesty! I swear I did not know. I do not even understand what they were doing—what I was doing."

One of the emperor's men says, "She ran with them but lagged behind. Could be she's telling the truth, sir." The emperor strokes his chin.

I snivel, letting watery snot run down my face to my mouth, and praying to gods I never quite believed in that Jonna killed all of those who had seen me fight. It hadn't been my best fight, but it would absolutely put the lie to the story I was weaving here.

"I didn't understand what they were doing, and it was scary in that rainforest back there. There were... There were things in it! Poisonous spiders, snakes, even tigers. And I left my antidote kit behind because I thought we'd be going back afterward. You may not be aware, Your Majesty, but poisons is one of the most complex areas of medicine. If I'd been bitten or stung, I'd really have needed a specialist, a scholar in the field, and me so far from civilization..."

I clear my throat as though embarrassed to be found lecturing an emperor. "So, I thought it would be better with the survivors. They gave me a sword..." I look around as if confused as to where it has gotten to. "They had big swords, even if they were traitors." I can only hope this performance is going to be enough.

Liv laughs lightly, as if this is excellent entertainment. "It's as I reported to you, Your Majesty. Too much the scholar. I'm not even sure she's seen anyone killed before. Imagine a life so protected." The soldiers around her laugh as well.

I spit in her direction.

"Whoa! Not so toothless, perhaps?" The emperor comments, but he's not really interested. His gaze keeps swaying to Squid, locked in its cage. He obviously wants to talk to the dragon urgently, or do something to it. Ice skewers my gut, but I keep my gaze on him. No cause for doubt, not from me.

Eventually, he nods. "Very well." He gestures to his men. They release me, and I fall to my knees, watching the tableau play out. "Someone get her a horse, I suppose. And that blade they gave her. She must make Pastira if she's to be of use as Lady Livinia suggests." The emperor turns to Liv. "Your service has been impeccable. Your role in capturing the dragon—though perhaps delayed beyond what we had expected—will not be forgotten. Here is your bounty, as promised." He holds out a velvet pouch that chinks meaningfully. "And, Lady Livinia ... I do hope our most recent arrangement remains appealing to you?"

Liv accepts the proffered purse and curtsies far more prettily than I have managed, then glances up at him through her lashes, thrusting her chest out to give him the best angle on her, well, everything. "Of course, Your Majesty! I am deeply honored to accept your invitation and your protection, as we discussed. It is a generous reward for my humble services. I only hope to serve you well as your... What was it? Foreign Adviser? In Ascelin." She giggles just enough. "This mission has been more trying than I expected. I look forward to spending time at your court. You do have baths there, yes?"

There's a ripple of laughter. She knows her crowd. "Indeed we do. Masseurs too! We are grateful for your sacrifice." The emperor bows in return, never taking his eyes from her cleavage. "We will send our own personal masseur to your tent this evening to loosen the worst knots."

Liv takes his proffered arm, smiling up at him as they turn away. "Your Majesty, you are too kind. I hope this does not mean I will be denied your company at dinner, though, for that would not be a sacrifice I would be prepared to make." She doesn't even look back.

And why would she? She doesn't even have to carry the guilt of my death now.

I despise her, at this moment, as I have never despised her before. It burns my gut, fury and fire filling my being as I have never known. But then, I have never known such a betrayal. She's taken everything I was seeking to protect, all that I'd sacrificed to keep safe, and thrown it away. Even in all the years she promised me faithfulness and slept with that long string of people, I never felt like this.

Only Squid's voice in my head keeps me from lurching after her and throttling her on the spot.

A soldier grabs me by the arm. "Right. We go," he says, his accent so thick I can barely understand. It is all I can do to stay in simpering, scholarly character as we lurch away, me dragging my sword like a plough. I watch Liv's pale shoulders disappear amongst the rows of soldiers, keeping my eyes dipped down to hide the fire I cannot quench.

Cascading in the aftermath is guilt. Because, of course, it wasn't just me she betrayed. It isn't just my trust. In fact—and the thought is like acid in my throat—it isn't even me who is going to pay for this.

Squid, I say to the dragon, and I almost wish I could grovel before it, to communicate how very awful I feel. The agony of this guilt. *Oh, Squid, I am so sorry. I had no idea she would... I had no idea...*

It is not your fault, small one, Squid replies calmly. *But you must fly away from here before they figure out who you are to me.*

Tears spring into my eyes. *But you are in a cage,* I wail internally.

I am, the dragon acknowledges. *But I am also one with my line. I know the answers to all our questions. And, more than this, I know what they intend.*

But if they kill you...

Squid sounds so much older. *They will not. I am the only living dragon, lass. And from what I can gather, I am essential to this emperor-child-grown man's plans.*

I cannot help the sob that tears from my throat, and I stumble on the uneven ground. My soldier escort harrumphs loudly, his hand closing like a vise on my upper arm, tight enough to leave bruises. *I cannot leave you in such danger,* I agonize, dragging my feet. *I cannot.*

And it's almost true. It feels like a tearing at me, like leaving a child—my child—in danger, if I knew what that felt like.

It is a long walk to the soldiers' encampment, uphill and through rainforest. My fury keeps me going when my body would give out. I slap at mosquitoes harder than necessary. Squid is silent, and all I can picture is Liv smiling up at the emperor who would kill all of Rescalin, having handed him our country, not to mention Squid and me, on a platter.

"How's about a quick one before you're on your way?" the soldier says to me, as we reach the edge of the camp where the animals are tied up. I stare at him puzzled, wondering what he could mean. He catches me around the waist with one hand and pushes hard against one breast.

I'd thought I was beyond feeling anything, but bile boils up into my mouth. At the stench, he pulls away, and I spit onto the ground. The acid burns. I must have scored a good one to the lip in the fight earlier. I touch it gingerly, and sure enough, it's puffy and split.

"Ugh." Disgust is writ large on his face. "A horse. Over there." He waves vaguely. "Get gone, woman. There's those here as won't care about your breath."

He walks off, leaving me sniffing back snot and tears and stumbling on in the dark. The rows of horses are quiet, but one keeps whinnying. It takes a long moment, but tears spike my eyes when I recognize it, and I lurch into a shuffling run.

Magically, as if some god out there decided to throw me a bone, it's Liza, pawing the ground and eyeing me sideways. She's obviously unimpressed but also worried about me. I sob, falling on her neck, and she nuzzles into me, all concern.

I pat her gently. "You were right, girl, you were so right. I should never have trusted her. She promised me everything, just to betray me." I weep as I haul myself awkwardly into the saddle, and Liza heads off into the rainforest without direction from me.

Part of me wants to stay, to work out how to take Liv down and how to save Squid. But most of me is broken, lost in an anguish I'd never felt before—even if I had known the source.

"I should have known." I find myself hiccupping as Liza takes the lead, heading the gods only know where. "I should have known."

CHAPTER THIRTY-FOUR

I am so sorry. The voice in my head awakens me. *I would let you sleep, but there are things you must know.*

Wakefulness is slow to pierce the fog in my head. Liza and I had stumbled around in the dark with me sobbing until she finally refused to go any further. Her saddlebags were well stocked, but it hadn't occurred to me how lucky that was until the moment before a sodden and unhappy sleep overtook me, curled up in a blanket, a long dagger clutched to my chest.

"Squid?" I say aloud, struggling to sit before I realize what I'm doing. The dawn just touches the tips of the trees and vines around me. I glance around. I have not a single clue where I am.

I lie back, groaning at the pain in all my limbs and the itch of mosquito bites, and the crushing events of the day before come surging to mind. I think of Liv, of her face when I promised to come back, when I promised that I would always love her, and then I force myself to think of her smiling up at the emperor, pleased as a cat with cream. The bag of gold. Bile rises in my throat.

I am sorry, Squid says again, intervening gently, *but I must tell you. We are traveling, and I am not sure how far it will stretch.*

I sigh and feel myself turn toward Squid, feel myself open up. *You can still... We can still ... communicate? We fled so fast, I'd have thought we were out of range by now.*

The dragon is faintly amused. *Our range is ... somewhat increased,* it says. *But I have things I need to tell you, and we are travelling, and I am not sure how much further we have. I am so sorry about how this happened. I know that you needed answers, as I did, and I couldn't let you go without giving them to you.*

I gulp. *About the ... immortality thing?* It's sour now. My biggest dread had been watching Liv die, and now it would feel like a gift.

You will live as long as I will, small one. There is no undoing the blood bond. I am sorry. The only way to break it is with my death. You may live beyond that day.

It says this like I might be glad of the fact, and it makes tears spring to my eyes. *I don't want it gone. No one is allowed to kill you,* I send fiercely. *I won't let it happen.*

They won't kill me, Des. The emperor won't kill me. He needs me.

For what? Dread spirals through me.

Only I can lay the next egg. And I think ... what he wants, more than anything else, is immortality. He wants a dragon so that he can be blood bonded. So he can live forever.

That's a long time, I say, inanely, and then I yank together my thoughts. *Why does... I mean, does he have something in particular that he wants to live forever for? Or does he just fear death?*

From what I can tell, that's not all he wants. He wants power. If he is the only immortal...

So he'll be coming for me? So he can blood-bond with you once I'm gone? My heart bounds into my throat, and I glance around at the jungle. *I don't know that I could stop him.*

Not yet. Not soon, I hope.

You hope?

He doesn't know who you are. I do not think he has shared but the barest beginning with me, but he has many plans. He tried to bond with me, and when it didn't work, he told me that I must lay an egg.

I swallow. *Alright. That gives you some small bit of control, I suppose, though...*

If I do, he'll likely kill me, so I must not. Because if he keeps the new dragon from Incorporating me, then my child would not have the knowledge I have just acquired, and without that... Without that, I am not sure how we will be able to keep peace between dragonkind and humanity. It would break the Accord. My child might even wind up making many eggs and bringing dragons back to your lands of chained time. We may not be able to keep dragons in the Everlands.

I blink in the dawn light at this. Liza gives a soft snort from where she's munching grass a short distance away. *The Everlands?*

Squid is mildly amused. *I'm sorry, I forgot that you lost consciousness in the midst of... Well, in the midst. Yes, the Everlands. Where we originate. Where time does not exist. At least, not as it does here.*

My mind reels, and the jungle around me spins as I try to take this in. *That's his plan? To bring back the dragons?* It also means that the emperor will likely use whatever he can to force Squid to his will. Sorrow threatens to overwhelm me. *Oh gods, Squid. How can you hold all that? What will he...?* Anger chases the sadness away, and my jaw tightens. *I cannot believe she gave you to him.*

Oh, small one. I know it is hard. But I am not sure it was a simple betrayal. She could have given you up to them, but she didn't.

Bile boils in my gut. *She gave him* everything *else. She betrayed me as thoroughly as it was possible to do, short of killing me. And I do not think it was selflessness that stopped her crossing that line. She's not capable of it. It's selfishness.* I can almost hear Squid sigh and decide to change the subject. It rankles, but I remind myself that this time is precious. *What else did you need to tell me?*

The dragon hesitates uncharacteristically. *I will not defend Liv, but do not forget she may now be our best in with the emperor.* It must hear all my anger because it hurries on before I can reply. *I... I know you fear the return of the Era of Storms. I know you fear... what I may become.* I have to gulp against a sob. Of course Squid could not help but know about my ambivalence since I read those texts at Scyless, but feeling such a sense of loss and revisiting this hurts. *But I need you to know this.* Squid is strangely cautious. *We are practically immortal. I know you humans fear death, but for us... For us, it is a great wrong. An evil beyond all others, beyond measure.*

I frown, trying to rope my recalcitrant mind into understanding this. *I had thought our fear of death was... I didn't think it was possible to fear it more!* I almost laugh. *No matter how long you live, there's only one death, no?*

It made us... Can I—can I show you?

I brace myself. *Will this be like when we Traverse?*

A little, Squid replies. *But I know more now. I don't think it will make you so sick.*

Alright then.

And then it shows me dragons, flying high above battlefields where men and women and beasts lie dying in a welter of blood and mud and suffering. For a moment, I see a dragon, gold and gleaming in the sunlight and suspended in the air, and then I dive toward it. Just as I pin my eyes shut against the collision, which doesn't stop me seeing anyway, I slip inside the dragon's head, and I am feeling what it feels, a little like I do with Squid.

And this is sorrow and horror beyond horror that these beings below me cease to exist for no reason, or for reasons so fleeting as to be nothing. For lines drawn on a piece of paper, or for insults that pass in a moment. Thousands, tens of thousands, dying because of who they follow. The dragon weeps, dripping tears onto the earth like rain. And then, so abruptly it's a shock, the dragon breathes out blue fire, and all below are incinerated in a split second.

I gape.

That's how it started, Squid explains. *It started with compassion. I'm not defending it, but that was the beginning.*

I don't understand. They killed them? My chest seizes in horror; I can't draw a full breath.

It looks like death, I know, but it's not so simple. I need you to understand, it wasn't malice. We are not simple destruction... I frown, guilt warring with horror over what it's shown me. Squid says the words as if they're almost painful. *It's the Burning. All those humans, all that life the dragons Burned into nothingness... Well, it wasn't nothingness, actually. I know you can't quite grasp the Everlands. A land without time—I know it makes little sense to you. I'm sorry it's confusing.* Squid actually feels apologetic. *I know it is hard to think of Burning as other than killing, but ... every single person and beast—every living thing—that was Burned off the face of the earth by a dragon ... all of them... They didn't die, not properly. They were* taken. *Into the Everlands.*

Its words are a rush now, quiet and hurried. *I need you to know this. I need you to know that I—that all of those before me—weren't simply crazy or murderous. So we sought to* save. *And we did. All those soldiers, all those people... They're all still alive. They're saved. They're just not* here.

They're in the Everlands. I swallow in the dim light, my mind laboring to comprehend this. But weary and heartsore, shivering and hungry and alone in the murky morning light, things feel like they have to be stripped back as much as they can be. I wish desperately for someone else, someone whose mind I can borrow to try to get around this strange, hideous, and overwhelming responsibility. *But what does that mean? I don't understand! I'm just a player,* I wail in my head.

I know it, the dragon says back. Then, with a droplet of humor, sounding older than the Squid I'd sent into poor Elimanesion's mouth, it adds, *but you did tell Elouise you could play at hero. And you have already.*

Some hero, I say, wiping my dripping nose, slightly embarrassed the dragon had seen that interaction with the duchess. *Not my most convincing performance.*

I was convinced, Squid says warmly, and the sense of its care fills me, settling the anger.

But what does it mean, with the emperor? About the Burning?

Squid sighs in my head. *It means I have to hold the line. I can't lay the egg. From all I can tell, he's seeking immortality, but that could all change if he gets what he wants—a bond with a dragon. If they Incorporate, then ... he'd learn everything I've just told you, and I'm still trying to work out what he might do with that knowledge.*

Would he not ... make more dragons?

Your—you humans'—stories about that time are not the worst, Squid tells me, and it sounds like its heart is breaking. It shows me again. This time, there are dragons in the sky, breathing great gouts of flame at each other. Over and over. Some with tiny humans borne on their backs, whipping through the sky like giant snakes, destroying each other and the armies that support them. Some on mountains and plains, hillsides and castles, ships and rivers and on and on, dragons attacking each other, attacking humans. On and on, the sheer quantity of death makes me nauseous.

This is why he cannot have his way. There was so much death. Squid, even now, sounds so bone-achingly sad that I send comfort before I think. *The human kings encouraged them,* Squid says, *and it's hard to know from whom the anger first came. Some say the first were two brothers—a younger who was blood bonded first, rousing the jealousy of his older brother, who sought out his own dragon to take revenge. Whatever the origin, dragons and humans fed each other's anger. In the end, it doesn't really matter where it came into being. It just matters that eventually, another way was found.*

The Quenchers' Accord, I say, grasping after the little I do understand here.

The Accord, yes. It is the one thing that has given us these five hundred years of peace. The chaos of marauding bands of humans and dragons giving way to relative calm. Of course, humanity has drawn yet more lines on the earth and given them undue weight, and there are still wars as a result, but they do not have the devastation they did when the dragons were tied to them. I fear if the child this emperor wants me to bring forth, or their child, does not Incorporate my knowledge, it will not understand why the Accord must not be broken. It will not understand how the Accord can remain unbroken.

Helplessness threatens to overwhelm me. *This is too big,* I say, unable to find any other words.

Squid sends comfort. It's almost everything. *But the thing is, he has no bond with me. He can't make me do anything, and he certainly can't make me feel the necessity of making eggs he can use.*

Wait... A bond can make you do things?

Squid's amusement echoes in my head. *Well, you can't command me, which I know you know by now.*

Not half, I comment, surprising myself with the shred of humor glimmering through.

But we can be ... influenced, I suppose you would think of it as, the dragon says. *From our perspective, it's not about power or command—it's that the very being of us alters when we are blood bonded. That's what happened before—why all the dragons were part of all those wars before the Accord. The anger of their humans mixed with their sense of the injustice of mortality... It was not a good combination. And that is exactly why we have to be careful. If you are no longer my blood bonded...*

He could sign up for the job, I finish.

Exactly. The dragon sounds worried.

That must be awful, I think timidly. *Not knowing what you might become part of if you're blood bonded to someone else.*

I understand a lot more about it now. I am grateful it was you who birthed me. I don't want to be changed, not like that man might change me.

We have to free you. I don't want you changed either.

I know, the dragon says. *But we need to be smart. The knowledge Elimanesion gave me, it's very ... dragony. I am likely the only dragon who has ever existed for any significant period of time without Incorporation, and without other dragons around, so my view on these things is a bit different, I think. Every dragon left here in this world longs for the impossible, Burning back home. This is... This world, living here, alone... It feels like exile, or it has to most of my kin.* I remember the feeling of loss I'd experienced before I passed out during Squid's Incorporation.

I blink. *Can we not have more than one dragon? Why not two? Why must they be alone?*

It's about the line of guardians. We hold the Accord in place, and it works only if there is one dragon. Squid explains that the first burned all the other dragons into the Everlands and then laid its one egg, drawing it through from the Everlands. When that egg hatched, the baby dragon Incorporated it, ensuring the Accord would hold on the dragons' side. The guardian dragon's body somehow connects to the eggs that are produced in the Everlands and brings them through. This has to happen one at a time, so that Incorporation can ensure the Accord remains.

But if more than one is brought through, only one could Incorporate, so it would break the line of our guardianship. A dragon who has not Incorporated the previous guardian would not be tied sufficiently to that history, to the Accord.

I swallow. *And that's the risk if he makes you lay even one egg. They might not… It might not Incorporate, and then they could use that dragon to make more?* I'm stating the obvious, and I get a vague thread of amusement from Squid, as well as affirmation. But the thought of the devastation weathered by the world during the Era of Storms makes me gulp. *Do you think the Quenchers might know how to intervene? I hope Liv didn't … and I do hope I haven't put Elouise and Twisty in danger, sending them to Scyless.* I think of the old and the tiny children and the injured. Of Iradine. Did Liv's betrayal involve them as well? Did they even make it to Scyless? I'm vague with weariness.

Des, I know you're tired. The voice is fainter. *We are traveling fast. I can play for time, but I do not think the emperor-child-grown man will prove to have endless patience. But maybe… with Elouise… you can work out how best to get me back without dying yourself… Get me back from … Ascelin…* My heart sinks. I shake my head. I can't even imagine how to get to Aredoma, the capital of Ascelin, or what it would take to mount some kind of sneaky attack to liberate a dragon… Liza snorts at me. I refuse to reply.

Squid is very gentle when it says, *Desta Mildue, the woman you love and hate is here.*

She sold us out, I remind it, the fury flaring, heating my bones. *You are now a slave to some insane imperialist, and I…* I cannot even find words for the pain of learning this love that had just started once more had become nothing more than a tool she'd used to gain favor with a new emperor. It's galling.

Squid almost smiles—I can feel it—but it's sad along with me. *It hurts. I know it, small human. But the woman you … hate, well, she is here with me. She may not be reliable, but I suspect it might prove useful to have someone you know in with the other side.*

Bile burns along with my anger. *She is treachery in a pretty package. She sold you into his hands, for fuck's sakes! Knowing he might kill you.* Intends *to!*

She also kept you out of those same hands.

Fury spirals through me. *Don't expect me to be grateful to her for that. She betrayed everything I hold dear.*

Squid is sad but hastens on without commenting. *Des, lass, I am essential to the emperor-child-grown man's plan. Alive. Without me, there are no dragons left in the world and no bridge to the Everlands to call through an egg. No blood bond. He will not risk that. It is the guarantee of all he's dreamed of: immortality. He won't kill me until I lay the egg, and he can't make me do that without the blood bond. As long as you remain alive, and as long as I can hold out ... I have to go now, Des. Call if you need me, alright? If I can reply, I will.* It's in a rush to go. Just as the connection disappears, I get a wave of pain that sends me curling into a ball, and then, abruptly, just as Squid is gone, so is the pain.

I swallow, alone once more. Squid is probably being tortured and trying to keep it from me. Tears sting my eyes. My hatred for Liv flares hot.

I lie there for a long time, thinking. Eventually, Liza comes to nose at my face, checking I'm still alive. "Sorry, girl," I say, patting her nose. "I'm just thinking."

Liza nudges me again with her nose, and I sigh and sit up. "Alright. You're probably right. The gods only know how far we got last night, and if we're aiming for Elouise..."

We face a long trip, overland this time, through rainforest and jungle and then confronting—well, fuck only knows which side we'll be facing on the shores by her home, but it's unlikely to be fun. I curse Liv once more as I tighten Liza's girth, and the fury is so intense I can barely breathe. Anger sits like a band around my chest.

But, as I haul myself into the saddle, I think of Twisty, of his easy loyalty and gentle thoughtfulness. And I think of Elouise—calm, centered, smart Elouise—and I think of her soft beds, and her sharing of my burden and taking it up, and her authority, both control and sacrifice.

And I inhale, deep and slow, allowing the jungle scent to fill my lungs, and angle myself toward the sun. Liza whickers.

On the road once more.

THE END

Join the Journey!

The best bit about embarking on this publishing thing is that I get to build a relationship with you, dear reader!

I save some of the tastiest treats for my newsletter subscribers. If you're wondering why Des put away her blade before this book started, you'll find all the answers in *A Hired Blade*, free on signup.

For those wondering just how spicy Des/Liv can be, there's an extended scene of their first encounter you'll also get on signup. Plus all the other tasty little treats—deleted scenes, bridging chapters, side stories, novellas and other cutting-room-floor tidbits. And you'll get details about where things are up to and a little of my ruminations on the state of the fantasy genre. It's a stack of fun, basically!

Plus, you get the opportunity to join my ARC, beta, and street team!

Sign up now!

Enjoyed this novel? You can make a big difference!

Reviews are vital to helping me bring my books to the attention of readers who might enjoy them. I'd love to have the connections and, let's be real, financial backing of one of the big five publishers, but I'm a baby indie author.

But I do have you! And that counts for almost everything.

Honest reviews are the best way for me—and you—to invite new readers to join Des on her journey. Well, reviews and word-of-mouth, of course!

Please leave me a review!

About the Author

J C Rycroft is an emerging author of fantasy, living and writing on Wadawur-rung Country in Australia. Their work draws on high and epic fantasy tropes, mixed with a dollop of queer romance, humor, and wit, flawed but fabulous feminist heroes, and diverse-in-all-the-ways characters, liberally sprinkled with philosophical concepts brought to life. She loves bringing together the apparent contradictions: high theory and silliness, profound political concerns with a rollicking good story, and ordinary people with unexpected demands to heroism.

You can find JC Rycroft online at: www.jcrycroft.com

Facebook: www.facebook.com/jcrycroft

TikTok: www.tiktok.com/@jcrycroft

Instagram: www.instagram.com/jcrycroft

Email: contact@jcrycroft.com

Goodreads: www.goodreads.com/author/show/24259731

ACKNOWLEDGEMENTS

The list of those I want to thank is long, but as with all of my lists, at the very top is mi novia, Maria, and our righteous babe, Ameyali. Thanks for your super-active support and tolerance of the time I spend in other worlds.

Also to my family-of-origin, especially my mama for reading the things, and my sibs for their thoughts on all things designy. Myf for the pictures throughout, Dan for saving my imprint logo from the horrors of almost-there images. And Demelza and Dad for all the encouragement. I couldn't have got this far without you all!

And to my wonderful friends, for their support and excitement as I took this newest deviation in a life filled with them. Extra thanks to Rosanne for helping me get a website functional for very little $$! So appreciated. And of course to The Rogue Writers, who got to see this MS first and were wonderfully encouraging.

And finally to my swiftly growing team—cover designer Fay Lane, proof-reader Nay, line and copy editor Rachelle Wright, and developmental editor, Cameron Montague Taylor—you are all such wonderful people to work with! Fay makes magic out of vagueness, and I am so grateful for it. Rachelle has an eye for detail I love, and teaches me all those bits of grammar I should probably have learnt a long time ago, as well as being an excellent foil for my occasional excesses. Plus she's *delighted* by my work, and that is *so* valuable by the time line and copy editing comes around! Thank you so much, Rachelle! And to Nay, whose presence is both ephemeral and ever-present – thank you for finding the terrifying number of typos that find their way into my work.

And many, many thanks to Cee—the first person I didn't already know who I shared work with. Cee manages to balance insight with encouragement, good humor with clear and practical advice, and somehow has such faith that they're excited about my *intentions*, even when the page isn't yet living up to it! I feel very fortunate to have lucked into your guidance on this journey, not least for your alphabet mafia chops which means I know my characters are going to be safe in your hands (even if they're not in mine).

CONTENT NOTE

Attempted murder

Blood

Child Death (off-page)

Cheating (off-page)

Death

Fire

Genocide (attempted)

Gore

Homophobia

Hostage

Kidnapping

Lesbiphobia

Misogyny

Profanity

Queerphobia

Sex (graphic)

Sexual Assault (attempted)

Sex Work

Torture (off-page)

Violence
War

www.ingramcontent.com/pod-product-compliance
Lightning Source LLC
Chambersburg PA
CBHW020330120726
47904CB00002B/348